BY C.E. MURPHY

Truthseeker

THE INHERITORS' CYCLE

The Queen's Bastard
The Pretender's Crown

THE WALKER PAPERS

Urban Shaman
Thunderbird Falls
Coyote Dreams
Walking Dead
Demon Hunts

THE NEGOTIATOR TRILOGY

Heart of Stone
House of Cards
Hands of Flame

WITH MERCEDES LACKEY AND TANITH LEE

Winter Moon

Truthseeker

Truthseeker

C. E. MURPHY

BALLANTINE BOOKS ∽ NEW YORK

SF

Truthseeker is a work of fiction. Names, characters, places, and incidents are the products of the author's imagination or are used fictitiously. Any resemblance to actual events, locales, or persons, living or dead, is entirely coincidental.

A Del Rey Trade Paperback Original

Copyright © 2010 by C. E. Murphy

Published in the United States by Del Rey, an imprint of The Random House Publishing Group, a division of Random House, Inc., New York.

DEL REY is a registered trademark and the Del Rey colophon is a trademark of Random House, Inc.

Library of Congress Cataloging-in-Publication Data
Murphy, C. E. (Catie E.)
   Truthseeker / C. E. Murphy.
      p. cm.
   "A Del Rey trade paperback original"—T.p. verso.
   ISBN 978-0-345-51606-0 (pbk.)
   ISBN 978-0-345-52302-0 (e-Book)
1. Murder—Investigation—Fiction. 2. Boston (Mass.)—Fiction. I. Title.
   PS3613.U726T78 2010
   813'.6—dc22

                                   2010014981

Printed in the United States of America

www.delreybooks.com

9 8 7 6 5 4 3 2 1

Book design by Caroline Cunningham

For Jai

who gave me the idea

Truthseeker

One

"—once upon a time, not so long ago, driven by a little old lady I know personally. She drove it to the store weekly, that's it, so its four thousand miles are gentle ones, ladies. It's six years old, but it has all the extras. You won't find a better deal here or anywhere else. Now, I know the sticker price is eighteen five and you're not looking to spend quite that much." The salesman leaned out from beneath his umbrella to get a better look at the deep V of Kelly Richards's T-shirt, and smiled. "It's cutting my own throat, but I think I can knock it down to seventeen flat. It's a bargain, ladies, a real bargain."

"Lara?" Kelly folded her arms beneath her breasts.

For a moment Lara found herself studying her friend's cleavage, too, if less avidly than the salesman had. Kelly had a lifetime's experience in using her assets to distract and command, whereas Lara's own figure had been described as a pirate's treasure: a sunken chest. Clinical curiosity made her wonder what it would be like to take control of a situation just by inhaling deeply.

"Earth to Lara, hello?" Kelly snapped her fingers under Lara's nose. "Are you in there?"

"Of course I am." Lara glanced at the yellow Mazda Miata the salesman hawked, but it was his quick patter that she concentrated on. The easy flow of words meant to distract and impress in the same way Kelly's T-shirt was—though Kelly had perhaps gone too far in her distraction techniques. She hadn't worn a coat, despite it being cold with a promise of serious rain. The salesman's gaze kept wandering to her chest. Lara shook her head, smiling. "He's lying."

Offense flew across the man's face and he clapped a hand over his heart. "How could I lie to two such lovely ladies as yourselves? But all right, all right, maybe a Miata isn't your style. Something with a little more kick to it, maybe something that makes a real impression when you pull up? I've got a Ford four-fifty over here, it gets thirty miles to the gallon—"

He broke off again as Lara and Kelly both turned incredulous looks on him. "All right, all right, maybe twenty-five in the city. But I can see discerning women like yourselves want better gas mileage than that. I've got just the thing for you. This way, please." He strode down the lot, Kelly at his side and Lara trailing behind, staying just close enough to overhear his routine. Kelly cast regular glances at her, and Lara shook her head each time.

Finally, exasperated, Kelly pointed at a ten-year-old Nissan with a four-thousand-dollar price tag. "What about that one?"

A spatter of rain hit the salesman's umbrella and rolled off in a pathetic dribble that matched his expression. "Decent gas mileage, but the engine was overhauled by an amateur."

"How's it run?"

He muttered, "Fine," and Lara nodded.

Kelly's smile lit up. "I'll take it."

Forty minutes later the Nissan sat outside a diner, Kelly whimpering with each raindrop that spattered against her new car. Her lunch, virtually untouched, no longer steamed with heat, and Lara waved her own half-eaten burger at Kelly's cooling french fries. "If you're bringing me out to the best diner lunch in Boston you might as well eat. Or is this a spécial new diet where you only inhale the scent of food?"

Kelly tore herself from the view to waggle a finger at Lara. "Technically, the Deluxe is in Watertown, not Boston."

Lara laughed. "Okay, fine. The best diner in the greater Boston area. You don't like it when I'm pedantic with you. How come you can do it to me?"

"Because you do it all the time. I'm just getting my own back. Anyway, lunch is for you, not me."

"So it's a new diet. One where you've given up eating?"

"Well, no, it's just, you know. I don't know how you can eat as much as you do and stay so slim." Kelly finally picked up her own burger, having been distracted from the car.

"Some of us get Mae West figures, others get fast metabolisms. Want to trade?"

Kelly glanced past her burger into the V of her own T-shirt. "Nah, I guess not. But thanks for coming along. You always know when salesmen are lying."

"Kelly, anybody who sells used cars is lying. You don't need me along to tell you that." Lara squished her burger until bacon and cheese oozed out of the bun, then sank her teeth into it with a blissful sigh.

"Yeah, but you also know when they're telling the truth."

Lara shrugged her eyebrows, grateful her mouth was full. Kelly was right, the correctness—the truthfulness—of her statement hummed under Lara's skin like a hive full of bees. She couldn't remember a time when lies didn't strike discordant notes. As barely more than an infant, Lara had heartily mistrusted her mother until Gretchen Jansen had learned to explain that Santa and the Tooth Fairy, among others, were simply stories that people told. Her mother's patient explanations had eventually allowed her to understand the idea of popular legends, but the truth-sensing ability had become even more awkward when her father died. There were no comforting lies to be shared with a child who was fundamentally incapable of accepting "Daddy's gone away for a while" as basic truth.

Since then—she'd been seven—she had understood it would be easier if she could instantly know when she was being lied to. It had never worked that way, though as she'd aged she'd learned to discern more and more about the probable truth. The Miata had almost certainly never belonged to a granny, and its four thousand miles were probably the result of someone tinkering with the odometer. But unless the salesman said so directly, she wouldn't know. Worse, she couldn't tell the difference between a truth based on misinformation or a genuine truth: if someone believed what he was telling her, it read as true.

As peculiar talents went, it was good for getting her out of jury duty—a frustrating perk, as she thought serving on a jury might be interesting—and not a great deal else.

"Hey. Hey, wake up." Kelly reached across the table to thump Lara's forearm. "Look, it's that guy from the news. The weatherman. Why don't you go ask him if he's single?" She nodded out the window, where a slender blond man in a long coat hurried past Kelly's Nissan, his shoulders hunched against bursts of rain. A cameraman followed, looking irate. "Poor guy, he predicted sunshine today."

"Oh. Is that why you're wearing a T-shirt? I thought you were just trying to keep the car salesman off his game."

"Merely a side benefit. No, I'd have brought a coat if I'd known it was going to be this nasty. Wow, there's a job that'd suck for you, huh? What if you had to predict the weather and kept getting it wrong? You'd give yourself the heebie-jeebies."

Lara, watching the weatherman cross the street, shook her head. "I don't think so. I'd be predicting on the best data I had, so it might be okay."

"Best data." Kelly snorted. "How many times have I watched the news and the weatherperson said it was snowing when it was raining, or when the prediction was windy when it was as calm as a crypt?"

"Calm as a crypt." Lara took her attention off the street and made a face at her friend. "Who says things like that? I don't know if you watch too much *Addams Family* or if you're just planning a career as an undertaker."

"I'm planning a career as a rich young widow," Kelly said archly. "See, if you were really a good friend you'd have already found me a rich old man to marry."

"Most of my clients aren't old."

"But they're rich, right?" Kelly's eyes brightened. "They have to be, to afford their spiffy custom suits."

Lara wrinkled her nose and put on a haughty accent. "Please. We at Lord Matthew's Tailor Shop prefer the term 'bespoke' to 'custom made.'"

"That's because you at Lord Matthew's are a bunch of Europhile snobs," Kelly said cheerfully, and Lara laughed.

"Steve's got three hundred years of tradition to live up to. Give him a break."

"Oh yes." Now Kelly put on the accent, sniffing disdainfully. "Steven Taylor, eighth in a line of tailors beholden to a Lord Matthew, whose name became so synonymous with quality that even during his lifetime men were referred to 'Lord Matthew's tailor' rather than the Newbury Street Tailor Shop. That's your party line, isn't it?" she said in a normal voice. "You have to admit it sounds snooty."

"It is snooty. But I love it. The way everything fits together flawlessly, it's like a true thing made real."

"A true thing made real. And you think I say weird things."

Lara grinned. "Someday I'll make your wedding dress and you'll understand why it's so fantastic. No patterns, just your body shape and your every whim conceded to. Except if you try to make a disastrous fashion choice, in which case I'll politely ignore you and make something suitable. At least I could do that with you. We've had clients with no taste at all. A couple of them were even famous."

"Fortune five hundred famous?"

"More like movie star famous."

Kelly brightened again. "Now, see, if I were even the tiniest bit interested in sewing, I would so make you get me a job. Intimately fitting clothes to movie stars. I want your life."

"No, you don't," Lara said with perfect confidence.

Kelly squashed her lips in mock irritation. "Shush. You're not supposed to call me on things like that and you know it. People say things like that, Lar."

"I know. But you don't mean it." If Lara's high school yearbook had had a category for least likely to develop a sense of humor, her teenage self would have been pictured there. It wasn't that she lacked one, but even as an adult, the line between teasing and telling lies was a thin one to her sense of truthfulness. She frequently had to stop and consider what she'd been told, investigate it for irony before responding. At the shop, her fellow tailors had such passion and joy for their creations they rarely joked about it; Lara's underdeveloped sense of humor fit in well there.

Outside, in the real world, she was grateful for people like Kelly, who had recognized Lara's ability on her own and wasn't bothered by it. Building friendships without the polite gloss of white lies was difficult. People simply didn't tell one another the truth all the time, or even often. When Kelly had protested that they did, Lara had arched an eyebrow and asked, "How often do you say 'fine' when someone asks you how you're doing?" Kelly had shut her mouth on further objections and rarely argued with Lara on matters of truthfulness again.

"Okay, I don't want your job. I want to hang out with you and meet the rich people you make clothes for," Kelly admitted. "Is that more accurate?"

Lara laughed. "Much. The trouble with that is most of them never even see me, Kelly. I'd have a hard time introducing you to somebody when I'm effectively invisible."

"I don't understand that. They're the dressmaker's dummies. How can they not see the dressmaker?"

"It doesn't matter," Lara assured her. "I don't need to be noticed."

"No?" Kelly cast a glance out the window. "Not even by him?"

Lara followed her gaze to where the weatherman, hair blown askew, shouted enthusiastically into a microphone as rain splashed over him. He was vividly handsome, with angular cheekbones and a pointed jaw, and a well-shaped mouth currently stretched in a rueful grin. His eyes were crinkled against the weather, features animated as he spoke. "Nah. Not that I'd say no . . ."

Kelly clapped her hands together. "Finish your burger. Come on, hurry up."

Lara picked up the sandwich and bit in, an automatic response to the command, then furled her eyebrows. "What's the hurry?"

"Look at him, Lar. He's a pretty-boy TV star, but that coat, those pants." She *tsked*, shaking her head, eyes wide with dismay. "The man needs a makeover to reach his full potential, and I know just the woman to give him one."

"You?"

Kelly gave an enthusiastic *pah!* of dismissal. "I like my men broad enough to fill doorways. Not that Mr. Weatherman doesn't have great shoulders, but my mighty thighs would crush those slender hips. I'm going to introduce you." She dropped a twenty on the table and caught Lara's wrist, tugging her up.

"Kelly! I'm not done eating! And you don't even know him!"

"Everybody knows him," Kelly insisted. "He's David Kirwen, Channel Four News weatherman, and they're shutting down filming. It's now or never. I'll buy you another burger. Come on, Lara. This is why you never meet guys. You never take any risks. Live a little!" She pulled Lara toward the door, ignoring her protests, and stepped out into the wind-driven rain, T-shirt soaking in a few seconds.

Lara muttered "He'll notice you, anyway," and earned a second dismissive sound from her friend.

"Huge tracts of land aren't everyone's fancy. Excuse me! Excuse me, Mr. Kirwen? My friend here wanted to talk to you about your wardrobe!"

"For heaven's sake." Lara spoke the protest under her breath as Kirwen turned to face them, amusement writ large across his face, animating thin lips and brown eyes into pure sensual charm. "I didn't," she said to him in embarrassment. "I mean, your trench coat is really well made. The stitches must be oiled, the way water's beading and rolling off. But really, I didn't want to talk to you. I'm sorry. My friend is—" She ran out of words, wrapping her arms around herself and shivering. The weatherman was dressed for the pelting rain; Lara, in a T-shirt and jeans—her coat was in Kelly's Nissan—was not.

"An enabler," Kelly offered. "This is Lara Jansen. She's a tailor, a bespoke tailor, I don't know if you're familiar with it, but—"

"I'm only a journeyman," Lara mumbled, but Kelly went on heedless.

"—it's custom tailoring, not even a pattern, I can't remember how it all works, but anyway, Lara can tell you about it, and she thinks you're cute and well dressed—"

"Kelly!"

"A tailor who thinks I'm well dressed. I'm flattered, Miss Jansen. It's a pleasure to meet you." He turned a megawatt smile on Lara, evidently unaware of its power. Bells chimed beneath her skin, ringing in the truth inherent in his statement, and Lara put her hand out automatically to meet his as he said, "I'm David Kirwen."

Pure tones shattered into discord.

Two

The hairs on Lara's neck stood against the rain and wind. The tones of truth rang with uncertainty, tremors lifting goose bumps on her skin. Her knowledge was usually an instant thing, one pure tone or a flat one, but the sound of David Kirwen's name went on and on, searching for a final note to settle on. They began to clear, shivering toward agreement, but even as purity took over, a dissonance remained. Lara felt her smile go fixed, felt her hand go icy in Kirwen's, and saw that he noticed it. Some of the light went out of his own smile and he retrieved his hand from her cold grip. "I'd hate to keep you out on an afternoon like this one. Thank you for saying hello."

"Lara and I," Kelly said briskly, "were going to stop for a cup of coffee down the street. Would you like to join us?"

Kirwen turned a slow, regretful smile on the invitation, looking at Kelly but leaving the sensation and weight of his gaze on Lara. There was a trace of apology in it, something more meaningful than the polite, obligatory refusal of, "I think perhaps I'd better not. Maybe another time, Miss . . . ?"

"Richards," Lara supplied. "Kelly Richards. We need to get going, Kel."

"But—"

"Now, Kelly." Lara pinched a smile toward Kirwen, wrapped her hand around Kelly's biceps, and tugged her toward the newly purchased Nissan up the street.

Kelly dug her heels in and pitched her voice low. "He's into you, Lara! What the hell are you doing? He's rich, he's handsome, he's famous, he's got a well-made trench coat, what's the problem? Let's get coffee! You could get a date! I mean, sure, dating with you is a little weird, but you could give the guy a chance."

"His name's not David Kirwen." Lara's answer cut across Kelly's good-natured spiel so sharply they both flinched. Kelly came to a full stop, and Lara puffed her cheeks. "Sorry. That came out nastier than I meant it to."

Kelly flicked a glance toward the weatherman. "S'arright. Look, Lara, of course his name's David Kirwen. He's famous. He's a TV personality. Everybody knows who he is."

"Everybody is wrong." Cold water slid down Lara's spine, highlighting the discomfort that slithered there as well. "It felt wrong. Can we just get in the car, please? I'm soaked."

Kelly scowled, first at Kirwen, then at Lara. "But everybody knows who he is. I mean, if you say so, but . . ."

"I know. But have you ever known me to be wrong?"

Kelly's shoulders drooped and she slogged toward the Nissan. "Only when somebody was making a joke that you didn't get. Lar, how can he not be David Kirwen? Who is he, if he's not? What happened to Kirwen, if he's not?"

Lara shot her a look of horror. "You make it sound like he killed somebody or something."

"Well!"

Lara slumped, blouse sticking to her skin. "I'm sure it's not like that. His name is David Kirwen. It's just . . . also not."

"How can his name both be and not be David Kirwen? You only get one name. It's the rules. One name each. Well, unless you take a stage name. Maybe that's what he's done." Fire sparked in Kelly's gaze. "I'm going to go ask him. Wait here."

"Kelly! Kelly! Wait!" Lara broke into a run after her friend, who splashed through puddles and caught Kirwen's elbow as he climbed into his news van. He came out of the van to look at her curiously, and Lara slowed to put the heel of her hand against her forehead, then gave in to a low laugh. Kelly was her perfect foil, acting on impulse where Lara overthought things. It seemed to be both a more interesting and more terrifying way to live. She wasn't sure if she envied it, but their ongoing friendship suggested she at least admired Kelly's madcap approach.

David Kirwen lifted a complicated expression to greet Lara as she approached the van. Curiosity and interest enlivened his features, and he spoke diffidently. "You think my name's not David Kirwen?"

"Lara has this annoying knack of always knowing if somebody's telling her the truth," Kelly said blithely. It sounded almost ordinary the way she said it, so matter-of-fact as to be unquestionable. "So she got the heebie-jeebies when your name sounded wrong to her. I'm sure she'd like to go out for coffee if you'll just explain."

Lara, despairing, said, "Kelly. I'm sorry, Mr. Kirwen."

Kirwen shook his head, complex emotions turning more toward hope. "No, it's all right. In fact, my name isn't Kirwen. It's ap Caerwyn, Dafydd ap Caerwyn." The difference in pronunciation was subtle, yet significant enough to send a rush of relief over Lara's skin as the name rang true. Kirwen's attention remained on her, intent, and she steeled herself against stepping back, out of his range of interest. "How did you know?"

"Dafydd ap Caerwyn," Kelly repeated. "It doesn't sound that different. Why don't you use it?"

"The spelling." Dafydd turned his TV-star smile on Kelly. A spark of envy startled Lara and she put her hand over her chest like she could push it down. "Americans usually pronounce it correctly if they hear it first, but if they see it written down they tend to call me Daffy-Did. It's Welsh, by most accounts."

Kelly spun around in triumph, fists against her rain-soaked hips. "There! See? Nothing mysterious at all! I told you!"

Astonishment dropped Lara's jaw and she gaped at her friend, who had the grace to look mildly ashamed. "Well, all right, I didn't tell you. But there was a simple answer! Now we can go out for coffee!"

"Kelly! No! We can't! For one thing, I'm soaking wet, and for another, I have to go back to work! And for a third I don't need you to—"

"Matchmake?" Kelly asked archly. "You need somebody to. Can you come out for coffee, Mr. Kirwen? You and maybe your . . ." She leaned past Kirwen to peer into the van. "Your cameraman?"

The van's door slid open to reveal a broad-shouldered man whose short hair was so wet and plastered to his head its color was indistinguishable. "If you don't say yes, David, I'm going to drown you in one of these puddles. I was gonna have a barbecue tonight, man, and look what the weather's doing."

"You should know better than to trust a weatherman, Dickon. And I'm afraid we really can't, Miss Richards. We're expected back at the studio in less than half an hour. Maybe I could make it up to you by taking you out to dinner tonight? Miss Jansen?"

Lara jolted, taken aback at being addressed. "What? Oh. No, really, you don't ha—"

"We'd love to." Kelly put her hand on Kirwen's arm and squeezed, then tilted to smile brilliantly at the cameraman. "You'll come, too, won't you? Since it's not barbecue weather?"

"Damn straight I will, especially if David's paying. C'mon, Kirwen, let's get back to the studio before they send an ark to pick us up." He slammed the sliding door closed and Kirwen got into the van as Kelly turned back to Lara, triumphant.

"There, see, that wasn't so hard, was it? Now we have dates for tonight!"

"Really?" Lara watched the van drive away. "Because I didn't notice any exchange of telephone numbers or a decision where we'd be eating."

Kelly's jaw snapped shut. "Well, we know where they work."

"Oh, you have got to be kidding." Lara looked to the heavens, beseeching, then spluttered and wiped rainwater from her eyes. "Seriously. Thank you for trying to salvage my love life, but I'm not quite that desperate. Look, I took a long lunch so I could go car shopping with you, but since we mostly skipped lunch, could you drop me off at St. Anthony's before I go back to work?"

Kelly sent another glance, this one defeated, after the van. "Yeah, okay. No dinner date and I pulled you out of the diner before we finished lunch. I'm the worst friend in the univ—" She broke off under the sound of Lara's laughter. "Okay, fine, maybe not the worst. But I'm up there!"

"I think you'd have to do considerably more than leave me hungry to qualify as even a moderately bad friend, much less the worst in the universe." Lara threaded her arm through Kelly's and tugged her toward the Nissan. "You can buy me lunch on Saturday. We're helping Rachel move, remember?"

Kelly kicked spray in the gutter puddles like a gloomy four-year-old. "Rachel's supposed to buy us pizza."

"For dinner! We're not supposed to be there till one. You can buy me lunch first." Lara knocked her hip against Kelly's, sending her around to the driver's side door. "This, by the way, is how I stay skinny. I never get to eat a whole meal at once."

"You're not skinny." Kelly unlocked the doors, dismayed as they got in. "My nice new seats, all wet!"

"It's your own fault," Lara said heartlessly. "You're the one who wanted to go chasing men in the rain."

"Just for that, I take it back. You *are* skinny." Kelly pulled out of the parking spot, shaking her fist at a pedestrian who walked into the street in front of her without acknowledging the car bearing down on him.

"As opposed to what?" Lara twisted water from her hair onto the Nissan's floor, where it puddled on the rough carpet.

"To slim. There's a difference. Are you soaking my new car on purpose?"

Amused guilt surged through Lara and she rubbed at the pool of water. "Not exactly. I was just trying to dry off a little. What's the difference?"

Kelly eyed her. "You know I have to believe you when you say that, even though I wouldn't believe anybody else, right?"

"It's one of the perks of being friends with me."

Kelly laughed out loud, sound filling the small vehicle. "I guess that's true. Anyway, skinny doesn't look good on anybody. Slim looks good on everybody. And you're slim." She glanced sideways at Lara and added, "David Kirwen thought slim looked good on you," in a sly, hopeful tone.

"We have no dinner date, and even if we did, we wouldn't." A mis-tuned chord warbled through her own words. Lara said "Hush," as much to herself as her friend, and tugged her seat belt on as Kelly plunged them into afternoon traffic.

The downpour had increased dramatically by the time they got back downtown. Wisdom said she should have Kelly drop her off at work, but she still had time on her extended lunch hour. Lara ducked out of Kelly's car and ran for Saint Anthony's Shrine, stopping beneath its arched entryway to wave as Kelly drove off. Then she slipped inside, bobbing toward the altar and crossing herself before scurrying down to a meeting room.

A dozen or so men and women were already there, gathered in a loose circle of chairs and listening intensely as a woman in her mid-thirties spoke. Lara offered a brief smile and took a seat, trying not to interrupt, but the speaker murmured, "Hi, Lara. Glad you made it," before continuing. "It's the credit cards, you know? They make it so easy. I only have one left, I cut the rest of them up—"

She broke off with a contrite look toward Lara, and one of the men—Matt—chuckled quietly. "Aw, hell, caught you out, huh? You know she don't mean to."

"I didn't catch anyone out. Go on, Paula."

"I've got one in the freezer," Paula muttered. "In a big block of ice. For emergencies, Lara, I swear."

"Hey." Lara shook her head. "I'm not judging you. You should know that by now."

"Not judging, just keepin' us on the straight and narrow. You know, I've met a lot of head doctors in my time, but nobody's as sharp as you, Lara. Donno how you do it."

Lara brought a finger to her lips in a shush motion. "The floor is Paula's right now, Matt. Let's let her talk."

She barely remembered the first time she'd been to a self-help meeting with her mother. It had only been a few months after her father's death. Her hazy memories of him were of a man outrageously boisterous at times and inexplicably sullen at others. It wasn't until she was ten or eleven that she'd really begun to understand that his moods had been exacerbated by alcohol, but in the aftermath of his death, her mother had started attending Al-Anon meetings. Lara, joining her, had found a certain relief in people trying so hard to tell the truth. They hadn't always succeeded, but their presence at the meetings showed a kind of dedication to truth that she found almost nowhere else. Her own life hadn't been badly set awry by substance abuse issues, but as a survivor, she'd been able to find a place in Alateen groups, and as an adult could hardly imagine her life without at least one weekly meeting.

"It's for emergencies," Paula was saying. "It's been in there two months and I haven't taken a hair dryer to it once. The other one has a really low limit." The woman's gaze came back to Lara. "I've got it all set up with the credit card company; I'm only allowed to make a payment once a month, so I can't pay things off and pretend I'm not spending, which is what I used to do. And yesterday I saw this pair of earrings . . ."

She trailed off into waiting silence, then knotted her fingers together and frowned at them. "I know it doesn't sound as bad as the alcohol or drug problems some of us have. I mean, it's just shopping, right? It's not like gambling. People think gambling is destructive, but shopping, everybody shops. Everybody's got a credit card. And it's not even like you can stop shopping if you want to, because you still always need food and sometimes you really do need clothes.

Maybe not sixteen pairs of Jimmy Choos, but shoes, anyway," she said to her lap, then looked up. "The woman behind the counter was really nice, too. She even let me try them on. They were these little moonstones with diamond drips. You would have liked them, Lara. They looked like something you'd wear.

"But I put them back." Paula loosened her fingers and sat up straighter, color burnishing her cheeks to a warm dark brown. "I put them back, and I swear to God my hands were shaking and I almost cried when I was leaving the shop, but I put them back, and when I got outside it was like this one little tiny chain had broken and I felt so much better. That was three hundred dollars that was going to go into paying off a debt instead of making a new one. I don't know, maybe it isn't a lot, but to me it felt like everything."

"Hey, babe, sometimes not a lot *is* everything." Matt leaned forward to clap a big hand against Paula's knee, then sat back again, folding his hands behind his head. "Three years, three months, twenty-six days, and . . ." He moved one arm to look at his watch, then said, "And seventeen hours drink-free," before shooting Lara a sly glance.

She laughed as wrongness jangled over her skin. "I know the years and months are right, Matt. It must be the days or hours you're fibbing about."

"Fourteen hours." He shook his head, grinning broadly. "Uncanny knack, uncanny knack. We gotta be the straightest, narrowest meeting in the city, with you keeping us on the line."

"You keep yourselves on the line," Lara disagreed. "I just drop by to make sure you're doing all right. How's it going?"

"Not too bad. You ever get a day when it's not so much the booze you want as it's boredom driving you to do something?" He raised his eyebrows and received a murmur of recognition from two or three of the others. "Sunday got bad enough I found myself another meeting to drop in to. Funny thing is I met a real nice girl there, and we went out to dinner after. I'm a cynic and I hate to say it, but maybe sometimes the Lord provides."

Lara, smiling, listened a while longer, then slipped out again, hurrying through the rain back to work.

Three

"And how is the suit for the button man?" Steve Taylor poked his head around Lara's open office door, startling her and garnering an embarrassed smile.

"Mr. Mugabwi's suit is coming along nicely. You're not supposed to know I call him the button man." Lara lifted one of the buttons in question, an antique ivory beauty with subtle age striations. "I can't help it, though. I get a thrill every time I work with these."

"Well, it's not every day we have a client arrive with a jar full of buttons as our starting place." Steve came in to sit on the edge of her sewing desk—Lara was on the floor like a proper tailor, legs folded as she judged one button's pattern, then another's, against the suit fabric—and grin down at her. "You did a good job, you know, convincing him to the browns."

Lara shook her head. "You convinced him with this fabric. I didn't even know we had it in." The brown wool weave was silken under her fingertips; yellow and red threads gave the fabric incredible rich depth. Mr. Mugabwi, in Lara's private opinion, should always wear browns; his skin tones were suited for it, and the sepia-tinged buttons he'd brought in would have been jarring against a black or gray suit.

"It was new," Steve said deprecatingly. "You would have selected it for him if you'd seen it."

"Only if I'd seen his bank book first." The fabric was a special blend, the makers having produced only enough for perhaps ten suits, and was priced accordingly. Not that anyone came to Lord Matthew's without deep pockets: bespoke tailoring was unabashedly expensive.

"Ah, yes." Steven nodded, expression deadpan. "After all, he came with hundred-year-old buttons. If he's recycling that much, he must be very cautious with money, indeed."

Lara laughed and mimed throwing one of the buttons at him, though she kept it safe in her palm. "The buttons are from his grandfather's suits, and you know it. It's not nice to tease me."

"I tease all my girls." Steve shifted off the desk and crouched in front of the suit, flicking away imaginary bits of lint as he examined her handiwork. Lara sat back, smiling. He was a master tailor and had four daughters of his own, ranging from a few years older than Lara to several years younger. That, more than anything, was what he meant by "my girls"—she had worked for him since her second year of college and, having watched her grow up, knew he half-thought of her as one of his own. She loved the sense of belonging, and worked harder than she probably needed to, wanting to make him proud.

"This is master class work, Lara. I'm sure you know that, but it's worth mentioning." Steve stood up again, lips pursed as he studied the suit. "Mugabwi's ordered three suits. I'll want you to make them all. But I also want you to discuss linen with him, when he's in for his final fitting. These will be perfect for corporate meetings, but a lot of his charity work is done in Africa. He'll need cooler material, even just for the high-level glad-handing he does."

"Maybe silk doupioni, not linen." Lara got to her feet, examining first her employer, then the suit before them, dubiously. "Linen's crisp and cool, but Mr. Mugabwi's job is asking corporations for huge amounts of money. I think his suits need a visual warmth that I'm not sure I'd get satisfactorily from linen. I mean, this cloth . . ."

She brushed her fingertips over the fine wool and shook her head. "The depth of color and the elegance of the buttons, when combined with the suit's fit, are going to warm people toward him instinctively. Wool can do that. So can silk. I'm just not convinced linen's the right fabric."

Steve was beaming at her. Lara trailed off, then ducked her head to stare at her feet a moment. "That was a test."

"And you passed with flying colors. I'll leave the design of the summer suits entirely in your hands, Lara. You can consider it your master test."

Heat rushed her cheeks and she put her hands over them. "Two years early?" Tradition expected a seven-year apprenticeship, and she'd only worked for Lord Matthew's for five.

Steve passed it off with a wave of his hand. "The modern world's a faster place. Besides, you were nearly at journeyman status when you started working for me, and you know it, Lara. Your portfolio was a lot stronger than most college sophomores' would be. You were doing body work on suits within eight months, and you know some of the others were still doing hems after eighteen."

Lara winced, but nodded. She was meticulous and always had been; the work came very close to making music in her mind, as if someone was whispering truth just out of her hearing. When errors were made, they reverberated sourly just as falsehoods did, and so she'd learned almost at the same time she'd begun sewing that it was far more worth doing well than quickly. Her coworkers hadn't always learned the same lesson.

"All right." Steve brushed the suit's shoulder once more. "Choose the fabrics you'd like to present to Mr. Mugabwi and we'll discuss them before he comes in again. Meanwhile, keep being a genius."

Lara laughed and waved as he left, then settled back down to work with a smile on her face. Gleaming pinheads marked the buttons' eventual locations; it was now only a matter of judging which buttons looked the most striking against the fabric. This was Lara's favorite part of her work, even more than the choosing of fabrics or the discussion of design: the fine details, most of which were invisible to the untrained observer, that finished a suit or gown to impeccable specification.

A knock on her office door pulled her out of her reverie as the last button went on. Pins in her mouth, she mumbled, "Mmm?," then extracted them from between her lips to blink at Cynthia Taylor. "Yes?"

"Someone's here to see you." Cynthia, at barely seventeen, was the only daughter interested in her father's business. She worked as a receptionist after school during the brief hours the bespoke shop was open to the public, but Lara was certain she would someday be a master tailor.

"Me?" A glimpse out the frosted windows said evening had fallen while she worked. Lara sat back on her heels and moved a cup of tea to be certain she wouldn't spill it. "I don't have any fittings scheduled this evening. I should probably already be gone. So should you, for that matter."

Cynthia rolled her eyes. "You should have told Dad that when he came by earlier. We're going to be late for dinner again, and Mom's going to kill us. But if we weren't still here, I wouldn't have been able to open the door for this man. I don't think he's a client. He's not wearing the right kind of clothes. But he did ask for you specifically, so maybe I'm wrong!"

"I don't know how anybody could even know to ask for me. I'm only a journeyman. Well." Lara climbed to her feet, brushed nonexistent dust from her knees, and put the tea on her desk. "Do I look suitable enough to be presented to a potential client?"

Cynthia pursed her lips, taking the question seriously enough that Lara bit back laughter: the girl's critical examination was better suited to a woman three times her age. "You'll do," she said after a moment, then lost her serious demeanor and dimpled. "You look wonderful. But you should probably put some shoes on."

Lara looked down at herself with a quick nod. She'd changed from rain-soaked clothing to a white silk blouse and gray wool three-quarter-length pants, their wide legs nearly a skirt. She'd been working in stocking feet, but she reached for knee-high boots now, slipping them on and adding another inch and a half to her height. "I don't have a suit jacket," she muttered. "I didn't expect to see anyone today. And my hair's all frizzy from the rain."

"Here." Cynthia scurried from the room, then returned moments later with a round hairbrush. "Brush the curls out and tie it back in a chignon and you'll be perfect, even without a jacket. Perfect," she repeated when Lara'd done as she'd instructed. "You look like one of those old paintings."

"Cracked and split?" Lara flashed a smile, patted her hair one more time, and followed Cynthia out of the office.

David Kirwen waited in the lobby, expression animated over whatever news his cell phone shared. Lara stopped in the archway leading from the private fitting rooms and offices, surprise slamming her heartbeat high. She curled one hand around the door frame for support, and wished, for a moment, that she could retreat and try her entrance again, this time knowing who awaited her. Cynthia slowed, peering at her, and Lara gave her a halfhearted smile of reassurance.

Kirwen looked up from his phone and offered a disarming grin. "Miss Jansen. I'm glad I caught you. I only realized after the fact that we hadn't set a time or place for dinner."

"I'd noticed that, too." Lara swallowed against a dry throat and gave Cynthia another smile, this one tinged with embarrassment. Cynthia's gaze brightened and she turned to give Lara a discreet thumbs-up before scurrying into the back offices and leaving Lara alone with David Kirwen.

He was considerably more handsome dry and smiling than he'd been dripping and cold on the street. That was her first thought: not *what is he doing here* or *how did he find me*, but *Kelly is right. He really is awfully good-looking*. More than good-looking: he bordered on pretty, features sharper and more chiseled than men's usually were. Men in general suddenly seemed rather blunt and thick when compared to David Kirwen, as if much of humanity were discarded rough drafts to his final sculpture.

A sculpture that could be far better dressed. Lara's palms itched with the desire to step forward and adjust his lapels, or better yet, to simply strip his clothes away and learn the canvas she had to work with. His stance suggested he would be beautiful in clothes cut to his form; as if he were meant to be dressed by someone like her, who could take the ordinary and trick the eye into believing it was extraordinary. Given the extraordinary to begin with, she could create such a vision that people would stop on the street, an emperor in new clothes.

She actually stepped forward to do that, to touch him and see if the gift she'd been given was real, before she remembered he wasn't a client. Curiosity lit his eyes, then turned his smile warm and amused. Lara, cheeks afire, stopped where she stood, and Kirwen's smile grew broader still. "Am I that bad, then?"

"No. No, I just forgot you weren't here for a fitting, Mr. Kirwen. I'm not used to men dropping by for any other reason." While true, the statement had a ring of pathos about it, and stung her into a straighter spine and lifted chin. "Really, I'm very sorry about Kelly's behavior this afternoon. She doesn't know when to quit."

"Occasionally we all need someone like that in our lives. I have Dickon finagling us a table at Troquet, so I hope that despite the unorthodox approach you might have dinner with me tonight anyway?"

"I—" Puzzlement took hold. "How did you *find* me?"

Kirwen laughed. "If I answer, will you say yes to dinner? No." He passed off the bargain with a wave of his hand. "Your friend mentioned you were a bespoke tailor. There are only a handful of shops in Boston that do that kind of work. I set my assistant on Google while I recorded the evening's weather report." He nodded toward a window, where rain still spattered against the pane. "Fortunately, it didn't require much guesswork as to how it would turn out."

An inkling of humor worked its way through Lara, though she kept her expression cool. "So you're a stalker, Mr. Kirwen?"

Dismay shattered across his face. "No, no, not at all. I just wan— Oh. You're teas— No," he said again, this time with more dignity.

"But my assistant takes stalking assignments as routine when necessary."

"I'm sure she does." Lara ducked her head, partially to hide amusement at Kirwen's story, but more to take refuge in the meaningless phrase. *I'm sure she does:* people usually meant it sarcastically, or as a way to pass off a topic they were uninterested in. It was one of a handful of things she could say, though, without triggering her own discomfort. Particularly when someone like Kirwen was making light of something but still spoke essential truth. Lara *was* certain his assistant took stalking, or at least Internet searching, in stride. She looked up, smiling. "I'm not sure, Mr. Kirwen. Your assistant was the one who did all the work. Maybe I should have dinner with her."

Genuine surprise filtered through his expression by degrees, and though they didn't stand close together, Kirwen fell back half a step. "I imagine that could be arranged, although I don't think Nat—my assistant—is, um, I don't think she typically dates wom . . ." He trailed off, peering at Lara in much the same way Cynthia had moments before. "This is impertinent, Miss Jansen, but would your friend have been trying to set us up on a date quite so enthusiastically if you preferred dating women?"

Laughter bubbled up and broke. "No, but it seemed like your assistant ought to get some benefit from doing your dirty work. She finds me, you get a date, and she gets . . . ?"

Kirwen, hopefully, said, "I could bring her the leftovers from Troquet? Okay," he admitted as Lara arched an eyebrow at him, "I wouldn't be impressed with leftovers, either. What, then? Roses? A paid holiday in Bermuda?"

"I was thinking more in terms of a box of chocolates, although if you're inclined to offer paid holidays to Bermuda, I think Kelly might want to talk to you about a job."

"Kelly? Not you?" Kirwen smiled. "I thought that kind of job perk would make anyone stand up to be counted."

Lara shrugged one shoulder, then glanced back toward her office.

"I like my job, Mr. Kirwen, that's all. I've never been inclined to say I'd want something that I don't. Even jobs whose side benefits include trips to Bermuda."

"How extraordinary," Kirwen murmured. Lara looked back at him and he shook himself, a hopeful smile reappearing. "Does that mean you've said yes?"

"I suppose it does," she said, surprising herself. Kirwen's eyes lit up, and Lara, truthfully and teasingly, explained, "Kelly would never let me live it down if I refused."

His face fell comically. Lara laughed, then gestured toward her office. "Let me get my coat and call her, and we can go."

Four

Kirwen hailed a taxi outside Lord Matthew's, and the driver's gaze locked on him as they climbed in. Almost before the door closed, the cabbie launched into a diatribe about the weather in general and David's inability to correctly predict it specifically, and ended with a plea for a sunny weekend, because his daughter's thirteenth birthday party was Saturday and he would go crazy if locked in the house with a dozen teenage girls all day. Lara exited the taxi wide-eyed and bemused to see Kirwen give the man a handsome tip. "Does that happen to you a lot?"

"Only on days I leave the house." The delivery was wry but honest. "I get blamed for the weather but rarely praised for it."

"And occasionally asked to intercede, like he just did?" Lara scurried for the door, throwing a rueful glance toward the sky. "I had no idea being a weatherman was so much responsibility."

"Neither did I, when I started. But it sends me interesting places at times. I covered the hurricanes last year." Kirwen reached over her head to push the door open, its weight coloring his fingertips white. Lara slipped under his arm and pushed the hood of her coat back, trying to shake off the rain.

"I remember. I remember thinking a job that sent you to Florida would be wonderful, except I'd want to go when the weather was good."

Kirwen grinned. "So would I, but the station doesn't seem to think sunshine and Disney World make for exciting weather stories. All right, if we're lucky Dickon's here before us . . ." He trotted up the stairs ahead of Lara, coat flapping dramatically, then waved and turned back to Lara with a bright expression. "And we've got the best seats in the house. Now, aren't you glad you agreed to come out with us?"

Dickon waved a greeting from a table beside enormous picture windows overlooking the Common. Even with the gray skies and rain, the polished wood floors reflected light, making the narrow room comfortable, and Lara smiled. "I think I am. I've never been here. Is being a famous weatherman enough to get you the best table on short notice on a Friday night, or does it just work mid-week?"

"I've never tried on a Friday." Kirwen gestured Lara toward his cameraman's table, admitting, "I doubt it's enough. Dickon, this is Lara Jansen. Miss Jansen, Dickon Collins, my cameraman and the only one with sense enough to come out of the rain."

"Nice to meet you, Miss Jansen," Dickon said over Lara's murmured "Lara is fine," then corrected himself: "Lara." He stood up to offer his hand. Lara nearly took a step back, astonished at the man's height and breadth, though he wasn't fat, only barrel-chested.

Rue crossed his face. "I have that effect, sorry. I look smaller sitting down. There's a reason they put David in front of the camera, not me."

"I was just thinking you'd look—" Lara put her fingers over her mouth, and he cocked an eyebrow curiously. "I'm sorry. I tend to re-dress people mentally as soon as I meet them. It can come across as rude, but I don't mean to be. I just like imagining people at their best." She flattened her fingers further over her lips. "I'm not making this better, am I?"

Kirwen, less reassuringly than Lara might have liked, said "It's all right" to Collins as he pulled Lara's chair out and invited her to sit. "She was dismayed at my clothes, too. You're in good company."

"I'm in your company, anyway." Dickon sat back down, grinning at Lara. "Probably giving you a hard time isn't the best way to make a good first impression, is it? But I figure we're safe, because everybody knows who David is, anyway. It's too late for a first impression."

That, at least, was true, if not for the reasons Dickon outlined. Lara glanced at David, who shed his raincoat and sat down beside her. "I wasn't dismayed. I just forgot you weren't a client for a moment. You have the kind of build clothing designers dream of. And," she added to Dickon, "I was only going to say, you'd be very imposing in a well-made suit."

"I'm imposing out of one." Collins pursed his lips. "That came out wrong. Maybe I better shut up now."

"I think that's probably one of your better ideas," David agreed. "We're not really rapscallions, Miss Jansen."

"Rapscallion," Lara murmured. The word sent shivers over her skin, not precisely mistruth, but a waiting on tunefulness. "A sort of rascal, a dishonest or unscrupulous person, though that's a darker definition than people usually mean. Popularly it's more like youthful wickedness. Mischievous. So I'd say you are that, Mr. Kirwen, but no harm meant."

Both men gawked at her, Dickon's smile coming to the fore more quickly than David's. "Wow, what are you, a walking dictionary? That was kind of cool."

Lara shrugged, embarrassed and pleased all at once. "I like to be precise with word choice. I have a pile of dictionaries and thesauruses at home so I can compare synonym definitions for precision." Color climbed her cheeks before she'd finished speaking, and she wished for a glass of water to hide behind until the heat faded. "It's more interesting than it sounds."

David Kirwen watched her with interest, though amusement played on his lips. "Actually, it sounds interesting. Whatever made you start doing that?"

"People don't use language very carefully, and it bothers me. Trying to change them is futile, but at least I can say exactly what I mean." It was an explanation she'd given before, all true without being all the truth. Lara smiled. "Besides, once in a while I can use it to tease handsome men who take me out to dinner."

"Handsome," Kirwen said with satisfaction. "Not well dressed, maybe, but handsome. It's a start. Is your friend as pedantic as you?"

"Kelly?" Lara glanced toward the stairs, as though Kelly's name might summon her. "No, but she doesn't get impatient with me, which is probably better. I wonder if I should call her."

"I don't think you'll have to." Dickon spoke with a new degree of admiration, and got to his feet as Lara turned to look toward the stairway again.

Kelly waved a greeting, thigh-length trench coat already unbuttoned over a figure-hugging green knit dress Lara was certain she hadn't owned an hour ago. She swept down on them, shook both men's hands, then seized Lara's upper arm with bright-eyed anticipation. "You know how it is, a woman can't go to the restroom alone. Come with me, Lar, please?"

A protest faltered on Lara's lips as the men laughed, Dickon asking, "What is it about women and bathrooms?" in a mutter he clearly intended to be overheard.

"It allows us to talk about you while pretending we're attending to nature's call. Pretending we're attending, that rhymed. C'mon, Lara. It's a feminine duty. Please?" Kelly dropped her coat over the back of a free chair and caught Lara's hand, tugging her toward the restrooms.

"Duty calls." Careful word choice, made easier by Kelly's laughing description of what duty was. Lara shook her head and, smiling, followed Kelly. "You look fantastic, Kel. The dress is great. Where'd you buy it?"

"I should've known I couldn't trick you into thinking I'd run home and changed clothes. You know my wardrobe better than I do." Kelly stopped inside the restroom door and turned to the mirrors, smoothing a hand over her hips nervously. "It's not too tight? I thought, wow, I look hot, but now I'm kind of all, wow, maybe I'm just fat."

"Not from the way Dickon stood to attention when you came in," Lara said drily, then smiled at their reflections. They were each other's opposites, Kelly tall and lush, Lara petite and conservative. "You don't look at all fat, Kel. You're beautiful. The dress is fantastic on you."

"God, one of the best things about being friends with you is I know you're not bullshitting when you say that. And Dickon did stand up, didn't he? I mean, I know you mean that literally, because you're you, but can I take it figuratively, too? He's cute, isn't he? In a big-redheaded-lug kind of way? Lara!" Kelly caught Lara in a hug, then set her back with equal enthusiasm. "Lara, you have a date! You have seized the bull's horns! Congratulations!"

Lara laughed. "I haven't seized anything. I just knew you would never stop harassing me if I said no, especially after he actually showed up at Lord Matthew's."

"You could have not told me."

"Except you would have eventually asked if I'd ever heard from that weatherman, and I would've had to tell the truth."

Impishness crossed Kelly's face. "That's true. You know, your weird truth-telling thing is handier for me than you."

"I do know. Did you have to pee, or were you just hauling me off to talk about the men?"

"Oh, I just wanted to talk about them," Kelly said blithely. "See, Lara, he liked you. He went to the trouble of finding you! Has he said anything that makes you go"—she clawed her hands and bared her teeth, physical action replacing words—"yet? So he's from Wales? I never met a Welsh guy before. What's he doing here? W—"

"Kelly!" Lara held her hands up. "I don't know. We've only been here five minutes. And if you don't have to go to the bathroom, I bet you'd find out a lot more answers by talking to him instead of me."

"Oh no. You talk to him. I'll keep Dickon distracted. And if he turns out to be a pathological liar you can knock your water glass on me so we can make an escape."

"If David does, or if Dickon does?"

"Ooh, she's graduated to calling him David," Kelly announced to their reflections. "That's a good sign. And either of them." She ran her hands over her hips again, then nodded. "Okay. We're ready to go now."

"We are?"

"I am," Kelly amended with a sniff.

"I don't understand why you're nervous, when you're the one who all but shanghaied me into going on this date." Lara nudged Kelly out of the restroom to the sound of mumbled excuses.

David stood again as they returned to the table, Dickon a beat behind him. "Someday," Kirwen said to his cameraman. "Someday I'll have you well enough trained that you won't need reminding to stand when women enter the room."

"At which time a woman will happily take him off your hands." Kelly moved Lara's coat from the back of her chair and took the seat herself, then smiled merrily at Lara. "You can sit across from David."

Dickon's eyebrows rose as Lara came around the table to sit by him. "I bet she's deadly at weddings, huh? Rearranges seating arrangements and shi—stuff?"

"As a matter of fact, she does. We know two couples who met at weddings because Kelly is a busybody."

"I am not!"

Lara smiled. "Yes, you are, but you mean well." She nodded thanks as a waitress offered menus and poured water, and for a few moments let herself become engrossed in nominally studying the choices, and actually peeking over its edge at David Kirwen.

He had a knack, like Kelly did, for putting people at ease. A more useful talent than her own, certainly; knowing the truth had never talked someone into joining her for dinner. The idea made her hide a smile behind her menu. Kelly would no doubt find a way to use the truth to get a dinner date.

Lara shook her head. It was easy to compare herself unfavorably to her boisterous friend, to envy Kelly's quick way with words and willingness to risk embarrassment in pursuit of the things that interested her.

Things like David Kirwen. Well, no: Kelly had gone after David purely for Lara's benefit, which she was certain of for two reasons. One, she'd have heard the lie if Kelly had been interested in Kirwen for herself, and two, the slender weatherman genuinely wasn't Kelly's type. His broad-built cameraman, though . . .

Lara hid another smile in her menu. Kelly would call it instant karmic feedback, trying to set Lara up for a date and finding a hunk of her own by doing so.

"You must have gotten a much more entertaining menu than I did." David Kirwen tipped Lara's menu toward him so he could peer down it. "It looks the same . . ."

Lara clapped the menu shut, then, flustered, opened it again. "Oh. No. No, I was just thinking. I hadn't even looked at it."

Kirwen flourished his fingers, coming up with a shining coin. "Penny for your thoughts, then?"

"Oh!" Lara reached out, startled, to catch the penny from his fingertips. "How did you do that!"

"You'd have me give away all my secrets on the first date?" Kirwen *tsked*. "You've taken the penny, so you owe me a thought now, don't you?"

"Ooh," Kelly said loudly enough to be heard, though her innocent expression suggested she didn't intend to be, "that implies there'll be a second date. That's promising."

Lara aimed a kick at her under the table and instead crashed her booted toes into the pedestal with a *thonk*. Kelly burst out laughing as Lara sank into her seat, face buried in her hands. "Way to be sub-tuhl, Lar. She was thinking a second date had better not be a double," Kelly told David. "Better not ask her while Dickon's around. He'll horn in on it."

"Only if my barbecue is rained out!"

Lara risked peeking through her fingers in time to see Kelly give Dickon a frankly lascivious once-over and lean in to purr, "Honey, I'll make sure your barbecue never goes out."

Dickon, brightly, said, "Check, please!" and beneath their laughter Lara murmured, "I was thinking it would be easier to be like you and Kelly. She makes friends in a heartbeat, and you seem to expect that, too. I'm not that outgoing." She held up the penny, smile turning wistful. "Was that worth a penny?"

"It was." David reached out to fold the coin into her palm, briefly cupping his hand over hers. "And if we were all as forthright as Kelly, then we would miss the delight of coaxing the shy out of their shells. Some things, Miss Jansen, are worth the wait."

"Good," Kelly broke in cheerfully. "Wait until Saturday."

David released Lara's hand, sending a rush of disappointment through her. She quashed it, feeling absurd, and frowned at Kelly. "We're helping Rachel move on Saturday."

"Exactly! David can spend the whole day coaxing you, *and* we'll have a couple of big strong handsome men around to help."

David turned to his cameraman solemnly. "I believe we've been hornswoggled, Dickon."

"I believe we have," Dickon said just as solemnly, then squinted at Lara. "Hornswoggled means tricked, right?"

"Oh no." Kelly looked dismayed. "You haven't already done your walking dictionary trick, have you? I swear, Lara, I leave you alone for five minutes . . . !"

Lara lifted her chin and sniffed, trying to dismiss Kelly playfully, and shook her head at Dickon. "It's like rapscallion. The real meaning is darker than the way it's used now. You have an old-fashioned vocabulary, Mr. Kirwen. Is that a Welsh thing?"

"It's certainly the way of my people," Kirwen replied lightly. "What time will you need us to help move your friend?"

"Us?" Dickon's voice rose. "Who said anything about us?"

"You wouldn't leave a fair lady in distress, would you, Dickon?" David gestured to Kelly, who fluttered her eyelashes and put on an unconvincing expression of helplessness. Dickon laughed and raised his hands in defeat. Lara smiled at the banter, listening as plans were made, and watched David Kirwen quietly, thoughtfully.

"It's the way of my people" was a very careful phrase. Lara thought even she might have overlooked it had it not highlighted something he'd said earlier, that his name was Welsh "by most accounts." He laid no claim to that account himself.

Curiosity blossomed in Lara's chest, stealing her breath. Handsome, witty, and not only mysterious, but cautiously mysterious. Very few people she knew could disguise the truth in such a way as to not trigger her sixth sense. Even fewer would have any reason to.

Disarmed by her own interest, Lara sat forward to rejoin the conversation and enjoy the prospect of dinner with a man who could keep a secret from her.

Five

"I haven't stayed up this late in months. I won't be able to see the pins tomorrow." Lara frowned at her feet, having difficulty focusing on where to place them, much less the more dubious prospect of fine needlework on the morrow. The steps leading down from the restaurant seemed distinctly more treacherous than they had upon arrival. "How much wine did you give me?"

"I believe you *asked* for that fourth glass," David Kirwen said in amused self-defense. "Careful, now." He offered his elbow and Lara clung to it gratefully as he escorted her down the stairs. Kelly and Dickon waited at the bottom, neither of them as impeded as Lara. She scowled lightly at Kelly, who made a dismissive sound.

"I drank as much as you did. I just have a lot more body weight to slosh it around in. You okay?"

"I think so." Lara released Kirwen's elbow and smiled up at him. "It was a lovely dinner. Thank you."

"My pleasure. I hope we can do it again sometime."

"Saturday." Kelly put on a winsome smile so transparent that Lara laughed. "Pizza after moving day. You don't mind, do you?"

"How could I resist such a heartfelt plea? We'll be there." Kirwen arched his eyebrows at Dickon. "Won't we?"

"Yeah, yeah, yeah." Despite his grumble, the cameraman didn't sound at all put out, and shook first Kelly's and then Lara's hands. "It was nice to meet both of you. We'll see you Saturday."

A chorus of farewells followed, and Kelly took up David's position of balancing Lara as they made their way down the sidewalk toward Kelly's car. The instant they were out of earshot, Kelly began singing, "Hey there, you with the stars in your eyes!"

"*Hnf.* The laws of physics don't allow for stars in the eyes, Kelly." She glanced over her shoulder as they climbed into the Nissan. "He is awfully handsome, though, isn't he?"

"If you like skinny blond boys with exotic accents, sure." Kelly grinned as they pulled into traffic. "You liked him. After all that fuss over his name this afternoon, you really liked him, didn't you?"

"He's interesting. No, I mean it!"

"Of course you mean it. You don't say things you don't mean. Define interesting, by Lara Ann Jansen's standards."

"He doesn't tell lies, but he's very careful about what he says. He never said he was from Wales, did you notice?" Lara folded her arms around herself and scooted down in the seat like a much younger girl. "I hate it when people lie to me, Kel. Not about the small things, you can't help that. But bigger things, it just feels so wrong. But he's not lying, he's just . . ."

"Interesting," Kelly finished triumphantly. "Who knew it would be the man she couldn't see right through who would catch her eye?" She pursed her lips, then shrugged. "Of course, if I put it that way it's kind of obvious, isn't it? Although, really, Lara, I think if you were trying to get him to slip up, you probably should have been pouring the wine into him, not into yourself."

"But I wasn't! I was just having a good time." Lara caught Kelly's fingers, squeezing, then released her so she could put her hand back on the wheel. "Thanks, Kel. I never would have gone if it weren't for you. I had fun. Thank you. And what about you? You and Dickon seemed to hit it off."

"It'll be a double wedding," Kelly said cheerfully.

Lara sang, "Slow down, you move too fast!" then laughed at Kelly's expression. "What? You started it with the stars in your eyes song, and how often do I get to sing something true?" When she could, or when she heard songs performed with genuine integrity, they always seemed strikingly powerful to her, but it was a rare occasion that either happened. Lara shook her head, smiling out the window. "I don't want to think about weddings, Kel. I'm just looking forward to Saturday."

"You remember how you were looking forward to this?" Kelly crouched beside another box as Lara put her hands into the small of her back and pushed forward, trying to pop her spine. A series of small clicks rattled her and she gave a breathless *oomph*, bending forward to touch her toes and finish the stretch.

"I wasn't talking about the heavy-lifting part, Kelly. But they say many hands make light work." Lara craned her neck, watching Rachel and her girlfriend stagger out the door carrying precariously balanced hatboxes. The four women would have been enough, but Dickon and David's presence sped things along: it only took the two of them to move things that all four women would have had to cooperate on.

"And it must be true right now, or you'd be saying too many cooks spoil the broth. Except there aren't any cooks or any broth here. God, you're literal."

Lara's eyebrows rose. "I didn't say a word, Kel. That deconstruction was entirely on you."

"Oh. Well, fine. Going to help me with this?" They took the box up together—filled with clothes, it was only awkwardly large, not heavy—and Kelly led the way toward the door. Dickon's shadow warned them to stop before a crash ensued, and he leaped aside, flattening himself against the door as best he could when he saw them.

"Want me to get that?"

"Hm." Kelly peered past the box toward the living room. "So far you've gotten the television, the computer, fifteen boxes of graphic novels, all the canned goods in the house, and an oak bed frame. I think we can manage one box of clothes. Go on." She jerked her chin, indicating he could go past them. He did a credible scurry for a man of his bulk, getting out of the way. They careened through the door and Kelly yelled a curse as she ran into David, who flattened himself more successfully and shot an apologetic look over the box. Lara grunted and they pushed past him, taking the stairs faster than wisdom dictated.

At the bottom, Kelly gave Lara a breathless grin. "Well, at least you can now say you've been in a tight space with him."

Lara pulled a face. "Not that I ever would. Kelly, I don't work like you do. It's all right, really."

Kelly laughed, guiding them out to the moving truck. "No, you wouldn't, but you could! I know you don't, Lar." They shoved the box into the truck, Kelly scrambling up after it to maneuver it into a tight spot. "I'm just afraid you're not having any fun, all hunched up there at the shop with your needle and thread. I want you to live a little."

"Your idea of living a little is throwing yourself off a bridge," Lara pointed out, relishing the opportunity to make a melodramatic and also absolutely honest statement.

"That was only the once! And I had bungee cords!"

"I know, but my point stands. He's nice, Kelly. He's interesting. You got us set up on a date. Let me take it at my own pace from here, okay?"

Kelly jumped out of the truck, arms akimbo and expression triumphant. "As long as you're actually going to, no problem."

"You," Lara said as severely as she could, "should quit the bra shop and go into matchmaking. Has anybody ever told you you're a busybody?"

"You do, regularly. And if I quit working there I'll lose my discount and will have to start going braless because buying them will bankrupt me. Nobody, least of all me, wants the girls bouncing around unslung. I'd say 'Ow, know what I mean?' except you don't."

" 'Some of us have fast metabolisms,' " Lara reminded her.

"I don't think that actually has anything to do with the difference between a B cup and a Q cup."

"You do not wear a Q cup."

"Well, you don't even have Q-tips!"

Lara threw her head back and laughed. "That's not true. All right, fine, don't quit. But if you're not taking up matchmaking full-time maybe you should stop pursuing it at all!"

"Lara, the only other excitement in my life is measuring women for bras."

"And jumping off bridges. And robo-rally racing or whatever that was you did a few weekends ago. And—"

Kelly ignored her, clearly not to be undone by minor details like truth. "I like a well-fitted bra as much as the next girl, but measuring acres of female flesh doesn't hold a candle to interfering in my friends' love lives. It'd be one thing if you could be trusted to it yourselves."

"Trusted to what?" Dickon and David came out of the stairwell, staggering under the weight of a king-sized mattress. Lara and Kelly scattered away from the truck, guilt staining Lara's cheeks pink. They'd only stood outside bantering for a moment or two, but others had been working while they played.

She wrinkled her nose. Kelly was right: she was too serious. Easier to admit than to change, though. Kelly's adventuresome streak had yet to rub off on her, and they'd been friends since college. "None of us can be trusted to run our own love lives, according to Kelly. But she won't give up her day job to become a matchmaker."

"The day job? Didn't you say you sell bras?" Dickon shoved the mattress the last few inches into the truck, then turned, panting, to Kelly. Lara clapped a hand over her mouth, cutting off a laugh. David appeared at her side to cock a curious eyebrow, and she let a smile slip through.

"Oh, Kelly's so . . ." She made an hourglass figure with her hands. "People would say she's the kind of woman men pant over. I thought it was funny to see someone actually doing that. I know he's just breathless from working, but—"

"People would say. But not you?"

"Well, I've never seen it really happen." Lara shifted her shoulders uncomfortably, and Kirwen's expression grew curious.

"And you only report what you see?"

Lara folded her arms under her breasts, keeping her eyes on Kelly and Dickon, the latter of whom was enthusiastic in his opinion that Kelly *shouldn't* give up her day job. "Kelly told you the other day. I have a knack for hearing the truth, so I don't like to stretch its boundaries. People don't usually literally drool or pant over one another. They might admire or gawk or be distracted, but actual drooling?" She shook her head.

"That's quite extraordinary." Kirwen sounded distant. Lara turned a concerned frown up at him, and discovered his gaze was as inaccessible as his voice. He seemed to be looking into her, through her, and beyond her, seeing something so far off as to be forever lost to him. "No wonder you have such a fascination with the precise meaning of words. Has it always been thus for you?"

Lara's eyebrows shot up. "Been *thus*? Rapscallion's one thing, David. Now you're getting all Middle English."

"Even Old, I should think," he said absently, then shook himself. "Sorry. It's a habit left over from a long time ago. But you've always known the truth when it was spoken to you?"

"Ever since I can remember. Kelly's right." Lara sighed and finally turned from the moving truck to go back upstairs. "It's annoying. I don't know if it's more annoying for me or my friends, but it's annoying."

David fell into step behind her, speaking so quietly she might have thought she imagined his words, but for the ring of truth in them: "No, Lara, it's a gift."

Lara's heart knocked in her chest, a dull thud that carried sorrow with it. She stopped, then pressed up against the wall to let Dickon and Kelly pass before turning to look down on David. "It's not much of a gift. Maybe if I could know what someone was lying about, or somehow make them tell the truth, it would be a gift. At least, if I wanted to be a lawyer, or some kind of advocate like that. But as it is, I'm a seamstress, and it just makes everyone, including me, uncomfortable."

"Gifts," David said quietly, "are rarely comfortable, and I believe truthseekers never are."

The word hit her skin like ice water, shivering and playing there. Lara caught a breath behind her teeth and held herself still, staring down at the weatherman. "What did you— Why did you call me that? *Truthseeker.* I've never heard that before."

"No." Sympathy colored his voice, warm and sad. "But it's what you are, isn't it? You're drawn to the truth. Drawn to its flawless lines, to the points it makes between one being and another. You live in a world made of truth's song, cradled by music, all the time. And it sounds so appealing," Kirwen murmured. "It sounds so appealing, when it's phrased that way.

"But what people forget is that music has a power all its own, doesn't it? A life beyond any granted to it by notes written on a page. Music, unleashed, can uplift and create and destroy, stripping away pretenses and leaving raw, exposed vulnerability behind. It's a gift, but not one to be envied." Kirwen's hands were knotted, urgency in them belied by the softness of his voice. His brown eyes were filled with helpless compassion, as if he understood what it was to know, always know, whether someone spoke the truth or not.

And he did. He understood in a way most people never did, not even Kelly. Lara's chest hurt, breath forgotten as Kirwen grasped truth in both hands and laid it before her unrelentingly. The music of his words soared, carrying hope that caught in her throat. This was a man who wouldn't lie to her, not for her sake, not for his own.

This was a man she could make a life with.

The thought was so unguarded Lara backed up a step and wrapped her arms around herself in unrealized defense. "Who are you? I don't even know you." The protest was more for herself than for the man who stood before her, a warning that she shouldn't trust a flighty thought of lifetimes, for all that her every impulse was to step forward and hide her face against David Kirwen's chest.

"I can tell you," he said, "and you'll believe me because you'll know I'm not lying, but it would be better if I could show you. I have so much to explain to you. So much to ask of you. And no right to do either, but I'm desperate, Lara. I've been searching for you for nearly one hundred years."

Six

"Time's treating you well." Lara could barely force a whisper, voice tightened by the feeling of her heart filling her throat and the sensation of air having fled her lungs. A rare phrase intruded on her thoughts: *I don't believe my ears.* Nearly everyone said that, but Lara, stripped bare of the pretenses shared by polite society, had always found it awkward. Now, despite the talent David Kirwen had just named *truthseeking,* she was hard-pressed to trust the conviction in his voice. No one lived a hundred years and remained young, except in fairy tales.

She looked away, suddenly and intensely uncomfortable. Preposterous truth was one thing; she'd encountered it often enough. Truth that was simply impossible, though, was beyond her scope, and she had no idea what to say to a man who presented it to her.

Her peripheral vision caught David's unhappy smile. "Do you believe in fairy tales, Lara?"

Lara jerked her gaze back to him, heart pounding. He hadn't—couldn't have—read her mind, but his question followed her thoughts so closely it seemed he had. She tightened her arms around herself and shook her head. "I don't like fiction very much. I know about learning lessons through allegory, but . . . no."

"It might be easier if you did. I—"

"Are you two down there necking?"

The question shattered David's solemn expression, and they both looked toward Rachel's apartment door to find Kelly peering down at them hopefully. "You're not. How disappointing. Well, get up here and help us argue over what kind of pizza we're ordering, then. Dickon wants anchovies. Rachel told him he'd have to have a pizza of his own in that case, but he seemed okay with that. So now we're trying to figure out if everybody gets one of their own." She disappeared inside, and Lara turned to David, who dropped his head in mild vexation.

"Maybe this discussion is better left for later." He made as if to catch Lara's hand, as if he'd pull her out of the hug she held herself in, but stopped before touching her. "Please. At least say you'll let me explain myself."

A tiny surge of disappointment caught her off guard and she frowned at her tightly held arms, feeling as though she'd somehow betrayed herself. All good sense told her to back away, to forget what he'd said and the unlikely truth in his words. No one lived for centuries, and no one would have any reason to search for someone like her.

Except, inconceivably, improbably, David Kirwen. "Dafydd ap Caerwyn," she said aloud, though softly.

Hope flashed through his expression. "The name I was born to, somewhere a very long way from here. Lara, please. An hour's time to explain, without anyone to interrupt. I beg you."

"Oh, well." Flighty laughter caught her chest and she threw a consulting glance upward. The stairwell lights offered no opinion, but she turned a nervous smile on Kirwen. *Caerwyn,* she reminded herself, and said, "If you're begging, it would be unkind to refuse you."

"Thank you." He did catch her hand this time, and kissed her knuckles to send a bolt of shy excitement and curiosity through her. "After supper, perhaps. Thank you, Lara. Already I'm in your debt."

Lara managed an uncertain smile. "In that case, you can buy my pizza."

He didn't, of course: it was Rachel and Sharon's treat, in thanks for help with the move. Despite Kelly's machinations, Lara sat across from David on the living room floor, more interested in watching than conversing. Kelly took it as a good sign and elbowed Lara more than once, making silly faces of encouragement. Lara smiled, but her attention was drawn time and again by the slender man regaling them all with tall tales of storm-chasing.

Mostly tall: there was enough basis in truth that she could tell when he veered into melodrama, though his description of their weather van being lifted up and spun around by a tornado had all the hallmarks of sincerity. It was more plausible than the idea that he'd been searching for her for a century.

More plausible, but no less genuine. Lara took refuge in eating a slice of pizza and trying to clear her whirling thoughts. Sherlock Holmes had said that when the impossible was eliminated, whatever remained, however implausible, must be the truth. It was one of very few axioms Lara liked, for no other reason than her own *truth-seeking* sense proved it right so often, regardless of what others believed. And so Dafydd ap Caerwyn was over a century old, because not once in her entire life had her talent told her wrong in the face of a direct statement.

She just didn't understand *how*. Curious impatience danced inside her, setting her heartbeat ajar. She took another piece of pizza, nibbling it to the crust and abandoning it as she came up with theories from fairy tales to Frankenstein, and rejected them. Divine touch, maybe: he was fair enough to be an angel, though an angel would hardly need a job. Lara laughed at herself, then snagged more pizza and shook her head as everyone glanced her way.

Kelly leaned over to whisper, "That's your fourth piece. I've never seen you eat this much at once. He's that discombobulating, huh?"

Lara blinked at the pizza slice, and at the remains of three others left on her paper plate. "Oh no. I won't be able to fit in my pants tomorrow."

"That's all right." Kelly nudged her again and dropped a wink. *"He'll fit just fine."*

"Kelly!"

Kelly cackled and sat up again to snag one of the last pieces of pizza herself. "You know what we forgot to order? Dessert. Where's the nearest Baskin-Robbins?"

"A few blocks from here. We should walk over," Rachel suggested. "Walk off some of the pizza. And then walk home to burn off the ice cream."

"I've already walked off the pizza by climbing those stairs four hundred times," Dickon muttered good-naturedly. "I'll need a six-scoop sundae just to keep even."

"After eating an entire pizza?" David asked both politely and incredulously. Dickon flopped the lid of his empty box closed, assuming a catlike expression of disinterested innocence.

"Maybe you could bring me something back." Lara carefully didn't look at David, but her pulse jumped to an alarming pace. Sour notes jangled beneath her skin, though what she said was technically true: "I thought I might start cleaning. Your landlord is due pretty early in the morning, isn't he?"

"Oh, God, you'll make us look bad." Rachel made a face. "Come with us, we'll all clean later."

"No, it's a good idea," David volunteered. "I'll stay and help Lara. We'll get a head start and you can bring us back an ice-cream cake. That won't melt on the walk home."

A little silence broke over the room as Rachel and Sharon exchanged looks that clearly said *oooOOOooh.* Together, and with obvious deliberate speed, they herded Kelly and Dickon out the door, leaving Lara with David and a few slices of abandoned pizza.

"Well." Nervous excitement made Lara draw her knees up and loop her arms around them. It was ridiculous to be nervous or excited: it wasn't as though she'd never been alone with a man before. Her job, in fact, required hours of that, and often the men in question were less dressed than Dafydd ap Caerwyn was at the moment.

On the other hand, none of them had ever claimed to have been searching for her at all, much less for decades on end. A little nervous excitement was justified. Lara tugged her knees closer to her chest and tried for a smile. "That wasn't quite as subtle as I hoped."

David laughed. "I'm afraid subtlety isn't a word I'd use to describe your friends. Is that something you like about them?"

"It is. They usually say what they think. It's its own kind of awkward sometimes, but at least I don't constantly feel like I'm battered by lies." Lara thinned her lips, fighting the impulse to leap up and run after her friends. Instead she swallowed hard and murmured, "I'd very much like an explanation, David. Dafydd."

He smiled and got to his feet. "You have a good ear. You say my name well. It's been a long time since I've heard it."

"A hundred years?" Lara tried for lightness and achieved tension, almost anger.

He heard it, and hesitated at the kitchen counter's edge. "In fact, yes, although I know you must be trying to figure out how I'm mocking you. I'm not, Lara. Not at all." He methodically emptied his pockets as he spoke—a palmful of change, a pocketknife, a set of keys—and put them all on the counter. Then he unfastened his belt, shooting Lara a sudden brilliant grin as he did so. "Don't be alarmed."

He set it aside, coiled neatly beside his other belongings, before his hands danced over his torso and upward, fingertips finally touching his left earlobe. His hair, Lara realized, was worn slightly too long, just enough shagginess to be sexy, covering the tops of his ears. A little bit rock star rather than the clean-clipped cut she'd so much expected in a weatherman that she hadn't seen how he really wore it. He removed two discrete earrings, put them on the table, then tapped a fingertip against it, looking himself over as Lara watched in bemused interest.

"Usually we'd discuss what you're looking for in clothing before I'd ask you to disrobe, Mr. Kirwen." Humor infused her statement, one of the times Lara felt comfortable with teasing: every word she spoke was absolutely true.

"You won't need your tape measure for this, I think. It's the metal," David said, explanation truthful, if not enlightening. "It holds the glamour in place, but it traps me, as well. It can't be undone while it touches me."

"Glamour? Undone?" Useless questions, parroted back. Lara pressed her lips together, waiting till she trusted herself not to echo him before she took another breath to speak and ask for clarification. Even as she drew breath, though, David turned back to her, and, as if the world snapped into focus, Lara saw through to the truth of what he'd hidden beneath his glamour.

Almost nothing about him was changed, yet everything was. The nearly pretty lines of his face sharpened and came into aquiline relief. His eyes, far more amber than brown, tilted more profoundly than any man of his pale complexion's might be expected to; that complexion, fair before, was porcelain now, making the sandy gold of his hair richer and darker by comparison. Certainty tightened in Lara's belly, that the too-long cut of his hair was deliberate so it hid the tops of his ears. Dizziness swept over her, preventing her from darting forward to examine his ear tips. It seemed as if it would be an unbearable intimacy. As if stripping himself to bare essentials that were literally beyond human were not already an intimacy that caught Lara with equal parts fascination and uncertainty.

Fascination and uncertainty, but no fear, and its absence seemed peculiar. A man—not a man; whatever he was—should have raised alarm inside her, not a slow release of tension, as if the changes that had been wrought explained a wrongness she hadn't been able to define.

His form, through the shoulder, the waist, the hip, was subtly different, ever so slightly more slender. His height seemed more dramatic for the narrowness of him, though he was no taller than he'd been a moment earlier. The clothes he wore, which had looked good on him moments earlier, now hung poorly on his frame, as if they had been made for a bulkier brother. Glamour stripped away, Lara could barely believe she'd been unable to see it before. He would never again be able to hide beneath his glamour, not with her.

She coughed on a question, unable to put the right words together. David smiled, and when he spoke his voice was lighter, filled with the music of tenor bells.

"My name is Dafydd ap Caerwyn. I am a prince of the Seelie court in the Barrow-lands, and I know you for a truthseeker because my people have legends of them. My brother has been murdered, Lara, and I need your help to find his killer."

Seven

Blood rushed through her ears, the sound of surf crashing in time to her pulse. "Seelie, what does Seelie mean? Elf? Are you an elf? You look like an elf, you're . . ." Nearly human. Nearly, yet he could never be mistaken for human, not like this, not with the indescribably ethereal aspect she now saw.

"Elf would do, though it has connotations in American culture that would make my people cringe. We aren't small woodland sprites, though we are a people of the forests." He spoke as he might to a wary animal: soft, calm, reassuring, as if the steady song of his voice was more important than the words.

Lara clung to them regardless, like they might be a lifeline back to a reality she hadn't intended to leave. She said, "No," hoarsely, and meant it as an agreement. "You're like the elves in the Tolkien books."

Astonishment turned his eyes to pure gold. "I thought you didn't like fairy tales. You've read those?"

"Of course not." Lara backed away until she reached a wall to lean against for support. To put her back against, like she could keep surprises from creeping up on her that way. "But I saw the film trailers."

"Ah." A smile flashed across his face, and Lara thought the images from the films were entirely wrong: those elves had seemed so solemn, where Dafydd's rapid-changing expressions held the capacity for undiluted joy. "More like them," he agreed. "More than the big-eyed, big-haired creatures with oversized swords that litter video games and cartoons, at least."

"And you're . . ." Words failed her again and she stood speechless against the wall before seizing deliberation in order to stave off panic: "I don't understand."

Dafydd took a step forward, then unexpectedly knelt, as if doing so was all that stopped him from chasing her across the room. His voice became something like a song, accent coloring it and turning the words liquid. "*Truth will seek the hardest path, measures that must mend the past, spoken in a child's word, changes that will break the world.*" Wry apology colored the third line, and the song, if not the accent, left his voice as he added, "Only my people would consider a woman in her twenties to be a child. Forgive us that. Our life spans are measured in centuries and millennia, not days and years."

"Dafydd." Lara had used the variant before, but *David* was easier to remember, easier to say, than the slight softening that *Dafydd* required. But the man, the creature, kneeling before her was by no means a mere *David*. Nor would he ever be again, she thought: like the glamour, once undone, she would always think of him as *Dafydd*.

Only after she spoke did she realize she said his name as if it offered answers. Her heart spasmed again, making an ache of tightness in her chest, but loosening her throat. "The beginning. You need to start at the beginning."

"There was a murder," Dafydd said without hesitation. "And that, among my people, is not done. A poet and prophet charged me with finding a truthseeker to hunt the killer with. I have been half-exiled ever since, unable to return home without the truth at my side."

Lara's laugh cramped in her throat. "With the truth at your side? I can tell if people are lying to me. That doesn't make me a-an archetype."

"No." The negative was an agreement, but Dafydd's eyes were

intense on hers. "But only because you're not at the height of your skills. Legend claims that a truthseeker in the grasp of her full power strips away all falsehood around her and lays bare the hearts and souls of everything that surrounds her."

Horror washed over her. "I don't want that. People are uncomfortable with me already. They'd hate me. Find someone else."

"There is no one else." Dafydd got to his feet again, slowly this time, as if she might startle and run. "There hasn't been a truthseeker among my people in aeons. I came to your world hoping I might find a half-blood child who bore the gift."

Lara pressed against the wall, cowardice far greater than curiosity. "I'm not—"

"You aren't," Dafydd agreed quickly, before she had time to struggle through the rest of the words. "Your gift is purely human. Almost," he said with a brief smile. "You could almost be part Seelie, from your figure and form. But there's a touch of something to the courts that—" He hesitated over the word, then made a pattern of rain with his fingers, indicating himself. "Glows."

Lara nodded jaggedly. With his glamour stripped away, an alien warmth cast gold through his presence. In another man she would call it charisma, but in Dafydd ap Caerwyn it was somehow more: as if his very breath could draw her in. She lacked that, and knew it as clearly as she knew her own name. "Then how can I . . . ?"

"Be a truthseeker? Your people have magic, Lara." David's smile went sad. "Not much, and not often, but it's always been there. You know the stories of your great wizards. Merlin," he offered, and Lara nodded again. "Or those with the second sight."

"Psychic hotlines," Lara said, and he shook his head.

"What would it feel like to you, if you took phone calls and money to tell people if something was true?" A shudder coursed over Lara's skin and David nodded. "Most psychics, real ones of any power, feel similarly. One of the prices of the magic. Come with me, Lara." He offered his hand, a smooth movement full of grace. "Help me find the man who killed my brother."

"You're cra—" Lara looked away, jaw clenched. *You're crazy.* A very normal response, perhaps even a true one, but not something she was often inclined to say. "You are crazy," she whispered after a moment. "You might be an elf, but you'd have to be a deluded elf to think a woman who's known you for a few days would . . ."

"Would cast all to the wind to help a stranger? Would you not, Lara? Do you not?"

"No! Not . . . not like this. I don't solve murders. I don't hunt down criminals. I just help a little where I can, Dafydd. And how do you even know that?" Anger burned away discomfort, Lara's cheeks heating. "I just go to open addiction meetings, to try to help people face their problems a little more truthfully, that's all. How do you *know* that?"

"I'm a snoop." Dafydd got to his feet, but stepped back to the counter, putting greater distance between them. "Kelly's comment about you knowing the truth intrigued me, Lara. I've been looking for you for so long. So I—"

"You followed me?"

Half-apologetic guilt slid across his features, still easy to read despite his changed aspect. "I followed you and I had Natalie look up what she could online. You have a degree in psychology. It made me think yes, perhaps you were what I was looking for. Does it help you understand people who see the world so differently than you do? I hope so. But I needed to know, Lara. I needed to know if you were a truthseeker. I'm sorry, but I'm running out of time."

A band of pain sprang up across Lara's forehead, throbbing in time with her pulse. She sank down to the floor, eyes closed and fingertips pressed against the thin skin of her temples. "What does that mean?"

"There are limits to the power that brings me here. If I tarry beyond one hundred of your years, the door will close. I'll be unable to open it again from this side, except perhaps at great personal cost. So I either return home with you—with one such as yourself—now, or I remain an exile here forever."

"Now?" Lara looked up sharply, trying to ignore the ripple of lights that followed when she opened her eyes. "What do you mean by 'now'?"

"I have a few days, perhaps a week. Within the scope of a century, the need is immediate. Will you come with me?"

"No! Go, get out of here!" Lara shoved to her feet, headache intensifying with the strength of her emotion. "I don't understand any of this and I don't want to!"

"I wouldn't ask if I had any other choice." Infuriating truth rang through Dafydd's quiet words, but he retreated, wafting a hand over his belongings on the kitchen counter. "I'll go," he said after a moment, quietly. His form shifted as he spoke, glimmers of change blunting the bones of his cheeks, the length of his fingers, the fineness of his form. They were lies, the things he pulled on over his elfin shape, and they danced and shimmered, making him hard to look at now that Lara knew the truth. She closed her eyes, and waited until his footsteps faded before she looked again. Waited, in fact, until all that was left were his words, echoing in her mind.

"I'm not difficult to find if you should change your mind. I hope that you do. You are my only chance, Lara Jansen. I am lost without you."

She was still sitting against the wall, head cradled in her arms as she tried not to think, when the others returned. Laughter preceded them, filling the stairwell and offering enough warning that she might have gotten to her feet, straightened her clothes, and greeted them with a smile.

With a lie.

It was the thing done in society, by polite people eager to keep others comfortable. Lara knew it, could do it if she had to, but with Dafydd's absence it seemed even more absurd than such rituals normally did. She could offer no easy explanation for why he'd left, and so to let her friends find her worn down was as simple an answer as she might find.

Rachel broke into raucus song—*for they are jolly good fellows!*—as she bumped the door open, all four of them trying to crowd through at once. Laughter and singing fell away as Lara lifted her head, wincing at the overhead lights' brightness.

Kelly gave Dickon an accusing, angry look and thrust an ice-cream cake box into Sharon's hands. Dickon protested, "What'd I do?" and the other two women turned half-suspicious, half-apologetic expressions on him as Kelly ran to Lara's side.

"What happened? What did he do? Are you okay? Where is he?"

"I'm . . ." *Fine* was inadequate; *fine* had variable definitions. "I'm not hurt, Kel. A migraine came on all of a sudden."

"Oh." Kelly thumped down on her butt. "Did David go to get medicine? God, you scared me there, Lara. I thought he'd hit you or something."

"David would never—!" Dickon's voice shot up in outrage and the women who weren't Lara hissed *shhh*s at him as Lara winced again. Dickon muttered, "Well, he wouldn't," sullenly, and Lara pulled a pained smile into place.

"I imagine you're right. It's nothing like that."

"Here, I always carry migraine medicine." Sharon handed the ice-cream cake off to Dickon and dug into her purse. "Why don't you call David and tell him to come on back, we'll save some cake for him."

"Yeah, all right." Dickon put the cake on the counter and Sharon offered Lara medicine and a plastic cup of water, asking, "Do you think you'll want cake?" beneath the sound of his call.

"Maybe a little piece." Lara took the tablets and watched Dickon over the edge of the cup as she drained it. His eyebrows crinkled into a frown, but he nodded, shrugged, and hung up to say, "David thinks he won't come back since he's already on his way out. He offered to pay for the cake."

"Well that's silly." Sharon stalked toward Dickon, a hand extended. "Give me the pho— Oh, he's already hung up? Well, for God's sake, what are we going to do with an entire cake?"

"Eat ourselves sick," Rachel suggested. "There's no such thing as too much ice-cream cake, a statement I will regret making about half an hour from now. We can all manage a fifth, right?"

"Well, give Dickon a third and we can split the rest among the girls. Lara's not going to want to eat an entire fifth of a cake."

"I already ate an entire sundae and you think I can eat a third of an ice-cream cake, too?"

"Are you sure you're all right?" Kelly asked under their good-natured arguing. "You look awful, Lar."

"My head hurts. The medicine will help." Lara leaned against Kelly as her friend settled down beside her. The racket of discussion over portion sizes, of disappointment at David's abrupt departure, of concern about Lara's headache, washed over her as thankfully ordinary commentary. Dafydd's image still lingered, elfin form too bright and uncontained to make sense within the context of a very human kitchen filled with entirely human bickering. "Kelly, do you ever wish fairy tales came true?"

Kelly shifted like she was trying to get a good look at Lara, who was too close to be seen. "That must be a doozy of a headache if it's sending you on flights of fancy. What do you mean, like dragons and princesses and heroes? Yeah, I guess, except I'd kind of like to be the one who fights the dragon."

Laughter escaped Lara's lips in a release of tension and pain. "And woe betide the dragon. I just wondered."

"You never just wonder anything. What?" Kelly nudged her. "Suddenly believing in love at first sight, are we?"

"No. No," Lara repeated a little less certainly. Curiosity and attraction didn't equate to friendship, much less love. *Intrigue* was the only word that came close to describing her feelings toward Dafydd ap Caerwyn. Her anger and fear had faded into something manageable while she'd waited for the others to return. Bewilderment still rang through her, but it was underscored by the talent and curse that defined her life: she was bewildered, yes, but she didn't *disbelieve*. She had not, as someone else might have, convinced herself that what she'd seen hadn't been real.

For a moment she felt painfully distant from other people, even

Kelly, warm at her side. Most people would, she imagined, be able to explain away Dafydd's transformation as some kind of trick, but it had sent such a song of truth through her that she couldn't doubt it even if she'd wanted to.

And now, with the initial shock fading, she wasn't certain she wanted to doubt it at all. He was something extraordinary, beyond the bounds of possibility and yet existing within it. She, of all people, had been given the ability to see that. A small, incredulous smile crept across her face, and Kelly snorted triumphantly. "Told you. Love at first sight."

"I thought he was a liar at first sight," Lara reminded her, and gratefully accepted a plate of melting ice-cream cake from Sharon. The cold made her headache recede a little, exhaustion following in its path. Her head lolled before she finished the slice, and Kelly rescued the plate as it slid toward the floor.

"Okay," Rachel said firmly. "Dickon, would you mind driving Lara home? She obviously needs rest, and we still have work to do here."

"Dickon?" Kelly objected. "Lara came with me!"

"I know, but I've known you for three years and Dickon for six hours, so you're the one I'm going to make stay and help us scrub the house. If that's okay, Dickon?"

"Take a pretty girl home or spend the rest of the night up to my elbows in soapy water. Hm. Hard choice. Wait, no it isn't." Dickon offered Lara a hand. "Let's go before they change their minds. Your steed awaits."

"Steed?"

"I drive a Bronco."

"How environmentally irresponsible of you." Lara clapped a hand over her mouth. "I shouldn't have said that."

Dickon laughed. "Call 'em like you see 'em, don't you? G'night, ladies. I'll give you a call soon, huh, Kelly?"

Kelly dimpled. "Yeah, okay. Drive safe, Lara's my best friend." She hugged them both, and Lara, before she was sent out the door, mumbled apologies for not helping clean.

"You get migraines often?" Dickon asked sympathetically as they left. "My sister gets them sometimes. Usually after too much dark chocolate or red wine."

"No, not often. I think mine are stress-related."

"David stressed you out, huh? He does that to people, but usually only the ones who listen to his weather forecasts." Dickon winked and helped Lara into his truck, then put her address into a sat-nav device so she could close her eyes against the streetlights and not worry about giving directions. "So is Kelly seeing anybody?"

Lara chuckled. "Yeah, I think so. Big guy. Works for the news station. Only I don't know if he knows it yet."

"Oh. Oh! Hey, cool. What's she in to?"

"Kelly's the adventure-vacation type. The bigger the experience, the better." Lara peeled one eye open, glanced at Dickon, and bit her tongue on a wisecrack. He saw the whole byplay and laughed aloud, filling the cab with sound.

"Good thing for me I'm big, then, eh? And you look so sweet and innocent, Miz Jansen. So maybe not so much flowers as, I donno, a bouquet of ice picks and crampons, to impress her?"

"Flowers probably wouldn't go amiss." Lara closed her eyes again, smiling. "Thanks for driving me home."

"No problem. Can I ask something?"

Lara, under her breath, said, "Can is a question of ability," and more clearly said, "Go ahead."

"David didn't leave to get you migraine medicine, did he? He sounded surprised when I said Sharon had some."

"I never said he did."

"Yeah, you—" Silence broke for a moment before Dickon cursed in surprise. "You didn't. Kelly did. So what happened? I thought you two were kind of getting along. Although with David I don't know, it's hard to tell about him and women."

An unexpected pang caught Lara in the chest. "Why? Does he have a lot of girlfriends?"

"No, he's never got any, he's just unfailingly polite and charming to every woman he meets. Between that and the way he dresses and, well, you should see him jumping over puddles. He looks like a god-damned fairy, and I mean like the winged kind you see on little girls' notebooks, not gay. Just kind of goes up and leaping like gravity doesn't mean much. So maybe he is, I can't tell."

"Is?" Lara asked, bemused. "Is gay, or is a fairy?"

"Either, take your pick." Dickon grinned. "Nah, he's not gay. We've been working together for five years, and he doesn't keep that much under his hat. I think I'd know."

"Well, then." Lara tipped her head against the window, watching through half-lidded eyes as streetlights and other cars whisked by. "He must be a fairy. Does he have any family?"

"He mentions a brother sometimes. I've never met him. I get the idea they don't see each other a lot, maybe because they're on opposite sides of the ocean. David came over here years ago, s'why you only hear the accent if he really turns it on." Dickon pulled onto Lara's street and squinted through the windshield at the apartment buildings rising up around them. "So how come he left early?"

"It's the last building before the corner. He made a shocking proposal," Lara added after a moment. "And then he left so I could think about it."

"No shit?" Dickon pulled up in front of Lara's building and rolled his window down as she climbed out of the truck. "What'd he do, ask you to run away with him?"

"Something like that."

Dickon whistled. "I didn't know he had it in him. So what do you think? Gonna run away with him and leave us all in the dust?"

Lara shook her head, waving as he pulled away again. "Truth is, I haven't decided yet."

Eight

The night passed in restless sleep, disturbed by Dafydd's anxious request. She woke early, unrested, to watch the sunrise, and answered an early-morning call with the feeling that she'd expected it; that she'd gotten up early so she might be awake when it came.

But it wasn't Dafydd ap Caerwyn who called, but rather a friend from one of the meetings, apologetic and hopeful all at once: "Hi, Lara, it's Ruth. I'm supposed to lead the meeting at Our Lady of Victories this morning, but both my kids woke up covered with chicken pox and their dad's never had it so he's been quarantined, and I know it's Sunday, but I was wondering—"

"I'm not a recovering addict, Ruth," Lara reminded her gently. "I shouldn't be leading meetings."

"I know, I know, but they like you, and most of it's about listening anyway, and Becky can't do it because she's got family in town over the weekend, and, well, please? They won't mind, not just this once."

"You called because you knew I'd say yes," Lara said with teasing rancor. "The meeting's at . . . nine?"

"You are an angel of goodness. It's at nine thirty, and the pastor usually unlocks the parish center doors for me at nine so I can get things set up. Is that okay?"

"It's fine. I'll be there. I hope the kids feel better soon." Lara hung up thinking the meeting was more blessing than bother. It would give her something besides Dafydd to think about for a few hours, and listening to other people work through their problems often gave her insight into her own. She suspected that was part of the reason people became psychologists, though Dafydd had detailed the reasons for her own degree accurately. Practicing psychology had never been her plan. She'd only wanted a better foundation for understanding those who were fundamentally unlike her.

Which, she admitted wryly, was very nearly everyone. Glad for the distraction, she got dressed and caught a bus to the church. It wasn't one of the usual locations she visited; after the first few months she had realized her regular presence stifled meeting participants. The occasional prod toward greater truthfulness was easier to handle than a constant edgy fear that basic honesty wasn't enough. A little of Lara went a long way; it was something she'd learned early and still worried about. Kelly and a few others had adapted to, or didn't care about, her pedantry, but in a delicate social situation like the meetings, it was better for Lara to be a periodic visitor rather than a regular. There were innumerable groups around Boston, and she'd made casual acquaintance with many of them. Ruth's group was one of her less-regular stops, but she knew enough of them to be comfortable stepping in at Ruth's request.

A blocky man with just enough grown-out fuzz to suggest he shaved his head to avoid obvious male pattern baldness got to his feet as she approached the church. "Miss Jansen?"

"Please, it's Lara. And you're Pete, right?" Lara shook his hand, smiling. "I remember you from the last time I was here. How's it going?"

"Sixteen weeks, three days. That meeting you were at was my first. It's not easy, Miss . . . Lara. My parole officer comes to these things to make sure I'm staying the course. No flippin' pressure. And he's an asshole."

Lara laughed. "All the more reason to prove him wrong by sticking with it. Ruth didn't tell me she'd have someone meet me. Thanks. It's nice to see a friendly face."

"It's no problem, I live around the corner. Hey, Pastor." Pete left Lara behind as a slight older man came up the road, a ring of keys in hand. "This is Lara Jansen, she's running the meeting for Ruth today. Ruth's kids have chicken pox."

"Ah, the poor woman. Nice to meet you, Miss Jansen. The door will lock behind you when you leave, so just tidy up a bit and you'll be set when you're done." He let them into a chilly open space littered with community projects, then departed still clucking over Ruth's misfortune. Pete turned the heat on as Lara pulled chairs into a circle and blew warm air over her fingers.

"I should have brought coffee for everyone. Maybe next time."

"It warms up fast," Pete promised. "I know you're not the regular leader, Miss . . . Lara, but I wonder if you'd take a minute to talk to my parole officer? He never believes me, he likes someone else to tell him I'm staying dry. I don't know how they'd know if I lied, but that's just how he is."

"Sixteen weeks, three days," Lara said comfortably. "I don't mind at all. I'm sorry he doesn't believe you. That must be a little undermining."

Pete shrugged. "The guys believe me, that's what counts."

"It's mostly what counts, anyway, hm?" Lara said to the faint discordant note in his voice, and he threw her a wry look that turned into another shrug.

"Mostly. Like I said, he's an asshole and, I mean, he's my parole officer, shouldn't really matter what he thinks, but it kind of does. I got in over my head when I was nineteen, a bunch of stupid shit and I deserved to go to jail, but I straightened up. The meetings are a condition of my parole, but I want to be here, you know?" He went on, comfortable honesty in his litany that didn't end as others arrived. He greeted them, introduced Lara, and left her smiling at his ease. Ruth had probably noticed already, but Pete would—did, in fact—make a good group leader, taking over most of the duties that Lara was in theory there to provide.

The only pall came near the end, when a chiseled blond man stepped into the meeting room. Pete's good nature faltered briefly and the others glanced toward the door, then subtly straightened and lost the edge of humor that had sustained them. Lara glanced from one suddenly tense face to another, then touched Pete's shoulder as she got up to talk to the newcomer. He put his hand out, and without bothering to keep his voice down as she approached, said, "Officer Rich Cooper. You're not the usual leader."

"Lara Jansen. Ruth's kids have the chicken pox, so I'm standing in today. Do you mind if we step just outside the door so we don't disturb everyone?" Lara shook his hand but walked outside, happy for once to do away with the pretense of polite behavior and insist, through action, that the officer oblige her. "Pete said you'd be dropping by. He's doing very well. He'll be a group leader if he wants to be, I think."

Cooper scowled over his shoulder as they left the community center, then scowled at her, though the expression smoothed over as if he was reminding himself that he was one of the good guys.

Or at least, Lara thought sourly, that he was putting on a performance as one of the good guys. She'd met any number of parole officers while working with the various twelve-step groups, and only rarely had they been as this man came across: eager to be a peace officer not for the sake of the community, but for his own perceived power. Pete, whose intention to stay straight was geninue, deserved a parole officer more willing to believe in him. Lara hoped he had the wherewithal to prove Cooper wrong.

"How can you tell, if you're not the regular leader? I think the guy is trouble."

Lara put on a smile she didn't feel, uncomfortable with the deception but certain anything else would be taken as aggressive. "I suppose he must have been once upon a time, in order to warrant a parole officer. I studied psychology. I know it's not the same as being an officer on the street, but I hope it gives me some insight into how people can and might behave."

Cooper hesitated, then looked pleased, taking her phrasing as a compliment. "I studied criminal justice, myself. Psych always seemed pretty soft to me."

"And you're clearly not soft." Lara bit back a laugh as the officer looked even more pleased, then put her hand on his arm and deliberately steered him a few steps away from the community center's front door. "Pete's at sixteen weeks and counting with the program. I'm confident your presence is a continued inspiration to him." She was absolutely confident, though not at all in the way she expected Cooper to interpret her meaning. "Thank you for checking in, Officer."

"My pleasure, Miss Ja . . ." Cooper trailed off, frowning, then walked away looking uncertain of how he'd lost control. Lara, pleased with herself, waved a good-bye and went back inside. Mindful of the pastor's warning, she pulled the door closed behind her, its locking *click!* loud enough to make people look around. Surprise washed over Pete's face and Lara shrugged as she rejoined the group, nodding encouragement to continue at the woman who'd been speaking.

Sometimes, she thought with satisfaction. Sometimes the truth, applied judiciously, could make someone's life easier, at least for a little while. Maybe it was all she could do, but some days it was enough.

That was it, then, the decision made. If it was what she *could* do, then it was enough. At the meeting's end, she closed up the hall, steadied her nerves, and called Dafydd ap Caerwyn.

Fashion dictated that modern men rarely came hat in hand to anything, but Dafydd, standing on Lara's threshold, looked very much as though he would like to have a hat to wring. Everything about him suited the old phrase: nervous worry in his expression, caution in his slightly hunched stance, as though he expected a blow. His entire aura was one of abject hope. Lara had seen similar demeanor before, usually on puppies who knew they'd done wrong and were pleading for clemency. Unexpectedly entertained by his attitude, she stepped out of the door and gestured him in. "Am I that frightening?"

He murmured, "You have no idea," then gave her a frown so curious it was clearly a question.

"No," she agreed, "I don't. You're telling the truth. Not even exaggerating, since I really don't have any sense of how or why I've become frightening."

"Your decisions stand between me and eternal exile," Dafydd said a little drily. "It awards you an astonishing amount of power and therefore no little ability to terrify."

"I suppose it would. May I take your coat?"

"Thank you." He slipped it off and she hung it in a closet as he surveyed her living room. Tidy, she thought: he would find it tidy and perhaps boring, with everything in its place and the colors well coordinated. But it suited her, all the pieces fitting together so when she glanced around nothing tore at her eyes or made jagged music play in her mind. To her surprise, Dafydd turned back with a smile. "I expected more neutral colors, I think, but it's how I imagined you would live. Beautiful form and function as one."

Disconcerted, pleased, she offered him a seat and took one across from him, drawing her arms in tight. "Thank you. Would you . . . would you mind taking the glamour away? My vision swims when I look at you."

Startlement washed over his features. "You can see through it?" Even as he asked, though, he began the same ritual he'd done before, removing all the metal from his person.

Lara grimaced and looked away, double vision made worse by his small rapid motions. "I almost didn't notice when you were outside the door, just standing there. But as soon as you moved . . . yes. I can see through it. It's like two people are trying to stand in the same place."

"Is this better?" His voice was once again lighter. Lara glanced back, and for a few seconds was arrested by impossible things.

Impossible that he should look so much more *right*, when everything about him was so clearly wrong. So inhuman, with his delicate bone structure, his alien eyes, his slim elfin form. But there was truth to him now, impossible or not, and he sat more easily in her gaze. "Much. Thank you. Although your clothes don't fit as well now."

He smiled. "You would notice that. They're made to fit the mirage, or I'd look like I'd been poured into skinny suits, and I haven't the height to carry that off."

"Skinny suits create the illusion of height. It's a very affected look, though, more rock star than weatherman. You could do it, but—" Lara broke off and shook herself. "I'm sorry. It's easier to think about your clothes than . . ."

"Than everything else? I am sorry, Lara. I wish I had an option other than utterly overwhelming you."

"But you don't," she said quietly. "Not if you're going to make it home again. Dafydd, you need to explain more. A lot more." She sat forward, clasping her hands together. "Begin with the power. You said humans don't have much magic," which sounded absurd, spoken aloud. Of course humans didn't have magic. A day earlier she'd have never dreamed it was a point worth arguing, despite her own strange skill. "But your people, you have magic, just not . . . truthseekers?"

"We do, yes, but I'm not sure why there are no more truthseekers." A faint wrongness rippled through his words and Lara tilted her head, trying to comprehend it. He saw her and breathed a sigh, almost a laugh. "How strange, to talk with someone who hears the subtleties of doubt in my voice. I have a theory. Truthseekers were never common, and their gifts were not particularly . . ."

"Welcome?" Lara offered, unsurprised.

Dafydd nodded. "I wonder if perhaps the ability was bred away, perhaps not quite deliberately, but not without purpose, either. Or perhaps it's just that there are too few of us, and the power too rare."

Lara pressed her eyes shut. "So you're left with me."

She heard him move, felt the warmth of his hands cover the knot hers had become, and only then opened her eyes. He crouched before her, gaze turned up, both earnest and apologetic. "I'm left with you, because in this world of six billion souls you're the one I've found with the gifts I need, but more important, because you've the courage to have called me back. I cannot imagine how unbelievable I must seem to you."

"You can't imagine how unbelievable you would be to other people," Lara corrected softly. "And neither can I, Dafydd, because I don't have the luxury, or the crutch, of easy disbelief like most people do. Tell me what the poem means, the one you quoted to me. Mending the past and breaking the world?"

"I don't know," he admitted. The ferocity of his confession tightened his hands over hers, and she freed one hand to touch the tense line of his jaw, unthinking of the intimacy until it was too late. There were profound lines around his mouth, aging him, but they eased under her fingertips as her touch lingered. Humans teased men who couldn't grow beards as being boyish, but there was nothing boyish about the slender man before her.

"I don't know what the prophecy means. Mending the past—the truth will set us free," he said, half-mocking. It sent a spasm of discordant notes down Lara's spine, sarcasm a close brother to untruth. "I can only guess that it means you'll be able to help us lay my brother to rest and bring his murderer to justice. As for the rest—" He broke off, shaking his head in frustration.

Lara tipped his chin up, studying the lines of helpless anger in his face. If she were Kelly, she thought, she'd let herself stop thinking and simply act on the impulse to bend and brush her lips against his, taste the glow of his skin and give in to the urge that had said *I could make a life with this man.*

You never take risks. That's why you never meet anybody. Kelly's words rushed her, and heat built in her face now, when it hadn't earlier. Maybe Kelly was right; maybe she was too cautious, her truthsensing ability holding her back when she might have been daring. Lara acted before wisdom could overwhelm her, and ducked her head to touch her lips to Dafydd's. "It's all right. You don't have to have all the answers." His breath caught, an unexpectedly rough sound, and she inched back to offer a fragile smile. "I'll come with you. I'll try to help."

The relief and shocked joy in his eyes was worth the price of her own internal agitation. A smile leapt across his features, so bright Lara laughed and touched his lips with her fingers again, then dropped her hand in uncertain apology.

He caught it before it had fallen more than a few inches and brought it back to his mouth, kissing her knuckles. "I owe you a debt I can never repay, simply for the act of trying. Thank you, Lara. Will you— The sooner we go, the better. Will you come now?"

"Now?" Alarm leapt in her chest and turned her fingers cold. "Don't I need to pack? Or something? How long will we be gone?"

"Time flows differently from my world to yours. The worldwalking magic will have ensured that very little has passed there, to so many years here. But in bringing you home with me, it will reverse. The time you spend there will be as moments here." He smiled again, bright and hopeful. "I should have you home in time for dinner tonight."

"Oh." Lara pressed her free hand over her stomach, trying to settle nerves. "I suppose I don't need to pack, then. We can—yes. We could . . . just go now." Her pulse was wild in her throat, unadulterated fear mixed with pure excitement that wanted to turn into uneasy laughter. "All right. Well. All right."

"Thank you. *Thank* you, Lara Jansen." Dafydd drew her to her feet, then turned half away from her to sketch a rectangle in the air. Lara arched an eyebrow and he winked at her, so blatantly trying to ease her anxiety that it worked, a tiny smile breaking through her worries.

With a showman's flair, Dafydd hooked his fingers in the top of the shape he'd traced, gold light bleeding around his hand. He bowed theatrically, and with the action, ripped open a door to another world.

Nine

Lara's vision flared to gold, color blinding before it faded out to leave shimmers around the edges of the doorway Dafydd had cut into the air. She caught a startled breath, stayed from making it a shriek by Dafydd's fingertips against her mouth. "This would be hard to explain to your neighbors, so please don't shout. I should have warned you."

Lara moved her head away and cast him a skeptical look. "Should have," she agreed. "But that would have taken all the fun out of it, wouldn't it."

Amusement creased lines into the thin skin around his eyes, then faded without leaving a mark. Rather than reply, he nodded toward the doorway, and Lara turned her attention that way, aware she'd been trying to ignore it.

Starlight shone through a sky of blue shadows and black trees beyond the door's golden edges. A grove of darkness, hollowed earth dipping low, lush-looking grass blue with moonlight. It invited with the cool comfort of an autumn night, wind rustling branches full of leaves. Even from the far side of the door, the quiet land seemed a sanctuary, drawing Lara to it. "Where does it go?" The question came out hushed, as if speaking aloud might disturb the world beyond the door.

"Wales," David said, utterly prosaically, and laughed as Lara turned an injured expression on him. His reply had the same wrong tone to it that his name did, playing on and on as it searched for accuracy in an answer that wasn't entirely wrong. "The Barrow-lands," he said more softly. "You don't like fairy tales, Lara. You might not know the stories of my people and our lands under the hills. Let me show you."

He took a step toward the door, extending his hand toward her as he moved. Lara slipped her fingers into his, surprised to feel that her own were cold with excitement. She thought the idea of stepping through a doorway made of magic to a world that wasn't her own should be terrifying, but the endless truth in Dafydd ap Caerwyn's words sang to her. All it left behind was the belief that she would forever regret not daring this exploration.

"Show me," she said, suddenly decisive. "I said I'd help. Let's go." She put words into action almost before she was finished speaking, stepping ahead of Dafydd to cross the door's threshold first.

Something changed as she stepped across, the weight of the world somehow releasing some of its hold on her. Misty, cool air swept Lara's cheeks, dew alighting in her hair, and the first breath she drew was tinged with its own sweet flavor, as if it had never gone through an endless cycle of breath. Under the starlight, silver sparkled off her skin, lifting hairs and sending a chill of delight through her. It felt like power, that sensation, lending Lara a confidence she'd never known. Curious, she tried to reach out with it, searching for what it could tell her about the alien truth of the world she now stood in. She felt Dafydd's weight shift behind her as he, too, crossed over, and she turned toward him with a smile already on her lips.

Hell unleashed itself.

The sky above Lara tore, wings and claws coming from the darkness, fiery eyes stealing the color from the stars to shoot bolts of heat at her. She screamed, flinging herself toward the door, but even as she did so its golden frame shattered under the weight of night. The space she pitched herself through held only nighttime and trees, no safe passage home. Momentum carried her forward into a dive, dew and grass staining her shirt as she skidded across the slippery meadow.

Dafydd bellowed in a language she didn't recognize, warning clear in his voice. Thunder clapped in the clear air, carrying his shout far beyond the strength of an ordinary cry. Lara twisted back toward him, her fingers digging into the dirt, fear a painful thing clawing at her chest in an attempt to escape.

Lightning came on thunder's call, shards of electricity shattering the night and briefly—mercifully briefly—illuminating the shadows that poured from the darkness. Lara had no name for them: demons were creatures of substance, not the wraith-thin shadows whose wings swallowed the lightning's brightness. They were barely more than wing and tooth and claw, a mockery of bats, black skin stretching from jaw to wing to foot, all distorted with each beat of the monstrous wings. One dropped its mouth open to gout flame and Lara screamed again, meaning it to be a warning to Dafydd.

He flinched, but didn't lose ground, only lifted his hands as if he held a sword. Lightning gathered between his palms, a blade of jagged brilliance cutting apart the horror's flame, splicing it to either side of him. His blade lasted no longer than that, fading as quickly as its element did, leaving him empty-handed once more. His voice, though, remained steady, almost cajoling, and Lara lurched to her feet, scrambling for the narrow window of protection offered by the Seelie prince's form. The breadth of his shoulders suddenly seemed much greater than it had in the confines of her home, his elfin delicacy abruptly filled with all the strength and confidence a warrior could need. Perhaps it was the same difference she'd felt in herself on stepping through to Dafydd's world: a completion that had been lacking in her own.

Lightning streaked the sky again, tearing Lara from her brief contemplation of Dafydd's shoulders. One of the monsters darted to the side too late, blue power exploding through its black form. It screamed, a birdlike sound of rage, then was gone, nothing more than a handful of sparks drifting toward the damp grass. Beneath the scream's echoes, Lara heard Dafydd's voice, soft and steady, making liquid words that meant nothing to her.

The air flexed around them, as if responding to Dafydd's calm speech. Another nightmare dove down, claws extended. Lara flung her hands up in a panicked attempt to protect her face. She only half-saw the monster bounce back with the same force it had attacked with, just a few inches away from Dafydd and herself. Dafydd staggered with the creature's impact, and the shoulder of his suit jacket dimpled, as if claws had hooked into it without managing to touch him.

Silence rose up, shocking as the screams had been, leaving nothing in the night but stars and moonlight. Lara dragged in a breath and stumbled from Dafydd's side, staring at the sky. "What the—"

"Lara!" Despair shot through Dafydd's voice and caution flared too late. Winged darkness fell from the sky again, red gaze searing into Lara's. Instinct went to war in her, the struggle between fight or flight leaving her frozen. Death awaited her in the clutches of vicious black talons, and even as she threw off paralyzing fear she knew she'd hesitated too long, that she could never move quickly enough to escape the nightmare. The admission rang with truth even inside her own mind, even barely made into words, and she thought she might be able to die well, not screaming.

Dafydd smashed into her, knocking her aside. Lara screamed after all, more surprise than terror, before horror tore another raw sound from her throat. The nightmare blackness didn't care which target it hit: Dafydd howled as its claws slammed into his ribs, ripping his clothes, tearing his skin. Lara closed a hand in the wet grass, furious that she found no fallen branch or stone to use as a weapon there, and surged to her feet, white rage replacing her fear. She tackled the nightmare, knocking it free of Dafydd. The world became pounding black wings and the scent of ashes in the back of her throat. She rolled with the monster, both of them trying to gain the upper hand.

She was somehow astonished when the winged blackness came out on top.

It slammed forward, jaw gaping, and she strong-armed it, driving her hand into what passed for the thing's throat, holding it back from tearing her head off. It was far more solid than she thought it should be, and much smaller when she had it in hand than it had seemed. From jaw to wing tip, from wing tip to clawed feet, it was less than the length of her arm, but she trembled holding it away from herself. For all its small size, for all that it looked like little more than a sheet of blackness cut away from the night, it had substance, a demon after all. It shrieked and swept its wings in, clawing at the ground around her, unable to gain purchase in her flesh with her hand at its throat.

Chimes sounded in the back of Lara's mind, clarifying and ringing together until they became the deep continuous toll of church bells, carrying with them a memory and an unquenchable sense of truth.

"I exorcise thee, unholy spirit." Lara could barely hear her own whisper beneath the captured demon's screams, but it flinched at the words. Confidence shot through her, strengthening her voice. She shoved herself forward, moving the devil's weight, and shouted, "I exorcise thee, unholy spirit, in the name of the Father, and of the Son, and of the Holy Spirit!"

The thing caught in her hand went first, an explosion of sparks that left behind a keening that raised hairs over Lara's body. From there light shot out, pure and white and hard, turning the trees to bleached daytime colors, it seared the nightmares, then faded again, leaving Lara blind in the wake of the banishing. Silence reasserted itself as her vision worked its way back to normal, before a new sound cut through the quiet, so rough and dry it took Lara a few seconds to recognize it as laughter.

Dafydd's laughter.

"Dafydd, oh my God, are you all right?" Lara slid across wet grass to his side, holding her hands above him uselessly. Another dry chuckle escaped him.

"An exorcism. I've brought a Roman Catholic among us." Dafydd laughed again, his forehead wrinkling with pain. "Someone's had a nasty shock. How wonderful." He took a careful breath, opening his eyes to study Lara in the moonlight. "How did you know what to counter the spell with?"

"I . . . I remembered the baptism ritual, the casting out of demons. They seemed like demons."

"They weren't," he assured her on a breath. "But my people, Lara . . . we don't bear the name of your creator easily. You couldn't have chosen a better counter to the attack." He hesitated, then said, delicately, "It would be easier on me if you didn't invoke that particular trinity again. The nightwing attack was quite enough. Staggering under the weight of your white god's name is more than any Seelie, prince or not, should have to face in a single night."

"Nightwings?" Lara's voice shot high with fear and confusion even as she recognized that she was focusing on one bewildering thing over another. She could hear the truth of what he said in Dafydd's voice, but his half-wry plea to keep her from repeating the name of the Trinity went beyond bizarre. Easier to focus on the monsters, on the brief battle. "Is that what you call those? What were they? Why did they attack me? How could they know I was here?"

"They didn't." Dafydd's reply was low with pain. "They couldn't have, Lara. The spell was set to detect my presence, not yours."

"But—" Confusion wrinkled Lara's forehead so hard her head began to ache. "I thought you were a prince. Why would anyone attack you?"

"Why would anyone murder my brother?" He reached for her hand, bringing it to his lips and imparting comfort when, Lara realized sharply, it should be she who offered kindness. Dafydd was injured while protecting her, and her thanks was to hurl questions so frightened and bewildered they verged on accusations.

"I'm sorry," she blurted, but he shook his head, accepting her apology but waving it off.

"Time in the Barrow-lands doesn't move the same way it does in your world. I told you I've been searching for you for a century. That's true. In your world, it's true. But in mine, I'll have been gone—ten days, perhaps two weeks, no more. The wounds of my brother's death are still fresh, and someone has a secret to protect."

"But why attack you? Why set a-a spell to sense your arrival?" Lara stumbled over the concept even as she understood that it was a true one; she'd seen magic used repeatedly in the last few minutes, alien but real.

"Because whoever is behind this has to know I wouldn't return without a truthseeker," Dafydd said quietly. "Because my return sets into play events that someone wishes not to see explored. Now." He took a cautious breath, tightening his hand around hers. "Now, if you'll help me sit up, and forbear from repeating that phrase again, I think I can take the edge off these wounds."

"That phra—you mean the Fa—"

Dafydd gave her such a sharp look that Lara clamped her mouth shut. "Sorry," she said after a moment. "What does it . . . do to you?"

"You saw what it did to the nightwings." Dafydd grunted as he sat up, strain making his hand tremble in Lara's. "I have thought, substance, presence that they do not. It might take a full exorcism to obliterate me. I'd prefer not to find out."

"But why?"

Dafydd lifted his gaze to hers, eyes weary in the moonlight. "Because I enjoy living, Lara." Amusement creased the corners of his eyes at her obvious exasperation, and more carefully he said, "Our courts, our people, are effectively immortal. We can die through violence but not through age. The—" He drew a breath through his nostrils, sweat against his cheeks, and Lara realized that as he spoke to her he was carefully exploring the edges of the nightwing-made wound against his ribs. "The price we pay for that," he said tightly, "is a lack of a soul, as your people see it. It makes the name of your creator painful to bear in the best of circumstances and deadly in the worst. Forgive me," he added, and ceased explanations to whisper again in the liquid tongue he'd used before.

Firefly sparks of gold glimmered and gathered with his words, until they seemed to reach a critical weight and dove beneath his clothing. Lara held her breath, leaning in to catch a glimpse of torn and bloody skin weaving itself back together under the light's guidance. Long moments passed, injury mending before Lara's eyes. Then Dafydd took a deep breath, straightening. "Better, I think. I'm sorry, Lara. I—"

Lara leaned forward and stopped his apology with a kiss.

Ten

Surprise widened Dafydd's eyes before they closed, before the light touch of his hand brushed Lara's jaw. It was long moments before she broke away, retreating only a few scant inches to gaze at him. "Have I earned this," he murmured, "or is it merely a human response to danger? It's not—"

A mix of amusement and chagrin coursed through Lara, ending in a smile. "Dafydd."

"Yes?"

"Shut up."

"That," he said, "I can do."

Her shyness fled in hunger's wake, and her tailor's hands were sure of themselves as she pushed his jacket from his shoulders. It was easy to open his shirt with quick twists of the buttons, though Lara knew, if she let herself think, that she was behaving more like Kelly than herself. Kelly would revel in high emotion and the passion of a moment, and understand what the tightening around her heart meant when she saw Dafydd's injuries. Kelly would know why watching Dafydd's miraculous healing sent fire burning through her body and desire riding every pulse of blood. Kelly, not Lara, would act the impulse to kiss the Seelie prince.

Kelly, Lara thought as the cool taste of Dafydd's mouth overwhelmed her, would be proud of her. And then she stopped thinking of Kelly at all as urgency swept her, fingertips exploring the newly healed gashes over his ribs. Heat emanated there, the warmth of accelerated healing, and he hissed a low sound at the comparative chill of her touch. She drew back and he caught her wrist, shaking his head. "It's all right. Your hands are cold."

"Your skin is hot," she countered with a tiny smile, then pushed him onto his back, dew soaking through his suit jacket and shirt almost instantly, and lowered her mouth to kiss the still-reddened injuries on his torso.

He was beautiful. She lowered her mouth to kiss the welts that had moments earlier been slashes in his skin. From so close, she could study the lines of his body without seeming to stare, exploring with fingertips and lips. Long, strong muscles under her touch, sensually male without being overdone. His stomach jumped beneath her kisses, just as a human man's might.

A sudden crescendo of certainty suffused Lara, bringing with it a reminder of the impulse that said Dafydd ap Caerwyn, human or not, was home. That he, among all the men she knew, was the one she belonged with. Smiling, she pushed up his body to find his mouth with hers again, and skimmed a hand to his waist, tugging open the button of his pants with ease.

His brief laughter made her hesitate, finding his gaze with her own and discovering a smile in it. "Not so fast," he murmured. "You have me at an advantage here." Humor lit his eyes, though an undercurrent of desire darkened amber to gold. A shiver of hope ran through Lara, an anticipation of seeing that controlled strength unleashed not in battle but with passion. *Feeling* its release, not just seeing it. He slid his fingers to the collar of her blouse, unfastening buttons, his gaze never leaving hers. She swallowed, trying to catch her breath, then offered a tiny nod that was all the permission

Dafydd needed. Her blouse and bra disappeared so quickly it might well have been magic, and Dafydd pushed her back until she sat above him, darkness swallowing the gold in his gaze as he studied her.

"Dafydd?" Her voice trembled, jitters resurfacing in the face of his intense examination.

"We have so little time, Lara—"

"Then maybe we should make the most of it." Lara touched her lips to his again, hopeful.

Dafydd groaned, then caught her again and rolled in the grass, putting himself above her. "You make an excellent argument. Lara, I—"

"Merrick ap Annwn lies dead and you dally with mortals in the glade, Dafydd?" A cold voice, sharp with disapproval, snapped through the darkness to drown Dafydd's words. Dafydd dropped his head, teeth bared as Lara stiffened and stifled a shriek.

"Some things," the voice went on, "never change."

"Please." Dafydd spoke through his teeth, eyes on Lara's. She glanced away, understanding his anger was for the rude interruption, not her, but still unable to hold his gaze.

He lifted a hand to touch her jaw, gentleness in the gesture making it an apology. Lara glanced back at him, then offered a feeble, embarrassed smile. Dafydd's answering smile was a grimace as he lifted his head to respond. "At least do me the favor of counting my crimes correctly. I've never before dallied with mortals, Emyr." He drew Lara's bra and blouse across the grass, returning them to her as he got to his feet, and made a barrier of himself so she could dress with some semblance of privacy.

The men and women beyond him were a dozen strong and mounted on white horses made blue by night shadows. They were armored, all of them, riders and horses alike. At their head was a man who could have been cut of moonlight, his gaze cool and sharp as the stars as he looked on Dafydd. "Have the years in mortal guise left you with no remembrance of how to greet your king?"

"My lord father." Dafydd bowed deep and low, dragging his fingertips across the clothing-littered grass and coming up with his own shredded shirt. "Forgive me. Crossing over was something of a trial."

The king's pale gaze slid to Lara, a smirk twisting his mouth. "So I see."

Discomfort more profound than embarrassment shivered over Lara's skin at his pointed sarcasm. There was no lie in his words, only a thick mockery, so strong as to set untuned chords pounding in her head. She tugged her shirt on as she climbed to her feet, still half-hidden behind Dafydd, and muttered, "There's no need to be nasty," as she buttoned it. Emboldened by being more or less dressed, she looked up to find the king's cold gaze on her.

Had Dafydd not called him father, Lara would never have guessed the relationship. Dafydd was golden where this man was ice. Straight silver hair poured over his shoulders, and his eyes were so pale blue as to be white in the moonlight. There was no gray in him, no warmth, and the angles of his face seemed blade sharp. Cold and cruel, Lara thought; not the kind of man to go to for comfort. His needle-straight posture and the arrogant lift of his chin warned even the attempt away.

Resplendent armor doubled his cool inapproachability. The breastplate and cuisses shone in the moonlight, so delicate and beautifully worked it hardly seemed they could protect the wearer from harm. He carried a helm tucked under his arm, though it had left no mark on the straight fall of his hair, and the sword he wore was unsheathed, ready for war. Beneath the armor he wore garments that might have been woven of newly thawed water, so fine that Lara studied their make with longing despite the man's arrogance.

"Dafydd is my son, and this my domain," he said. "I will be . . . nasty . . . where I choose."

Lara tasted pleasure in the absolute truth of the words, and astonished herself by sniffing dismissively. "Not if you want me to help you figure out who killed your son."

The harshness of her own response struck her too late, but the king seemed a far cry from a father in mourning. His regard snapped back to Dafydd, who was beautifully composed, in spite of being bare-foot and shirtless in the grass while his father rode in resplendent garb. A smile pulled at Lara's mouth, then fell away as the monarch spoke.

"My . . . son?" Incredulous disdain filled the fine voice.

Dafydd stood his ground, one hand fisted in the shirt he'd retrieved. "My brother. Born of your blood or not, Father, Merrick was my brother more than Ioan ever could be. I knew Merrick," he said more softly. "Ioan is a stranger to me."

A hiss rippled through the attending host, angular eyes narrowing, color coming to sharp cheekbones. Some made distasteful faces, looking away, as though Dafydd had said something unexpectedly repugnant. To Lara, though, the truth of his words rang strong, like church bells in her mind, so loud she could barely imagine no one else heard it. Painfully aware that she was the stranger here, among people who had known each other for lifetimes, she pulled a deep breath and took a step forward, determined to defend Dafydd.

The king made a sharp gesture, cutting her off before she spoke. "Merrick ap Annwn was no more than a hostage for good behavior. It shames me that you speak of him as a brother."

"It shames me that you do not." Dafydd's voice was low with anger, emotion turning the chords of truth to harsh sounds. But unlike his father, who spoke as truly, there was something more to Dafydd's words. The king's truth was sharp to the point of brittleness, almost discordant. Dafydd's was tempered, as if compassion rendered conflict to music.

Lara fell back the step she'd taken, shaking her head with quick violence. Subtleties in truth were beyond her talent's scope: all she could tell was truth from lies.

But Dafydd had called her talent immature, not as an insult, but as a promise. Her gaze returned to him, slender and golden in the moonlight, then went to his father, whose offense was writ large on his angular face.

Her every instinct told her to placate the anger of a powerful man, and her job had taught her to tread gently. Treading gently, though, was not the same as backing down; her talent, after all, was in making them look their best. False flattery did neither the tailor shop nor its clients any good.

Nor would it do an elfin king any good. The thought gave her confidence, the same unexpected surge that had come on her as she'd crossed through the Barrow-lands door. Lara made her hands into fists and stepped forward again, moving quickly so courage couldn't fail her. "Dafydd's telling the truth. He thinks of Merrick as his family, and wants to find his killer."

The king's gaze returned to Lara's, mild with unpleasant amusement. "And you are so certain of this because you carry a truthseeker's power. A mortal. A child," he said disdainfully. "When neither has ever been so blessed or cursed in my memory, which stretches back beyond the dawn of mortal time."

Hairs rose, prickling Lara's arms and neck. She tilted her head, searching his words for the untruth. "Do your people only become truthseekers when they're adults?"

Skin tightened over the bones of his face, making him ghoulish. "We do not reckon childhood the way your people do."

"You're not answering me. I've been able to do this my whole life. When does the power show up in your people?"

The king's lip curled. "In childhood."

"Hah!" Lara rocked back on her heels, pleased with herself. The motion brought a sensation of warmth, Dafydd closer to her than he'd been. Siding with her, she thought; protecting her. It took an unusually long moment to tamp her smugness over catching the Seelie king in his exaggeration. In her own world she wouldn't stand her ground against a man like him, but in this one, he was expected to—did—inherently understand her gifts. "There's not much point in being theatrical. If you're familiar with truthseekers at all, you should already know dramatizing just sets my teeth on edge."

"But the truthseeking talent does not mature for centuries." The king sounded petulant, like a child unaccustomed to being thwarted.

"Maybe among the Seelie," Lara said. "But I'm human." It took everything she had to not glance back at Dafydd, seeking reassurance for that statement. His hand touched the small of her back, warm and comforting, as if he understood her hesitation. Bolstered, Lara went on. "I don't have centuries to mature. My talent would have to grow up faster, too. I can stand here all night picking apart your half-truths, but I'm here for a reason. Dafydd thinks I can help you find a murderer. I'm willing to do that."

She lifted her chin, eyes narrowed as she studied the king, and the certainty of knowing when to make a challenge came over her. "I mean, unless you don't *want* to find the killer."

Eleven

Ice built in the king's eyes, turning them from pale blue to clear. Lara felt color rise in her face and wondered abjectly if the Seelie blushed, or if she looked all the more human and alien for the sudden color in her skin. But she refused to look down; refused even to blink, meeting the monarch's fury with her own forthright challenge. She was an invited, if not entirely wanted, guest. She wouldn't lose face and risk her tenuous status, not when she had only one certain ally in a very strange place.

Dafydd might have warned her, though. The dour thought sent a trace of humor through her and her blush faded as she glowered back at the Seelie king.

Whose gaze faltered, just briefly, lids shuttering his eyes. A trace of tension left Lara's shoulders, surprising her; she hadn't known she had the ability to stare a man down, much less recognize when he so subtly capitulated.

"What I wish," the king snarled, "is to have an end to battle. We do not ride to greet my wayward son, but to make haste back to our citadel ahead of the black armies that dog us. Tell me, Truthseeker. Can you see an end to our battle? Can you tell me who is victorious?"

Lara's spine straightened, drawing her taller than she normally stood. "All I know is if someone's telling the truth. I'm not a prophet."

The king sneered. "There were once truthseekers of such power they could speak a thing and it would by force of their will become true."

Dafydd, at her side, stepped forward as if to defend her, but Lara lifted her fingers to stay him, studying the king cooly. "Really. And what happened if both sides of a war had a truthseeker predicting they'd win?" She turned away, feigning disinterest, though nerves clutched her stomach.

Dafydd caught her eye, and laughter blossomed within her, burning away the fear created by her boldness. She saw herself suddenly from his eyes, saw them both from his perspective, and from the king's as well.

She was merely mortal, and had the audacity to turn her back on an elfin king. The man who'd brought her there was half naked, wounded, and had been caught dallying with her very mortal self. It took very little imagination to name them both a disgrace, and yet in the face of good sense, in the face of soothing his father, Dafydd ap Caerwyn grinned at her. It was a broad, open expression, full of approval, and she tried not to laugh as she wondered how often anyone put the king in his place, never mind a human woman chastising an immortal monarch.

Shock seized that monarch, leaving a silence into which Lara said, "You didn't say anything about a war when you asked me to come here. Do you think that's why we were attacked?" with accusation carefully tamped out.

Almost, at least: there were notes of anger and fear well buried in her words, but airing them would show a weakness that she didn't want the king to see. Guilt twisted Dafydd's expression, washing away his glee, and he shook his head, honest admission of fallibility. "I didn't know it had come to this. If I'd known—"

He broke off, visibly aware of his phrasing and of Lara's interest sharpening on him. "I still would have asked you to come," he finally said. "But I would have warned you. I didn't mean to bring you into a hornet's nest."

Lara pursed her lips, studying him, then nodded. "Good choice," she said quietly. "Platitudes and reassurance wouldn't have been as good an answer, even if you meant them well." She turned back to the king, well aware she'd dismissed him once already and that he would be unhappy with her.

Fair enough; she wasn't especially happy with him. "You don't look like you've been fighting, and this doesn't look like an entire army. Are you really at war already, or are you just a vanguard?" *Just,* she realized an instant too late, was a poor choice of words: a king would not appreciate being *just* anything.

"My host and I have ridden to see our enemies' numbers," Dafydd's father said tightly. "They're far greater than our own, and the magics I have left behind will only stymie them for so long. Until dawn, if we're fortunate. The battle will happen then. You spoke of an attack." His attention went from Lara to Dafydd, as though she was unworthy of answering.

"Nightwings," Dafydd said. "At least a dozen of them. When was the last time they plagued us, Father? Not since Rhiannon died, I think."

The king went still, as though his iciness had taken over even himself. "They have come forth a time or two since then, but never in force. They're mindless creatures and must be controlled by someone of strong will."

"You mean royalty," Dafydd said softly, and his father's lip curled.

"The Unseelie court is a blight on this land. Come dawn, we will wipe them from it."

"Dawn," Lara repeated. "How many hours away is that?" She heard Dafydd's indrawn breath, and wondered at it before realizing she had repeatedly spoken to the king as an equal. That was almost certainly not to be done, and he gave her a cold look before deigning to respond.

"Some ten or eleven. Moonrise is not so far behind us yet."

"Then by your majesty's leave," Lara said, and for a rarity was able to revel in sarcasm and sincerity as one, "I'd like to go to your headquarters and see if I can't get to the heart of this mess before an army shows up on your doorstep."

Any sensible choice, Lara thought, would have put her on horseback with one of the armored guard who rode with the king, and Dafydd on another. One unarmored person riding with an armored one had to be more comfortable than two armored people riding together.

Still, one of the guard had chosen to ride with another, leaving her horse free for Dafydd and Lara to share. Lara was mostly grateful: her sole experience with horses was a childhood memory of one stepping on her foot. It hadn't hurt much. The ground had been soft and its broad hoof had simply pushed her sandaled toes into the earth, but it had left a lasting impression of the animals' size and strength. She had been wary of them ever since, much to the disapproval of her horse-crazed classmates in elementary school.

Gratitude, though, was mixed with pique. She was almost certain she'd been saddled with Dafydd because none of the elfin riders were willing to sully themselves by riding with a human, and that the one who'd offered up her horse had chosen discomfort over contamination. Lara would have been offended, if the arrangements hadn't granted her the chance to mutter, "I think you'd better fill in the blanks," at Dafydd as they rode. "Starting with who are the Unseelie, why are they coming to war, why you called Merrick your brother when he's not, and why it didn't sound like a lie."

"Because he is," Dafydd answered softly, and there was no discordance in his voice, though there'd been none in his father's, either, when he'd disavowed Merrick ap Annwn as his son. "I have a blood brother, Ioan ap Caerwyn, who is my father's son by my mother, Rhiannon. Merrick is—was—the son of Hafgan ap Annwn, the Unseelie king, and they've been hostage to the courts' good behavior their entire lives. Merrick grew up with me. I've barely met Ioan."

A dozen questions crowded through Lara's mind, and the one that came out was the least important: "Are they second sons?"

"Firstborns. Ioan and Merrick are heirs to the thrones. It was when I was born that the treaty was made. Emyr's luck in having sons worried Hafgan. With a second heir, my father might have risked trying to push the Unseelie back into the waters they came from."

Lara closed her teeth on a second rush of questions, frowning at the horse's alert ears. There was no visible road ahead of them, only forest and meadows, but the animals went with confidence, following a path she couldn't see. The horse flicked an ear, as if aware she was paying attention to it, and Lara shook herself, trying to clear her mind. "The Unseelie are . . . ?"

"The other peoples of the Barrow-land." Dafydd drew breath to explain further, and Lara raised a hand sharply, cutting him off. Then she snatched at the saddle—there was no horn, the leather cut more like the English saddles she'd seen in a few movies than like the Western ones she was more familiar with—and clenched her stomach, uncertain of her balance.

Dafydd slipped an arm around her waist, warm and reassuring. Lara released her white-knuckled grip on the saddle carefully, relaxing incrementally against Dafydd. "Thanks. I'm not used to riding. And the Unseelie came from the ocean?" Her voice went up dubiously on the last word, earning Dafydd's chuckle.

"So our legends tell us." For a second time he started to say more, and Lara shook her head, not trusting herself to raise a hand again. The horse snorted, sounding for all the world like it was making commentary on her fear. She blinked, then, daring brought on by amusement, she patted the animal's shoulder.

"I don't need all the history. I just need enough to understand. Why did they exchange their firstborns? I thought second sons were more usual." Insofar as she'd ever thought about it at all, at least. Lara could hardly imagine anyone in the modern world participating in exchanges of that nature.

"We—both Seelie and Unseelie—live a very long time. One of the prices we pay is that we have very few children. When Ioan and Merrick were the only heirs, warfare was rarely devastating, because neither king would risk their only child. When I was born, Emyr had an advantage. It was Hafgan's idea to exchange the firstborns."

"Better to not raise his own son than to risk losing him in battle?" Lara shook her head. "Wasn't 'not fighting' an option?"

"The Barrow-lands are small," Dafydd said with a shrug. "Before the Unseelie came from the oceans, there was enough land for the Seelie. Since they came, though, we've fought over the earth time and again."

"How long ago was that?"

Dafydd shook his head, movement felt rather than seen. "As long as I can remember."

Lara twisted to see him, wondering how long that might be. The horse side-stepped and snorted irritably. One of the guards, another woman, caught its bridle with an easy grip. "It is time immemorial to most of us since the Unseelie came from the oceans and began to fight us for our green growing places. I am Aerin," she added with the air of someone unaccustomed to introducing herself.

"I'm Lara. It's nice to meet you." The perfunctory phrase was one Lara had learned she could say without discomfort creeping over her. Aerin's hair was blue in the moonlight, and her eyes yellow, disconcerting colors that emphasized a lack of humanity. Lara glanced away, then back again, not wanting to be rude either by dismissing the woman or staring at her.

"And you," Aerin said after a moment's silence. Then she inclined her head toward Dafydd, murmuring a phrase Lara didn't catch, then saying his name in a more familiar manner.

"Aerin." Dafydd loosened his arm from around Lara to take the Seelie woman's hand briefly, a smile in his voice. "How long has it been?"

A sting of envy stiffened Lara's spine and the beleaguered horse huffed again, obviously displeased with her seat. Chastened, she tried to relax again. She'd met Dafydd only a few days earlier, and could hardly hold old friendships against him.

Her own thoughts chided her with dissonant tones, and Lara gave a huff of her own, quiet echo of the horse's. She couldn't *reasonably* hold old friendships against him, and with that half-amused amendment, the off-key notes in her mind subsided.

"Longer for you than for me, I think," Aerin said. "Ten days, Dafydd. Ten days with no answers, and a week of that with skirmishes along the valley borders. Merrick's death must be answered for, or we'll all pay the price."

"Which is what? War?"

"War," Aerin said crisply. "The ruin of our people. The drowning of the lands." Her attention slid to Lara, then back again, and it was with a note of affected diffidence that she asked, "And how long has it been for you?"

"The drow—" Lara looked away, trying to hide her face as a spasm of triumph seized her. War, the ruin of her people, and the drowning of the lands evidently came secondary to Aerin's personal concerns, which suggested Lara wasn't the only one fighting envy.

Dafydd, though, gave no hint of recognizing it in either of them as he said, "So little time we wouldn't mark its passing, here, and yet so much time in the mortal land that I no longer recognize what it became from what it was. A century," he added, so lightly the long years might not have had any meaning to him. "A decade there for every day here, it seems."

Horror banished jealousy and its petty triumphs as Lara twisted to stare at Dafydd again. "That's not going to happen to me, is it? You said I'd be home in time for dinner!"

He shook his head hastily. "No, no. You will be. The worldwalking spell has been charmed on your behalf. For a little while we can hold time in step, one world to the next. You'll be gone no more hours at home than you spend here, but for my part, there was no knowing how long it would take to find a truthseeker. Even after only ten days here, we're on the brink of war. A century might have seen the ruin of us all."

Lara exhaled noisily, slumping in the saddle. "I think there's too much you didn't tell me." The horse whickered agreement, turning with its fellows down a trail that became, as she watched, a broad avenue lined with trees that reached for the stars. At its far end, both impossibly distant and mirage-close, rose a building that looked like it had been carved of moonlight, pale and stunning against the foreground of green-black trees.

"Where did that—" Lara straightened again, eyes rounding. "I didn't see us coming up on—" Despite her poor riding seat, she bent to look over Dafydd's arm at the fading path they'd taken. "I should've been able to see that a long time ago. Why couldn't I? What is it?"

"The citadel of the Seelie," Dafydd murmured. "Welcome to my court."

Twelve

"Your court." Aerin made a sound remarkably like the horse's regular snorts. "Watch your tongue, Dafydd. You don't want your father to hear you say that."

"Our court, then," Dafydd said affably. "I meant nothing by it. It's my home, after all."

"As it is all of ours." Emyr's cool voice broke over their conversation, warning that he'd overheard Dafydd's claim. "You are not appropriately dressed for court, Dafydd."

Dafydd managed to sweep a bow around Lara, whose eyes were all for the citadel. It glowed in the moonlight, pouring so much brilliance from its white walls she couldn't understand how she hadn't seen it as they approached. A fanciful answer, *magic*, leaped to mind, then remained there, its honesty ringing true. Certainly its lavender-hued light was unlike any earth light Lara had ever seen, and even from the ground she could see the delicacy of tall towers winding their way toward the sky. The path beneath their feet had turned to flagstones, though the horses' hooves made no sound on them, like they still walked on grass.

"I will remedy that, Father, never fear. And as for you, Lara,

I think Aerin can help you." Dafydd swung down from the horse with more grace than Lara could imagine having, then helped her down and made her graceful, too.

She was unexpectedly stiff as she hit the ground, as though they'd been on horseback far longer than it had seemed. Startled, Lara cast a glance toward the moon, trying to gauge its travel through the sky. It had crossed more distance than she'd realized, pushing the hour very late. Still gazing at the moon, she rubbed her back and asked, "How long was that ride?"

Dafydd hesitated, not so much reluctance, she thought, as struggling for words. "It's the horses," he finally said. "They choose the easiest path, and only some of it is . . . noticeable. We've ridden for perhaps two and a half hours."

Lara turned to him, gaping, and his smile turned apologetic. "The Barrow-lands are not much like your world, Lara. I'm sorry, but I swear the lost time won't count against us when we bring you home. Are you all right?"

"I'm . . ." Lara wobbled her head, knowing she looked silly but unable to express herself more coherently. "Yeah, I guess so. I just thought we'd been riding about twenty minutes. Is everything here like that?"

"Rather a lot of it, I'm afraid." Dafydd gave her another crooked smile, then gestured to Aerin. "She has a sister not much taller than you. Would you like to borrow an outfit to meet the court in?"

Lara held her breath a moment, searching for her equilibrium, then let out an explosive sigh. Clothes that weren't wet and grass-stained would help her regain her balance, if nothing else. "Please. That would be great. Thank you."

Aerin dismounted with the same dismaying grace Dafydd had shown. She was taller than he was, and brisk as she said, "We have only a little time before the court is gathered. Will you come with me?"

"Of course." Lara shot Dafydd an uncertain glance; then, at his nod, hurried after Aerin.

The Seelie woman made no allowance for Lara's shorter legs,

striding through phosphorus halls whose permeating glow had no apparent reliance on torches or other obvious light sources. Lara caught glimpses of open spaces within the citadel, stretches where forest seemed to break through china-white walls and become part of the building, but she had no time to linger and wonder: it was clear Aerin would leave her far behind if she didn't focus on keeping up.

It was clear, too, that she would be hopelessly lost without the taller woman's guidance. By the time Aerin gestured her through doors to what proved to be her private rooms, Lara's stomach was tight with nerves bordering on panic. She had crossed into a world that wasn't her own, a world where time and space bent to a horse's will, and she had just left the only person she knew here. Kelly may have teased her about not taking risks, but this one now seemed like idiocy. No one in her right mind would have taken the chance Lara had just taken.

An untuned violin's sour notes screeched through her mind, objecting to her last thought—Lara did, at least, believe herself to be in her right mind. "Most of the time," she breathed aloud, and cast a glance upward, taking in the room Aerin had led her to.

It soared, distant ceiling edged with delicate cornices that made earthly gingerbreads look gross and squat in comparison. Globes of light, emitting the same soft glow the halls did, swung around each other near the ceiling, shifting the room's shadows. Tapestries hung down the walls, picked with silver and gold and blue, as though someone had threaded moonlight and sunshine and water to weave them. Subtle patterns teased Lara's eye and faded again when she looked directly at them, the tapestries becoming nothing more than shimmering imageless cloth.

This room was clearly a sitting room, a public area. There were recognizable chairs and couches, though, staring at them, Lara became convinced their wooden frames were grown, not carved or fastened. The padding was of pale soft cloth, cool colors everywhere.

Which made the emerald-clad girl in the middle of the room all the more remarkable. She was vivid, the first Seelie besides Dafydd whom Lara'd seen wearing anything but moonlight shades. Her hands were gathered in her skirts and her green eyes were wide with excitement, making her look rather like Cynthia Taylor when her attention was caught by a new project at the bespoke shop. Lara offered a swift, surprised smile to the girl, whose own smile lit up with youthful delight. "I'm Myfanwy, Aerin's sister. She said you wanted to borrow one of my dresses?"

Lara gave Aerin a startled look, and the other woman shrugged. "We aren't, with close friends and relations, relegated to mere vocal speech. Impulses, ideas, emotions can be shared, if not words. I sent ahead to let Myfanwy know we were on our way."

"I think I have the perfect dress," Myfanwy said breathlessly, and within minutes Lara found herself in the unusual position of playing dressmaker's dummy. She had spent so many hours as the tailor that she was surprised to discover she was self-conscious, and kept stiffening as the sisters adjusted a gown meant for a taller woman. It wasn't, she told herself with some despair, that she was *short*. The Seelie were just unnaturally tall. Aerin, kneeling to stitch a hem, was still more than half Lara's height.

"How long have you known him?" Aerin glanced up at Lara with studied nonchalance. Pretending to try to put Lara at ease but in reality testing the waters; it was very much the same indifference Lara had affected when Dafydd had offered Aerin his hand. Faintly amused at their awkward camaraderie, Lara smiled.

"In hours? About eleven, over the course of five days."

"Oh," Aerin said with an odd note. "Our stories tell us we find your kind easy to glamour and pull into our world at a cost to your own lives. If that's what Dafydd's done, I'm sorry."

"He didn't."

Aerin's eyebrows shot up. They were nearly white, like her hair: the blue tones had faded once moonlight was left behind, and her yellow eyes had proved spring green. "Would you know?"

The question hung between them, marking out the silence between heartbeats. Lara felt heat crawl into her cheeks, an admission of uncertainty broken by a light tug on her hair and a shy, fascinated trill of laughter as her ears were uncovered.

Aerin reached around Lara and smacked her sister on the thigh without losing hold of the work she did. "Behave. The Truthseeker is a guest here."

The words twisted in Lara's ears, the sense of them clear, but the language itself wholly unfamiliar to her. She shook her head once, a sharp motion, and frowned at the woman kneeling in front of her. "What did you say?"

"I said behave." This time Aerin's speech was clear again. "I apologize for Myfanwy's impudence."

"But I heard—" Lara drew a slow breath. "You're not speaking English, are you. Of course not. Why would you be? What *are* you speaking? Why do I understand you?"

"It will be part of the spell Dafydd's cast to bring you here," Aerin said after a moment. "If you didn't understand me, it's because I used our high tongue to scold her."

"I understood what you meant." Lara pressed her lips together as too many thoughts fought for precedence. Aerin's question was a good one: she had come so willingly she might well have been influenced, unknowingly, by magic.

Might have been. There was one clear risk to that gambit, one that she put into words slowly. "I understood what you meant," she repeated. "Not the words, but the idea of it. The truth behind it. If I can sense the true idea behind words I don't even know, you tell me: Would you dare cast a glamour to trick me into coming to your world?"

Aerin folded her hands in her lap, studying Lara. "Perhaps not. Not if I thought there was any chance you might realize it, and I would assume a truthseeker would. You should still be cautious of us, Lara. All of us. Even Dafydd."

Chimes poured from her words, ringing true and clear. Lara, fist still knotted in the fine fabric, nodded, and Aerin lifted a hand to gently loosen Lara's grip on the skirt. "Then I think you're ready to greet the court."

✒

She had not expected Dafydd to be at his father's side.

In the moment after she assimilated the sight of the slim golden prince beside his father's iron throne—no, it wouldn't be iron, a small part of her recognized: fairies weren't supposed to be able to bear the touch of iron, and so for all of its cold metallic weight, the king's throne could not be iron. His father's *silver* throne, and that was an idea even more overwhelming than Dafydd's cool remote presence at the king's side. The throne, tall and spired and shining, engulfed Emyr. Lara felt embarrassingly mortal for being so impressed at a chunk of precious metal.

A very *large* chunk of precious metal, to be sure: more than most humans might expect to see in a lifetime, much less displayed ostentatiously at the head of a courtroom. Lara shook herself, not caring that every eye would see her do it: she had no reason for pretense. She was a stranger and meant to be awed.

It would have been all right, though, if it hadn't worked quite so well. And Dafydd, as if catching a hint of her thoughts, quirked a corner of his mouth, which went much further in restoring her equilibrium than she had imagined possible.

He would, of course, be at his father's side. He was a prince of this realm, and for all she gathered he wasn't precisely the favored son, there was nowhere else he could be without presenting the appearance of a schism within the royal house. Lara knew enough of politics to understand personal feelings fell a distant second to the illusion of a united front. And they did: the rest of the Seelie court rippled away from them, fading into obscurity when viewed alongside the king and prince. There were hundreds of people pressed into the throne room, all of them slim and ethereal and inhuman, but it was the royals who arrested Lara's attention.

She, though, held everyone else's. She'd known she would: that was the purpose of being presented to the court. Knowing it, though, and feeling the weight of so many gazes were different things. If it weren't for a fear of doing her elegant gown an injustice,

Lara thought she might turn and flee. She was a tailor, almost invisible to even the people she worked for, and she had spent most of her life trying not to call attention to herself or the discomfiting gift she possessed.

A gift that every person in the room knew she had, and which they all hoped might give them the answers they sought. Lara, quite certain royalty was supposed to break the silence, cleared her throat and squeaked, "Look, if I'm supposed to ask everybody in this room if they murdered Merrick ap Annwn, we'd probably better just get started."

A ripple of subdued laughter turned Lara's hands into slow fists beneath the long pointed sleeves of her borrowed dress. She looked the part of one of Dafydd's people, or very nearly: she'd seen that in Myfanwy's mirror.

The gown was probably the finest thing she had ever worn, despite having been made for someone else. Its tall, open-throated collar brushed her jaw and plunged to a narrow *V* that spilled down the bodice, making the most of her height. The bodice was wound gold and russet velvet, woven alternately until it made a textured cinch that shaped her figure to remarkable slenderness. It loosened at a dropped waist to float into the long, light lines of the skirt, layers upon layers of thin silken gauze. The colors were perfect for her, bringing vitality to her pale skin, and in the gown, she might well have been one of the Seelie, if unusually petite.

And then she opened her mouth, and marked herself as absolutely and unquestionably alien to the Seelie realm. The king stiffened, becoming a blade of ice. Dafydd touched a hand to his father's shoulder, murmuring, "She means no offense. Her country has no king and no protocol in speaking with royalty. She's afraid, and trying to hide it."

The king relaxed fractionally, evidently satisfied by the idea that Lara feared him. She wondered if Dafydd had been as impossibly arrogant as his father when he'd left the Barrow-lands to roam the mortal world, and wondered, too, how deep and shocking the change in him must be, if that were so. He must have lived half a dozen human lives in the century he'd spent in Lara's world, but only a matter of days had passed here, in his own. He may well have returned a stranger to the life and people he'd known. The idea sent a pang through her, as though an unexpected wound had opened and left her with no way to heal it.

"If I may, my lord," Dafydd offered, as much to Lara as his father. The king sniffed and lifted a finger in agreement. Refusing to be sullied by speaking with a mortal, truthseeker or not, Lara thought. She caught Dafydd's gaze, struggling against the urge to roll her eyes. The Seelie prince's mouth quirked, but he replaced the beginnings of a smile with solemnity as he lifted his voice to address the court.

"I have brought to you the truthseeker we sought. Born of the mortal world and carrying mortal magic, Lara Jansen has chosen to come here, a place so foreign to her home that it's a thing of legend and children's tales. She knew me from the moment we met: knew me to be other than what I claimed to be, and in so knowing proved her magic. We are all in her debt, myself most of all." His voice softened as he brought his attention to Lara.

"Myself most of all, for the scant days that have passed in the Barrow-lands have been a full century in her world. Her willingness to join me and search for the truth of Merrick ap Annwn's murder has ended an exile that has left my heart bereft. I would ask you to do her an honor, and offer her the thanks of all our people."

A thunderous chant answered him, and Lara flinched straight. She patted the noise down with her palms toward the floor, embarrassment burning her cheeks, and mumbled, "Thank you."

"I think you might be able to ask us as one, Truthseeker," Dafydd said as the calls faded away. "Only if you sense discordance in the answers would you have to trouble yourself to ask us individually if we are guilty of this foul deed."

Lara's eyebrows shot up, her distress wiped away by Dafydd's sheer pomposity. He pursed his lips, clearly judging what he'd said by her terms, and amusement creased his features as it had moments earlier when the king had been equally haughty. The impulse to tease him rose, then faded again: she was there to fulfill a duty she'd agreed to. "Dafydd, there ha—"

Another gasp rushed around the hall and Lara's gaze went to the gathered courtiers, her eyebrows wrinkled in confusion before exasperated comprehension swept her. She'd breached protocol by using his name so casually. Well, the Seelie court would have to adapt: she wasn't, despite an outward similarity, one of them. "There must be a thousand people in this room, Dafydd. There's no way I can tell if a handful of them don't answer, and if they don't, there's no truth or lie to sense."

"A compulsion can be laid," he offered. "One that will oblige speech, though it cannot force the truth."

Lara's eyebrows shot upward. "I take it you don't have a Fifth Amendment. You can—" She turned away from the throne—turned her back on the king, eliciting yet another shocked intake of breath around the room—and put her fists on her hips. Only Dafydd, she thought, would see how her nails bit into her palms: how she used the bold stance to hide her own worry. "And you'd let him?" she demanded of the court at large. "You'd let him compel you to speak?"

"He is our prince," Aerin said into a silence no one else seemed willing to break. "We have nothing to hide from him. Of course we'll allow it."

Lara, loudly enough to hear in the quiet of the courtroom, muttered, "You really aren't human," and turned back to Dafydd. "All right. If that's acceptable within your justice system, it's all right with me. But if it's not someone here, what are we going to do about the rest of the Barrow-lands?"

Another smile spilled over Dafydd's face. "We'll cross that bridge when we come to it."

Thirteen

Elves obviously didn't say "we'll cross that bridge when we come to it": a rumble of comprehending bemusement rolled through the court before their prince began murmured words of enchantment. As when Aerin scolded Myfanwy, the sense of his words became clear to Lara. Then recognition leapt in her: it was the same tongue Dafydd had spoken in the fight with the nightwings, and she hadn't understood it at all, then. A few hours in the Barrow-lands *had* changed her, had deepened her talent already. Lara folded her arms around herself, warding off a cold that came from within. A murder investigation might take days. By the end of that time, she wasn't sure she'd recognize herself as the same woman who'd walked through a portal torn in the air.

Though, truthfully, she had already stepped so far beyond her customary boundaries as to be unrecognizable. *I contain multitudes,* she thought, and wondered if the poet who had written those words had ever found himself torn between worlds and choices.

Dafydd's incantation ended and the court gave a collective sigh, their attention turning to Lara again. She tightened her arms around her ribs, then imagined how fragile and afraid she must look, huddled like that. It was the stance of a woman who didn't want to be noticed, but she'd come here to offer help. She straightened, taking a breath deep enough to strain her tight-woven bodice, and met the eyes of those closest to her.

Light eyes: they all had light eyes, water blue to golden hazel and clear green, but none of them even close to the brown of her own. Lara stared from face to face for a few seconds, taken aback by uniformly translucent skin, pale hair, and eyes without a hint of darkness to them. For an instant their willowy forms and high-cheekboned faces looked not ethereal but inbred. Nowhere on earth could she imagine corralling a thousand passersby from any handful of streets in that city and finding such an unbroken similarity from one face to another.

They were dying, she thought very clearly, then threw the idea off with a shudder. "Is there a way to test if the compulsion is working?"

Dafydd made a nonplussed sound. "You'll have to trust me. Or ask everyone individually if they're obliged to answer, in which case we may as well have not bothered."

"Fair enough." Lara backed up until her heels touched the first step of the throne dais, then stood on her toes. "I wish I could see you all. All right. I think I'm going to have to ask a lot of very similar questions to cover all the bases, so I'll start with . . . did anyone here murder Merrick ap Annwn?"

She braced for a tide of answers similar to the thanks offered moments before, but was instead greeted with a thousand chimes, like single notes struck from distant triangles. They lifted her, played at her skin and the fine hairs at her nape, making her tremble with their music and taking her weight from her feet. "No," she whispered back into the purity of their response. "No one here murdered him."

A sigh of relief tempered with concern washed over the court. Lara felt a stab of sympathy. It would have been easier if one false note had played; if one person had come up untrue and therefore offered an end to their uncertainty. At the same time, the truth reverberating in their answers meant none of their friends was guilty of murder, and that was soothing, too. Lara bit her lower lip. "Is anyone here responsible, in any way, for Merrick ap Annwn's death?"

Sour notes echoed in the court's response. Lara pressed her fingers against the sides of her nose and bared her teeth behind the steeple of her hands. "That was an awkward question. Let me try this: Does anyone here feel guilt over his death?"

Pure tones rang out in disparate answers: hundreds upon hundreds answered *no*, truthfully, but a handful more said *yes* with as much truth. Glances were exchanged, frowns and sharp looks, and in a few places the courtiers shifted, making distrustful space around those who had answered in the affirmative.

Lara nodded, lifting a hand as though she conducted music. "Will those of you who said yes please answer this next question, and the rest remain silent: Why do you feel guilty over Merrick ap Annwn's death?" Repeating his full name felt necessary, like anything less might allow the men and women she interrogated to squeak by with a truthful answer that didn't address what Lara wanted to ask. Her heartbeat was sick and fast in her chest, full of worry that she might let something slip by unnoticed. She was a tailor, not a lawyer.

Answers flooded back, more than one word this time, many of them mumbled with shame. *I didn't like him*, or *I wished him ill*; *I wanted him out of our court*—all true answers. Dafydd stood rigid with tension at Lara's side, his gaze lingering on those who responded truly with an answer he didn't like. He looked betrayed, Lara thought, as though those who hadn't liked Merrick struck at him personally with their distaste.

Lara nodded again, more to encourage herself than the court. "The same group, please answer this: Do you believe your feelings may have created a situation that led to Merrick ap Annwn's death?"

Some did, or were, on further questioning, afraid they might have. The spaces around them grew, their comrades distancing themselves from association with possible murder. Those who stood abandoned did so with grim pride, their eyes warning that such slights would not go unforgotten.

Lara put her teeth together, searching for the right questions to ask: Were those fears rational? Fear wasn't, by its nature, rational, but most people could separate out a fear of heights from the conviction that the bridge they crossed was going to fall into the water below. Finally satisfied that it was, indeed, fear driving guilt and dissonant answers, Lara brought her questions back to the whole: *Does anyone know who is responsible for Merrick ap Annwn's murder? Does anyone have suspicions? Motives?* That got a bitter laugh, and one clear voice out of hundreds: "He was Unseelie."

Silence, abrupt and strained, followed the accusation. The courtiers, so willing to edge away from those who confessed to dislike, went still, as if afraid they would otherwise all look to whomever spoke, and in doing so condemn him.

But there was no condemnation to be made. Even the repugnance with which the words had been spoken wasn't enough to mask an inherent truth. Merrick's Unseelie heritage may have seemed, in melodramatic terms, to be reason enough to destroy him, but there was dissonance in the words: it was not, in truth, reason enough. It had not driven any of the gathered court to kill.

It made her aware she knew too little and that Dafydd had diced his language carefully when he'd asked her to help him. That, in turn, reminded her of Aerin's warning to be cautious, and Lara trembled with both exhaustion and nerves as she finally turned back to the throne. "I honestly don't think anyone here is responsible in any way for your brother's murder, Dafydd. I don't know what that means, where we go from here, but if anyone here is guilty I can't think of a question to ask that'll resonate with me."

"A truthseeker worthy of the name would have looked among us and known instantly," the king said coolly.

There was no profit in angering powerful men. Lara's chin dropped to her chest, weariness overcoming wisdom. "Dafydd said my talent hasn't matured. If you're not in any hurry, I could come back in a few years and we could try again then. I'm trying my best, though, and there is something I *did* notice, even if I'm not as good as I could be."

Impatient fingertips rattled a drumbeat against the throne's arm. "And what is that?"

Lara lifted her head, meeting the elfin king's eyes. "Neither you nor Dafydd answered any of my questions."

Emyr came to his feet in a silver shot, offended power blazing off him so strongly that Lara's next breath showed on suddenly chilly air. As one, the gathered courtiers moved back, showing the respect and awe due a monarch whose temper had been ignited by insult.

Panic leapt in Lara's stomach, driving the impulse to do as the courtiers had done: to escape the king's reach and his wrath. She wasn't certain it was bravery that held her in place; it could as easily have been a fundamental inability to move. But she forced her chin up, forced her gaze to be cool, and told herself that in the face of her calm the Seelie king's response was overblown and gauche. That he made himself foolish, when all he'd had to do was respond evenly in order to retain his own dignity.

"I'm sorry," she said mildly, and meant it, though more as an expression of surprise than apology. "Is the king above the law in the Barrow-lands?"

"The king is not expected to participate in common courtroom displays," he said through his teeth. Ice crystals grew around his feet, marring the silver craftsmanship of his throne and creeping toward Lara like a physical threat. For a long moment her attention was drawn to their inching progress, and a shiver rose up from her core. Regardless of how much courage she drew on, she could never hope to match an anger that was literally elemental.

The leading edge of ice turned to water as it moved beyond the immediate area of the king's effect, and a prosaic curiosity knocked fear out of her: she wondered how the silver remained unblackened, if the Seelie monarch was prone to fits of temper. There would have to be servants to mop up the melt water so it wouldn't oxidize in hard-to-reach crevices, since Lara couldn't imagine Dafydd's father stooping to do such menial work himself.

Equilibrium restored by ordinary matters of pragmatism, Lara lifted her gaze back to the king and arched an eyebrow in deliberate, if moderate, challenge. "In private will be fine, then. I do most of my work behind a closed door anyway."

"I have nothing to hide." Dafydd's voice surprised her, but nowhere nearly as much as it shocked his father, who flinched so hard a spray of frost cascaded from his shoulders and fell white against the throne. "I should have thought to include myself in the compulsion, or at the least, made answers to your questions. The prerogative of royalty," Dafydd explained. "I'm afraid even a century among humans didn't eliminate my assumption of *carte blanche* once I returned home."

The king's jaw locked, fury paling his eyes. Dafydd met the expression with an artless expression of no concern, but subtle tension changed the set of his shoulders and the way his clothes fell. He was forcing his father's hand, Lara realized and, looking between them, had an instant's clarity. The king wasn't above the law: he *was* the law, as he would have been through much of human history. It was therefore almost impossible to suggest the law might be in any way corrupt without also implicating the crown.

She'd come to the Barrow-lands to help, not to sow the seeds of civil war. "It's all right, Dafydd. I probably wouldn't have thought to include myself, either. And I imagine no one would expect the queen of England to be subjected to mass questioning, either. I do think it's necessary to put you through it, though, your majesty, if for no other reason than to allow you to face the Unseelie king with the absolute truth at your side."

The phrase "your majesty" came more smoothly than she'd feared it might. It was deliberate mollification, as deliberate as her earlier attempt to infuriate him, but the wealthy and powerful were frequently easy to assuage by paying them the due they thought owed them. And, to be fair, the man was a king. Insufferably arrogant, perhaps, but a king.

And, just like a highly sensitive shop client, he relaxed a little, some of the cold inching back from where it had grown around him.

"Hafgan would never believe me to be in any way responsible for his son's death. To be so would be to risk my own child Ioan's life. Even so, the assurance would not go amiss." He took one step down from his dais, approaching Lara, though it was his court he addressed.

"I am Emyr, king of the Barrow-lands, and I tell you this now: I have had no hand in the death—the *murder*—of Merrick ap Annwn, child of Hafgan of the Unseelie. I neither nocked the arrow nor drew it nor released it." His gaze went to Lara, and quietly but sharply, he added, "And those words are both literal and figurative in their truths. I am not part of the plot that designed his death. I did not shape it, nor do I have any knowledge of who did. I only wish I did, if for no other reason than to assure my oldest son's safety." The ice that had left it came back into his voice. "Now, Truthseeker, are you satisfied?"

Lara tilted her head, eyebrows furrowed as she considered the king. Then she took a handful of skirts and dropped a brief curtsy that felt unnatural, but which she meant with as much genuine respect as she could muster. "I am. You were very thorough, and I don't think I have any follow-up questions." She released her skirts and turned to Dafydd much less formally. "Which only leaves you, I guess."

"Why bother?" Aerin stepped forward from within the courtiers. "There's no one among us who doesn't know Dafydd ap Caerwyn was the murder weapon himself."

Fourteen

Ice erupted in Lara's stomach and froze her breath as surely as though Emyr had cast a spell to chill the air. Bravado had pushed her through facing his anger; bravado and the certainty that if she let herself admit to the awe she felt, she would crumble in a whimpering heap at the throne's edge and never get up again.

Even that narrow strand of willpower deserted her, resonating pure tones in Aerin's charge stripping what strength she had to draw on. She swung toward Dafydd, the ice in her belly spreading to her arms and legs and leaving her a clumsy marionette. Only the way the skirts crumpled in her hand promised her gown was still gossamer: its weight was such that it might have turned to stone. There was nothing to her voice, only a protest of disbelief she knew would go unanswered: "Dafydd?"

Unanswered, at least, in the way she wanted it to be. Weary regret in the lines of his body told her everything she already knew to be true: that Aerin's accusation held merit, and that the son of the Seelie king had somehow lied to her.

"I nocked the arrow." Dafydd's shoulders slumped, all his slender alien beauty wiped out with such a human stance of defeat. "I drew the bowstring and loosed the arrow that ended my brother's life."

"And you didn't think to tell me this?" Venom melted the cold in Lara's chest and carried heat to her cheeks. Worse than blushes, bitter water stung her eyes. She knotted her fingers more tightly into the thin fabric of her skirts, willing herself to not draw attention to tears by dashing them away, and wondered sharply if the Seelie cried from frustration or anger. It was a human fallibility she'd be glad to give up. "What the hell did you want me here for, if you killed him?"

"He claims himself innocent of the crime." Emyr spoke again, disdain in every word. "Our poet and seer insisted he be given the chance to clear himself, and that can only be done through a truth-seeker's talents."

"I loosed the arrow." Dafydd's hands slowly turned to fists, his body taut and his face downcast. His gaze, though, remained on Lara, fiery with desperation. "But my actions weren't my own, Lara. I remember still—I will never forget—the thickness that came over me. I can see what I did, can feel my arm bend and take the arrow from its quiver, can feel the weight of the bowstring against my fingers, and in nightmares I watch the arrow fly true while my mind screams against my actions. I was the weapon, but I am not the killer. I swear it."

Strain released him abruptly, as though offering his explanation had been a battle of wills that, once ended, left him drained. "I'm sorry," he added in a whisper. "I should have explained it all, but I was afraid you wouldn't come with me, and I have no other way to prove myself innocent."

Lara sat down gracelessly, scraping her hip painfully on the edge of the throne dais as she did. The wince that crossed her face was excuse enough to cup her hands around her forehead, shielding herself from the curious light eyes of so many strangers while she caught her breath.

Shielding herself, too, from showing confusion and relief and dismay, though she knew hiding her expression was as much a giveaway as sharing it would be. The courtiers' silence pressed on her, unforgiving in its interest, inhuman in its patient extension.

She broke before they did, shivering under the weight of their anticipation. "He's telling the truth. At least he believes it's the truth. He was the weapon, not the murderer." Aerin had named Dafydd the weapon as well, a distinction that had meant nothing to Lara a few moments earlier. She folded her fingers down, searching for Aerin's willowy form among so many others. "Is that possible? Dafydd just laid a compulsion to answer on all of you. Can one be laid on someone to make them act against their will?"

Hesitation clouded the Seelie woman's clear eyes. "I would have said no. That there must be a part of the one enchanted that wishes to act as the enchanter wishes him to."

"But?" The single word echoed sharply in a hall too filled with bodies for reverberations to sound at all. Discomfort crawled over Lara's skin, raising hairs, and the muscles in her neck creaked with the effort of holding her head still. Magic was being employed, making her voice carry. She was almost certain of it, but looking around to question Dafydd or Emyr's hand in it felt, somehow, like losing ground.

"But I've known Dafydd and Merrick all their lives," Aerin said. "I saw rivalry between them, as with any family, but I can't believe there's any part of Dafydd that wished Merrick harm. Either I don't know him as well as I think, or there's a magic that can force a man's hand against his will."

"Unseelie magic" came out of the gathering, accusing words spoken in more than one voice. Others nodded, muttering agreement as a spasm of uncertain concurrence shaped Aerin's mouth. Lara released her self-imposed stillness and twisted to glance first at Dafydd, then Emyr. Her neck ached from the angle, but getting to her feet seemed risky: tremors rattled her, Dafydd's confession still leaving marks.

"A few more questions, if you will, your majesty. Am I right in assuming you're one of the most skilled magic users of your people?" A trill of body-weakening absurdity ran through her, making her glad she hadn't risen. A week earlier she hadn't believed in magic at all. Now she was interrogating a monarch on his talent for it. She felt as though a bandage had been torn off, the sting fading so long as she didn't look too closely at the wound it had covered.

Emyr stared down at her, impassive enough to be threatening. He finally nodded, a single short action that informed Lara as to her rudeness in asking. She sighed and climbed to her feet again, feeling more able to face Emyr's acidic gaze that way. "Then for the purposes of this trial, I'm going to consider you an expert witness. As such, would you say it's possible to enchant someone into doing something he didn't want to?"

"I have never tried," Emyr said after a lengthy silence, "but I believe I could." The faintest emphasis lay on the final "I," making it clear that he doubted it was a skill owned by all.

"So it's not necessarily Unseelie magic?" Lara used the word cautiously, uncomfortably certain that the Seelie court regarded it as synonymous with *evil* or *dark*.

For all his pale icy colors, Lara saw fire rise in the Seelie king. "Not," he said with too much precision, "necessarily. But that court has made use of their magics before in ways that this court and these people had never considered and would not condone. This is such a use. I think it more likely, if my son has been used as a weapon, that the wielder is of the Unseelie court, and not this one."

"Even though they'd be killing their own king's son? Why would they do that?" Even as she asked Lara knew, and answered her own question: "To provoke war. To create a chance at seizing the land they want. How long did you say you've fought over the Barrowlands?"

"It has been this way for—" Dafydd shrugged, spreading his hands. "Forever."

"Forever," Lara heard herself say in a light, disconcerting tone, "is a very long time, to immortals." Her dress suddenly wasn't warm enough, cold rushing over her as though she'd stepped into a northern wind. Uncertainty crossed Dafydd's face, a sign that the strangeness in her voice wasn't something only she had heard, but it was his father who answered her.

"It is, and yet even I would rest easy with saying it has been this way forever to a truthseeker."

"And have there been wars over it before?" Lara folded her arms around herself as she turned back to Emyr, not caring that it made her look small and defensive.

The first hint of humor she'd seen in him ghosted across the king's pale features. "Not in forever. Battles, yes, but never war. The Unseelie have never gathered in such force as will greet us in the morning." Humor passed, leaving sharpness in its wake. "All of us who live in the citadel are gathered in this room, Truthseeker. If you cannot point us at a murderer tonight, then we who must fight on the morrow will retire, the better to protect our lands and people with dawn."

"All I have right now is Dafydd," she said bitterly. "The same as the rest of you. He believes utterly that he was the weapon but not the killer, and no one else in here has even a hint of guilt about them. You might as well go to bed."

Courtiers scattered away from Lara, from their disgraced prince, and most of all from their bleak-eyed king. Lara watched them break into groups, gossip rising up in whispers before they'd escaped earshot. Even Aerin slipped into the heart of a small gathering, ducking her head to catch the murmurs and speculation of those around her. It was easier to watch them, to wonder at what they said, than to look at Dafydd again, knowing he had betrayed her trust with full and deliberate intention.

Oh, he hadn't lied, and Lara perversely admired that, but it did nothing to ease the cut of betrayal she felt. He hadn't lied, but neither had he told her anything like the whole truth, nor laid out the clues that might have led her to asking questions he couldn't refuse to answer.

Kelly would call him a piece of work for that particular success. Lara cast one hard glare at the floor, then made herself lift her gaze to find Dafydd's, to see what she could read in his expression.

Humility, even self-disgust, marred his handsome, alien features, and his glance skittered away guiltily before he brought it back to her, seeking forgiveness he in no way deserved. She met that plea coolly, feeling the same well-controlled condemnation in her gaze as she'd laid on him the first time they'd met, in the moment he'd given her a false name.

She ought to have been wiser from that moment on. Subtle complexities of truth were so rare as to be intriguing and exciting to pursue, but at the heart of it he had lied to her from the moment they'd met. When she had been so uncomfortable over his name, she should have known better than to trust that he had been wholly honest with the story that had convinced her to join him in the Barrowlands.

"Don't tell me you had no other choice." Her voice was as clipped as Emyr's had ever been, and she wondered if she could be as arrogant as the Seelie king. "You could have said you'd been framed. I'd have heard the truth in it."

"But would you have come with me, knowing I'd murdered a man? You just said I believed what I told you was the truth. That's not exoneration, Lara. It's only enough to hang the jury."

It was a curiously human expression from the Seelie prince, and had her anger been a little less, she might have smiled. Instead she snapped, "Do you even have juries here?"

"No." Emyr stepped down from the throne dais, regal presence needing no other clarification: he was the beginning and end of the law, uninterested in troubling with juries or trials. "Take your truthseeker away, Dafydd. I have magics to work, and I would have them removed from her influence."

"And her mortal taint?" Lara asked under her breath. Emyr's shoulders pinched and he turned a sharp look on her. Lara scowled back, sullen in her defiance and not particularly caring. Nor did she expect an answer, and a touch of her outrage was mollified by the fact that he bothered.

"Yes. Your nearness pulls at the warp and weft of Seelie magic. Oisín was not *cursed* with immortality without youth; that he ages was the unintended price of magics worked on a man of mortal birth. Now go, as far away as my son can take you without leaving these lands."

"Who's Oisín?" For the second time, Lara forwent Emyr's answer, turning to walk away, arms folded under her breasts. Dafydd scrambled after her, offering an answer she wasn't certain she wanted, given that it offered him an excuse to talk to her at all.

"Oisín is our seer, the one who sent me to your world to look for you. There are stories about him, legends."

"I don't like fairy tales."

Dafydd, ill-advisedly, breathed, "And yet here you are, participating in one."

"You son of a *bitch*." Shrieking discordance rushed through Lara, infuriating talent picking apart impossibilities and untruths. Furious, frustrated, she spun and rushed away from him, strides just short enough to not be called a run. A moment later she pushed through the audience chamber's great doors, the violent slap of her palms against them shocking through her elbows. They were obviously meant to open with a mere touch: under her thrust they flew back, startling everyone but her with their bang.

Wind, as if affronted by the assault, snatched at her gown and hair, making her feel like she'd been transformed into a wild thing in the space of an instant, and then fell away again as abruptly as it had risen, leaving Lara with the impression that the air itself was shocked by her mere mortality and how easy it was to rumple her.

"Lara . . ." Dafydd's placating voice came after her.

She turned back to him in such a snap of skirts it seemed the wind hadn't left her at all. "Don't try to charm me right now, *your highness*. You're right, maybe I wouldn't have come here if you'd told me you'd killed Merrick yourself. But you should have given me the choice. Or did you just think you were being clever, hiding things from the naïve human truthseeker?" Her lips peeled away from her teeth, her expression feral enough that it drove Dafydd half a step backward.

Lara's snarl turned to a sneer, belittling his cowardice in the face of her wrath. "I'll help," she said. "I'll help because I said I would, but I'm going home the second this is over. In the meantime, stay out of my way." She whipped around again and stalked away, leaving Dafydd to stand alone on the citadel's steps like Cinderella's prince.

Fifteen

Within minutes, embarrassment outweighed Lara's anger. Running away was a child's trick, and like a child, she'd failed to pay any attention to her path. The citadel's vast ghostly shape above the trees wasn't enough to guide her back on the path she'd taken, though she might be able to work her way back by heading toward its graceful spires. Might: the idea of briar rose patches and moats, things of fairy tales, presented themselves to her as likely deterrents surrounding the heart of the Seelie court. The forest seemed improbably thick so close to the palace, wild and grown-over rather than the widespread oak trees and soft under-growth she'd seen surrounding ancient castles in photographs.

But those were images captured in a different world. Magic bent the rules here; there was hardly any reason to suppose things like forests or landscaping would follow the same patterns they did at home.

The thought felt too big, too unwieldy to be accepted. Lara, over-whelmed, sank into a huddle of moss and branches that softened to make a comfortable seat for her weight. For long minutes she sat with her head in her hands, eyes dry as she stared at the forest floor.

She had no way home except through Dafydd's goodwill. Scorning him, despite his treachery, had been a mistake, though even as she admitted that, irritation washed through her. He ought to have followed her, for all that she'd told him not to. The contradiction pulled a reluctant smile to her lips: men, whether human or fae, were right to be confounded by women.

"And so we are," came a voice from the forest. Lara jolted in her mossy chair, too entangled to come to her feet. "Forgive me," the voice added. "I forget how silent the forest is until the silence is broken. I am Oisín."

He came out of the trees as he spoke, a bent and ancient man with a heavy staff and filmed-over white eyes, though his step was more certain than Lara's had been as she'd run from the palace. Like everyone she'd seen, he was dressed beautifully, but there was nothing ethereal or inhuman about the soft robes he wore. The collar was high, the shoulders winged, the colored wraps around his middle of the finest material: each piece was as richly made as anything that graced the Seelie, and yet the whole was somehow imbued with a solidity that made the old man as human as Lara herself was.

Oisín settled into a hummock across from her, smile flitting across lips thinned with age. "It's only in our youth that they can dress us and make of us a semblance of what they are. You carry Myfanwy's gown well, better than I ever wore their fashions, and I have not been young for a long time."

"How long?" Lara cleared her throat, trying to erase the crack in her words and her discomfort at asking the question.

Another smile danced over the old man's mouth. "Oh, forever, to be sure, by the reckoning of those such as you and I. Eight hundred years," he added more softly, and gave a shrug as easy as a younger man's. "Perhaps longer. Time here is not the same."

"Eight hun—" Lara broke off, staring at the old man.

He spread his fingers, promise of a story, and made a song of his answer. "Another truthseeker of human origin might have sought the heart of ancient legends, delving into their truths, but that seeker would have lived a life unfulfilled, Lara Jansen. Legends are born of men, and men must die, and with them the truths only they can tell. Not even the strongest of magics can draw honest tales from the dead: memory is too fragile, and deeds done to greatness are easier remembered as wonders, even by those who did them. You've chosen a wiser path, creating beautiful things for the world around you. There is joy in that, where there is rarely joy in truth.

"But here I am neither dead nor mortal, and so I can give you a truth that no one in the world we both came from will know or believe: it is, after all, only part of another story.

"There are things that open passages between the worlds. Magic, such as that which brought you here, but mortal words, as well: poetry or song, when it's crafted just so. I was a poet even before I came here, and that gift let me glimpse my lady Rhiannon across the breach between the Barrow-lands and our own home world. I followed her here. They will say in the stories that I fell back to my own world a blind old man, but in truth I stepped back a youth with all my own strength still mine."

"But time had passed you by," Lara whispered. "How much time?"

"Enough. Enough that I no longer knew the young men, or even their grandfathers. We were less careful in the keeping of years then, but when I heard my own name in a song about the fair folk, I knew that it had been time enough that I no longer belonged with mortal kin. I began to write again," he murmured, "and in time the walls faded a second time and I returned to the Barrow-lands. Here I was granted immortality, but even Seelie magic isn't enough to hold youth on a once-mortal frame.

"I have not been young in eight hundred years," he said again, then smiled on a sigh. "But I lived among the Seelie, not yet old, for such a very long time before that."

"Forever," Lara said in a small voice, and the unwelcome ache of truth rang through it.

"Forever," Oisín agreed. "There's my tale, Truthseeker, and now I have yours to spin for you. It's my own fault you're here, and for that I offer apologies and gladness. If we have time, I would like to hear what's become of the world I left; there have been no visitors in so long that I've lost all sense of it."

"I don't think I'd know where to begin."

The old man's smile came again, a comfortable expression, as though he'd long since given up regrets and found pleasure in each moment as it passed. "My story for you is the more important. Did young Dafydd tell you of the prophecy?"

Lara's eyebrows arched. "Young? How old is he? And, yes, some kind of chant that I don't remember. Except the part about breaking the world. I can't do that. How could I do that?"

Oisín, wryly, said, "Here, everyone is young except for me." His voice dropped into a singsong, losing the music of his earlier tale. *"Truth will seek the hardest path, measures that must mend the past. Finder learns the only way, worlds come changed at end of day.* I know," he added, amused. "The poetry lacks. My own work is, I like to think, better, but these are words that come to me in fits, as visions of the world to come."

"But that's not what Dafydd said. He said—" Lara pressed her fingertips to her eyelids, trying to draw up the memory. "The first part was the same, but the second part changed. Something about . . . *spoken in a child's word,* because he apologized for that. Spoken in a child's word, changes that will break the world. That's what he said. Why did it change?" She glanced up to find a frown etched between Oisín's eyebrows.

"Prophecy . . . flexes. It alters as circumstances do. Changes that will break the world, spoken in a child's word, or finder learns the only way, worlds come changed at end of day. There's something gentler about the newer version, is there not? Though I fear either way this land will not be what it was, Lara Jansen, when you are finished here. If you meet any other seers, ask them for a foretelling. The differences may be important."

"If I meet— Am I likely to?" Lara stared at him, uncertain if interest or fear dominated her emotions.

"No," Oisín said, suddenly genial again. "The gift is as rare as truthseeking, and no one else in the Seelie court bears it. Still, you'll return to our world, and we mortals have a knack for surprising even ourselves."

"I think I've had enough surprises for one day. What do the rhymes mean?" Lara shook her head before the ancient poet spoke. "You can't tell me, can you?"

"Not the way you would like me to, no." He leaned forward, offering a hand. Lara put her fingers into his, surprised at his warmth, and at the strength with which he imparted comfort with a squeeze. "I could tell you of mystical journeys and unfolding power, but I think even the most literal-minded of truthseekers might gather that much from the prophecies."

"I did finally learn to understand metaphor," Lara admitted. "'Truth will seek the hardest path' sounds straightforward even to me. Truth is always a hard path. But if I'm supposed to be truth, then what about the new line you just said? Who's the finder? Do your visions show you pictures?"

"Only words, I'm afraid. Stories have only ever been words to me, even before I lost my sight to age. Your path will lead you to the finder, or you will become what you seek, and we will bend or break with the changes wrought." A finality came into his voice, like a bell tolling the end of some solemn service. Lara caught her breath, searching for questions that could be given quick, easy answers, but the music and the moment passed before she could voice any. Rueful with defeat, she looked around the wooded copse surrounding them and shook her head.

"Well, right now the truth is going to have a hard time seeking the path out of here, because I wasn't paying any attention when I came in."

"That," Oisín said lightly, "I think I can help you with, Truthseeker. There is a path, a true way through these woods, and your eyes should be able to find it. Most could not."

"All I can do is tell if someone's lying, Oisín. I can't even do that if they think they're telling the truth."

"Have more faith," murmured the old man. "Close your eyes and look for the light."

Lara shot him a skeptical look that went unheeded, his blind gaze serene enough to hint at laughter. She pulled a face, drily certain that Oisín would know it, and closed her eyes as she muttered "Look for the light" to herself.

The forest's silence closed around her as her lashes came together. Wind trickled through trees, disturbing leaves, but there were no other sounds: no distant traffic, no whine of airliners, no voices raised in laughter or debate as there were at any hour in Boston's streets. She had never known quiet to be overwhelming, but in the Seelie forest it had a presence of its own, surrounding her, cushioning her, pressing at her.

Look for the light, she reminded herself, but truthfulness had never come to her as light or dark; it came as music. Music didn't, as a rule, make paths, though "follow the yellow brick road!" popped into her mind at the thought. She smiled, imagining such a road unfolding a brick at a time in front of her, though in an instant its color faded to white: yellow brick was simply too much at odds with the deep forest surrounding her. The music changed as well, shying from the perky traveling tune to a more subtle ringing, so deep inside her that for long seconds she didn't recognize it as a tone.

Silver: moonlight on silver, so pure it had no earthly counterpart; that was its sound, and in her mind's eye the brick road she'd built shot forward, drawing a line through the trees. She opened her eyes, unsurprised to find Oisín gone, and even less surprised to find a path leading straight and unbroken toward the ghostly white palace.

Heartbeat queer with the chime's power, Lara got to her feet and followed her magic back into the heart of the Seelie court.

The glimpses she'd had going to and from Aerin's chambers had been accurate: there were open spaces large enough to be called parks within the city's heart, wilderness of the forest beyond tamed by ivory walls and open arches that, had it been a human park, Lara might have called gates or fences. They were neither: even the contained stretches of forest were too much a part of the city to be bound by such words, as if they had all grown up together, part and parcel of one another. She saw that clearly as the sound of the chimes drew her through the citadel's halls.

Her sure feet led her to an arched doorway more elegant than any she'd seen so far. The music fell away suddenly, leaving silence broken by voices that seemed sharp and uncomfortable after the strength of chimes: Emyr, making demands. Demanding her presence, in fact, in such short commanding words that good sense deserted her and she stepped into the filigree doorway.

The king's private chambers were chilly, silver-woven tapestries on the walls doing little to catch heat and keep it from escaping. The windows were rimed, and the floor beneath her feet crackled with hoarfrost. Heatless light rained from the tall ceiling as Lara had seen everywhere in the citadel, but in the heart of Emyr's domain it caught silver and ice and brought the room to a shining, cool brilliance that only reinforced its chill. Looking around, Lara wondered if Dafydd had any real desire to assume his father's icy mantle, or if he would as happily let that relentless cold power pass to Ioan. But then, they were Seelie: immortal in almost all ways, and perhaps a king's heir was that in name only. Neither child might ever rule.

The second son stood a few yards away from his father, his whole body tensed for action: he was already turning toward the door, no doubt to do Emyr's bidding, when Lara said, drily, "Don't bother. She's here."

Both men flinched, a more gratifying response than Lara had expected. A smile swept Dafydd's face, then disappeared, leaving a boyish hope in its wake. He didn't want her to be angry with him, and Lara, searching for the emotion, found that it had largely washed away in the forest. Wry exasperation rose in its place: Kelly would say a man she couldn't stay angry at was a keeper.

There was no such friendliness in Emyr's gaze. He turned away from a basin-topped pedestal, mouth tight with displeasure. "How far did you go?"

Lara caught her fingers in the delicate archway to keep herself from backing up. "I went into the forest. I don't know how far. Ten minutes or so, before—"

"Before?" Emyr glared down at her, such a picture of lordly pique that the impulse to retreat faded. She'd been second or third tailor to men who reminded her of the Seelie king: men whose self-worth was so invested in how they looked that they jumped on imagined slights. Emyr, she had no doubt, had the confidence those men didn't, but the similarity was enough to let his irritation sluff away without bothering her.

"Before Oisín found me," she said steadily. "We talked for a little while and then he showed me how to find my way back."

"Oisín." Distasteful resignation slithered across Emyr's features. "That explains much." He returned his attention to the basin, silver hair falling over his shoulders as he leaned in.

Lara muttered "Oh good," and felt discordance race over her skin, inborn talent not caring for the sarcasm in her own voice. "What's explained?"

"The Barrow-lands have only known one kind of mortal magic for a very long time. Yours is new, and disruptive. When it met Oisín's—think of it as two waves coming together to create a larger one." Dafydd brought his hands together in demonstration.

Lara looked between father and son, her gaze finally settling on Emyr's stooped shoulders. "So you can't do magic? I'm sorry. Is there anything I—"

"You do too much already," Emyr snapped. "I had thought a simple spell to isolate your power would do, but with mortal magic met, there is a tide that would take a great binding to hold back. To work it would require the willingness of the land, and the land," he said bitterly, "is very fond of Oisín. I cannot fight it to set you apart and work the scrying magic at the same time."

"Can't Dafydd—"

"The scrying spell is one of ice and water," Dafydd murmured apologetically. "Neither is my element."

"What is?"

The golden Seelie prince turned his palm upward, fingertips curved in. Electric sparks flew between them, lightning made miniature before it faded away. Lara made fists against sudden embarrassment. "Right. The sword you fought the nightwings with was electricity. I should've known."

Dafydd arched an eyebrow, the expression sympathetic. "Hardly. Truthseeking gives no hint to the elemental strengths and weaknesses of Seelie magics."

"But the doorway you made to bring us here. And you healed yourself. Those weren't lightning."

"The healing is a matter of what we are. We die, Truthseeker, but not easily. Poison magic felled Merrick. And the doorway," Emyr said sharply, "is a magic of the Barrow-lands itself, as setting you apart would be. Without its agreement, Dafydd would never have opened a passage to your world or back again. It's a deeper magic than any he has ever worked, and it is an unwelcome one. Once we passed easily between the worlds, but no longer. The iron and steel of your world damages ours, and to open a pathway risks our very being."

Lara swallowed an *oh* and wet her lips, hardly daring to look at Dafydd. "I'm sorry. I didn't know. Am I—" Nerves closed her throat and she swallowed a second time, trying to clear it. "Am I going to be able to go home?"

"Oisín wouldn't have sent me for a mortal truthseeker if he believed traveling between your world and the Barrow-lands would endanger us," Dafydd said with quiet confidence.

Changes that will break the world. The last line of the rough poem whispered in Lara's mind, freezing her thoughts. Never mind being *able* to go home; she wasn't sure she'd dare, with the truthseeker prophecy hanging over her head. The life she'd lived there was hardly worth risking an entire world over.

Regret seized her at the idea, sudden tears blurring her vision. Her life *wasn't* worth risking a world for, but the idea of never saying good-bye cut deeply enough to take her breath. Her friends, Kelly and Cynthia especially, would never understand; her mother would never stop grieving.

The need to move, to break away from the promise of a future that threatened to lock her in place, seized Lara in its grip. She jerked forward as though she'd been pushed, crossing the room with rough steps and only stopping when she came to Emyr's side at the tall basin. She caught its edge, cold rising through her palms to make her wrists ache, and she lowered her head, blinking furiously to force tears away.

They fell regardless, striking the frozen surface of the pool and hissing. Heat spread, thinning ice, and Lara caught a glimpse of her own wide-eyed expression before blinding sunlight shot out of the basin. The reflection was painful, ricocheting migraine auras through her vision, and she jerked a hand upward, trying to cover her eyes.

Instead, Emyr's hand came down over hers in an icy, unforgiving touch that forbade her to move. She yanked, trying to pull free, and his grip tightened, numbing her fingers until she thought they were frozen against the basin's edge.

He nodded, one sharp silent motion, when her eyes met his: nodded toward the basin, returning her attention to it. Both furious and frightened, she gave up trying to free her hand and looked back into the brilliant water.

Sunlight still glared around the basin's sides, but it had faded from the center, leaving a gem-blue sky over fields seething with green and black and white and red. It took long seconds for the writhing images to resolve in Lara's mind.

Then, as if someone had taken blinders from her eyes, the inexplicable mass became men and women, hundreds of them, even thousands, all clashing together beneath the clear sky. Fewer than half the warriors had the light-colored hair that marked the Seelie. The greater number had darker hair, black and brown and deep copper red: the Unseelie army, Lara guessed, whose coloring made them look like the other half of the too-pale Seelie people to her eyes. They looked complete, even coming together as enemies instead of as a homogeneous whole.

And to play up their differences—it could only be deliberate—the warring factions wore armor of moonlight and of sable, drawn together by nothing but the spatter of red blood as bodies fell. In the abstract, it was beautiful.

In truth, it was terrible. Lara cried out, a sound of protest she couldn't stop, but her hands refused to obey a command to release the basin's edge. Across the battlefield, the warriors stopped, looking skyward, as though they'd heard her voice and were searching for its source. Heartened by the idea that she could be heard, Lara drew breath to demand they stop.

Her words were blocked by fingertips over her lips, Dafydd's eyes regretful as he shook his head. Lara jerked her head away, looking back to the basin, but the moment was lost: on the field, battle heat overtook the brief pause, and soldiers again began to fall beneath swords and arrows.

An arrowhead of midnight-armored warriors appeared, coming out of the massed ranks as though magic had guided them to thrust deep into Seelie territory. It wasn't impossible that magic *had*. Seelie warriors fell on the dark-clad soldiers, but their leader caught Lara's eye, drawing her attention.

The images in the basin shifted, closing in on the arrowhead like a lens pulling in for a close-up. Once; then a second time, narrowing down to a youth in black armor who used his sword as though it were a part of himself. It took a moment for Lara to understand why he'd caught her attention, and then her breath disappeared from her lungs. He was fair-haired, fair-skinned, and leading a host of fighters much darker than he was. She *knew* who he was, knew it with the ringing clarity of truth that dogged her even when she might have preferred ignorance. Knew it, and knew that Emyr would not forgive her for showing him what they all now saw.

Ioan ap Caerwyn, son of the Seelie king, led the Unseelie army against his own people.

Sixteen

Lara flung herself back, escaping Emyr's grip. The images in the water ruptured in a burst of ice and fog, Ioan's face lingering for a few seconds in the shards that fell to the floor. Dafydd stared at them, then jerked his attention to Emyr, and to the failed magic of the scrying pool. Lara, trembling, looked from man to man, and whispered, "What happened?"

"It shouldn't have happened," Dafydd said when it became clear Emyr would not speak. "The pool, the magic, they belong to the king, but he didn't—" He broke off, staring at Lara again, then passed a hand over his eyes as if trying to pull composure together by hiding his face. "He had not yet cast the scrying spell, Lara. He couldn't, with your presence pulling the warp and weft of the Barrow-lands' magic."

"Scrying spell," Lara breathed. "That's what that was? It was— It was like somewhere else came to life in the ice."

"As you say." Dafydd carefully didn't look toward his father, but Lara did, and cringed at the coldness of his expression. "No one should have been able to awaken what is Emyr's to command, Lara, least of all a mortal. And even if someone else had the power to awaken it, you shouldn't have been able to call forth future visions."

"Fut— Is that what that was?" Not for the first time, Lara thought it would be easier to take refuge in disbelief, but the strength and tenor of Dafydd's voice brooked no room for lies.

"It was." Dafydd crossed to the pool, staring into its waters again, and spoke more to Emyr than Lara, but more to himself than anyone else present, she thought. "Truthseekers could once predict a thing, and make it true through force of will."

"The pool," Emyr said icily, "is meant to show things that are, not what may be."

"Is it so different?" Dafydd kept his gaze on the still waters. Lara retreated from them both, falling into silence in lieu of disappearing from their presence entirely. "Perhaps in a truthseeker's hands it's as easily a tool to show what will be. I wonder what it might have shown had Merrick lived."

"You mean would it show him fighting for our people as Ioan has chosen to fight with the Unseelie?" Sarcasm ran thick through Emyr's voice. "You would expect him to don our moonlight armor and fight at your side, and be betrayed should he choose otherwise. And yet I am betrayed that Ioan sides with his foster family." He released the basin and stepped away more slowly than Lara had, expression too remote to be angry. "What have you done?" he said softly, and the question was for neither Lara nor Dafydd. It might have been for Emyr himself: he, after all, had sent his son away as hostage, and in so doing had, it seemed, given Hafgan a coveted second heir.

"You never saw Merrick as your son," Dafydd whispered unexpectedly, hearing something in Emyr's question that Lara couldn't. "You never dreamed that Ioan might accept another as a father. He was a child, Father. He was a boy when you sent him to the Unseelie court. They were the family he knew. Yes, I would have expected Merrick to fight by my side, and so I can believe that Ioan might fight by Hafgan's. That's what he's done. Why he's done it." Silence drew out before he murmured "I'm sorry" with such an ache Lara's heart hurt to hear it.

Lara found her voice in the echoes of Dafydd's speech, and pushed herself away from the wall, determined to understand more clearly. Emyr focused on her as she moved, and Dafydd made a short, awkward motion, like he wanted to warn her away from coming to his father's attention. Too late: having captured it, she stood tall and met the monarch's gaze. "Why wouldn't you let me go, or let me talk?"

"Because when the pool is awakened only the spellcaster can guide or release the magic, and I had things I needed to see before you let it go." There was no anger in Emyr's voice, but his control, his containment, was worse. Dafydd, apparently liking it no more than she did, stepped forward a second time, almost putting himself between Lara and his father. Emyr gave him a withering glance, then looked back at Lara. "Speech travels through the scrying spell, and we looked on a day that has not yet dawned. You couldn't be allowed to speak and perhaps affect that day through what you do not know of its making."

"How do you know it was the future?" There was no doubt in either man's voice, but hope flashed through Lara and died again at Emyr's cold look.

"It could hardly be the past. I can assure you I have never yet seen my son ride against me in battle. And it could hardly be the present." He gestured toward a window, where dark-leaved trees whispered against the night. "It was a day yet to come, and I do not thank you for showing me what it holds."

His bleak gaze turned on Dafydd, pinning him in place. The Seelie prince shifted uncomfortably, casting his gaze downward. It struck Lara that she found it easier to meet Emyr's eyes than his own son did, and wondered what it said that she could stand under his gimlet glares as calmly as she did.

"It seems you are my only heir," Emyr said to Dafydd. "As such, you will ride with the army tomorrow."

Dafydd lowered his head, shock whitening his face, but his whispered "Your will, my lord," was nearly lost under Lara's incredulous, "That *can't* be a good decision!"

Emyr turned on her, angry enough that spots stood out on his cheeks, but she stepped into his space, frustrated beyond thoughts of caution. "Send your only heir onto the battlefield? Especially when, given that he's now leading an army that I assume wants to wipe you out, Ioan is the most likely candidate for having murdered Merrick ap Annwn in the first place?"

From their expressions, it was clear neither of the men had considered the possibility, which did nothing to change the ring of truth Lara heard in her own words. "It wasn't someone *here*," she said, exasperated. "Not in the citadel, anyway, if you really did gather them all into the courtroom earlier. And you did," she added, "at least as far as you know, you did. I'd have known if you were lying. But come on."

She looked from king to prince and back again, hands opened in demanding supplication. "Aerin didn't think a spell could be cast that would sunder someone's will, but isn't it starting to add up? You said you might be able to do it, right, Emyr?"

Too late she realized she should have used an honorific. Emyr's expression, dark to begin with, blackened entirely. Lara ground "Your majesty" through her teeth, and judged she'd done very little to alleviate her error. It didn't matter that much; the worst he could do was kill her, and it was far more likely he'd send her back home. "You thought you might be able to do it, because you've got greater scope to your power than most people do. Ioan is—was—your heir. Wouldn't he have to have talent on the same level you do?"

Emyr nodded grudgingly. Buoyed, Lara went on. "And he's been raised in the Unseelie court, which is where most of *your* court thinks that kind of magic would be condoned."

"But why?" From another, the question might have been plaintive. From Emyr, it somehow bordered on a threat.

"Power. Sympathy for the people he's been raised with. Even just trying to save his own hide. I don't know. He's your son."

"No longer. Dafydd—" Emyr swung toward his son, dismissing

Lara. Incensed, she stepped closer, almost daring to catch his sleeve. It wasn't necessary: he went still, then turned his head toward her incrementally, clearly disbelieving her audacity.

"If I'm right, and I don't know if I am"—Clarity rang in that, too: her talent couldn't differentiate between reasonable possibilities and the genuine truth—"then Dafydd is the only thing standing between you and the Barrow-lands falling into Unseelie hands. It is *not wise* to put him on the field, Emyr."

"And yet it must be done," Dafydd broke in.

Lara gaped at him and he sighed. "If Ioan leads the Unseelie army, a fair number of our own people will refuse to fight unless they have a banner of their own. The choices are myself or my father, and I'm the more expendable."

Music chimed, giving weight to what he said. Lara folded her arms under her breasts. "I know you believe that's true, but—"

"And," Dafydd said, more strongly, "if Ioan's hand was the one that directed mine in slaying Merrick, then it is my wish to meet him on the field and exact the price from his flesh."

"And what if it was?" Lara snapped. "What if he does it again? You're not going to be much of a banner to the Seelie army if you suddenly turn around and start hacking at them."

"I'll be prepared against it this time, Lara. It's much more difficult to bespell someone who is prepared for you."

"So, what? You're going to ride up to him and say, 'By the way, Ioan, did you possess me and make me kill Merrick?' Do you really think he's going to openly confess to murder?"

"Of course not," Emyr said softly. "Which is why you'll be riding at Dafydd's side."

Lara, wearing armor that had been fashioned for her while she slept, glowered at Dafydd's shoulders around the edges of her fine, lightweight helm, and wished herself somewhere, *anywhere*, else. It had no effect: magic wasn't that accommodating.

She had argued, partly from fear, partly from dismay, partly from barely knowing which end of a sword to hold, until the glint of exasperation in Emyr's eyes had turned to a wall. She didn't remember being sleepy, but one moment she'd been arguing and the next he'd said, "You must rest before dawn," and she had known nothing after that until an already-armored Aerin awakened her and strapped her into moonlit armor of her own.

She had been fed, put on a horse, she was told, bespelled: she literally *could not* fall off unless the animal died beneath her. Aerin had shoved her hard a couple of times to prove it true, and split a wicked smile when Lara, sullenly, had pointed out that she could hear the truth in the explanation and didn't need to be pushed around.

Now she scowled at Dafydd, honing anger so it would outweigh fear. He had come to her once she was on horseback, wrapping an armored hand around her equally armored calf: metal, light as this stuff was, did not make for easy intimacies. "I do need you," he'd said quietly. "I would not kill my brother without knowing for certain that my actions were just, and there is no one but you who can tell me that."

Lara had bit her tongue on the question *"Is that all you need me for?"* and had instead glared down at him. Even sick with terror, her face overheated and her hands cold, it was hard to be angry with him, especially seeing him prepared for war.

The bright pale armor could have been worked moonlight, for all she could tell: it was that light, and that beautiful. Even in the coming dawn its shadows were blue and purple, intricate designs etched into it whispering stories of the night. The fanciful idea that the Seelie were a night people had caught her, and had stayed with her as she watched the men and women around her armoring up and taking saddle. They were so pale, so fragile-looking, as though daylight took their strength and the night returned it.

Dafydd was no different, and clad in armor he seemed both dangerous and delicate, a description Lara was certain he wouldn't appreciate. She wanted, against all sense, even against understanding, to send him to safety, even if she herself had to face a battle to keep him from it.

Warring music rang through her head, mocking her dramatics as half-truths and reigniting her pique. "You could capture him," she'd muttered. "Bring him back to me to question." It was an argument she'd tried the night before, and had sullenly conceded when Dafydd pointed out there was no guarantee of catching Ioan.

"We might," Emyr had said, in a tone that had put her instantly on edge, "if I were to use a greater magic."

Lara, through her teeth, had said, "But I disrupt your greater magics," and Emyr had given her a beneficent smile that managed to be a falsehood all on its own.

"And so you must be as far from me as possible, and you will be of the most potential use at Dafydd's side."

It was almost immediately after that that he'd bespelled her to sleep.

Dafydd hadn't forced the point again, had only squeezed her calf—she could tell from the scrape of metal against metal, rather than feeling pressure—and mounted his own horse, leaving her to frown at his shoulders and wait for the signal to ride.

It came with the clarion sound of horns, both in truth and in her mind. She had never imagined there might be a purity in riding to war, but the music of the calling horns told her there was. They lifted her, tightening her chest with anticipation, even enthusiasm, and brought unexpected fierce tears to her eyes. It was the being part of something that did it, she thought: the purposefulness of their actions becoming larger than any one rider. For a brief, bewildering moment she felt connected to a legacy older than history.

Then her horse surged forward and she flailed, keeping in the saddle only through the spell that stuck her there. Anticipation failed in the face of panic and horror. She was human, and this wasn't her fight, even if she'd known anything about making war.

The avenue outside the citadel broadened as the Seelie army thundered out, widening to encompass the breadth of their front lines. The forest itself receded, responding to their need, and there were suddenly miles of clear land before them, leading down into the heart of valleys Lara hadn't even known existed. In the far distance she could see a dark wavering mass: the Unseelie army, for now nothing more than a blot on the land.

The sun jolted through the sky, rising too fast and making the time it took to reach the Unseelie army shockingly brief. Certainly briefer than the speed of armored horses could allow for, and Lara thought of Dafydd's explanation that the beasts took the easiest route, one that somehow slipped through the edges of time. In a way, it was good: it gave her less time to think, less time to be afraid. She couldn't reach exhilaration again, not even with the sound of hooves pounding and armor rattling in her ears. It needed a sound track. She had never seen anything like what she participated in now except in film, with rising music to bring the audience where the director wanted.

That idea sustained her until they crashed relentlessly into the Unseelie front lines.

The heat was terrible. The sun hadn't yet reached its zenith, but bodies and horses were already wet with sweat. Lara's breath came hard, tightness squeezing her chest so each gasp felt like it brought too little air to her lungs. Dafydd had left her buried in a contingent of men and women whose duty was to protect her, and had surged ahead, Aerin at his side, to meet the enemy. A lunatic part of Lara resented that: she wanted to be where the Seelie woman was, fighting as Dafydd's equal, though she knew perfectly well that in this matter, she was not.

He moved like he'd been born to the sword; like he knew the mechanics of fighting as well as he knew the act of breathing. Aerin was faster yet, smoother and more certain with her blade. Through flying dirt and blood and the surge of bodies, Lara saw the white-haired woman cast a concerned glance at Dafydd.

That, Lara thought, was entirely unfair. It had been a century, in all likelihood, since Dafydd had worked with a sword. Even immortals must lose their edge, if they had no need or chance to practice. She fought off the urge to press closer to Dafydd, to scold Aerin for her disapproval, not that she had a chance of breaking through the tightly bunched guards around her.

They moved even more beautifully than Dafydd did, if she could ignore the results of their actions. There were never fewer than two on all sides of her, though she could tell the riders and horses shifted places as black-armored Unseelie rode against them. Lara clutched a sword in her hand, feeling absurd, but there was no chance of using it as her guards' blades glittered and darkened in the sunlight. For whole minutes at a time she was aware of nothing but them, of nothing but trying to stay in their midst.

Dafydd was closer than she expected, when a moment's lull in the battle gave her a chance to look up. His face was pulled in a grimace, worse even than the weariness beginning to mark her guard. For a few long seconds she was arrested by him, watching without care to the resurgence in fighting surrounding her.

There was a thickness in his body, a deadly slowness and weight to his arms. Even Lara, who knew nothing at all of fighting, could see that attacks he should have blocked scraped off his armor. Frustration contorted his features, and he lifted his gaze to catch hers across the field. Relief shattered across his face and he wheeled his horse toward her, abruptly moving against the tide of battle.

The weight came off him, his sword arm moving more easily, and a vicious joy lit his eyes. Lara saw herself through his eyes, stiff and awkward on her horse, holding an unfamiliar sword in an iron grip, and could hardly blame him for riding to her side. Maybe truthseekers of legend could make a reality in which they remained safe through their will alone, but she had nothing of that power.

Aerin crashed into Dafydd, her teeth bared as she jerked her chin at the black-clad warriors around them. The command couldn't have been clearer if she'd spoken it in words: *pay attention!* Lara's spate of envy at their shared battle skill, at Aerin's ability to fight at Dafydd's side, faded. She, truthfully, wanted to be safe and protected. Aerin's strength in battle was admirable, not enviable.

Dafydd drew up, bewilderment etched across his face before he shook himself hard and nodded. Then he urged his horse forward again, toward Lara again, instead of back into fighting.

Aerin shouted loudly enough to be heard over the general noise, and cuffed him alongside the head. Armor or no, he swayed, and Aerin grabbed his horse's bridle to haul the animal around, forcing Dafydd to face the Unseelie troops. He hesitated, and Aerin, clearly irritated, slapped his horse's hindquarters and sent it leaping forward into battle.

One stride, no more. Then he pulled it around again, pushing himself back toward Lara, but now an expression of rage and fear strained his features. Lara heard panic strengthen his shout, and saw the name he cried was Aerin's, not her own. And despite the need to reverse herself, despite the press of men, despite swords clashing and metal ringing all around them, Aerin was at his side in an instant.

He handed her his reins in an ungainly motion and spoke, words drowned out by distance and noise, but the tension in his body said speech wasn't easy.

Aerin's head came up and she shot Lara a sharp look across the field, then came back to Dafydd with an expression darker than Lara had ever seen. Nerves turned Lara's stomach to a writhing mass and she urged her horse forward, forgetting the battle, forgetting danger. Her guard slowed her and she shouted wordless frustration, sound lost to cacophany.

She was still an impossible distance away when Aerin knocked Dafydd's sword from his hands and severed his horse's reins with her own blade. Lara, gaping, watched helplessly as Aerin wrapped the long strips of leather around Dafydd's wrists, and leaned forward to speak in the Seelie prince's ear.

He knotted his fingers in his horse's mane and hauled it around to drive it forward with a kick.

Forward, into the heart of the Unseelie army.

Seventeen

"Dafydd!"

For an instant the battle went still, Seelie and Unseelie alike looking to the sky, as though Lara's scream had come from far above. She had cried out the night before, looking into the scrying pool, and she wondered which had arrested the soldiers: her horror then, or now.

Aerin, undisturbed by Lara's shriek, straightened in her saddle, watching as whatever she'd said drove Dafydd into the enemy's waiting arms.

Rage turned Lara's vision red. She forgot the men and women around her were meant to protect her; forgot that she knew nothing of swordplay; forgot everything except evidence of her own errors in Aerin's actions. She didn't know how Aerin had escaped the compulsion Dafydd had laid on the courtiers to answer, nor how she had missed the lies in the white-haired woman's voice. Maybe, if a spell could force a man against his will, another could hide falsehood from a truthseeker, especially one as infantile in her talents as Lara was.

In the moment, none of it mattered. Her horse rushed forward, Lara's fear forgotten as she stood in her stirrups and shouted.

She should have fallen off, but the magics Aerin had placed on her were to Lara's benefit. She *couldn't* fall, and she couldn't be expected to do as she was doing.

That, then, was the only reason she scored a blow across Aerin's kidneys at all.

Lara had seen others take hits that looked harder, but the moonlight armor screamed and bent under the force of her strike. Aerin whipped around, pain shattering beneath shock as she recognized Lara. Lara swung again, wildly, as momentum sent her past Aerin. The Seelie woman didn't even have to parry to avoid it, but she lifted her sword to block a third attack as Lara hauled her horse around in a tight circle.

Metal scraped metal, Aerin drawing her blade down the length of Lara's to tangle the guards. A quick twist wrenched the sword from Lara's hand, and Aerin grabbed the edge of Lara's breastplate, hauling her close. "What mortal idiocy drives you now, Truthseeker?"

Lara balled her armored fist and threw the first punch of her life at Aerin's beautiful face.

Aerin's head snapped back satisfactorily, blood pouring from her nose and upper lip. The nosepiece of her helm had caught the brunt of the blow: it was bent, and a cut leaked red down the bridge of her nose to mingle with the rest of the mess.

Lara, still standing in her stirrups, shoved Aerin backward, snarling "Arrest her" to those nearest to them. The command broke their stillness, drawing their attention from the echoing cry that Lara had voiced both seconds and hours earlier. Within moments the sounds of battle roared around her again, chaos personified by glittering swords and splashing blood. The sun was in her eyes, blinding and somehow, gratifyingly, reducing her fear. Emboldened and not waiting to see if she'd been obeyed, Lara pulled her horse around a second time and sent it into the Unseelie battalion. Chasing Dafydd; chasing hope.

She broke through their defenses by speed and surprise, not skill, but it was enough. Surprise let her knock men aside with kicks and once with a bash of her fist, and that was all the time she needed.

Time enough to see that, just beyond the Unseelie front lines, Dafydd's silver-bridled horse stood empty-saddled and startled-looking amid surging black-clad warriors.

Dafydd was gone.

In defiance of what she saw, in defiance of what she was, a single thought hung in Lara's mind: Dafydd *could not* be gone. It rang false, but it wouldn't leave her. It wasn't possible that he had disappeared. She'd seen no brilliant door open in the air, nothing to take him away from the Barrow-lands. But then, she'd seen very little, with the sun in her eyes, and the transition had taken hardly any time when Dafydd had brought her to his world.

There were suddenly dozens of Seelie around her, their bright armor splashing in a wave against the Unseelie dark. She remained unmoving, stuck in her saddle even as she recognized that they were protecting her. They were obeying Dafydd's order, even though he was no longer there. She stared at the earth, half afraid she would see his slim body trampled beneath hooves and Unseelie feet, and then another thought struck her: that he'd become invisible. She redoubled her search of the ground, hoping for signs of such a thing— maybe footprints appearing in the earth—even as the larger part of her rejected the possibility. She had seen his magic. It was electricity, not the manipulation of light that might allow him to hide in plain sight. Perhaps others among the Seelie had that skill, but not, she thought, Dafydd ap Caerwyn.

Which led her back to the impossible: that he had vanished.

She was still struggling with that, searching for another answer, when an arrowhead contingent of Unseelie rushed through the surrounding Seelie army and fair-haired Ioan ap Caerwyn clobbered her alongside the head with a gauntleted fist.

Later, she thought she had not, quite, lost consciousness. Nor had she fallen from her horse: Aerin's magic was thorough. Dazed, she'd been surrounded by Unseelie warriors, and they'd ridden through the army at an oblique angle to the fighting. The battle thinned, then suddenly turned to nothing, grasslands becoming forest as her escort picked up speed. By the time the ringing in her head—for once not born of truth or falsehood, but from simple, painful trauma—had faded, they were well beyond the battlefield, and she had lost any hope of finding her way back on her own.

Ioan was not among her captors. They were all dark-haired, their helms removed once they'd left the field behind. Three of the group were women; and a part of Lara was bemused they felt she required eight soldiers for escort. They had more faith in her than she did.

A crescendo came over her at the thought, piano chords pounding in her head. Truthseekers, she imagined, could be dangerous, if confronted at the height of their power. She had no doubt they knew what she was—why else take her at all?—but they wouldn't necessarily know that her talents were meager.

That might be her sole advantage. Lara bit back questions, certain her armed guards wouldn't answer them, and tried to bury fear under the strength of her magic as they rode. They left the forests behind, climbing upward, the land becoming less hospitable as they did. Lara built a vision of their destination in her mind's eye: a granite citadel as imposing as the Seelie court's home, cold and unfriendly as the barren mountaintops they strove for. A wall rose up in the distance, hinting that her imagination was true; impenetrable and unscalable, it drew her eye upward, searching for an impossible palace built at its farthest reaches.

There was no such thing nor, as they came closer, any hint of a path rising along its sheer face. Its foot was buried in darkness, and they were nearly upon it before Lara realized it was a chasm cutting hundreds of feet down into the rock.

She had time to scream as the horses launched themselves across the terrible divide. Above her scream, the leader of her escort shattered the air with a piercing whistle.

In the instant before they smashed into the vast mountain wall, it ruptured, rock twisting and exploding before them. A gaping mouth opened, a black maw that roared with the sound of tearing stone. Lara's stomach rebelled, as if it had been wrenched sharply to the left, though her vision insisted she still rode straight ahead.

Hooves clattered against the cave's broad stony tongue, which angled down at a desperate degree, as if swallowing them. The horses barely slowed, finding their pace again as what had been a diamond of riders around Lara became a long line with her in the middle.

A road stretched before them, a narrow strip of stone leading down. Rock face shot upward on their right and plummeted on their left: one misstep would see her at the bottom of the very chasm they'd just leaped across. Lara dared a brief glance over her shoulder. There was no glimpse of the ledge they'd jumped from or the cavern they'd come through, only their thin road melding seamlessly back into the rock face. To their left, across the broad divide, rose the canyon side they had leaped from.

Lara, grateful that she didn't have to watch in order to stay safely on her horse, closed her eyes hard, and considered the possibility that the Seelie might be unable to find the Unseelie court if they were unwilling to be found.

She remembered, too, how the avenue leading to the Seelie citadel had also appeared only when they were already on it, apparently at will. They both seemed to be hidden people, Seelie and Unseelie alike, both inclined toward isolationism and the black and white boundaries it drew. She wondered how the two courts had even managed to communicate enough to make a bargain over their firstborn sons. She would have to ask Dafydd.

If she ever got the chance.

A new wave of nausea clenched her belly, fear rather than the twist of magic. Lara swallowed against it and raised her eyes to the path in front of them, shocked to see they'd nearly reached the bottom. Within seconds the leader disappeared, though not through magic this time: the road simply curved sharply at its base, delving deep into the rock.

They burst out its other side into a cavern so immense that Lara reined up her horse in awe, too goggle-eyed to care whether her escort disapproved.

The rock face they'd just ridden down had to be little more than a shell, so vast was its open interior. Walkways, most of them cordoned, ran up and down the walls, interrupted every few yards by balconies carved out of living stone. At the far end, distant enough to seem small, a waterfall crashed through the rock, its thunder a low comforting echo throughout the enormous chamber. Mist cooled the air, and the smaller sound of a river was nearer to where she sat astride, but the floor of the unending cavern was what held Lara's eyes.

A town of black mother-of-pearl spread out before her, oily rainbows scattered in its curves. At its heart was a palace, the Seelie citadel's antithesis, low and rambling, where the bone china city ran high and pale. They were both alien, both beautiful, both unwelcoming, both compelling. The leader of her escort barked an order for her to continue, and she edged her mount forward into the gleaming walkways with an eagerness that belied good sense.

Almost no one stood watching as they paced through the streets. A handful of children in bright colors; a handful of adults whose presence bespoke great age, though their faces were as youthful as any others. The rest had gone to war. Lara wondered if any of the children would lose a parent on the green battlefields. There was an emptiness to the city that reminded her of Emyr's citadel, although she hadn't seen that stripped of its people. It seemed possible that both courts simply lacked some spark of life that gave their homes heart.

At the palace door—there were no gates, simply a shining courtyard that joined the town to its castle—her escort dismounted. Lara stared at the ground, uncertain. Aerin hadn't mentioned whether she'd be able to dismount if she wanted to, only that she couldn't fall off.

Maybe if she was certain not to *fall*. She grabbed the saddle's front with both hands, not caring how awkward she looked, and concentrated on swinging a leg over her horse's broad back, all her weight on one stirrup. The feeling of being pinned in place vanished, and she reached for the ground, dismayed at how far away it was before her toes finally made contact. Pleased with herself, she disentangled from the stirrup and stepped back to discover her eight guards all looking somewhere else, as if they were trying not to laugh.

A thought flew through her mind: this would be her best opportunity to attempt an escape. If, at least, she had a weapon, an idea how to use one, or a plan. She had none of those, and shrugged with resignation as the Unseelie mastered their expressions and fell in around her again, guiding her into, and through, the palace.

Gardens sprang up with the same regularity as they did in the Seelie citadel. These, though, were of metal and stone: trees had marble trunks and golden leaves, and vines of emerald wended their way around them. Sea-clear pebbles littered the garden floors, and when a nightingale sang, Lara was certain it was a mechanical wonder, and not a real bird. Her guard followed the path of a silver-bedded stream, its color that of a northerly ocean, as it fed into a pool set with the same silver shimmer.

A man stood before the pool. He was broader than Seelie men, partly in fact and partly thanks to the doublet he wore: heavier material than any of their costumes, with rounded stuffed seams at the shoulders. Practical, Lara thought; the cavernous city was chilly, cooled by the waterfall and perhaps by being too close to the surface to retain a steady temperature. The handsful of people who'd watched them come through the city had been similarly dressed.

But this man wore black, and it suited him. His hair was inky beneath an ebony and ruby circlet, and his skin golden in comparison to the pale Seelie. He held up a hand, and Lara instinctively obeyed the command, freezing in place.

Irritation swept her before he gave her permission to move. She made fists, surprised at how stiff her fingers were inside their metal casings, and walked forward. "What do you want with me?"

The Unseelie king turned to face her, eyebrows elevated in surprise. He was handsome, Lara realized with her own small shock of surprise. More handsome by far than Emyr, whose coldness left its mark, and better-looking than Dafydd in a classical sense, though she preferred Dafydd's angular lines. He studied her a moment, then bent to make a cup of his hands and scoop water into them. When he straightened, it was with a worked silver goblet in his hand, which he offer to her. "I am Hafgan ap Annwn—"

Wind instruments shrieked objection, turning Lara's skin to ice beneath her armor. "You are not."

The Unseelie king stopped midword, staring at her. Lara thrust out her jaw and glared back, anger flaring high enough that she hardly knew herself as she snapped, "I don't know who you are, but you're sure as hell not Hafgan. I'm a truthseeker. There's really no point in lying to me."

A long silence met her accusation, ending, finally, in a twitch of the crowned man's eyebrows. "I had not meant to test you, but it seems I have done so regardless. I have been Hafgan for many centuries, Truthseeker. Long enough that even the oldest among us have forgotten that someone else once bore the name, and that he now lies above the salted earth and below the bitter sea. Drink," he added more prosaically, "and I will do my best to explain. Drink," he said again, when she hesitated. "You must be thirsty."

As he said it, Lara became aware of how dry her throat was, how sticky her tongue was in her mouth. She scowled at the cup, determination very slightly greater than thirst. "Who are you?"

The man sighed. "I am, and have been, for a very long time, the king of the Unseelie people. But once upon a time, and this is the name I think you seek, I was called Ioan ap Caerwyn, and I was the son of Emyr on the Seelie throne."

Eighteen

Lara's heartbeat thudded in her ears, drowning out all other sound. Thumped at her skin, for that matter, washing away cold and replacing it with heat, but also bringing a static numbness to every inch of her body, as though she'd received one shock too many and could no longer feel anything at all.

Truth, though, wouldn't let her go. Its power pecked at the numbness, soundless chimes cracking armor her mind needed, until it shattered and left her able to move, if not to think clearly. She shuffled forward and took the silver cup from the king's hands, then drained it. The water was cold and bright-tasting, and the cup disappeared as she drank, until the last sip swallowed the last curve of silver and she was left staring at a trace of water on her gauntleted fingers. An insipid comment welled up, the only thing she could find to say: "That was really cool."

Ioan smiled, a rueful expression that made him look much more human than any of the Seelie court. More human, even, than Dafydd, who'd had a century of pretending to be one. "Merely a trick so old that it no longer holds wonders for our kind."

Lara, still feeling dull-witted, said, "It's a good trick," and pulled her helm off. She put it down by the pool, then sat beside it and stared toward the black pearl palace. Shock was good for one thing, at least: she had no fear left at all, only utter bewilderment. "Who was on the battlefield, then?" she asked eventually. "The blond Unseelie, I mean."

"Another trick. A glamour to dishearten Emyr, or so I hoped. I haven't looked like that for a long time." Ioan sat beside her. Peculiar behavior, Lara thought, for a kidnapper and the leader of an enemy people.

"Start there," she said after a while. Putting words, thoughts, together was taking a long time, but a sense of the absurd rose at the idea. The people of this world lived forever. A mortal taking a few minutes to scrape intelligent conversation together would hardly be noticed. "Start with being dark-haired and dark-eyed and golden-skinned. Nobody in the Seelie citadel is. Nobody at all."

"Nor was I when I came here. I was as my seeming was, there on the battlefield, pale-skinned, light-eyed. I chose to become what my friends and family here were." Ioan gestured to the far-distant cavern ceiling and to the myriad dwellings littered along the towering walls. "We lived under the sky, once, and this land was known by another name."

"You did? It did?" Lara bit her tongue as Ioan chuckled.

"We did, and it did. It was called Annwn, which meant 'the land beneath,' and I think once upon a time your people found your way here through fairy mounds and underground paths."

Uncomfortable truth left Lara's skin a mess of goose bumps beneath her armor. "I wouldn't know. I don't like fairy tales."

Ioan gave her a strangely sympathetic glance, far gentler than the one Dafydd had given her when she'd said the same thing to him. The unexpected kindness felt like a punch, and she looked away, searching for something else to say. Static was fading, leaving her thoughts clear, though she still felt as though she'd been sent to an advanced class in a subject she hadn't studied the basics of. "Annwn's the name you said was yours. Hafgan ap Annwn. Your last name."

"My father—Hafgan, not Emyr—would say that he had no last

name, and that he simply was *of* Annwn. That word has become less than it was, though, and if it carries any meaning now, it is perhaps only 'the people of the earth.' The Unseelie were once as fair as the Seelie. They—we—lived on and worked the lowlands of the sea, and were colored silver and blue and gray and green, all the shades of water. But we have dwelled so long under the earth that it has stained us, and so Emyr named us Unseelie, the dark ones, and we took the name as our own."

Lara blurted "That's not possible" over the hum of truth in his words. "I mean, people don't— That would take generations of evolution. It doesn't work that way."

Amusement creased lines around Ioan's eyes. He scooped up another goblet full of water, offering it to her with a cocked eyebrow. "And in your world, I think it doesn't work this way, either."

Lara stared at him, then, realizing she was still thirsty, accepted the cup and drank it into nothingness. "No," she said when it was only droplets on her gauntlets. "No, it doesn't. And I'm having a hard time with that." She'd questioned her talent more in the past twelve hours than she could remember doing in her life, though each time she'd recognized the basic truth of the situation she faced. Dafydd *had* disappeared in front of her; the Unseelie *had* undergone physical change in a way that humans simply would not. Ioan himself had, evidently by choice.

For the first time, she felt a twist of compassion for those who didn't share her gift. *I don't believe it* had never been a phrase that made any sense to her, not when someone was confronted with irrefutable truth. She'd always been impatient with it, unable to understand why someone would deny what was real, even when the reality was terrible. If she could hold on to the fumbling sense of disbelief this world had confounded her with more than once, it might make her relationships at home a little easier.

If she ever got home. Lara pressed cold metaled fingers against her mouth, and felt the weight of Ioan's hand on her armored shoulder.

"This is Annwn, Truthseeker. These are the Barrow-lands. What governs your world does not hold true here. Best keep that in mind, if you can."

"You're not what I expected," Lara said distantly. Aerin had given her a similar warning, though about the people rather than the place itself. Hearing it echoed in the Unseelie king's advice made her consider more sharply why she'd agreed to come to the Barrow-lands. Kelly's teasing had been part of it, and Dafydd's appeal another part. But she'd had no idea at all what she was agreeing to, and now Dafydd was missing and Lara had been taken from the people who ostensibly had a reason to protect her. She wasn't afraid, but neither did she imagine there was much she could do to help, anymore.

"I am not, or we are not?"

"Either. Both. You're not much like Emyr."

"My father would have reminded you more of Emyr. He was of that generation, though life for our people is so long it scarcely seems it should matter." Ioan studied the pool waters. "My father might have known the answers I now seek, but the pain of lost Annwn drove him back to the sea long ago, and he left no secrets behind. Without him, I need your help, Truthseeker. It's why I brought you here."

"Brought me, is that what you call it? Did it occur to you to ask, rather than kidnap me?"

"No," Ioan said with shocking honesty. "How might I have asked? In the midst of battle, or by hunting down Emyr's citadel and knocking politely on the door? Emyr barely tolerates his own kind, much less Unseelie."

"You're his son!"

Ioan gestured at himself. "If he saw me like this, he would reject me. He would say I'd turned my back on my people."

"Which is true," Lara said, startling herself. Extrapolation lay outside of her talents.

Or it had; Ioan gave her a wry look that suggested she was right. "Why should I not? I was a child when I came here, and what I found, as I grew, were a people who had lost their history, lost their sense of selves. Legend that laid blame for that at Seelie feet."

"The Seelie think all their problems are your fault, too. That you're overrunning their land."

"And perhaps somewhere in the middle lies the truth."

The words were a challenge. Lara's spine straightened, though her armor didn't permit much slumping. "If I help you figure it out, are you going to let me go?"

He, after a moment, bowed his head. "Perhaps."

Lara laughed, surprised at the truth for all that there was no point in him lying to her. "That's not very convincing."

"I know." He glanced up again, dark-eyed and earnest. Kelly, Lara thought, would find him incredibly attractive, although even Kelly's libido might stop short of falling for a man who'd kidnapped her. Lara felt her expression shadow at the thought, and watched Ioan's earnestness fade, as though he recognized he was playing his hand too far. "I would like to say I'd release you, but you'd know if I lied. If you can help me find the clear path of our history, the truth is I may need you further."

"To do what?" Lara lifted a hand. "Wait. First tell me what you *think* happened in your past, and then tell me why you can't remember. I thought you were supposed to live forever."

"Living forever doesn't mean remembering forever. The past fades as it does for mortal memory as well, but for us, it stretches so far back that our own lives become legend. Only a truthseeker can strip away the fog and tell us what truly happened."

"Which you think is . . . ?"

"I believe—my people believe—that we were once, if not masters of this land, at least equals in its governing." Ioan fell silent, leaving an air of expectation that Lara sighed into.

"And? Do you know what that answer sounds like, to me? It sounds like a half-tuned orchestra. The strings are groaning against each other and the wind instruments are creaking like they're falling trees. Whatever it is you're *not* saying makes what you *have* said sound like a lie. Half-truths aren't enough."

Ioan pulled his face long, another expression that seemed more human than the Seelie usually indulged in. "Very well. We also believe it was Emyr, or his court, who called worldbreaking magic and drowned our lands and drove us underground."

Lara interrupted, "Worldbreaking magic." Oisín's prophecy danced through her mind and sent hairs rising over her skin. If the power was something that lay outside her, it suggested there was some hope of returning home, rather than her very travel between worlds presenting a threat. "What kind of magic was that? How do you break a world?"

"With a weapon long since lost to us." Ioan shrugged, hands spread in loss. "If such a thing existed outside of legend, I think it can no longer be in Annwn. I've searched," he said more softly. "What can break a world can perhaps heal it as well. But without it, all we have are stories that say we've been persecuted by the Seelie for longer than memory allows us to recall. Without it, only a truth-seeker's help may permit us to regain our rightful place in this world."

"Only a truthseeker's help." Something in the words stood out, making their obvious content so shallow as to be meaningless. Lara got to her feet, suddenly uncomfortable. "Tell me what you mean by that."

"If our legends are revealed as history, then I'll need a truth-seeker's vision to turn the tide of war in my favor."

"Emyr mentioned that," Lara said thinly. "That truthseekers could say something and through force of will make it true."

"The most powerful, yes. If your skill isn't that great, then I would give you maps of our lands so you might show me ahead of time where our enemy will strike, and give us the advantage."

Lara lifted her gaze to the far side of the pool. She heard music, not in Ioan's words, though his conviction rang there, too. No, it was a chime, a warning that seemed to start behind her heart and fill her chest. "And if your legends are just that? Legends? If there's no lost worldbreaking magic, if the Unseelie are trespassers on Seelie land?"

Ioan's silence drew out long enough to answer her without words. Lara's heartbeat fluttered, a butterfly sensation that clawed her breath away. Her ears pounded with the relentless thin tone of bells, almost drowning out Ioan's eventual response. The words came slowly, as if he was only just coming to realize the truth: "I'm sorry, Truthseeker, but I can't let you go."

A breath hissed through her teeth. "So you're not such a good guy after all. You're very reasonable, but not a good guy. I can't let you keep me." She recognized the music now, recognized the feeling it built in her, though it had been far less intense in the forest outside the Seelie citadel. It rang so loudly a path appeared, striking its way through her heart and leading into the pool, where it reflected hard against silver stones.

"I think you cannot stop me."

Lara whispered, "But I can," and stretched out a hand toward the water. "There's a true way through these woods. A true way home again." Laughter akin to panic knotted itself in her throat, and she reached for the only phrase she could think of that would unlock a magical door: "Open, Sesame!"

A silver-shot door tore apart the bottom of the pool, water draining at a tremendous rate.

Lara dove in, leaving Ioan's shout of protest behind.

She hit muddy earth with a squelch, breath knocked away. Silence rang out around her, more than just a cessation of music. It had a quality that said an instant earlier the air had been full of voices and laughter, and that surprise had taken delight away.

She ached with the impact against the ground, armor jabbing her uncomfortably, but not badly enough to force her to move. For a brief eternity she lay where she was, facedown in damp earth, struggling for breath. She thought she might be glad to lie there forever, except an uncertain voice said, "Lady, are you okay?"

Lara flipped onto her back in a spray of wet sand. Sunlight burst in her eyes, blinding her before a ring of children leaned over her, curious faces blocking out the sun. A dozen or so, more children than she'd seen in total within the Barrow-lands, and all of them with ordinary round human ears and varied skin tones and eyes that ranged from brown-black to pale blue.

"Are you okay?" a little boy asked again. He was dripping: all of the children were, despite the brilliant sunlight.

"I think so." Lara sounded hoarse, but no discordance rang with her answer, relief in itself. "Where am I?"

"The farm park," the boy said. "Where'd you *come* from?"

"Fairyland," Lara said without thinking, and a little girl smiled brilliantly.

"Are you wearing fairy clothes? They're all shiny!"

"That's armor, dummy," the boy said scornfully. "Like the Power Rangers wear."

Lara sat up, the ring of children moving slightly to keep her surrounded. Sunlight glittered off a metal slide only a few feet away, her landing-place the sandbox at its foot. Swing sets and jungle gyms were strewn about, children arrested in their playing to watch the gathering around Lara. "The farm park? Is that in Boston?"

The little boy looked nonplussed. "We live in Arlington. Are you crazy?"

"I don't think so. Thank you for . . ." Lara trailed off, words lost under a barrage of fairyland questions from the girls and a growing interest in her possible insanity from the boys. Her hand went to her hip, looking for a cell phone that was still back in her office at Lord Matthew's. She encountered an empty scabbard instead, and dismay seized her. "I really must look like I'm from fairyland."

The children scattered as running footsteps heralded an adult's arrival. Lara lurched to her feet in time to be greeted by a scowling, worried woman who snapped the children farther away before demanding, "Where did you come from? A pool full of water fell out of the sky, and then you did. I didn't seen a—an airplane?" She looked skyward, and Lara did, too, remembering urban legends she'd read about scuba divers found in the middle of forest fires, dropped there by helicopters scooping seawater to battle the fires with. She wished she had a similar story to explain away her arrival.

"I'm not sure how I got here. I'm sorry, but could I possibly borrow a cell phone?" she asked, abruptly hoping she could brazen it out. "I left mine at work yesterday."

The little girl grabbed the woman's hand. "I think she's magic, Mommy. She says she was in fairyland."

Lara winced, painfully aware that "being in fairyland" sounded like a euphemism for drug use. The woman pursed her lips, looking Lara up and down, then wordlessly drew a cell phone out of her purse and offered it. "Thank you," Lara whispered, and edged out of the sandbox to sit on the bottom of the slide as she dialed the only phone number she had memorized.

"Lord Matthew's Bespoke Tailoring Shop. This is Cynthia, how may I help you?"

"Oh thank goodness, Cynthia." Lara laughed in relief. "This is Lara. I've had the most incredibly strange night, and I'll tell you about it, but right now I was wondering if you could grab my jeans and shirt from yesterday and bring them to, um, the Arlington farm park? I really need a change of clothes."

"Lara?" Cynthia's voice cracked, then turned angry, clashing with the sound of bells. "This isn't funny. Who is this?"

"It's— What? This is Lara, Cynthia. Lara Jansen. How many other Laras do you know?"

"I don't know who the hell you think you are, but call this number again and I'll report you to the police," Cynthia snapped. "Lara Jansen disappeared seventeen months ago."

Nineteen

The phone went dead, leaving Lara to stare sightlessly across the playground. Details filtered in, unattached from active recognition: things she'd noticed without thinking about them. The children wore shorts, T-shirts, sandals. The sun was high in the sky, pouring warmth over the city. There was no cold breeze, no slush, no leaden gray skies. The only dampness was in a ring around her.

Lara handed the phone back. "It's summer, isn't it."

The woman gave her an odd look. "Yes."

It had been winter when she'd left. Lara nodded, the action mechanical. "Thank you. And thank you for letting me borrow your phone."

"You're welcome." The woman put her hand on her daughter's shoulder and drew her away.

Lara watched them go, Cynthia's angry words cutting through the rush of white static in her mind. *Lara Jansen disappeared seventeen months ago.* Tones of truth in the statement, deep melancholy bells that rang out slowly.

Seventeen months. She would no longer have an apartment. No

clothes, no credit cards, no cash. Her mother would be mourning; Kelly would have moved on with only the occasional regretful look back. And Dafydd had lied, twice. First about his own part in the murder, then about the magic that would hold the passage of time in her world to match the time in his.

The music of truth flattened, souring with the last thoughts. Lied, Lara amended, or had been mistaken. She could bend that far, though doing so felt brittle. It hadn't been his magic that sent her back home, but her own. Maybe truthseeker magic wasn't meant to open paths between worlds, and had warped the spell.

The *how* didn't matter. Cold with disbelief, Lara stepped out of the sandbox and shuffled away from the playground toward a life that no longer existed.

It took almost an hour to hail a taxi: most drivers looked right through her, and Lara, clad in Barrow-lands armor, couldn't blame them. She wore a tunic and leggings under her armor, but she was reluctant to discard it: it was the sole tangible thing she could offer in explanation, or excuse, for her disappearance. She did tuck her gauntlets, awkwardly, into the belt meant for her sword.

The cabdriver who eventually picked her up regaled her with stories about fighting somewhere called "Pennsic" with a reenactment group specializing in medieval costuming. Lara, too grateful for words, listened silently and wondered what he would think of the real battle she'd seen.

He was now parked outside of the brassiere specialty shop Kelly had worked at a year and a half earlier, waiting for Lara, who pushed the door open with nerves making a pit of sickness in her stomach. A blond girl she didn't know looked up with a smile that turned plastic with astonishment. "Um, hello. Can I help you?"

"Hi, I'm—" Lara blushed, stumbling over an explanation she knew wasn't necessary, but couldn't help offering. "I'm not here to shop. I don't need a bra. I'm just a thirty-four B, it's not like it's hard to find bras that fit, and I know I look really weird—" She bit her lower lip, trying to stop babbling. "Sorry," she said after a moment. "I was wondering if Kelly Richards still works here?"

The girl's smile had turned increasingly panicked all the way through Lara's fumbling explanation, and turned to a squeak of relief at the eventual question. "Yeah, she's my manager. Hang on and I'll get her." She disappeared into the back and Lara returned to the door, waving to let her driver know she was still there. He was on his cell phone, chatting, she imagined, to some other reenactor, telling him about her armor.

"Hi!" Kelly's voice came from behind her, loud and cheerful. Lara's hands went cold and she turned jerkily. Nerves seemed ridiculous when it had been only a day or two since she'd seen Kelly, but she still heard Cynthia's anger. *Seventeen months.*

Both color and cheer drained from Kelly's face. She said nothing, only stared with disbelief so profound it didn't even allow for hope. In her wake, Lara saw the shop assistant shift uncomfortably.

"I need to pay the cabdriver," Lara finally whispered. "I'm sorry, I just— I don't have any money, and I didn't know who else to come to. Mom's so far out of the city. . . ."

Kelly jolted like someone had run electricity through her, flipping from shock to business in an instant. "Right. Right, hold on." She grabbed a purse from behind the counter and swept out of the shop.

Lara reached for a display rack as her knees failed, relief stronger than nerves had been. The assistant squeaked and scurried toward her in concern, but Lara waved her away. "I'm all right." Polite fiction, not exactly a lie, but not true enough to sit comfortably on her tongue.

The shop doorbell jangled as Kelly charged back in. Lara turned halfway around and Kelly caught her by the shoulders, her color returned and burning hot in her cheeks. "What've you— Where've you— What're you *wearing*? Oh my God, Lara, is it you?"

She burst into tears before Lara could answer. Heart aching, Lara pulled her into a hug and sought the shop assistant's gaze. "Can we go in back?"

"Yeah. Yeah, of course." The blond girl ushered them toward the back of the store, Lara guiding Kelly as she sobbed. The assistant—Ruth, Lara finally saw on her name tag—whispered, "I'll get some coffee," and rushed out again. A moment later the doorbell rang again, and the distinctive click of a lock told Lara they were safely alone and wouldn't be disturbed.

With Ruth's retreat, Kelly dragged in a hiccuping breath and swiped tears from her eyes. "I'm sorry. I just thought I'd never see you again. Lara, what happened? Where have you been?"

"It's okay. And . . . Kel, this isn't something I say a lot, but you wouldn't believe me if I told you."

Kelly grabbed her hands hard enough to hurt, eyes wide, like if she blinked Lara would disappear again. "Of course I'll believe you. You never lie."

"I know. It's just that it's unbelievable."

"We thought you were dead," Kelly whispered. "You're not. Anything's believable, if you're alive. My God, Lara. What— You have to tell me. You *have* to tell me." Then dismay contorted her features even more, words tumbling on top of one another: "Unless, I mean, unless you don't want to. If it's been horrible and of course it probably has been—"

"It's only been a day," Lara blurted, stemming Kelly's apology more thoroughly than she'd imagined possible. "I know," she said as confusion and worry overwrote the dismay on Kelly's face. "I know, it's impossible. But it's not like I have amnesia or am missing a year and a half of my life. It's been barely twenty-four hours since we helped Rachel move, as far as I'm concerned. Do you still have the Nissan?" she asked wistfully.

"Yeah, it's been a great little . . . Lara, it's been seventeen *months*. You can't go around telling people it's only been a day. That's insane."

"It's true."

"*How?*"

Lara pulled a smile into place, feeling it fracture around the edges. "David Kirwen turned out to be a prince of fairyland, and he brought me there for a day."

"Da—" Kelly gaped at her, then grabbed her hands. "Lara, David Kirwen was arrested on kidnapping charges two days after you disappeared. They indicted him within a week, and flagged him as a flight risk because of his dual citizenship. He's been in jail all this time. The trial's coming up soon."

Only then did what Lara had said seem to catch up with her. Her hands loosened, something Lara saw more than felt: her own fingers had gone cold. She whispered "Arrested?" at the same time Kelly said "Fairyland?"

"Two days after I disappeared?" Lara got up and began shedding her armor, an awkward enough task that she was glad she hadn't tried it at the playground.

Kelly, visibly restraining herself from questions, got up to help. "The last anyone saw of you was at that AA meeting on Sunday morning. When you didn't show up for work Cynthia was worried, and I went over to your apartment and no one was there. The door wasn't even locked, Lara. The last person you'd called was David Kirwen, and the next morning you still weren't anywhere, but he came parading down Cambridge Street in a ridiculous—"

Her hands flew from the binding straps on the armor to her mouth, eyes large above her fingertips. "In this ridiculous suit of armor," she said through her fingers. "My God. It looked just like this, Lara. It was just like this."

Lara unlatched the last bit that held the arm pieces in place and set them aside, then loosened the breastplate. Her next breath came easier, for all that the moonlit armor was as weightless as metal could be. "We'd been in battle."

"Battle," Kelly said after what felt like hours of silence. Lara heard the attempt to hold back disbelief and caught Kelly's hands again, squeezing her fingers apologetically. Diamond glittered, catching the light and fading again as she made herself meet Kelly's eyes.

"Go ahead. Say it." Then her gaze jerked back down to the clear jewel in the ring on Kelly's finger. "Oh my *God*, Kelly, are you *engaged*?"

"What?" Kelly looked at her own hands as if they belonged to a stranger, then pulled them back from Lara's grip, hiding the solitaire ring. "No. I mean, yes, but this didn't really seem like the time to mention it."

Lara sat down in a clatter of armored legs, light-headedness sweeping her. The summertime heat, the phone call to Cynthia, Kelly's reaction to her appearance—she had believed months had gone by, but the evidence presented by a half-carat ring brought home the passage of time in a way nothing else had. "It was only yesterday," she said faintly, and it rang with a dichotomy of truth and falsehood. "Who is he? An undertaker?"

Color rushed along Kelly's cheeks. "No. That stopped seeming funny after you disappeared. It's Dickon, Lar. Dickon Collins, David's cameraman. We were both looking for you, he was determined to find you to prove David was innocent, and I don't know, I'd liked him in the first place and . . . I wasn't going to have a maid of honor," she whispered. "I wasn't going to, because there wasn't anybody but you I wanted to ask."

"Oh, God, Kel." Lara leaned forward to hug her friend. "Congratulations. And I would love to be your maid of honor, if you're asking."

"I am." Kelly returned the hug hard, then sat back with tears staining her cheeks again. "I am, and I want to tell you everything about Dickon and the wedding and everything, but *fairyland*, Lara? Battle? I know you don't lie, but that's . . ."

"Delusional?"

"Crazy talk," Kelly agreed. "Seriously, Lar. Fairyland?"

"I know. I do know, Kelly. But he was looking for me, for someone with my stupid ability to hear the truth. That's what upset me so much a couple nights ago at Rachel's. He'd asked me to go with him, to help him at home. He called me a 'truthseeker,' and it felt like it fit." Lara muffled the words in her hands as she told the story of the past day, ending with the clarity of power that had allowed her to open a doorway back home. Kelly listened in expressive silence, her eyebrows and lips shaping comments she didn't give voice to.

"Well," she said eventually, "you're going to have to come up with a different story for the papers. Yes, the papers," she said before Lara asked. "Your disappearance, the kidnapping, it was huge, Lara. Kirwen's a celebrity. Maybe just a local one, but still. Local weatherman arrested for kidnapping? Everybody was talking about it. So you're going to need a story."

"You believe me?" Lara asked through her fingers.

Kelly heaved a sigh. "No, but yes. If anybody else told me this, I'd never believe it. But it's you, so." She shrugged.

"Thank you."

"Yeah, well, what are friends for?" She studied Lara, eyebrows drawn together. "So what do you do now, Lar?"

"I don't know. I make up a story for the papers." The idea sent atonal vibrations under her skin. "I get Dafydd out of jail."

"Can you do that? I mean, with your . . ." Kelly trailed off, then, brightness coming into her eyes, giggled. "With your, um, your magic powers." She laughed again, contagious enough to make Lara smile, too. "Sorry. I always kind of thought of it as your spooky power, but I never wanted to say that. And now it turns out it really is like magic."

"Just like," Lara said drily. "Don't worry. I'm not used to it, either. What were you going to ask?"

"Oh! Can you do that, get him out of jail with your magic?"

Lara blinked. "I don't know. I was more thinking that I'd just tell them I wasn't kidnapped. I mean, I'm back and I—"

"Have no explanation for where you've been." Kelly's eyebrows rose. "It might not be that easy, Lara. David pled not guilty, but he wouldn't say anything in his own defense. The only reason he wasn't prosecuted for murder was nobody could find any evidence of foul play except that you were missing. And none of us wanted to have you declared dead," she said more quietly. "It was too much like giving up hope."

"Oh, Kel." Lara leaned forward to hug her friend again, mumbling "I'm definitely not dead" against her shoulder. "I'm just going to have to make them believe me somehow."

"Can you do that?" Kelly asked for the second time. Lara sat up, frowning, and Kelly spread her hands. "Look, all I'm saying is if you can make a path between Boston and fairyland, then just *making* somebody believe you weren't kidnapped seems like small potatoes. Especially if it's the truth." A wobbly smile creased her face. "You've always been good with the truth."

"I don't know if I have that much power here." Lara's protest shriveled under a rising chorus of song that lent credence to Kelly's suggestion.

Emyr and Dafydd had both made it clear that her magic was purely human, and even the little time she'd spent in the Barrow-lands had strengthened not just her ability, but her confidence in it. There was no reason an earth-born magic shouldn't be as strong—perhaps stronger—here as it had been in the Barrow-lands. She pursed her lips, then turned her hands palm-up toward Kelly. "On the other hand, there's really only one way to find out."

Kelly got up decisively. "I'll bring you down to the station. Dickon and I got to know the detective on your case, Reg Washington. He'll be the best place to start."

"What about—" Lara broke off both speech and action, stopping halfway to her feet, then sat back down abruptly, fingers steepled hollowly in front of her mouth. "What about my mom, I need to call her before I turn up on the evening news. And Cynthia, she didn't believe me when I called. And . . . and look at what I'm wearing," she whispered. The light woven shirt and breeches she still wore under the armored leggings would draw curious glances in the best of circumstances, which she didn't foresee in her immediate future. "And I should call Dafydd. See him. Something. He must think I'm . . ." Dead. Lost. She wasn't even certain what words to use. "Seventeen months," she whispered into her palms, and Kelly, slowly, crouched to pull her hands away from her mouth. Lara let her, trying to control the trembling that rushed through her.

"Okay. It's going to be okay, Lara. Look, you stay here for a minute, okay? I'm going to call my boss and see if I can leave Ruth in charge, or if she can come in, or if I can close the shop early. This is an emergency," she said gently. "I'll take you home, we'll get you changed, and we'll go from there. Okay? Okay." Kelly squeezed Lara's hands, then went into the front of the shop to make the necessary calls.

It was absolutely absurd, Lara thought, to fall apart now. She'd traveled between two worlds, ridden in battle, and commanded more power than she'd ever imagined possible. The prospect of dealing with a handful of mortal details shouldn't be overwhelming enough to shut her down entirely, but even the endless music of truth was barely a static rush at the back of her mind. It was the disappearing time: that was the worst of it, the most bewildering. Lara put her face in her hands again, waiting silently for Kelly's return.

It was preceded by "God, you look awful. Here," and as Lara looked up, Kelly rustled a candy bar from her purse. "When was the last time you ate?"

Lara whispered, "Apparently about a year and a half ago," and took the candy hungrily.

Kelly snorted laughter and sat, looking like she wanted to hug Lara again but was trying to let her eat. "Trish is on her way. We can leave Ruth in charge, so you eat that and we'll go back to my place. I kept some of your clothes." A wistful smile played over her lips. "I just kept thinking how sad you'd be if you came home and it was all gone. So I kept some of them, and look, you came home, and now you don't have to be sad." Her voice broke on the last words and, candy bar or not, Lara surged forward to give her an awkward hug.

"S'okay," Kelly whispered into her hair. "S'okay, Lar. We'll get it figured out. C'mon. C'mon, let's go, okay, hon? It's going to be okay." She drew Lara to her feet and led her out of the back room, repeating, "It'll be okay."

And Lara, grateful, heard nothing but truth in the promise.

Twenty

Boston's streets were unimaginably loud after a single day in the Barrow-lands. Lara stood on the tiny balcony that Kelly's apartment sported, red and white lights of traffic blurring in her tired vision. The day had disappeared into reuniting with her mother, whose disbelief and relief at Lara's return had led, for the second time, to the telling of where she'd been. The second and, Lara expected, the last: no one else would accept the truth for what it was.

She had more than half imagined her mother would tell a story of some old family legend, a story of some ancestor who claimed she'd been stolen away to fairyland, and had borne a child to an elfin lover. It would be the sort of tale Gretchen Jansen would never have told her truth-sensing daughter for fear of upsetting her in the same way stories of Santa Claus had.

But there had been no such story, nothing to laugh or wonder over. If such a thing had ever happened, it was long lost to history, but Lara thought it more likely that Emyr and Dafydd were right: that her magic was only human, and all the more unique for it.

Gretchen had reluctantly returned home as night fell, leaving Lara both glad to have seen her and utterly exhausted. There would be more of the same tomorrow and, she feared, for days to come: she hadn't even yet been to Lord Matthew's, much less to the police. Sharing her story with her mother and Kelly was by far the easiest of what she would face over the next several days. They knew her well enough to accept it, even in all its wondrous impossibility.

Her bones ached from weariness, and probably from having ridden horses and carried swords and flinging her armored self through a breach between worlds and landing hard in a sandbox. Despite tiredness she let out a rough laugh and leaned hard on the balcony's iron fence. Sleep evaded her: the streets were too loud, or, more likely, her emotions were too high. She, who had spent a lifetime rooted in pedantic truth, who had never believed such a thing could happen, had become a time traveler, and was lost in both the awe and horror of that fact.

The clothes Kelly had kept for her had been tucked into boxes whose lids were dusty, and the tissue paper her jewelry had been wrapped in was fragile and creased with a year's disuse. Proof, in small ways, that yesterday had been a long time ago.

And there were other matters to dwell on, too, if she let herself. Not just Dafydd's imprisonment, but the history Ioan had hinted at. There'd been no mistruth in what he'd recounted, but she was unaccustomed to trying to sort history from legend. The way humans turned men into legends often rang false with her; she had no idea what the reality behind Robin Hood was, but no version of that story, passed off as history, had ever struck a true chord in her mind. By those lights, Unseelie legend might have been born of fact, which opened a window on a much larger landscape than she'd originally been asked to see.

She said, "Changes that will break the world," to the street below. Ioan's worldbreaking weapon nagged at her; if it was something she could find, or wield, it might help bring answers to light. But it was long lost, whatever it might have been. Or lost, at least, to the Barrow-lands; that was what Ioan had said. Lara's gaze went unfocused, city horizon turning to a blur.

Lost to his world, and what better place to lose it than hers? They were linked, but only royalty could work the worldwalking spell, and if Emyr had cause to hide a weapon in her world, it would shed more light on why he was so displeased with Dafydd's hundred-year sojourn across the breach.

"Lar?" The bedroom door opened, Kelly's voice pitched just loud enough to carry. Lara waved from the balcony and Kelly came in to lean in its doorway. "I heard you talking. You okay?"

"I don't know. I'm confused."

"I can't imagine why." Kelly made a face as she came out to the balcony. "Sorry. I lost the habit of not being sarcastic out loud."

"It's okay. I've been gone a long time, and you only ever had to do it with me."

"But I'm probably a nicer person when I keep the snark on the inside." Kelly peeked down at the street nervously, fingers knotted around the rail. "I never come out here."

"I know. I don't understand why you're willing to spend an extra hundred dollars a month for an apartment with two balconies when you're afraid of heights."

"Hundred and fifty. Rent went up. But Dickon and I are moving in together soon, so it won't matter." Kelly gave the railing a tentative shake. "You could probably stay here, if you wanted. Move in, I mean, and have the place to yourself when we get married. It'd be easier than looking for a new place to live."

Surprise cascaded through Lara like cold water pouring down her insides. "I hadn't thought that far ahead."

Kelly chuckled and stepped back to the safety of the doorway. "Are you lying to me, Lara Jansen?"

Lara opened her mouth and shut it again, Kelly's teasing jangling at her nerves. "Yes and no. If I had thought that far, I thought—"

"That you were going back to the Barrow-lands with David?"

"Yeah." Truth, for once, wasn't a comfort, drawing a note as discordant as lies under her skin. "And no, Kel. I can't quite believe it's been a year and a half. I can't quite believe I won't just get up and go to work in the morning. That my job's not even there anymore, probably. It was just yesterday."

"Wow," Kelly breathed. "That must be really bizarre. Not believing, I mean. That must be like gravity stopped working."

"Or like magic started." Lara shook her head. "I have no idea how anybody lives with this level of uncertainty. I thought always knowing if something was true or false was hard, but this is worse. So beyond getting Dafydd out of jail, I just don't know. I think they might need me, in Dafydd's world, and I'm starting to think maybe there's something I need to find here, in this one. And I don't know what happens if I do. This is my home." Lara sighed, pulling herself back from the larger scope of worries. "And this is a great apartment. It'd be a good place to move in to."

"Plus that way I could leave as much stuff here as I wanted and just stop by to pick things up when I missed them," Kelly said cheerfully.

Lara laughed. "But you're only thinking of me, right?"

"I would never say that. You'd call me on the terrible lies in my voice." Kelly reached for Lara's elbow, pulling her back toward the door to hug her. "Look, it was just a thought, okay? You don't have to make a decision right now. First things first. Get your weird-ass boyfriend out of jail, and we'll figure out the next step after that."

Lara grunted at the strength of Kelly's hug and returned it just as hard. "Okay."

"Ooh. I note she didn't deny the 'boyfriend' part of that sentence." Kelly waggled her eyebrows as Lara spluttered a protest, then pointed at the bed. "Get some sleep, Truthseeker. You've got an elf to rescue tomorrow."

"I can't do this." Lara reached across the car—the same little blue Nissan she'd helped Kelly pick out barely a week ago in her memory and nearly a year and a half earlier in Kelly's—and grasped Kelly's wrist. "I can't do this."

Kelly pried Lara's fingers off her wrist. "Your hands are freezing, Lara, jeez. And you have to do it, unless you want to let David rot in a jail cell for the rest of his life. How long do elves live, anyway?"

"Dafydd," Lara whispered, correcting the hard American way Kelly said the name to the softer Seelie pronunciation. "They live forever."

"Well, somebody's going to notice if he lives forever in jail, so let's go."

"But *look* at them."

Dozens of reporters crowded around the front door of Boston police headquarters. They were barred from entry by a couple of grumpy-looking cops, but mostly they didn't appear to want to go inside. They were waiting, and Lara had a too-clear idea of what they were waiting for. "How could they even know I was here?"

Kelly's eyebrows shifted upward. She killed the Nissan's engine and took the keys out of the ignition before leaning on the steering wheel and pointing, with the keys, toward the crowd of cameramen and microphone-bearing press. "I can think of at least six different ways they found out. The woman you talked to in the park. The cab-driver. Either of them might have eventually recognized you from the news. And you said you called Cynthia. Or there's Ruth, or me, or your mom. Hey!" She sat up, lifting her hands in a protestation of innocence. "I said I could think of six ways, not that they were all likely. I didn't tell anybody, and I'm sure your mom didn't, either. But Cynthia could've called the cops."

"Cynthia didn't believe it was me."

"Doesn't mean she didn't call the cops and somebody didn't make a note of it. Look, Lara, I told you. You're a news story. You're going to have to face these people eventually. Might as well get it over with."

"Would you be this phlegmatic if you were in my shoes?"

"Of course not, but all I've got to do is have your back, sister. Come on." Kelly cracked her door open and elbowed Lara to do the same. "It's only forty feet. How bad can it be?"

Lara, climbing out of the car, shot her friend a despairing glance. "That's one of those questions you should never ask."

Kelly's apology was lost beneath a triumphant, "There she is!" from within the midst of the press corps. Dozens of faces turned her way, and Lara squeaked with dismay, fumbling for the Nissan's door handle. Kelly, much bolder, all but slid across the car's hood to grab Lara's hand and pull her forward as reporters surged toward them.

"They're not as bad as a dark elf army," Kelly whispered. "Come on, you can do it."

It hit Lara like a gong, like *she* was the gong, her chest reverberating with a truth so obvious it became understatement, and then became funny. A day earlier she'd ridden into actual battle, albeit reluctantly. A mob of men and women armed with cameras and microphones was nothing, in that context. Chin lifted, she stepped ahead of Kelly, meeting a tide of bodies and questions with a sudden calm that felt like arrogance.

Even with newfound determination, there were simply too many reporters, all pressing close and shoving microphones or cameras into Lara's face. Questions made the air thick, shouts hurting Lara's ears, but she set her jaw and pushed forward.

And hit a wall, jostling bodies vying for position and creating a deadlock. Even the battlefield hadn't been quite like this: there, though they wanted to hold a line, the soldiers had also wanted a chance at their enemy, and had let people slip and step through so they could fight.

They might well still be fighting, that same battle not yet ended, given the radical differences in time's passage between her world and Dafydd's. If she could get through, if she could obtain Dafydd's release, they might yet be able to make a difference in his world; might yet stop that fight before it became a genocide. Chords sounded in her mind, thunderous sounds that made truth of the possibility.

But the reporters wouldn't make a path.

Lara drew breath and focused the pounding music in her mind into her voice, turning it to an answer for the most-oft asked question: "I was *not kidnapped!*"

Power burst in it, opening a passage through the mob. Lara

surged forward, driven by Kelly's hands in the small of her back. She stumbled into the small empty space at the police station doors and turned to face the press corps with indignation boiling through her.

For a few astonished seconds, they gaped in silence. Kelly lurched to her side, and the officers who'd been manning the doors stepped up to flank them.

"They believed you," Kelly whispered. "Keep talking."

Lara wasn't certain at all that they'd believed her, but they had let her through, and had gone quiet, which was enough. A distant part of her found that interesting: typically she would have been deeply concerned about the truth, that it be accepted, but not now. She stared from face to face in the crowd, and just as the power of her voice started to wear off, she spoke again.

"David Kirwen and I are friends. I know I've been missing for months, but that wasn't by his design." Technically true: Dafydd's intention had been to bring her back very close to the time she'd left. The language could be used to play fine notes, a tuning Lara had never cared for. No one else would hear the dissonance in the words in quite the way she did, though she could see many of the reporters latching on to her careful phrasing. A new wave of questions inundated her before she could say anything else. Exasperation reached its breaking point and snapped.

"Of course I don't have Stockholm syndrome. How could I, when the man who supposedly kidnapped me has been in jail for the last year?"

Another silence, this one considering, seized the press corps for the briefest moment. Lara whipped around, her pride too great to let her actually run inside, though it was a near thing. Another barrage of questions rushed after her, and exasperation rose up a second time as she pulled the door open. "Yes," she said over her shoulder, in response to something half-heard. "Yes, as a matter of fact, I *did* disappear off the face of the earth. I'm sure that'll be a very exciting mystery for you to solve. I have nothing more to say to you, not now and not ever."

The door closed behind her, cutting off the inquisition. Lara let out an explosive breath that loosened her anger, and Kelly applauded. "That was impressive. You told them off *and* you told the truth."

"Sometimes I amaze even myself," Lara said without a hint of irony. She straightened her skirt—she'd gone shopping that morning, instinctively searching for a black suit skirt and a red silk blouse, and had thought nothing of it until Kelly'd looked at them and said, "Battle colors, eh?"

Caught out, Lara had almost exchanged the blouse for a blue one, but in the end had kept the red. She *was* preparing for battle, after all, though of a different sort than had seen her strap on moonlit armor. Confident she was presentable, she approached the front desk, where a stout officer in an ill-fitting uniform looked her up and down. "Yeah, I know who you are. Washington'll be out in a minute." He went so far as to pick up the phone and send a message to make certain that would happen, and Lara, feeling somehow chastised, retreated to wait on the detective's arrival.

"I've never been in a police station before," she whispered to Kelly. "Have you?"

"More than I'd like to think about, the last year and a half." Kelly leaned against her for a hug.

Embarrassment flooded Lara's chest. "Right."

"Hey, don't worry about it. All's well that ends well." Kelly smiled, and Lara's discomfort faded.

"Miss Jansen?" A tall, good-looking man in a suit—off the rack, Lara thought, but well-cut and long enough in the arm for his height—came through a side door and extended a hand to Lara. "I'm Detective Washington. I was assigned to your case last year. Kelly," he added. "Good to see you again. How are the wedding plans going?"

"Better than they've ever been. I've got a maid of honor now." Kelly, beaming, stood on her toes to kiss the detective's cheek after he shook Lara's hand.

"Congratulations. I hope I'm still invited."

"Of course you are. We got to be friends," Kelly said to Lara, more shyly than she'd admitted to being engaged. "Neither Dickon nor I would leave him alone. I wouldn't give up hope and Dickon wouldn't accept David was guilty."

"And you were right. You have no idea how glad we all are to see you back safely, Ms. Jansen. Can you come this way?"

Lara looked between Washington and Kelly, her eyebrows lifting as a feeling of loss worked its way through her. A day, she thought. A day, and seventeen months. Her world had changed, even if she hadn't. Or hadn't much: her talent was stronger than it had been, but in comparison to the differences in Kelly's life, that seemed like nothing. Lara murmured, "Sure," and fell into step behind the detective.

He led them through a labyrinth of halls whose cream-colored paint was sallowed by aging fluorescent lights. A few officers smiled as they passed by; more nodded, and one or two did a double take, clearly recognizing Lara. "I feel like an exhibit," she breathed to Kelly, but it was Washington who answered.

"Sorry for saying so, but in a way, you are. People don't usually turn up after going missing for a year and a half."

"Not usually," Lara echoed. "But sometimes." She stepped through a door Washington opened for her, looking back at him for an answer.

"Sometimes, yeah." Washington gestured her to a desk in the midst of a dozen others, then looked apologetically at Kelly. "Sorry. I only have the one chair."

She grinned. "I know. I've been in it often enough. I'll go grab a cup of really bad vending machine coffee. Want me to bring some back for you?"

"If I give you five bucks will you go to Starbucks instead?" Washington reached for his wallet, but Kelly waved him off.

"My treat. Celebrating Lara's return. You want anything, Lar?"

"An iced tea, please?"

"Will do. And try to remember everything you say, because I'm going to want all the details later." Kelly winked and hurried off, leaving Lara feeling oddly fortified. She sat down, smiling, and Washington returned the smile as he pulled his own chair out.

"That woman's a firecracker. Never gave up on you."

"I hope I wouldn't, either." Lara held her breath a moment. "Detective, I really wasn't kidnapped. I don't know what the legal proceedings are to get someone who's been wrongfully imprisoned out of jail, but I hope you'll help me. He hasn't actually been convicted yet, right? So maybe it's not too hard?"

Washington lifted an eyebrow. "Well, if you can convince me, that'll help when we bring it to a judge. Where did you say you'd gone?"

"I didn't."

The words fell flat, Washington's mouth thinning as it became clear that was all Lara would say. "Ms. Jansen, we scoured a tristate area. We studied every security tape, every Greyhound station, every car rental agency, every airport, and found nothing. No activity on credit cards or bank accounts, no sightings at Seven-eleven convenience stores, no hitchhiking encounters. Children disappear that way, Ms. Jansen. People with no links, no friends, no family, disappear that way. People like you don't."

"All evidence to the contrary."

The detective beat a rhythm on his desk, then nodded. "All evidence to the contrary. You disappeared off the face of the earth."

Lara spread her hands, a thread of amusement working its way through her. "That's what the media outside said, too, and I'm content to leave it at that." She softened her tone as irritation darkened Washington's face. "I know you want answers, Detective. I think you even deserve them, but I also know you wouldn't like the ones I have to give. Not knowing might eat at you, but if I told you anything, you'd think I was lying, and that would only make you angrier. You won't believe me, but you'll be happier if you just let the whole thing go."

"You practice this story, you and Kirwen? He said damned near the same thing when we arrested him."

"I imagine detectives have to be pretty good judges of character. Either we practiced, or we're independently telling the truth. You make the call."

Curiosity sparked in Washington's eyes. "You're not quite what

I expected, Ms. Jansen. Everyone I talked to, even your mother, described you as shy. Nonassertive. Given that kind of billing, I'd say you just read me the riot act."

"It's been seventeen months, Detective Washington." Seventeen months, or one day. Lara shrugged a little. "People change."

"I guess so." Washington studied her a few moments more, finally pulling a hand over his face. "I don't know what to do with you, Ms. Jansen. Never had a kidnapping victim turn up and say no, sorry, didn't happen. If I had, I'd expect her to have an explanation. Without one—"

"With or without one," Lara said steadily, "with my reappearance, you have no reason to hold David Kirwen. I've read news stories every once in a while about how people who were supposedly murdered have reappeared, and the person convicted of killing them has been released. How is this any different?"

"They usually have an explanation for where they've been. A story that checks out."

"And if I don't? Does that negate the fact that I'm here, healthy, and will swear in court that I wasn't kidnapped?"

Washington scowled. "No, it doesn't, but I don't like it, and neither will anybody else. You'd better be damned sure about being willing to take that oath, Ms. Jansen. You're going to have to."

Twenty-One

The warning in Washington's voice stayed with Lara, even hours later. She'd sent Kelly to work and borrowed the Nissan to drive out to the state correctional facility in Concord on her own, thoughts spinning.

It would be easier by far to offer Washington and the press a story they could sink their teeth into. Even given her lack of talent for falsehoods, it would be easier. But she could think of nothing that would stand up to investigation short of claiming she'd gone into the wilderness, built a cabin of trees she'd felled herself, and hunted for every bit of sustenance required over the past year and a half.

She caught a glimpse of herself in the rearview mirror, heart-shaped face and soft hair, and huffed disbelievingly. Anyone who would accept that story probably deserved to be lied to. In desperate circumstances, maybe she could survive in a remote cabin. In desperate circumstances and armed with enough library books, almost certainly. But she didn't look like a desperate woman, and she doubted anyone would accept such a tall tale. For that matter, some intrepid reporter would probably search for the hand-hewn cabin, and make a story of failing to find it. Saying nothing remained the most practical option, for all that it wasn't a comfortable one.

She showed identification at the prison gates—her driver's license had expired, but Kelly had kept her passport—and was relieved that the guard took no particular interest in her name. Maybe Concord was far enough out of Boston that neither she nor Dafydd were quite local celebrities, or perhaps the job inured one to oddities. Even so, it took a long time to get out of the car after she parked: not so much a fear of being recognized as painfully aware of being a stranger in a strange land.

As if she could belong at the doors of a human prison any less than she could belong in the fairyland called Annwn. The Barrowlands, though, had beauty on their side, making them enticing, which no correctional facility could be. But she wanted Dafydd to know she'd returned before he got a call from his lawyer, and so, nervous or not, Lara climbed out of the car.

The blocky prison doors opened as she did so. A uniformed police officer escorted a young man through, the youth's expression torn between relief and nervousness at his parole. Lara sympathized: freedom was as frightening as captivity, in its own way. She had had careful constraints on her own life, intended to measure and control her exposure to the lies of well-meaning strangers, and Dafydd had torn those constraints apart. She had never imagined herself a prisoner, but watching the youth's gaze flicker from the sky to the horizon, watching it linger on her in one part desire and one part apology, she thought she wasn't so different from him.

"Lara Jansen," the officer beside him said, incredulously, and Lara's attention flinched to him.

Two days: it had been little more than two days, and well over a year, since she'd seen him. It still took a moment to fumble his name to her lips, surprise working against her more than the passage of time: "Officer Cooper. What are you doing here?"

"What am I—!" Cooper actually released his prisoner and stepped forward to seize Lara's shoulders before remembering his duty. He retreated again, still incredulous. "I'm collecting my parolee. What are *you* doing here? God damn, Miss Jansen, but I was damned near the last upright citizen who saw you. I got interrogated inside-out over you."

"I'm sorry." Lara knotted her hands in front of her stomach, partially in self-defense and partially to prevent herself from blurting offense at his phrase. The twelve-step group members deserved better than relegation to second-class citizenship, though from her previous encounter with this man she doubted an argument would do any good. "Of course you did. I'm sorry, I didn't realize. I'm back now. I just had to . . . go away for a while." *Had to* carried too much weight, jangling her already-stretched nerves, and Cooper seized on the words, though for a different reason.

"Had to? It wasn't family getting sick, it wasn't you getting sick, what kind of 'had to' makes you disappear entirely?"

"I'm sorry, Officer Cooper." Lara struggled for an explanation, then sighed and gave up with a shrug. "It's nothing I can talk about."

That, astonishingly, worked where a flatter refusal to explain hadn't. Curiosity flashed through Cooper's expression: curiosity, then answers he supplied himself. Lara, following flights of fancy, imagined stories ranging from terrible brutality to government operations, and bit back laughter. She ought to have tried that tactic with Detective Washington, rather than insisting he wouldn't accept the truth. At least now she knew it was a truthful way through the questions and could use it in the future.

"Sure," Cooper said awkwardly, then shouldered his charge toward a nearby police car. "I'll see you, Miss Jansen."

"Officer Cooper," Lara murmured, and watched them go before drawing herself up and entering the prison.

Dafydd ap Caerwyn, immortal prince of the Seelie court, looked awful. The jewelry he had chosen to wear in the outside world had all been silver and gold, Lara recalled, not iron: not the heavy-looking stuff that weighed him down now. She wondered if it damaged him, though surely the glamour he wore must offer some protection against mortal metals.

The glamour, though, seemed shabby. It would never fool her eyes again, but watching him shuffle wearily into the visitor's room, Lara wondered how it could fool anyone. His hair, cropped short now, did nothing to disguise the upswept tips of his ears, and she couldn't trust her shimmering vision to tell her whether the glamour truly disguised them to human eyes. More than that, though, he simply looked fragile: his color was bad, and made worse by his orange jumpsuit, and his skin looked parched and thin, like it might break with a touch. His slender fingers were sticklike, and he'd lost muscle from his slim form. Even by Seelie standards he seemed delicate, and by human expectations, he looked so weak it was a wonder he'd managed to survive within the penal system. He shuffled to the glass phone boxes and sat without looking up, motions awkward as he lifted the phone with cuffed hands.

"Hey," Lara whispered into the phone, and pressed her palm against the glass that separated them.

Dafydd's head jerked up, sudden life flooding him. The glamour strengthened, making Lara dizzy, but the astonished brightness in his eyes was worth the oncoming headache. "You look awful," she whispered through a damp smile. "Orange isn't your color."

"Truer words were never spoken." Relieved laughter marked lines in Dafydd's face as Lara crinkled her nose. "Very well," he whispered back. "No doubt many things far truer have been said. But orange isn't my color, and— How did you come here? You're here, you're *alive*, Lara, I've been so afraid. It's been so long." His voice broke and he kept it low with obvious effort, bringing his hand up to match Lara's through the glass. "Did my father send you back?"

"No, I . . . brought myself home. How did *you* get here?"

"You—!" Dafydd curled his fingers into a fist against the glass, slow motion filled with uncertainty. "How?"

Lara glanced toward the security cameras, shaking her head. "I don't think this is the time to explain. I'm sorry, Dafydd. I'm sorry about how much time passed. I'm sorry you're in here. I've gone to the police already—"

"Already? How long have you been back?" His face set like he awaited injury, and mild insult washed through Lara.

"Barely a day. I had to see my mother, and I went to the police this morning, then came out here. I haven't been ignoring you for weeks."

Embarrassment replaced subtle injury and he flattened his hand against the glass again. "I'm sorry. How long . . ." His gaze went to the cameras, too, then came back to Lara. "How long were you gone?"

"I came back a few hours after you did, Dafydd. I don't know why it was so long here. I thought the . . ." She didn't want to say *magic* or *spell* under the cameras or on the phone, uncertain of whether their conversation was being recorded. "I thought it was supposed to keep time the same."

"It was, but you were never meant to come back by yourself," Dafydd said just as circumspectly, and for a delirious moment Lara felt badly for anyone trying to interpret their cryptic discussion. Dafydd met her eyes, intent with apology. "That could have changed things. I'm sorry."

"It's not your fault. It's *Aerin's* fault, I don't know what happened, she lost her mind and threw you to the Unsee—to the enemy. I had her arrested."

"What!" Dafydd blurted, then cut himself off with a strangled sound. "Lara, it was the compulsion. The one that made me—" He broke off again, glared at the cameras, then looked back at Lara, clearly hoping she followed his thoughts.

"The one that got you in trouble with Merrick."

"Yes." Dafydd pressed his eyes shut, then leaned in to the glass, fingertips colorless against it. "She wasn't throwing me to the hordes, Lara, she was acting under my orders. All I wanted was to be at your side, and I couldn't control my actions. I was afraid what would happen if I reached you."

Cold slithered inside Lara's chest and thrummed out to her fingers, rendering the glass warm beneath them. "Oh." Silence drew out before she added, "I suppose I shouldn't have broken her nose, then."

Dafydd, astonishingly, laughed aloud. It restored vivaciousness to him, making his skin look less like aged parchment and brightening his eyes. "No, nor arrested her, but I find I can't hold it against you, when you were acting in my best interests. Thank you. I think."

"You're welcome. Dafydd, I came here to tell you I'm all right and that I'll get you out of here. They can't keep you here for kidnapping if the victim shows up and says she wasn't kidnapped." Determination turned Lara's voice to steel.

"Can they not?"

"They won't," she said flatly.

Something curious came into Dafydd's expression and Lara glanced away, discomfited. The strength in her words was unfamiliar to her; she was accustomed to being quiet, unnoticed, and gentle in her interactions. She had thrown some of that away simply by entering the Barrow-lands, and had been obliged, once there, to push herself far beyond where her confidence might usually have lain. She knew it, but Dafydd's recognition of her changes said they ran both deeper and more clearly than she'd imagined possible in such a short period of time. But it was necessary, if she was to succeed in getting Dafydd out of prison, much less face the questions the Barrow-lands offered. "I don't know how long this will take. Not too long, I promise."

Dafydd smiled. "Promises spoken by a truthseeker are not to be taken lightly."

"They're not given lightly, either." Lara couldn't remember the last time she'd made a flat promise; absolutes were too difficult to deal in. "Dafydd, I'm sorry, but I can't stay. I need to find a lawyer for you, for me maybe, in order to make this work."

"It's all right. I've endured these long months here. Another few nights won't harm me."

"They'd better not," Lara muttered. "I don't want to explain to your father how I lost you to the American prison system."

"I can hardly imagine how he would react to that," Dafydd said drolly, then, more softly, "I'm glad you're well, Lara. I was worried."

Lara smiled and pressed her hand against the glass. "Me, too." She thumped the glass, then stood abruptly. "We have so much to talk about and none of it can be done here. I'm going to go before I get indiscreet. Dafydd, I—" Audacity took her breath and left her wondering at the intensity of emotion she'd been about to voice. "I'll get you out of here," she whispered instead. "As soon as I can."

He nodded, and she left with her final image of his amber eyes in a grateful face.

It was late enough when she returned to the city that it made a viable excuse to return home, pretending the day was over. The temptation to do so was great enough to keep Lara idling at a traffic light, distant with thought as the light turned to green.

An impatient beep behind her jolted her into action, knocking the turn signal on and making a decision for her. She made the turn and entered an underground parking lot that others were deserting as the hour ticked past five. It was only a few minutes' walk to Lord Matthew's, and Lara rang the entrance bell stiffly, wondering if Steve still worked long hours that would make him late for dinner.

Cynthia's voice came through the intercom system, polite and more mature than Lara remembered: "One moment, please, and I'll escort you in."

Lara took a breath to offer her name and a protest that she didn't need an escort, and let it go again in silence. The radio or one of the ubiquitous twenty-four-hour news stations might have announced her return by now, but Cynthia was unlikely to have heard either between school and work.

The door opened, and Lara felt her expression go slack-jawed. The high school senior she'd known was nearly nineteen now, probably in college, and had left the last vestiges of childhood behind sometime in the past year and a half. Instead, a poised young woman in a high-fashion shirt and skirt, beautifully made but catching the edge of exuberant youth, stood before her with her eyes going increasingly round.

Then Cynthia blurted, "Oh my God, it *was* you, I'm so *sorry*," and fell on Lara in a teary hug. Lara caught her, almost laughing with relief and not especially caring that they were making a scene on Lord Matthew's doorstep. It took several sniffling moments before Cynthia pulled her inside and demanded, "What *happened?*" in such a high-pitched voice that Lara thought perhaps the high school senior hadn't been left so far behind, after all.

"I can't talk about it," she answered softly. "I will if I ever can, Cyn, but right now I just can't. I'm okay, though. I'm all right, and I'm so sorry I disappeared like that. I didn't know it was going to happen."

"Well of course, nobody *knows* they're going to disappear. I'm just so glad you came back and you're okay and oh my *God*, Lara! Dad! Dad! *Daddy!*"

Lara winced. "If he's with a client—"

"He isn't, he's just going deaf. Daddy! Lara's back!"

For a man purported to be going deaf, Steve Taylor appeared with remarkable alacrity at Cynthia's last shout. He looked older, too, Lara thought: more gray at the temples of his curling hair, and circles under brown eyes. He stared at Lara a moment, then, much like his daughter had, swept her into a hug. "Thank God. Are you all right?"

"I am."

"Okay." Steve set her back, hands on her shoulders, and looked her up and down as if making sure she was telling the truth, then nodded. "Okay. That's all that matters. That's all that matters."

"Steve, I hate to do this, I can't explain where I've been—"

"It doesn't matter." There was so much passion in his voice that Lara faltered, overwhelmed by the music of his conviction. She'd known he cared about her, but hearing the depths of his relief told her that Steve Taylor was, in truth, the closest thing to a father she'd had. Suddenly teary-eyed, she stepped forward to hug him again, and his reassurances were murmured over her head: "You're alive, you're safe, you're home. I mean it, Lara, that's all that matters. We've missed you."

"I missed you, too." The answer came automatically, not even a lie, though all the missing she'd done had been crammed into the twenty-four hours since she'd learned she had been gone for well over a year. She wiped her eyes surreptitiously, stepping back to look up at him. "Steve, I need a lawyer. Dafydd—David, David Kirwen, he didn't kidnap me, he didn't hurt me, nothing like that happened. I need to get him out of jail, and you're the only person I know who even has a lawyer. I'm sorry to ask, especially like this, but—"

"Lara." He squeezed her shoulders and spoke more gently. "Listen to me. I don't care if you took a vacation to the moon. You're home, and nothing else is important. If you need a lawyer, then I can help you. There is no 'especially like this' for you to apologize about."

"*I* care if she took a vacation to the moon," Cynthia said abruptly, though not seriously. Steve stepped back, taking his cell phone out, and spoke beneath Cynthia as she continued, "I want pictures, at least, and I want to go with her next time because one-sixth gravity would be awesome."

Lara giggled, aware it was a surprisingly pathetic sound. "I didn't go to the moon. Sorry. No Earth-rise photos from me. I didn't even have a camera."

"I'd say bring one next time but I don't want you to disappear again *ever*."

"I'd rather not myself," Lara admitted, and Steve closed his phone with a snap.

"My lawyer's on her way. Welcome home, Lara. Everything's going to be okay."

Twenty-Two

Law and Order, Lara was convinced, had an uncanny ability to zip back and forth through time: all the cases took place simultaneously, rather than one at a time as they were portrayed. There was no other explanation as to how the legal proceedings shown could take place with such apparent rapidity. Steve's lawyer, a handsome, no-nonsense woman named Marjorie Oritz, had seen a ray of hope in Dafydd's case because he hadn't actually been put on trial and convicted yet. Otherwise, despite Lara's reappearance, it could be months, even years before he might be released. Like Detective Washington, though, her mouth had drawn thin and tight at Lara's refusal to explain her whereabouts. She had left the office with a grim, but not hopeful, promise to see what could be done, and Lara had retreated to Kelly's apartment feeling defeated.

"You're going to have to stick to your guns," Kelly said helplessly. "I'm a much better liar than you are and even I can't think of a story that would stand up to investigation. Unless you want to say you were kidnapped by the government and held at Guantánamo for the last year and a half. You could be a terrorist."

"Armed with a needle and a box of pins?" Lara smiled, surprising herself. "I think the government would deny it, Kelly."

"Well, that would be the point! It's not like they'd throw open Gitmo's doors and invite people to come take a look to prove they hadn't been holding you. So your best bet is to either accuse the government of something outrageous or keep your mouth shut."

"I think I'll keep my mouth shut." Lara tucked her feet up onto Kelly's couch and curled her head down against the arm with a sigh. "Marjorie said with a miracle this could take days, but it was likely to take weeks. I don't want to leave him there that long, Kel. Prison's not good for him."

"Prison's not good for anybody."

Lara muffled a short laugh in the couch arm. "No, but it's worse for him. It's an iron cage and it's making him sick. So I have to find a way to make this move faster."

"I take it you won't be going back to Lord Matthew's, then."

Regret made a knot around Lara's heart. "Not right away. Which might mean never. I don't know. I have to—" Her stomach rumbled and she put a hand over it. "I have to eat something. I don't think I even had lunch."

"Thus reminding me of how you stay slim. Never fear, I anticipated this. Dickon will be here within half an hour, bearing an enormous bag of Mexican food." Kelly caught her lower lip in her teeth. "Lara, about Dickon . . ."

"I'll tell him the truth," Lara offered quietly. "He's not going to believe it, but he's your fiancé, Kel, and he's been Dafydd's friend for a long time. He's going to have to talk to Dafydd to believe it, he's going to have to *see* Dafydd to believe it, but it's not fair to keep him all the way out of the loop."

"I've told him about you and the truth. Maybe he'll believe you." Kelly sounded dubious. "But thanks in advance for trying, even if he'll think you're insane."

"I'm willing to be considered insane as long as he brings dinner." Lara pulled another tiny smile, then glanced around Kelly's cozy apartment. "Are you sure I'm not in your way here? I don't know how long this is going to go on."

"The wedding's in a month. I can handle having you as a room-mate that long, Lar. Then if you want the place, it's yours. What're you going to do, if you're not going back to work?"

"Find Emyr's worldbreaking weapon." Lara spread her hands as Kelly's eyebrows went up. "I'm going to try, anyway. Ioan thought maybe it could be used to put things right in the Barrow-lands, so if I get Dafydd freed and we go back, it might be good to have it."

"Ioan the kidnapper? That Ioan? And you belie—" Kelly broke off and made a face at the ceiling. "Well, Kelly, it was a hypothesis on his part, and not an outright lie, so of course Lara, *who senses the truth,* is going to give him the benefit of the doubt." She reversed her gaze, smiling ruefully at Lara. "Sorry. I kind of forgot who I was talking to there for a minute."

The door swung open on her last words and Dickon said, "You're back after a year and a half missing and she's forgetting who you are already? Lara, you need new friends." His joviality sounded forced, and Kelly jumped up to get plates from the kitchen as he mustered up an awkward smile for Lara. He'd lost weight since she'd seen him last, though it did little to reduce his imposing size. The worry etched between his eyebrows, though, removed any thought of cau-tion he might have inspired. "Holy crap, I'm glad to see you, Lara. I, um. Can I, like, hug you?"

A trill of strained laughter broke from Lara's throat. "That would be great. I'm glad to see you, too."

Dickon crossed the room in two steps and put the sack of food on the coffee table before hauling Lara off the couch into a bear hug. "Man, I knew David couldn't have hurt you, but holy *crap* am I glad to see you in one piece." He put her back down on her feet, expres-sion so tight it looked headache-inducing. "Look, I know I'm sup-posed to give you time to settle in, Kelly made me promise not to come after you or harass you but what the hell *happened,* Lara? Where have you been?"

Kelly wailed "Dickon!" from the kitchen. He looked faintly abashed, but not enough for the curiosity in his eyes to fade.

"It's okay," Lara said, loudly enough for Kelly to hear, then smiled lopsidedly at Dickon. "Dinner first, and then I'll explain everything, okay? I'm famished, and it smells fantastic."

Dickon nodded jerkily. "Yeah, of course, okay. Kelly said you'd forget to eat."

"She knows me very well." Lara took the armchair Kelly had abandoned as Kelly came out of the kitchen armed with plates and silverware. Moments later a picnic dinner was spread across the coffee table, all three of them ladening their plates.

"Eat fast," Dickon suggested. "I got sopapillas but they get tough as they cool."

"We can soften them up again with honey and ice cream. Except I think I only have chocolate." Kelly frowned toward the kitchen and Lara made a dismissive noise around her first bite of tamale.

"I'm too hungry to eat slowly anyway. I'm sure I can get to the sopapillas before they're cold." For a few minutes they were silent, eating quickly, and Lara finally gave a sigh of contentment as she took a couple of still-warm pastries. "Okay, Dickon. Tell me six things about yourself, and make two of them lies."

He blinked at her, then took an overly large swallow of soda. "Um. Okay. My name is Dickon Edward Collins, I'm thirty-two, um, I drive a Harley, my mom was born in Scotland, I went to film school in Manchester, that's where I met David, and I'm nuts about your best friend. How many was that?"

"Seven. And you don't drive a Harley and your mother wasn't born in Scotland." Lara grinned as he straightened and looked suspiciously between her and Kelly.

"Kel could have told you either of those things. And you've been in my Bronco, so you knew I didn't drive a Harley."

"But I didn't! And you do have a Yamaha," Kelly pointed out. "Which I never told her."

"Try me again," Lara said. "I know Kelly's told you about my truthseeking ability. Try something Kelly doesn't know or wouldn't have any reason to tell me."

"I broke both my legs jumping out of a tree when I was seven."

Mistruth jangled across Lara's nerves, the same uncomfortable wrongness Dafydd's Americanized name had produced, though much less intense. "Part of that isn't true."

Curiosity turned up the corner of Dickon's mouth. "I broke both my legs."

"True."

"I broke both my legs jumping out of a tree."

"True. But you weren't seven."

He laughed. "I was six. My brother was supposed to catch me. I think he got in more trouble than I did, but I paid for it. I spent the whole summer sweating in a cast. Oh my God, it itched. Okay, how about this: I met the Dalai Lama once."

Kelly's jaw dropped. "You did?" Her gaze snapped to Lara, whose eyebrows went up.

"He did."

Kelly smacked Dickon's shoulder. "How come you never told me that?"

"It never came up in conversation! I mean, you want to talk about name dropping to impress a girl? I don't think so. It was at a peace conference in New York a while ago. I was part of a film crew. He was just like people say he is. Serene, happy, compassionate. He was amazing. That was pretty cool. Okay," he said to Lara. "I still think Kelly could have told you most of that, or you could even have found out about me meeting the Dalai Lama online, but I don't know why you'd look. So okay, we'll say I believe you always know when people are telling the truth, and that you don't lie because it bugs you."

"Gee, thanks," Kelly said sardonically, voicing what Lara would never have said aloud. She laughed, though, and said to Kelly, "This must be why I don't *tell* people about the truthseeking."

Kelly sniffed. "Some of us are clever enough to notice it on our own."

"Some of you have known Lara for years," Dickon said. "This is only the fourth time I've met her."

"And you hardly believe me, which I understand. It does mean you're almost certainly not going to believe where I've been, but I think you should be told anyway."

"I'm all ears."

Lara felt a pained expression cross her face, and Kelly picked up the laughter Lara'd given in to a moment earlier. "You can't say things like that around Lara, Dickon. Now she's imagining you as a great big pair of Dumbo ears."

"More like hundreds of little pairs of ears, like butterflies, but close enough," Lara admitted. "Dickon, do you remember asking if Dafydd had asked me to run away with him?"

"Yeaaaah . . ."

"He actually asked me to go home with him, and I did." Lara set her untouched sopapillas aside, gathering herself for Dickon's disbelief. "And as far as I'm concerned, only a day passed. Rachel and Sharon moved last Saturday, in my calendar. I met you and Dafydd a week ago."

"You went to Wales and think you came back again in a day? What the hell happened, were you in a coma?"

"No." Lara shrugged, vividly aware there was no way she could couch the truth to make it palatable. "Dafydd's not Welsh. He's from a place called Annwn, and to us it's a fairyland. He took me there, and was thrown back here without me. I had to make my own way back, which we think is why I got thrown out of time."

Dickon stared at her a long time, expression so smooth it seemed like a falsehood in and of itself. Finally he said, "Kelly, can I talk to you?" and got up, leaving Kelly to look helplessly between him and Lara as he headed for the apartment door. Lara nodded, wincing at the idea she was giving Kelly permission to follow him. But it released Kelly from her place on the couch, and a few seconds later the door closed behind them. Tense, sharp voices came through, though the words were indistinguishable. After less than a minute Lara got up to clear the coffee table and clean the kitchen, glad of any kind of physical activity that would let her escape the semi-audible conversation.

Kelly banged back in several minutes later, took a look at the sopapillas Lara had reheated, and got a plateful for herself. She doused them liberally with chocolate ice cream and honey and stuffed most of one into her mouth before saying, "He's gone home. He thinks you belong in a mental hospital."

An out-of-place bloom of cheer rushed through Lara. "I suppose at least that tells us exactly how people would react if I told the truth. That's something."

"No, I mean it, Lara, he actually literally thinks you need mental help. He's sure something so traumatic has happened to you tha—"

"I believe you, Kelly." The good humor remained intact, a sense of the absurd so profound it couldn't be shaken. "As long as he's not calling the paramedics it's fine. And if he does, I'll be obliging and check myself in to whatever mental hospital they want me to."

Kelly choked on a bite of pastry. "Why would you do that?"

"Because if you voluntarily enter a mental health institute you can voluntarily exit, and they can't stop you," Lara said cheerfully. "Kelly, he was always going to think I was crazy, and we both knew it. I'll find a hotel or stay with my mom if he's worried I might be dangerous to you."

"I don't think that occurred to him." Kelly slumped against the counter. "I don't know, Lar. I thought he might just . . ."

"Accept it?" Lara shook her head, oddly relaxed. She'd spent a lifetime trying to avoid situations like this one, but in finally facing it, it was less distressing than she'd imagined. Maybe it was the confidence that had burgeoned while she was in the Barrow-lands, or it might simply have been a sign of maturity, both in herself and her gift. "You said yourself if you didn't know me you wouldn't believe it. I'm not even sure you do believe me, exactly. You just don't quite *dis*believe me."

Kelly looked guilty. "Your mom believes you."

"My mom had to deal with me being hysterical over the Tooth Fairy, Kel. From where she stands, if I come home believing a story about fairyland, it's not possible I'm lying. We're just going to have to get Dafydd out of jail so he can show Dickon the truth."

"Do you think that'll help?"

Lara caught her breath, searching for a true answer, and finally shook her head. "I really don't know. Dickon's worried, right? Not angry? So maybe if we can prove I'm not lying it'll assuage his worry. Is he worried about *you*, Kelly? I mean, you believe me. Enough to be participating in what he must see as a farce, anyway."

"He thinks I shouldn't be encouraging your delusions. Me! Do I seem like an encouraging-delusions sort of person?" Kelly eyed Lara. "Don't answer that."

"You seem very straightforward, Kel. That's part of why I'm able to be friends with you. What did you tell him?"

"That I didn't think you were deluded, obviously. I don't know, maybe I should have lied. Maybe I should've said I thought it was better to let you stay in your bizarre little comfort zone for a while. That maybe when you got used to being home you'd be able to shake it off and deal with what really happened. And I can't believe I'm telling a truthseeker I think I should have lied."

"Believe it, because you are. What's more unlikely is I think you're probably right." Lara turned a hand up as Kelly blinked at her incredulously. "I don't want him to be upset with you, Kelly. Maybe you should call him tomorrow and say you think he's probably right, you're just so used to me telling the truth you couldn't wrap your mind around me lying."

"And when David turns out to be an elf and you were in fairyland?"

"Then you can refrain from saying 'I told you so.'"

"Lara Jansen, I do believe you've lost your mind."

"See?" Lara, grinning, turned her attention back to the cooling sopapillas. "You and Dickon *are* on the same page."

Twenty-Three

"When in doubt, go to an expert." The platitude, murmured under her breath, had a ring of truth to it. At Kelly's suggestion Lara had begun an Internet search for mythological weapons. Within minutes she'd found herself lost in a maze of fictional weapons from online role-playing games. Living, breathing humans, she'd decided, were likely to be much more helpful, and she'd borrowed Kelly's car again to make the journey up to Cambridge.

The building that housed Harvard's Celtic Studies Department was a beautiful old pillared home. Lara peered at it through the Nissan's windshield, wondering if she would be able to hold a discussion about legendary weapons without compromising her truth sense, then shrugged. She would certainly never find out sitting in the parking lot. A sense of propriety made her knock on the building's front door, though she let herself in immediately.

A young woman with her hair in a ponytail blinked up from where she sat reading on a comfortable-looking couch. "Hello?"

"Hi. My name's Lara Jansen. I'm here to see . . ." Lara hesitated, unwilling to even attempt the jumble of letters that made up the director's name. She glanced at the office listings instead, where "Pádraig hÉamhthaigh" was emblazoned in the leading slot.

A sympathetic grin flashed over the girl's face. "It's pronounced 'Heafy,' if you can believe it. Pawrick Heafy, pretty much. He's from Ireland himself, from one of the areas called the Gaeltacht, where people still speak the old language as a matter of course. I think he keeps the Irish spelling just to make people panic when they see his name written down." She got to her feet as she spoke and led Lara to the converted house's upstairs, where she knocked solidly on a closed door. "Professor Heafy, Lara Jansen's here to see you."

The door swung open a few seconds later to reveal a slender older man with a beaky nose and thick white hair. "So she is. Have you finished that translation yet, Alison?"

The girl waved the book she'd been reading. "Still working on it. It'll be done by week's end."

"*Which* week's end?" the professor asked drily, and Alison grinned as she scurried back downstairs. "Well, come in, Miss Jansen. You're the young woman who went missing in Boston, are you not?"

Lara tried not to wince at the recognition as she followed Heafy into his office. "I am."

"And you returned with an abiding interest in Celtic folklore. I suppose you won't be telling me how that came about." He gestured to a well-worn leather chair, its arms and seat alternately shining and dull with use, and sat down on the other side of his desk. Lara spent a few seconds studying a wall of haphazardly arranged books, then shook herself and offered the professor a brief smile.

"I was exposed to some while I was gone. I have a lot of questions, Professor, and I think some of them are probably a little strange." Music chimed disapprovingly, and she made a face. "Maybe very strange. Do you know anything about a place called Annwn?"

Heafy's eyebrows elevated. "The Welsh land of eternal youth, sometimes called the Deep or Drowned Lands. The underworld, or fairyland, if you like. There are an infinite number of interpretations."

Notes jangled again and Lara ducked her head, trying to dismiss the exaggeration of infinite interpretations. "How did they drown?"

"Ah, sure and you'd ask me that." Heafy got up and pulled a book off the shelves, though he didn't appear to read anything from it as he flipped through its pages. "One legend says a priestess of a fairy well let it overflow. Another says the man sent to guard the dikes was a drunkard and in his spirits left the sluices open. Here, this is a grand version of the story."

Lara jolted to her feet as he offered her the book, and glanced through its pages. "Um. I'm sorry. I don't read French."

"Oh." Heafy took the book back, examined it curiously, then returned it to the shelves. "I didn't notice it was in French. That version tells how the drunkard seduced the priestess and that was why she let the well overflow. In all likelihood, of course, it was only the end of a miniature ice age, and the sea level simply rose."

Lara sat back down with a sigh. "So there are no stories of magical weapons that broke the land?"

"That's more an Arthurian kind of tale." Heafy returned to his own seat, looking thoughtful. "The Arthurian legends come out of Wales, mind, so I can see tangling the two. A sword, I suppose, would be what you're after?"

"Not Excalibur." Lara smiled faintly. "No, I was told about a weapon that might have been lost. Something with the power to drown the land and subjugate a people, maybe."

"Excalibur would have been lost and found and lost again, to be sure, but its mythology is more to unite a land and free a people, wouldn't you say? No, tell me more, me love, if you know it. Perhaps you'll shake something loose in this old mind of mine."

"I don't know very much else about this version. There are two rival kings, Emyr and Hafgan—"

"Now Hafgan was a king of Annwn, that I know," Heafy interrupted. "Emyr's not a name I'm familiar with."

Breath knocked out of Lara's chest like she'd been hit. "That's interesting," she murmured, the phrase so inadequate as to send dissonant chimes over her skin. "They fought, and the lands were drowned, and this legend says the power behind the drowning was a weapon. Legend says the weapon was cast out of Annwn after that, because it might have the power to heal the land, too, and the victorious king, Emyr, didn't want that."

Heafy's eyes were bright. "It's not a tale I know, but it has the hall-marks of proper mythology. Who did you have it from?"

Lara exhaled again, as sharply as before. She had managed to skirt lies succesfully so far, but the direct question was hard to avoid. Harder, when Ioan, who had told her the story, was unlikely to be a name to trigger mythological memories. Finally, jaw set against the jarring dissonance of a flat-out lie, she said, "A man called Oisín."

Heafy leapt to his feet again, eagerly sorting through books. "Oisín the poet. Plenty of lads today carry that name, but I give yours credit for telling a good tale. The first Oisín, though, now there's a story I know well, and that reminds me of something. He was an Irish poet stolen away by the fairy queen Níamh—"

"Her name was Rhiannon, I think, in this version."

"Ah, Rhiannon of the white horse, that's all and well, too. Stolen away and when he returned thinking only three years had passed, three hundred had gone by in Ireland. He returned to Tir na nÓg, that'll be the Irish name for Annwn, or close enough, to live out his days, but there's a story I have here, me love, that tells of his second return to Ireland."

"He only—" Lara bit her tongue. Oisín had only told her of one time he'd returned home, which didn't mean that had been the only time he'd gone. "When did he come back the second time?"

"Upon Níamh's death." Heafy seized a book from the shelves, flipped it open, and plunked it triumphantly on the desk in front of her. "It's a favorite story of mine, crossing two great legends of Irish mythology as it does. Do you know of Saint Brendan?"

"The one who crossed the Atlantic in a leather boat?" The last word turned into a squeak and Lara leaned forward to study the book. This one, at least, was written in English, but Heafy spoke more quickly than she could read.

"That's right, searching for the Isle of the Blessed. There's more than one tradition, me love, where that might mean Annwn or Tir na nÓg itself. Now why, I ask meself, would a Christian priest monk be searching for the fairylands? There are stories that say an angel sent him sailing as punishment for disbelieving the word of God, but a prophet and an angel might be thought the same."

"And Oisín was a prophet," Lara murmured.

Heafy beamed at her. "Just so. A prophet from the land of youth. Now doesn't that sound a wee bit like an angel from Heaven to you? Sending a holy man on a holy quest? But here's my thought: maybe it's not *to* fairyland, but far *from* it that Oisín sent our man Brendan."

Lara flattened her fingers against the book, though she was watching the professor. "Away from Annwn with the weapon that nearly destroyed it."

"And Brendan," Heafy said gleefully, "came to America."

Lara laughed out loud. "Would you happen to know where he hid the weapon?"

"Ah." Heafy sat down, as suddenly defeated as he'd been exultant. "I've never thought to sort that, no. You'd have to speak with one of my colleagues in the Native American Studies Department, perhaps. I can ring them up and make an appointment for you, if you like?"

"That would be great. Thank you."

Heafy nodded and dug out a phone directory from within his desk, muttering and flipping pages until he found what he was after. He lifted a finger to admonish Lara to wait a moment as he dialed, then was clearly transferred twice before getting to the person he wanted. Lara's search was explained in a few quick sentences, before his eyebrows rose and he offered the phone to Lara. "Professor Cassidy wants to speak with you."

Lara lifted her own eyebrows, but accepted the phone curiously. "This is Lara Jansen."

"Hi, Miss Jansen. I'm Ellen Cassidy, one of the department heads. Look, I don't want to waste your time, so if you're trying to find pre-Columbian contact in the Americas, you're going to want to go to Canada. The Viking settlements and trade agreements there are the only halfway verifiable data we've got, and that doesn't go nearly as far back as Brendan's legendary voyage. I'm really sorry, but we've heard this all before and it's just got no basis in reality. I wish people could accept that the Native American cultures were entirely capable of complex societies and interactions without European interference."

Uncertain notes trembled under Lara's skin, finding issue with some aspect of Cassidy's rant, but she nodded into the phone anyway. "I understand. Thank you for your time, Professor." Lips pursed, she handed the phone back to Heafy, then smiled wryly. "I hit a sore spot there, I think. I didn't mean to imply native cultures were in need of Western guidance."

"Perhaps you can find someone else more willing to talk mythological theory," Heafy said with a smile. "I'm afraid it's back to work for me, me love, unless there's something else I can do for you?"

"I don't think so. Thank you very much, Professor. This was more helpful than I expected." Lara took her leave, Cassidy's words still buzzing in her ears. A phrase stood out: *it's just got no basis in reality*. That was opinion, Lara realized. Informed opinion, no doubt, but as with any facts from a prewriting society, it was at best an inference, a leap of logic. It was no more certain to be possible Brendan *hadn't* made it to America than it was to be sure he had.

And her immature truthseeking talent, only a matter of days ago, would have taken Cassidy's firmly believed opinion as gospel truth. Lara climbed into the Nissan and sat there awhile, staring sightlessly through the windshield. The magic was strengthening. Eventually she might be able to do as she'd always thought would be helpful: *know* the truth even when someone told her its exact opposite with their full confidence behind the telling. For now, though, the sour notes suggested there was still a path to be followed.

Her heart suddenly quick with anticipation, she turned the Nissan on and headed back to Boston. The research she needed to do now could be done in a library, free of most slants of human prejudice.

"Do you have any idea how many sacred Native American sites there are just in New England?" Lara dropped an inch-thick stack of photocopies on Kelly's kitchen table and put her fists on her hips, as if explosive actions would cause Kelly to have the answers.

She didn't. Instead she eyed the papers, then Lara, then went to stir the macaroni and cheese cooking on the stove. "Not a clue. Are you going to drive around to all of them and see if any of them sing to you?"

"I hope not." Lara sat down and flipped through her stack of papers. "I narrowed it down to places on or near rivers, for right now. Brendan came back from his Atlantic journey, so I'm working on the idea he never abandoned his boat anywhere."

"And that doesn't make you itch?" Kelly waved the macaroni spoon as Lara frowned at her. "You usually look like somebody dumped itching powder on you when you hear lies. So I figure a badly wrong theory would make you twitchy."

"I'm counting on the idea that it would." Lara held her breath, looking at the papers again. "This is over my head, Kelly. I've never tried using this power to discern before. What if I can't?"

"Then Annwn's screwed," Kelly said helpfully. "'Spoken in a child's word,' Lar. Your superpowers are just starting to mature. Maybe you'll be surprised what happens if you push them a little."

"It's not a superpower."

"It totally is. It's not quite as good as Wonder Woman's golden lasso, but that's only because a little bit of bondage can be fun. You're totally a superhero, and you're going to save the world."

"The horrifying thing is you believe every word you just said."

Kelly grinned as she poured mac and cheese onto plates. "Look, if I can't be a superhero myself, at least I can be the plucky faithful sidekick. Do you want tartar sauce?"

"With my macaroni and cheese?"

"With the fishsticks I'm about to take out of the oven. Oh, crap, I forgot to make vegetables. I tell you, I should not be let loose in a kitchen. Thank God Dickon can cook."

Lara got up to root through the freezer and came out with a bag of corn. "You make tartar sauce, I'll cook the corn. Vegetables will be accomplished. Did you talk to him?"

"Corn is technically a grain." Kelly laughed as Lara gave her an exasperated look. "You have no idea how much fun that was. All these years of you saying things like that, and now I get to get my own back. I did, yeah." She took the fish out of the oven and slid the sticks onto the plates. "I said what you suggested, that he was probably right but it seemed safer to let you work through it on your own for a while. He was kind of tense, but then we had great makeup sex so I guess it's okay."

"I did not need to know that."

"Oh, but I think you did. Is that enough corn for two people?"

"It'll have to be. It's all you've got." Lara put the pot on to boil and went back to her papers. "I also have this idea that because the weapon was used to drown Annwn it might have an affinity for water. So I think if Brendan brought it here, it would be hidden near a river or lake or something."

"Look at you, Ms. Extrapolatey. Here, let's try something." Kelly came over to pick up the top sheet of paper, then cleared her throat dramatically. "The worldbreaking weapon is hidden at—you actually had to photocopy pages about Niagra Falls? You couldn't have remembered that one?"

"I was being thorough." Lara lost her scowl as Kelly laughed.

"Okay, okay. Ahem. The worldbreaking weapon is hidden at Niagra Falls in upstate New York," she said decisively, then looked hopefully at Lara, who gazed up at her in astonishment.

"That's one of the strangest things I've ever heard. There's no music with it. It's completely neutral, like you don't have any idea of the truth of what you're saying."

"Well, I don't. But damn, I hoped maybe there'd be some kind of inherent truthiness you'd pick up on." Kelly went back to the fridge, taking mayonnaise and pickles out to make tartar sauce.

Lara shook her head. "I guess the power's not that well developed yet. It was a good thought, though. It's okay. I'll just read all of these carefully and see if anything strikes a chord."

"And if it doesn't?"

"I don't know. Maybe that just means this is the wrong way to go about it. I'll keep trying to think of other approaches, too."

"Are you really sure it was only a day, Lara?"

"Of course. Why?" Lara looked up with a frown to see Kelly studying her with an odd expression.

"Because you've always been quiet and shy. The only thing I've ever seen you strongly opinionated and decisive about is clothing. And here you are acting like"—Kelly shrugged a shoulder and smiled— "a superhero."

Lara glanced down again, half wanting to hide herself in the paperwork. "Yeah, I know. It's partly that I was so scared in the Barrow-lands just in those first few minutes, Kel. I had to pretend I was brave so I wouldn't completely fall apart. And then dealing with Emyr, I kept having to stand my ground, and it keeps getting easier."

"Well, that's good. I think that's good. You're going to need all the confidence you can get your hands on when we go to court. In the meantime . . ." Kelly drained the corn and plonked spoonsful onto the plates, then slopped tartar sauce down beside the fishsticks. "In the meantime, a delicious repast prepared by yours truly, and you can spend the next week or two honing your truthseeking skills by finding the worldbreaking weapon."

Twenty-Four

More accurately, it seemed, she could spend the next week or two giving herself headaches trying to find the worldbreaking weapon. It seemed extraordinary that being called into court could be a welcome relief, but Marjorie Oritz's call that Dafydd had been granted a hearing was the first time since she'd come home that Lara felt a surge of real hope.

For a woman who couldn't get taken on for jury duty, she had spent a surprising amount of time in courtrooms recently. One, true enough, had been Emyr's palace court, but if he were to be considered the judge there, he was a far less forgiving one than the woman who presided over Dafydd's reentry hearing. She, at least, had a glint of humor behind her expression of distaste for the array of petitioners gathered in her courtroom.

Lara knew she made a good impression: her boxy-shouldered, short-sleeved dress was of a classic style, popular for its elegance and its practicality in the summer heat. It lent her slight form a degree of determination, making a statement that she wasn't a victim. The judge would very likely see it as just that, but Lara had thought it an important effort to make, regardless.

Dozens of other people were gathered as well. Lara's mother was there, watching Dafydd with an open curiosity that Lara doubted had been present any other time they'd been in each other's company. Kelly was at Gretchen Jansen's side, and Dickon Collins was at Kelly's. Worry niggled at Lara when she glanced Dickon's way: he had tread very lightly around Lara the time or two she'd seen him over the past two weeks. It would take Dafydd to prove herself to Dickon, and whether Dafydd would be willing to do that remained unknown.

Cynthia and Steven Taylor were there as well. Cynthia looked astonishingly adult in tailored gray, while Steve maintained an expression of reassuring calm. Beside them, on the courtroom aisle, sat Detective Reginald Washington, whose off-the-rack suit looked uncomfortably hot and ill-fitted compared to the tailors at his side.

Unexpectedly, parole officer Rich Cooper was also there—though after his comment about being turned inside-out by questioners after her disappearance, Lara supposed she ought to have expected his attendence. She might, after all, let slip some detail of where she'd been, instead of the mysterious refusal to discuss it that she'd left him with.

Dafydd himself looked better than he had in prison. He still had nothing of the vitality Lara was accustomed to seeing in him, but he seemed stronger. His suit had been purchased for him hastily, rather than taken out of storage. Lara breathed a promise to herself that he would soon enough be free, healthy, and returned to the gorgeous clothes of his home court.

Lawyers, security, and a court stenographer were there, but unalarming. It was the reporters gathered in the room who made Lara's heart palpitate with nervousness, and she was grateful there were no cameras allowed within the courtroom itself. The bailiff called for order and the judge leaned forward, elbows on her desk as she brought her forefingers together to point accusingly at Lara.

"I'm given to understand that you're here to petition David Kirwen's return to polite society, young lady."

"Yes, your honor." The title came much more easily to Lara's lips than "your majesty" had, and she schooled her expression, certain that laughter wouldn't stand her well just then. "He didn't kidnap me, and he certainly didn't kill me. There's no reason for him to be incarcerated."

"Yes, so I understand. And yet you've given no one any explanation as to where you were for the past . . ." The judge made a show of tipping her wrist and examining her watch, as if it had a calendar of all the days Lara had been missing. "Seventeen months, three weeks, four days, I believe?"

"Seventeen months, one week, and four days, your honor," Lara said with a touch of asperity. "I've been back two weeks now, after all."

"Don't get hoity with me, young woman. You've cost the state a remarkable amount of money in terms of manhunt hours, nevermind the cost of incarcerating a man you claim has done you no harm. One more remark like that and I'll present you with a bill for our time."

Lara inclined her head sheepishly. "Sorry, your honor."

"As well you should be. Well, Miss Jansen." The judge waited until Lara raised her eyes again, then spoke acerbically. "I'm afraid you're going to have to provide some sort of explanation for disappearing so thoroughly and frightening the wits out of your friends and family. I would be delighted if it encompassed the reasons Mr. Kirwen opted not to speak in his own defense at his indictment, if he's not responsible for your disappearance."

"I didn't say he wasn't. I said he hadn't kidnapped me." Lara reached for the confidence she'd developed over the past weeks, pushing away the embarrassment that had briefly overtaken her. She couldn't afford to be mild, not when she had nothing but unpalatable truth on her side. She had to make them believe, regardless of the cost.

The judge's eyebrows lifted. She glanced from Lara to Dafydd, then turned a thin-lipped, sharp smile back at Lara. "Do go on. We're all abated waiting to hear the details."

"Your honor." Lara took a breath, then steadied her voice as she met the judge's eyes. "Your honor, you wouldn't believe me."

Truth rang through the words, making them sharp enough to cut. Fanciful phrase, Lara thought, but even it had precision to it: it was as though the truth, forced into being spoken aloud, actually made the air clearer, made it ring and shape the world. She heard it, and so, clearly, did the judge, whose face went lax, a telling show of surprise before the muscles around her eyes and mouth tightened again. "Perhaps you'd be so good as to let me be the judge of that, young woman."

Lara swallowed and deliberately opened her hands, refusing to make them fists. It took concentration: everything took concentration, even breathing, but it was only with that effort she felt she could invest her words with truth. And she had to be believed; she, who had spent a lifetime hearing the truth, *had* to make it heard now. Anything else would be insufficient; anything else would lead to Dafydd's exposure, and that was not a risk she was willing to take.

But she could do it. Her talent had stretched well beyond where she'd once imagined its boundaries lay. She remembered the nightwings, destroyed with a prayer, and drew on the strength of belief and voice she'd had then.

"You wouldn't believe the details, your honor. They would make you angry. You would think I mocked you. I wouldn't, and neither would Dafydd if you sent him from this room and heard his side of the story separately, but you would believe we were lying. That we'd practiced it, though you wouldn't be able to figure out when."

The words hurt. They scraped at her skin, exposing muscle, and went deeper, digging for marrow. There was none of the music she associated with telling or hearing truth, but rather a harsh uncomfortable strain to everything. Maybe that was what relentless truth was to other people; at its worst it could be that way for her, too. She wished abruptly she had another way: a translation of truth into song, the way she sometimes heard lyrics on the radio. It still cut deep that way, still hurt, but music tempered truth in a way raw forced words couldn't.

Rustling in the courtroom made her dare a glance over her shoulder. Both policemen wore deep frowns, and the gathered reporters had given up scribbling notes or holding out their recording devices to instead stare uncertainly at Lara. Kelly, sitting beside Lara's mother, had her arms wrapped around herself, face pinched with unhappiness. Gretchen herself wore an expression of terrible sorrow, her gaze on Lara speaking a desire to somehow save her from herself.

"I'll tell you." Lara looked back at the judge, keeping her voice soft. Soft as shark skin, and so razored in its way. "But it will not satisfy you, it will not make you happy, and it will not change the fact that David Kirwen is not a kidnapper, and should be released from jail. I am *sorry*, your honor, but this is not easy on any of us. Please let it end now."

The judge's fingers, once pointed so accusatorily, were now knotted together, less an action of distress than frustrated rage. She wouldn't be accustomed to such flaunting of her authority, and even if she was, she would never have encountered something like Lara's talent. She gathered herself, spitting a question that came forth hoarse, despite the attempted strength behind it: "What are you?"

Lara bowed her head and sighed. Not who, but *what* was she, and there was no satisfactory answer to that. She tried anyway, looking up and speaking as softly as she dared while keeping the truth's razor edge in her voice. "I'm someone who hears truth and lies when people speak to her. And I can make others hear the truth, too, if I have to. Please, your honor. David Kirwen is guilty of no crime. Let him go."

She did, after that. Had him taken away, technically, to fill out paperwork, but the intent was clear: he would be released.

It was also clear almost no one understood why. Kelly did; Gretchen Jansen did. Dafydd ap Caerwyn, of course, did, but the others let their gazes skitter off Lara and shifted away from her if she came too near. Even the reporters backed off, retreating from the courtroom with low-key agreements that they would interview her on the steps outside. It didn't surprise her: Lara felt her own presence and actions like a weight in the courtroom, and was as grateful as they were to escape it.

Kelly was waiting with Gretchen Jansen and Dickon when Lara exited the room. Both women offered hugs, and Lara sighed into her mother's shoulder before turning to face Dickon, searching for something to say.

Detective Washington strode up to them, a step ahead of Officer Cooper, before Lara found a way to break the silence, and did it for her: "What the hell was that?"

"The truth." Her answer was so simple it almost made Lara laugh. Instead she passed a hand over her face, and more quietly, said, "It's what I said in there, Detective. My whole life I've known when people were lying to me. Today I had to make you hear the truth. I'm sorry. I really am."

"You can't make somebody . . ." Washington trailed off unhappily as Lara lifted an eyebrow in challenge. "Excuse my French, Miss Jansen, but that's a load of bullshit."

"Okay." Lara shrugged as discomfort raised the hairs on her arms. Small enough recompense for what she'd put the court through. "Then find an interpretation you can live with, Detective. I told you none of this would make you happy."

"You still haven't told me what happened to you."

Lara looked up at him, studying his dark eyes and the deepening lines around his mouth before she shook her head. "The only way you would believe me would be if I did what I just did in there, Detective. If I made you hear the truth. And I think you hate what just happened, am I right? So maybe you should let it go." She glanced at Cooper, standing silent behind Washington, and sighed. "Both of you. I'm sorry."

"You say that a lot. Do you mean it?"

Kelly gave a sharp, bitter laugh. "Lara never says anything she doesn't mean. Reg, you really wouldn't believe her. Let it go, okay?"

His scowl darkened. "You know where she's been?"

"Yeah. And believe me when I tell you that you'd think she was lying to you. God," she added explosively, turning to Lara. "Is this what your life is like all the time?"

Lara, under her breath, said, "It's not usually this dramatic," but nodded. "With the truth? Yes. It's always complicated."

"I'm sorry for ever giving you shit," Kelly said fervently.

"You're forgiven." Lara caught the hostility on Washington's face and sighed. She'd spent a lifetime with that kind of emotion directed at her, even without forcing people to acknowledge a truth they didn't want to hear. Maybe it was strength to be able to stand in hostility's face, but the idea of its relentless weight never lifting exhausted her.

"Here's our man." Relief swept Dickon's voice. He broke away from the uncomfortable huddle to pound Dafydd on the back. "Good to see you in something other than an orange jumpsuit, man."

"It's good to be in something else. I'd have never admitted it in prison, but they chafe." Dafydd wrinkled his nose delicately, earning a laugh as Dickon released him to the rest of the group.

His mortal glamour slipped and slid in Lara's vision, but she jolted forward to catch him in a hard hug. His arms, at least, felt safe and strong around her, and his breath stirred her hair as he murmured, "Thank you."

She mumbled "You're welcome" into his shoulder. "Thank God. I don't know what I would've done if that judge hadn't agreed to release you." She knew she should let him go, make some effort to smooth things over with Washington, but she remained still, trying to convince herself everything would be all right now.

"You'd have told her the truth." Kelly sounded wry. "And then she would've locked you in a looney bin. David, I owe you an apology."

"Not at all." Dafydd released Lara to shake first Kelly's then Gretchen's hands. "The circumstances were impossible."

"They still are." Distortion crawled across Officer Cooper's face and darkened his eyes. "I want the straight answer."

"To hell with you, man," Dickon said with more conviction than humor. "How about me? Am I ever gonna hear something other than Lara's delusions?" He added, "Sorry," perfunctorily, and Lara ghosted a smile.

"No, you're not. And Dafydd will explain—" She broke off to wait on his approval, then continued at his nod: "But not here, okay, Dickon?"

"You mean not in front of the cops?" Washington's jaw rolled aggressively enough that Dickon stepped forward, pitting himself against the detective. They reminded Lara of gladiators, determined to end—or maybe bring on—a confrontation at any cost. "Right now I don't care if it's on the record or off, Miss Jansen. I just want answers."

Dafydd exhaled loudly. "At the very least I think we should extract ourselves from these surrounds before arguing about it. Perhaps if we retired somewhere more private?"

"Well, we can't take the elevator down to the parking garage," Kelly said. "There are about a million—" She broke off, looked at Lara, and said, "About twenty reporters waiting around it. Is there a way we can sneak out without being seen?"

Her no-nonsense tone coupled with the effort to be literal sparked Lara's amusement. Washington, looking both irritated and accepting, gestured them toward a hall. "I can walk you out the same way they brought Kirwen in."

"I'll use the public elevator," Gretchen said unexpectedly. "The press know who I am. They'll be happy to get a statement from me, if they can't have one from Lara and Dafydd." She embraced Lara, gave Dafydd a brief smile, and hurried toward the elevators.

Dafydd watched her go, then turned to Lara with a bemused expression. "I'd hardly think I deserved that from her."

Lara shrugged and took his hand. "I told her the truth. She believed me. So she has no reason to blame you for anything."

"Even so," Dafydd murmured, then nodded as Washington gestured impatiently down the hall.

Silence fell over the little group as they hurried for the cavernous concrete lot beneath the court building. Half a dozen police cars were parked in the area they entered, and Washington slowed before reaching the floor-to-ceiling fence that barricaded the police area off from the rest of the lot. "I don't suppose this is private enough for your little discussion."

"Sorry." Lara glanced upward at the security cameras. "I'd rather not be someplace where there's surveillance."

Exasperation flashed over Washington's features. Lara imagined he thought her paranoid, but Dafydd's safety was worth that. Cooper, trailing along behind, muttered "Give me a break" as Washington waved a keycard at the gates and they began rattling open.

"We'll go back to my place," Kelly said. "I'll get my car, and, I don't know, Reg, can you take a police vehicle? There's not enough room in the Nissan."

"We'll manage. Go on." He waved at the doors.

Dafydd, at Lara's side, stiffened. She turned a worried glance on him as warning widened his eyes and caught an alarmed sound in his throat.

And then it was too late, as concrete walls and massive pillars rended with magic that let nightwings pour through the gaps.

Twenty-Five

"Down! Down! *Down!*" Lara tackled Kelly, laying her out on the concrete. Kelly screamed, more surprise than fear, and Lara rolled off her, reaching for Dickon's hip. "Get *down!*"

She suspected it was instinct rather than her orders that made him duck as winged blackness shrieked and flew at his head, but the effect was the same. Lara grabbed a fistful of his shirt and let her body become deadweight, dragging him further down. "Keep Kelly safe! Don't fight them!" The command and confidence in her voice were alien to her, but Dickon responded, flattening himself above Kelly, whose eyes rounded with outrage as Lara scrambled to her feet.

For an instant she saw everything as though it had been flash-frozen, an indelible image stamped in her mind. The glamour that made Dafydd appear human was gone, and a scattering of objects lay around his feet: loose change, his belt, a ring. No doubt his earrings lay somewhere on the concrete, too small to see as lightning shattered from his fingertips and threw the garage into stark relief. Against that inversion, gunfire flashed repeatedly.

Nightwings squealed, ripped apart by lightning, thrown back by bullets. It seemed ludicrous that human weapons could damage the nightmare creatures, but Lara was glad they did; glad that Washington, whose eyes were as round as Kelly's, had the nerve to stand his ground and fire into the seething blackness over and over again. She glanced around wildly for Rich Cooper and found him at the open gate, his own duty weapon flashing gunshots into the mass of nightwings.

Some kind of distortion altered the appearance of the nightwings. A shadow, a ghost, nothing more: if Lara looked straight on she couldn't see the wrongness at all. A part of her was ready to look away, so she might pretend the nightwings hadn't followed them at all.

But fury bubbled up: fury that they *had* been followed, fury that her friends were in danger, fury that someone was trying to kill her to hide the truth of an investigation she'd promised to see through to its end. That anger wouldn't let her look away, not even to study their ruined shapes—though with monsters scattering around them, anywhere she *did* look let their broken forms tease at the corners of her eyes.

Lightning and gunfire erupted again, reminding her sharply that she had a weapon of her own to use. She flung her hands up, as dramatic a gesture as Dafydd used, and threw familiar words at the nightwings: "I exorcise thee, unholy spirit, in the name of the Father, and of the Son, and of the Holy Spirit!"

The black-winged creatures nearest to her flinched, then surged forward, swarming her. Kelly screamed again as Lara went down beneath a rush of nightwings, too astonished for fear. She knew nothing about fighting: it was an instinct for survival that straight-armed a fist into one of the monster's throats. That had more effect than the exorcism had. The thing fell back, clawing and coughing as if it were a mortal beast instead of a magical horror.

"Your world!" Dafydd bellowed, and light blew through the words, illuminating their meaning to far beyond their simple content.

In *his* world, calling on the trinity of her faith was a spell of significant power: the godless Barrow-lands were vulnerable to it. In *hers,* a world of many gods and faiths, the simple exorcism she'd called on was only the beginning of a ritual that could banish demons. "But I don't know the longer version!"

Dafydd was there, cutting through nightwings with a blade of electricity in one hand and offering help up with the other. Lara seized his hand and flew to her feet. For the space of a breath they were nose to nose, and Dafydd's voice was quiet under the screams of monsters and mortals alike: "Call on the heart of your magic. Nightwings fail before the light."

"I don't know how," Lara whispered, but he was gone, pulling lightning from the air and wielding it with faultless precision. It had to exhaust him, Lara realized abruptly: his magic wasn't natural to her world, forcing him to fight against the same faith and laws that had weakened her attempted exorcism.

But the nightwings still drew power from the Barrow-lands, its magic feeding their strength as much as the bleak riders on their backs pushing them forward. Lara could see it in scatter-shot glimpses, truth ringing short sharp chimes in her head.

The heart of her magic was the music of truth. She had wished, earlier, for a way to couch harsh words in softening song, and it suddenly seemed a viable path. She dropped to her knees—making herself a smaller target, putting herself in a position of prayer—and began to sing, a thin weak version of the only song she could think of.

"Amazing grace, how sweet the sound, that saved a wretch like me . . ." In the space of a breath Lara whispered, "Kelly, I need help. I need faith."

Kelly's screams broke off, replaced by astonishment. "You know I don't believe in God."

Forget God! Lara wanted to shout. *Believe in* me*!* But there was no time: she sang the next words, still struggling to put power behind them. "I once was lost, but now am found . . ."

Big hands folded over hers. Lara's eyes popped open and Dickon gave her an embarrassed smile. His baritone, though, was deep and powerful, lending strength to Lara's voice as they sang, " . . . was blind, but now I see."

The nightwings etched into brilliant white light, coming vividly clear in Lara's gaze. They were warped: that was the impression of riders she'd glimpsed. The creatures she'd encountered in the Barrow-lands were sleek killing machines: these leeched back to the breach between the worlds, as if the Barrow-lands pulled them back. They became more ephemeral the farther they were from the split, though the leaders still struck with vicious, painful attacks.

Lara lurched to her feet, forgetting the words to the hymn herself, but Dickon continued to sing, strong and certain. A second voice joined in over the rupture of gunshots: Washington, singing harmony to Dickon's melody, their voices entwining like they'd practiced in choir a hundred times.

Buoyed by the song, by the tones that rang through it—not just what they sang, but the passion and conviction beneath it—Lara walked forward, eyes on the rip in the air. The bleached-out night-wings shrieked and wheeled to escape her, as if her presence was anathema to them. Some drove back through the black tear, but more simply scattered, tearing away from the hole that dragged them back. Those who escaped it snapped into the sleeker shape she'd seen in the Barrow-lands and winged forward, skreeing tri-umph. Where they broke free, the breach bled thick black ichor that spat and sizzled when it hit the concrete floor.

Power leaped in Lara as she stared at the rip, chimes ringing with such violence there could be no music to it. It grew worse as she lifted a hand, bringing it nearer still to the rip.

The raging bells told her the doorway wasn't *true* in the way an arrow might not be true: it was warped, a thing not meant to be. That was what the worldwalking spell did, created a mistake be-tween two disparate lands that allowed them, briefly, to touch. It could be set right, the magic undone, closed off again, by one who understood the inherent untruth of its making.

Lara put her hand over the tear in the world, drew breath, and sang it closed.

Power rushed out of her, clashing bells turning by slow degrees to chords, then to single notes, and finally to a thin sweet sound of purity as the gash shriveled and shrank to nothing beneath her palm. Lara sagged against a concrete pillar, dizzy with exhaustion as she tried to focus on the fight.

Dickon's song stopped, his jaw fallen open as he knelt where Lara had left him. Kelly was crouched a few feet away, knees drawn up so she could just barely see over them. She'd never begun screaming again, though her eyes looked like she still might decide to.

Dafydd and Washington stood between Lara and her friends, each fighting in their own way. The attacking nightwings paled as Lara watched, turning gray with the sudden break in the link to the Barrow-lands. Dafydd roared triumph, lightning cracking from his hands to destroy dozens of the creatures at once. The survivors screeched, making a flurry around Dafydd and falling back again as fresh electricity snapped around him.

Under the sound of wings, of screams, of lightning leashed, a familiar click rang loud in Lara's ears. Familiar, but only from film; a quiet sound, something she shouldn't have been able to hear in the noise. The sound of a gun chamber coming up empty, no bullet to fire.

Lara screamed, much too late. The nightwings wheeled away from Dafydd and descended on Washington as if they sensed his vulnerability. Dafydd bellowed and spread his hands, but this time no lightning came, nothing to tear black beasts away from the detective's fighting form. Claws dug into his flesh, the nightwings struggling to steal him as they fled.

His weight proved too much: almost as one, they dropped him, one straggler with tangled claws crashing to the concrete with him as he fell. Kelly screamed this time; Lara's hands were fisted against her mouth, cutting off any sound.

She could not, from the small distance, see if the detective still breathed. Gashes and punctures tore his body, made a red bleeding mess of his clothes, and his eyes were open, staring at the ceiling, mouth pulled in a rictus of pain.

The nightwings grew increasingly pale as they spun together, their amorphous mass darting from one exhausted form to another. Kelly shrieked and slashed at their cloud as they came toward her, but Dafydd threw lightning and they retreated with a howl. A funnel formed, rushing the sole open path in the garage.

Rich Cooper stood in the gates, duty weapon still lifted but emptied of rounds, and had no chance at all as the nightwings slammed into his chest, and disappeared.

The silence left in the wake of their screams was astonishing. Cooper broke it with a faint sick sound, fingers plastered against his chest as though he could find, or draw out, what had entered him. Then he snarled; a feral expression that showed too-long teeth and nightwing-dark eyes before he flung his gun away and ran.

Lara managed one step after him, then caught herself on the pillar again, utterly drained of energy. The door she'd torn to return home hadn't exhausted her as much as closing this one had. But then, the Barrow-lands were meant for working magic in. Earth was not, and she paid the price for that.

They *all* paid the price for that. Dafydd took a step forward, staring down at Washington and drawing all their gazes. Lara, abruptly, saw what Dickon and Kelly must see: a slim form, alien with arrogance. The angular lines of his face, the inhuman slant to his eyes and the upsweep of exposed ears, were all pronounced as he looked down an aquiline nose at the detective as if he was an inexplicable thing, lying there bleeding as he did.

"I have no talent for healing others," he said. It sounded absurd in the aftermath of the fight, Lara thought; absurd in the face of his elfin form. Anything that looked like that should command magic as easily as breathing; he *should* be able to heal a wounded man. And he knelt, as though he'd try.

"You can't." Lara barely knew her own strained voice. "I'm so sorry, but you can't. I did it, Dafydd. I broke the world."

"Broke?" Dafydd looked up, expression drained by incomprehension.

Lara put her hand against the pillar for support. "The worldwalking spell, it's bad for the Barrow-lands. I could feel it, and when I closed it . . . 'changes that will break the world,'" she reminded him. "I think I closed it for good. You saw what happened to the nightwings, how they went gray when the door closed. They were cut off from the magic, and so are you. And you said they're creations," she whispered. "They don't have magic, energy, of their own. I think that's why they went into Cooper, so they had sustenance. I'm sorry, Dafydd. I think you're stuck here, and all the power you've got left is what's inside you."

Kelly crawled to Washington and put her hand against his chest, then whispered, "He's still breathing." She glanced at Dafydd, flinched, and looked away. Injury flashed across his face and sympathy surged through Lara. He had saved them all with his magic, and it was neither fair nor surprising that Kelly should look away.

Especially given that Lara's blurred vision had disappeared. "The glamour, Dafydd. It's gone."

His hands were always long-fingered, elegant, but his gaze snapped to them, and then he lifted his hands to his ears, tracing their elfin shape with clear shock. Lara shook her head. "It fell away as soon as the fight started. And I don't think you're going to be able to put it back now."

"I had to get rid of the earrings to call the lightning. But the glamour should have stayed—"

"Dafydd, you're not strong, you know that. Being in jail did something to you, you haven't looked right—"

"This is all very touching," Kelly said through her teeth, "but we have to go. We have to go right now, Lara. We have to leave Reg." She got to her feet, face tight with determination as she pulled keys from her pocket.

Lara, gaping, turned her attention to Kelly, and Dafydd staggered as though only her gaze had kept him in place. Kelly, despite her earlier flinch, caught Dafydd with an arm around his waist. "There were gunshots. There'll be cops here inside another thirty seconds. We have to go right now."

"Kelly, are you nuts?" Dickon sounded thunderstruck.

Kelly propelled Dafydd away from Washington, driving him toward the gated doors even as she answered Dickon. "Do you see any choice? How are you going to explain what happened to Reg? How are you going to explain what David looks like? We have to go. Cops'll take care of Reg, but we cannot be here."

"It's too late," Lara whispered. "I hear them."

Fear so potent it became fury filled Kelly's eyes. She pushed Dafydd off her and caught his shirt in both fists. "Lara told me everything about you. You've been here a hundred years. What do you think happens if the cops find you, *Dafydd ap Caerwyn*? What do you think happens?"

"I die," he said in a remarkably clear voice. "If I'm lucky, I die quickly."

Lara let go a low cry of dismay, but Kelly snapped a nod, then pointed toward voices and lights that were now coming close. "You have about fifteen seconds, and that glamour trick you do is going to have to hide all of us. Do it. Do it *now*."

"He can't! Kelly, he'll—"

"Die?" Kelly shouted. "Maybe, but if he doesn't try we're all going to jail and he's going to be the most exciting lab rat anybody's ever seen! Lara, you know I'm right, we can't be found here!"

Dafydd whispered, "She's right," and wrapped them all in magic.

The world went wrong.

The double vision of Dafydd's glamour, worked on himself, had nothing on the way the parking garage folded in on itself as magic swept over them. The air turned red and twisted around, smearing the garage's contents into a shattering landscape. The usual unending song of truth became knife stabs of piercing noise, short and sharp. Even Dickon and Kelly were horrible to look at, bleeding pieces of themselves into the concrete.

Dafydd, though, was worse. If she saw any truth at all with his magic surrounding them, it was *his* truth, and that was a story of agony. Power sheeted off him, weakening him with every heartbeat: in very little time, he would be unable to recover, but he would die, if necessary, to get them to safety.

"Quick," Lara grated, and the sound made her stomach turn, distorted by the veil of falsehood Dafydd held around them. She caught his arm, supporting him as they ran for Kelly's car.

He arched in agony as Kelly yanked the Nissan's front door open and propelled him inside. Silent agony: whether he had the presence of mind to stay quiet, or simply hurt too much to give it voice, Lara didn't know. She ran to the driver's side, climbing into the backseat beside a whey-faced Dickon, and Kelly took them out of the garage under cover of magic before snapping, "You can let it go."

Dafydd jerked violently, then collapsed, and the ear-bleeding madness of the world faded. Lara whimpered, then bit her knuckles to calm herself, and reached forward to tug Dafydd's seat belt around him. It would be foolish to let a detail so small give the police an opportunity to stop them.

"Straighten him up, too," Kelly said in the same short tone. "Can you reach the glove compartment? There are sunglasses in there. I don't know what to do about his ears, I don't have a baseball cap with me."

"Some people's ears point," Lara whispered. Kelly gave her a sharp look in the rearview mirror, then nodded, allowing Lara her illusion. It was true: some people's ears did point, but not usually with the fine-tipped delicacy Dafydd's did. She got the sunglasses out and fitted them over Dafydd's face.

Kelly made a satisfied sound. "All right. I'm stopping at my bank to withdraw as much cash as I can before they put a lock on any of our accounts or a trace on the cards. Dickon, we're going to have to abandon our cell phones, and thank God you thought the ten-year-old Nissan was a good bet at that car lot, Lar, because that means it hasn't got GPS installed."

Lara's voice cracked. "Get rid of the cell ph— Kelly, when did you turn into an undercover sleuth? This is insane."

Kelly scowled at her in the mirror. "We just ran away from a crime scene, Lara. One where, if we're really, really lucky, there's a police detective who's only dying instead of dead. The cops are going to come together to find us, and being incredibly easy to track is a price tag of modern society. I'd get rid of the car if I knew another one I could get to, one that wasn't associated with any of us."

"I have one." Dafydd sounded as though someone had taken razors to his throat, cutting his speech to a rough whisper. "Up north, in Peabody. If we can get out of Boston . . ."

"You're sure?" Kelly asked sharply. "It's not registered in your name?"

Dafydd chuckled, low raw sound. "I've been doing this for a hundred years, Miss Richards. I'm sure."

"This is fucked up," Dickon said abruptly. "Kelly, I can't do this. Stop the car."

Twenty-Six

"Dickon . . ." Lara spoke at the same time Kelly did, then bit her lip. She barely knew Kelly's fiancé, and was all too aware of how little he'd been told over the past weeks.

"Dickon," Kelly said again. Her knuckles were white around the steering wheel, jaw tense in the rearview mirror's reflection as she met Dickon's eyes there. "Please don't. Let us just get out of town first, okay? So we can talk?"

Dickon raised his hands like he was blocking a physical assault. "We went way past talking about it already. I don't know what the hell David is, I don't know what the hell Lara is, but Washington's probably dead because goddamned *monsters* attacked us, and I *can't handle that.*"

"If you can just let David explain—!"

"Explain what? That Lara really was in some kind of fucking fairyland? That my best bud for the past five years is some kind of alien freak? I think I needed an explanation a long goddamned time ago."

Lara put her hands over her mouth, caught Kelly's despairing glance in the mirror, and tentatively reached for Dickon's wrist instead. He jerked like she'd branded him, and she pulled back, ashamed. "I know you didn't believe me, Dickon. I'm sorry. I thought pushing it would be worse until you could see it was real."

"You should have tried making him believe you, like you did the judge today." Kelly's gaze danced between the road and the mirror, miserable accusation in her voice.

"No!" Dickon pulled further away. "I don't know what the hell that was in there—"

"I've never tried that before today, Kel. And they all hated it. It wouldn't have helped if I'd tried it with Dickon."

"It sure as fuck wouldn't have."

Crescendos of broken crystal, pure shattered tones, slivered into Lara's skin and burrowed deep, scores running to the bone. It *wouldn't* have helped, but knowing that, even for an absolute certainty, didn't make her feel any less as though she'd failed. She whispered "I'm sorry" and turned her face away, unready to meet Kelly's eyes in the mirror. Traffic lurched by them, horns honking, windows rolled down, all the normal things expected on a warm city afternoon. Lara wondered how many of the rolling rooms around them encapsulated their own singular dramas, played out in solitude close enough to touch.

"Dickon, please," Kelly whispered, and Lara saw a faint reflection in her window as the big man shook his head.

"Please what, Kel? Please let you explain? Please let you tell me why it's okay we just left somebody to die on a greasy concrete floor? Kelly, I thought I loved you, but now I don't think I even know you. How could you have done that?"

Lara looked back at her friend, whose eyes were wide, fixed on the road, though tears spilled down her cheeks. Her voice was distorted, struggling for calm through sobs that hiccupped her breath. "I could do it because we weren't guilty of anything and because there was no explanation and because Reg might live if the paramedics got there in time, but there is no way they would have let David live. He's not human—"

"And you're okay with that?" Dickon cried out. Kelly hit the brakes instinctively, as though his shout warned of danger. A car behind them honked and she flipped them off, a burst of obscenity accompanying the gesture. Lara flinched and ducked her head, searching for something to defuse the situation, but Kelly spoke with unnerving calm.

"I'm really not in the least freaking bit okay with it. Lara told me, but believe me, knowing and seeing aren't at all the same thing. But we had to get out of there. I couldn't exactly stop to have a fit. I still can't. I'll fall apart later."

"You didn't stop to think about the trouble we're gonna be in?"

"It doesn't have anything to do with thinking!" Kelly slammed the heel of her hand into the car horn, its pathetic beep doing less to shatter the tension than Lara thought it might. "I was just trying to make sure we all survived!"

"What about Reg?"

"We couldn't help him!" Kelly yanked the blinker indicator up so hard Lara was surprised it didn't break, and cut off traffic as she jerked the car toward the sidewalk. "You want to get out? Fine, get out! I don't care!"

"Just lend me the car," Lara whispered. "I can get us out of the city. You two don't need to be any more involved in this."

"Oh like hell." Kelly threw the emergency brake on and her seat belt off, twisting around. "No, Lara, look, at the very least you need somebody with a driver's license at the wheel if you run into any cops—"

"You let me drive your car without a license before," Lara objected quietly.

Kelly glared at her. "I know you can *drive*, Lara, that's not the problem. There weren't likely to be police looking for you before. And I know you haven't gotten a new license, so you need a driver, and he," she said, jabbing a finger at Dafydd, "can't drive right now. More to the point, you need somebody who can tell lies if it's necessary. David's in no shape to talk and you, well." She snorted, making a mockery of the anger and fear in her eyes. "This is the most universally fucked-up situation I've ever been in, but I'm *right*.

We couldn't do anything for Reg, so the best I can do is protect you. You're my best friend," she said more softly. "What else am I supposed to do?"

"Maybe choose me over them?" The accusation had gone from Dickon's voice, leaving him defeated as he unbuckled his seat belt, too.

Fresh tears tracked down Kelly's cheeks, but resolution tightened her jaw. "I'm sorry, Dickon. I didn't know getting David out of there meant I was making a choice between you and them. I thought I was choosing all of us, to get out of a situation we were never gonna be able to explain. But if it's one or the other, I'm sorry. Right now it's them."

"You're going to get arrested," Dickon said quietly. "We're all going to get arrested."

"No," Kelly said, clarion horns in the single word. "Worst-case scenario, three of us are going to get arrested. But first we're going to get David to safety, because otherwise he's going to die. And, Dickon, I love you, I really do, but I'm not going to let somebody die just because he's not exactly human."

Dafydd, unexpectedly, let go another soft chuckle. "Not human at all, but I play one on TV. Dickon" —he rolled his head back, tilting his sunglasses so his amber eyes were revealed— "a useless confession, my friend: I was going to tell you. This morning, in fact, I thought, 'he should know.' I'm sorry I was too late. Secrecy is an old habit to break."

Dickon's gaze skittered to Lara. "Is he telling the truth?"

"He is."

"Hnh." Dickon rolled his jaw, then jerked his head at Kelly. "Let me out."

"Dickon—"

"No, you know what, Kel? Just let me out. I'm going to the hospital. I gotta see if Reg is okay."

"But what about—"

"I don't know, Kelly. I don't know. Maybe if I'd had a week to get used to this, but I don't know. You . . . you go do your thing, this thing, whatever it is. Save the freak. Call me when it's over, maybe. I don't know."

Kelly, hollow-eyed, opened her door and stepped out of the car without saying anything else. Dafydd, though, spoke into her silence. "A week ago," he murmured, "a week ago you were my champion, Dickon, and Kelly was my doubter."

"I know, man." Dickon pushed the Nissan's seat forward, shouldering out. "A lot's changed since then."

Everything, Lara thought. Everything had changed since then. Kelly got back in, rebuckled her seat belt, and pulled back into traffic, all of them trying not to look at Dickon's reflection receding in the mirrors.

"Maybe it's a good thing. They're looking for two women and two men in a Nissan, not two women and a man in a Toyota." Kelly, still driving, turned the radio off with a resounding *click,* her jaw still set. According to local news, an unnamed detective had been rushed to the hospital and police were looking for four suspects to question. Lara's stomach turned to lead as their names and physical descriptions were announced, along with Dafydd's recent jail time and her peculiar disappearance.

"Maybe it's good," she echoed, dissonance running over her skin. It wasn't a lie, but she didn't believe it any more than Kelly had.

They'd stopped at Kelly's bank less than five minutes after Dickon left them, and Kelly had withdrawn most of her savings. "Eight and a half thousand," she'd said when she got back in the car. "I left about forty dollars in the bank. This is all we're going to be able to get, unless you've got accounts in other names." The last was directed at Dafydd, who nodded vaguely, as if he hadn't understood the implied question.

The Seelie were, by Lara's estimation, a fragile-looking people to begin with, but even so, Dafydd's weakness frightened her. His bones seemed to shine through parchment-fine skin, as if he faded before their eyes. He'd burned up too much power: the truth of that rang through her in ceaseless waves, like water at the shoreline. Whether he could recover with time and rest, she didn't know. It seemed all too likely that, cut off from the Barrow-lands, he would never regain his strength.

He'd given them the address of his storage unit in Peabody, and at Lara's urging, the combination to its lock, before fading into a restless drowse he hadn't fully woken from. The car they'd found there was new enough to be unremarkable, but old enough to lack the global positioning system that most new vehicles were automatically fitted with. With luck it wouldn't matter; with luck no one would trace their change of vehicles and be looking for a mid-range blue four-door Corolla. Lara glanced behind her to where Dafydd sprawled gracelessly across the seat as he dozed, and said "With any luck" aloud.

"I'm not going to assume luck is on our side. Lara, look, not like any of this was planned, but do you have any kind of . . . plan?" Kelly's fingertips tapped the wheel, quick nervous rhythm. "I'm running on adrenaline and spy movies here. I know about not using credit cards and sticking to blue roads instead of interstates, but beyond getting us out of the greater Boston metropolitan area, I don't know what to do."

Lara pressed her temple against the window, watching the roadside scenery turn to a blur of green. "I keep thinking we need to go to Wales."

"Wales? What, like in Britain? Not a chance, sister. I don't think eighty-five hundred dollars is enough to buy us fake passports, even if I had any idea where to go to try to get that kind of thing. *Wales?* Are you serious? Why?"

"Because it's where Dafydd said he was from. That the Barrowlands are close to it, in terms of how his world and this one map to each other. Ioan said something about how once upon a time people from this world were able to cross to the Barrow-lands through underground paths."

"Long ago," Dafydd murmured from the backseat. "Long ago.

Even in Oisín's time it took royal blood casting the worldwalking spell, and that was a long time ago."

Lara twisted around, hooking her arm over the back of the seat. "Hey, you're awake. How do you feel?"

Dafydd took a breath, held it, and on the exhalation admitted, "Terrible."

"You look awful." Lara wrinkled her nose at the raw truth, but it got a chuckle from Dafydd. She smiled wanly in return, then found herself echoing his deep breath and long exhalation. "Have you ever heard of a worldbreaking weapon? Not me, but something that might have been used to destroy Unseelie territory?"

He frowned. "The Unseelie lands have been drowned as long as I can remember, Lara. Having spent so much time in your world, I'd say it was probably just a result of climate change."

Unexpected burrs ran through his words, pulling their truth out of tune. Hairs stood up on Lara's arms, reinforcing the feeling of wrongness, and she blurted, "No," without meaning to. "Whatever it was, it wasn't climate change. My power's getting stronger, Dafydd. I'm starting to hear it now when people are wrong even if they believe it's the truth."

Delight lit his face briefly, pushing his weariness away. "Truth-seeker indeed." Then a touch of dismay creased his features and he relaxed into the seats again. "But I'm wrong?"

"I need you to try and remember any legends or stories Oisín might have told you. Did he ever mention someone named Brendan?"

"There's a mortal name," Dafydd said absently. "Brendan, ah, Brendan the sailor. They were friends from before he came to the Barrow-lands, I think."

Lara, under her breath, said, "No," as the words soured in her mind, but Dafydd continued undisturbed. "I remember, just barely." His eyes closed and he sank further down, voice rising and falling in a soft murmur. "He was blind with age already, Oisín was. I never knew him as a sighted man. But he used to carry a stick, a walking staff. Carved bone, I think. A gift from my mother, I think. I only re-member him having it after she died. I asked once if I could have it, because I barely remembered her and I hoped it would remind me. But he said we had to give it to Brendan, to take across the sea."

Hope surged in Lara's stomach, making a knot as nauseating as fear. "Did he say *where* across the sea?"

"I supposed he meant to Tir na nÓg, the lands to the west. I never asked."

"But Brendan was Irish," Lara whispered. "Across the sea to the west was America, for him."

"So it *is* here," Kelly said triumphantly, then made a face. "Or it was at some time."

"No." Music had turned to a crescendo with Kelly's first statement. Lara turned to grab the dashboard with both hands, as if she could direct the car through will alone. "No, it is here. Still is. It felt *true* when you said that, Kelly. Pull over, can you pull over?"

"Uh, yeah." Kelly pulled off, tires scrabbling over gravel as she went too near the ditch. "What are you going to do?"

"It's here. It's here somewhere. I found a path through the Seelie forest back to the palace, maybe I can find one here. It's got to have some kind of similar feeling, doesn't it? They're both magical constructions."

Dafydd climbed out of the car as she spoke, leaning heavily on it as he pulled Lara's door open as well. He offered her a hand, and a faint smile as she looked up at him in concern. "We can share a little of thought and emotion with those we're close to," he reminded her. "And I hold the image of the staff in my mind. But I can't do it within the confines of that vehicle."

"You can't at all! You don't have very much power left!" Lara got out, more to herd him back into the car than to accept his help, but he caught her hand.

"If there's an item of Seelie, or even Unseelie, power here, Lara, it's more likely to lend me strength than anything else in your world. It may mean my survival."

"Even if you burn out looking for it?"

"I believe the risk worth taking."

"Either way," Kelly said from within the car, "make a decision.

We're not exactly in suburbia, but I don't like you standing around outside the car when there's an APB out on us."

Dafydd tipped his head toward the vehicle. "Kelly makes a compelling argument."

Lara raised a palm in defeat. "All right. If you can give me the image, I think that'll help me build a path. How do you do this, like with a . . ." She trailed off, but lifted her free hand to Dafydd's face, approximating a gesture she'd seen in film trailers.

Dafydd laughed out loud. "A Vulcan mind meld? Would that make it easier?"

Color rushed Lara's face. "Actually, yes, I think so. It's sort of familiar."

Kelly leaned over the passenger seat, peering up at Dafydd as he confidently settled his fingers against Lara's cheek and temple. "Today has been one hundred percent full of suck, and yet at this exact second I gotta say I love my life, because I'm watching somebody perform a mind meld for real."

Enough truth ran through that to make Lara smile. Dafydd, looking into her eyes, smiled as well, then gently tugged her forward to put his forehead against hers. "Proximity eases the sharing. Close your eyes. Think of sandy beaches, cloudy skies."

The clear white path truthseeking had created when she'd searched for her way out of the Seelie forest filled her mind, as neutral an image as she could come up with. It had song to it, distant tolling like water against a shore. Oisín appeared on the path, less frail than he'd been when she'd met him, though he was by no means a young man. He still wore fine Seelie raiment, but now he carried a staff taller than he was.

If it was bone, it came from the largest animal Lara had ever imagined. Even an ivory tusk seemed inadequate for its height, and it had no curve to it at all, standing slim and ramrod straight. Intricate carvings along its length showed that it was hollow, and though the carvings were delicate in design, the staff itself warned of strength and power. In Oisín's hands it had no bent toward either destruction or creation, but the sense of it said it could be used for both.

And it was here, in her world. Choir music filled her, a host of soprano notes striking a triumphant path forward. Lara staggered as power splashed through, and out of, her. It leaped forward, racing across the countryside to briefly illuminate the image of a roaring waterfall pouring from a narrow point in a broad river. Surprised laughter broke from her throat, and Lara opened her eyes to flash an exultant smile at Dafydd.

He whispered, "Lara," and her clarity of vision faded in a rush as he collapsed in her arms.

Twenty-Seven

"Dafydd? Oh my God, Dafydd!" His weight was in-consequential, even though Lara didn't think of her-self as physically strong. Kelly sprinted out of the car and around to the passenger side, helping Lara to pour him into the backseat.

"Buckle him in," Kelly snapped. "We're leaving. Now."

Lara, mute, did as she was told, then took her own seat, barely able to pull the seat belt on as Kelly pulled away from the curb. It took two tries to clip the belt in place, and she buried her face in shaking hands when she'd managed it. "I don't think our world is really meant for using magic. Closing the breach in the garage wiped me out, and this was worse," she said into her palms. "And I think I just ripped away most of what Dafydd had left to power my own search. Kelly, if he dies—"

"It won't be your fault," Kelly said shortly. "Where do we need to go?"

"West." Lara parted her fingers to stare at the road in front of them as she tried to bring the clarity of vision back. "It's hidden in a waterfall west of here, a big one. It's got to be on the Connecticut River."

"West and what? North? South? It's a big river, Lara."

"Almost due." A hint of music returned, merely a thin bell tone compared to the earlier song. "It's almost due west of Peabody. There can't be that many waterfalls on that parallel."

"We'll get a map." Anything else Kelly intended to say was interrupted by Dafydd's sharp intake of breath. Lara twisted to find him pressing both hands against his temples.

"I'm sorry," he murmured after a moment. "I seem to have fallen asleep."

"Lara put a whammy on you," Kelly said over Lara's apology. "When was the last time you ate?"

"This morning, I suppose," Dafydd murmured, then continued in a hazy voice: "Some unpleasant second cousin to oatmeal, a last meal by the standards of the Massachusetts penal system."

"Well, it's about four o'clock now. Your blood sugar's probably low, besides everything else. We'll hit a drive-thru."

Lara's stomach, reminded of something as mundane as food, rumbled loudly enough for Kelly's tension to break into sharp laughter. "Yeah, me, too. All right, we have a plan. Fast food, then a waterfall in western Massachusetts where there's a weapon of unimaginable power." She added "Tally-ho" in a mutter, and Lara squeezed her shoulder.

"You're a rock, Kel. Thank you."

She got a crooked smile in return. "Don't thank me. I'm . . . what's that kind of rock that breaks off into a million slivers? Shale? I'm like that. I look really solid but any minute now I'm going to fly apart. I just want to get somewhere quiet and safe before that happens. David, do you have a hideout anywhere?"

"I never thought I would need one. I had always thought if I couldn't return home, if I was in danger, that I'd go . . ."

Lara turned to look at him when he trailed off, catching a grimace marring his features, though he smoothed his face as she frowned in turn. "To a great wilderness," he said. "Even in this world, the wild places are kind to my people. I could have remained undetected in the Catskills forever, if necessary, but that was alone, and with all my skill." His voice hardened at the end, hiding nothing from Lara: he was denying fear, denying so much as considering what it meant that he was cut off from the Barrow-lands.

Kelly, though, startled and straightened, looking at him in the mirror again. "You know, that's a brilliant idea. It's a thousand miles from Wales—"

"Three thousand," Lara said pedantically, as mistruth shivered over her skin.

"Okay, fine, three thousand, whatever, but my point was aren't the Catskills haunted? Like Rip Van Winkle plays ninepins up there and stuff. If there's anywhere on the East Coast that's got any kind of connection to David's world, doesn't it seem like it might be them? So we get the staff, we head for the Catskills, and you two figure out how to power it up and get David home by sunset." She made her lips thin, scowling down the two-lane highway they were on. "Well, if we could take the interstates, anyway. It'll take longer on the back roads, especially since I have to find one that'll get us pointed west. I was kind of going to Canada."

"So we could be arrested at the border?" Lara wondered. Kelly turned an injured look on her and she shook her head apologetically. "No, you're right, it was a good idea. There must be some little roads you can cross over without border patrol noticing. Or at least we could abandon the car and walk across through the woods."

"Perhaps as a second choice," Dafydd murmured.

Kelly flashed him a tense smile in the rearview mirror. "Second choice, not last resort?"

"As you say. Let us hold making our way to Wales as the last resort, and for our first choice, explore the Catskills." His voice wavered and he closed his eyes, suddenly more fragile than he'd been. "Though, Lara, even if we should find the staff, my magic—"

"You have royal blood, and I have the ability to find a truthseeker's path," Lara said fiercely. "We'll *make* a world-road if we have to."

Deep bells rang through the words, carrying, for the first time, the weight of prophecy.

✌

"Okay, where are we?" Kelly wolfed down a cheese-covered hot dog and slurped at a soda as Lara unfolded the map Kelly'd bought along with the food at a local grocery store. Lara's own meal was cooling, but she'd argued that she could eat it while Kelly drove, whereas eating and driving invariably turned messy. Dafydd, still in the backseat, ate a green salad straight from the bag, alternating with long draughts of bottled water.

"Here's Peabody. We're . . ." Lara tapped her finger just below a green spot on the map. "We're about here, because I just saw a sign for this forest." She drew a line westward across the map. "If you head due west, the only reference to a waterfall I can find is Turners Falls."

"I'm pretty sure that's dammed up, Lara. I don't know if there are any major falls on the Connecticut River that aren't."

"No, it's this one." Confidence jangled over Lara's skin, its music imbuing her with hope. "If it's dammed up, there must be a way to get beneath or behind or inside it. Something," she said with less certainty.

"You're the navigator. Okay, let me see that." Kelly shoved the rest of her hot dog into her mouth and took the map, studying the thin road lines. "The thing is, we know they're looking for us in Boston," she said around her mouthful. "We don't know if they'll have spread out. Still, I don't want to take the direct route. If we drive north a little ways farther we can get onto one of the smaller roads and come around and head south. Nobody'd be looking for us from that direction."

"Your friend has the makings of a criminal mastermind, Lara." Dafydd's color and humor were both improved, though Lara thought it would take escaping the vehicle's metal frame to really see a difference in his health. "Did you know this about her?"

"I had no idea."

"C'mon," Kelly muttered. "It's the kind of adventure everybody dreams about, right? You think of all the ways you'd prepare. You just don't expect a cop to end up dead and your fiancé to dump you along the way."

"Oh, God, Kelly." Lara reached for Kelly's shoulder and was shaken off, though not rudely.

"No, forget I said that. It doesn't make it any easier."

"We don't know Detective Washington's dead," Lara offered in a small voice. "The news hasn't said so."

"Yeah, well, Dickon didn't technically dump me, either, but I'm kind of thinking we should consider this a worst-case scenario situation. Anyway," Kelly said ferociously, "I thought everybody made up melodramatic plans about how they were going to survive the plane crash or how they would disappear after stealing a hundred million dollars from Wall Street or whatever. Don't they?" She looked up and Lara gave her an uncertain smile.

"I never did, but you're the one who was always telling me I never took any risks."

"Start smaller next time," Kelly suggested, and twisted to pop her back. "If we go the long way around we're probably not going to get to Turners Falls until after dark, but that might be to our advantage. It's easier to sneak at night. And then whether we find this staff or not . . ." She looked in the rearview mirror. "The car makes you worse, doesn't it, David. Can you handle us taking the long way?"

His silence was more telling than the answer he gave: "I'll manage."

Kelly shot a look at Lara. "Is he telling the truth?"

Lara shivered, listening to the resolute notes lingering in Dafydd's answer. "He'll manage, but you don't need my power to know it won't be good for him."

"Yeah." Kelly blew a raspberry and gave Lara the map, then put the car back in gear. "Hang on till we get there, David. Then you can get out and go lie down in a forest or something while Lara and I do the heavy lifting."

"I would be grateful." Dafydd spoke quietly. "I don't need shelter, but I think even a few hours under the moonlight, in a green and growing place, would restore me greatly."

"Okay." Kelly pulled back onto the road decisively. "Lara, you navigate. Keep us off the blue roads, even, if you can, and push us west."

The dam blocking the river at Turners Falls was massive enough to make Lara laugh. Despairing humor, she thought, but humor regardless. Three enormous walls— levies, blockades; she didn't know what to call them—pooled the river behind them into a glittering black lake. The grounds around the lake, at least where Kelly had found parking, were well-kept lightly forested greenlands. Dafydd had gratefully stumbled from the car to sit beneath a tree while the women got out to study the dam in dismay.

"There's no way you're getting behind or under that thing, Lara. There can't possibly be any artifacts left under it anyway. They'd have been pulverized when it was built."

"But it's here." Lara turned in a loose circle, wishing her conviction would offer more information. "Someone must have taken it before they built the dam," she said slowly, testing the idea for veracity. It rang true, though uncertainty caught her for a moment. With the way her power was changing, it seemed possible that if she wanted it to be true badly enough, she might convince herself of the lie.

Or she might force a true thing back to before the dam's construction, changing the time line that had led to this moment. That idea was vastly more appalling. Lara groaned, dropping her face into her hands, then let out an explosive breath as she looked up. "Okay. I'm going into town and see if I can find out when the dam was built. If it was recently enough, maybe there was some kind of preservation work done first."

"You're deluding yourself, Lar." Kelly's dry response sounded unfortunately accurate, but Lara spread her hands in semi-defeat.

"Do you have a better idea?"

"Not really. David, can you handle the car again?"

He pushed to his feet, using the tree for support. "Reluctantly."

"Then we'll drive in. C'mon." Kelly headed for the car, Lara stepping up to Dafydd's side to help him back. His weight was negligible, as though he might blow away in a strong wind, and she frowned at him.

"If we can't find a clue or a hint somewhere fast, I want Kelly to take you back into one of the forests we just drove through, okay? You need the rest more than I need the help searching."

"Lara, if the staff is what you say it is, it's not meant for mortal hands. It could be very dangerous to you."

"Oisín carried it for years," Lara argued. "It might be less dangerous in mortal hands than in Seelie. And this isn't up for debate. You're—" She broke off, unwilling to finish the sentence. Unwilling to voice the truth that the Seelie prince was dying, as if letting it go unsaid might let him eke out a few more hours.

He hesitated beside the car, looking down at her before his shoulders slumped and he nodded. "Very well. I would prefer we find it rather than split up, but I . . . am not strong. I don't want to burden you in your search."

"You're not a burden, Dafydd. I just have no intention of explaining to your father how I got his son and heir killed on a world not even his own."

"You're very sweet," Kelly said from inside the car. "Now stop mooning over each other and get in. The longer this takes the more wasted David's going to be."

Dafydd murmured, "Again to the heart of the matter," and accepted Lara's help getting in the car. He shied away from metal, even forgoing the seat belt, and Lara kept a nervous eye out the window for patrolling police who might notice the minor transgression.

There were none on the short drive into Turners Falls, nor any readily visible as they reached the town center. Village center, Lara read on a tourist information sign minutes later. The township was Montague, made up of five smaller villages, of which Turners Falls was the largest.

"Oh, *great*," Kelly said from the other side of the sign. "Welcome to beautiful Turners Falls, named after Captain William Turner, who slaughtered a village full of sleeping Indians in this location three hundred and forty years ago. I bet anybody who knew where your staff was has been dead since then."

Lara came around the sign with a laugh, and chagrin crossed Kelly's face. "I mean, okay, yes, obviously, they'd be dead by now anyway. You know what I meant."

"The dam was built in the eighteen sixties," Dafydd read from where Lara had left him, a note of discouragement in his voice. "Certainly there was no hope of preservation work having been done so long ago."

"No, but there were survivors of the massacre." Lara picked up the history where Kelly had left off, tracing the words with a fingertip. "Maybe there are still a few descendants who might know something about a legendary staff."

"And how are you going to find them?" Kelly asked with curious exasperation. "Go around knocking on doors? 'Excuse me, were your ancestors murdered in their beds by an army captain? They were? Great! Do you know anything about Saint Brendan's visit a thousand years ago, or about a staff he brought here?'"

Lara glanced down the street at storefronts already closed for the evening and restaurants doing late-dinner business. "If we have to, but there must be some bars off the main street here that are less trendy and more local. We could start by talking to people at them, instead of knocking on doors."

"And if any of them watched the news and recognize us?"

"Recognize me," Lara said decisively. "Dafydd's glamour won't hold, so he can't go anywhere people might get a good look at him, and I'd rather not leave him alone. So if you guys want to hole up in—" She turned back to the tourist poster and tapped a green square a block and a half away from where they were. "In Peskeomskut Park here, then I'll catch up with you later, okay?"

"Lara . . ." Worry creased a line between Kelly's eyebrows. "You're not very good at sweet-talking people. Maybe I should—"

"Much as I would like to retreat to a wooded place with Lara and allow you the search," Dafydd murmured as he joined them on their side of the sign, "I suspect that if Lara should find anyone who knows of Brendan or the staff, her truthseeking talents might be critical in establishing herself. You've been extraordinarily helpful, Kelly, but I fear in this you and I may be relegated to the sidelines."

Kelly's frown increased, then slid away in a rueful smile at Lara. "How does he make that sound so reasonable?"

"Because it *is* reasonable," Lara said, but Dafydd put his hand over his heart and bowed elegantly, if more shallowly than full-blown theatrics might call for.

"Centuries, even aeons, of practice, my dear Miss Richards. Now, if you would be so good as to escort me to this mouthful of a park, I would be grateful for rest among some greenery."

Kelly severely said "You be careful," to Lara, and "'Peskeomskut' isn't that hard to say," to Dafydd as they headed for the park, leaving Lara behind.

Twenty-Eight

Bars and dance clubs were not Lara's natural or comfortable habitat. In the one or two trendy clubs, she was at least the right age; in the more local bars, she stood out as both too young and too touristy.

And, she decided, probably too determined to broach a particular topic of conversation. Films always showed locals closing ranks when a stranger came in to talk, and that representation felt dismayingly accurate. Still, she nerved herself beyond the front door in more than one bar, ordering a glass of wine and putting on a shy smile for the bartender. By the third bar she wished she'd ordered soda all along, though it did seem to be getting easier to broach her awkward topic. Amused at the realization, she leaned forward to explain herself for the third time.

"I'm doing research on Native American legends. I—"

"You'll probably want the Discovery Center, then," the bartender said. So had the previous two, and Lara nodded with familiarity.

"Probably, but I got into town after it closed. I thought I'd see if there were any locals willing to share stories, especially about the falls." Unrelated statements, both true, meant to sound like together they meant something. If someone else had done that, it would make hairs stand up on Lara's arms, but her truthseeking sense allowed it to slip past, this once at least. "I'm on a tight deadline, so I hope I can skip going through the Discovery Center."

A hint of sympathy tempered the barman's smile. "Put off a college research paper, huh? Look, you can try Old Jake. He's usually down at the Canal Bar—you know where that is? Head west three blocks, until you get to the canal, then go north two. He'll tell tall tales as long as you keep buying him another drink. I don't know if any of them are true, but you're looking for legends, not the truth, right? And if you're looking for a place to stay, the bar's got rooms, too. Canal Bar and Inn, you can't miss it. New building, part of the revitalization work going on here, not one of the old mill buildings."

Lara, grateful, said, "*Thank* you," and drank her wine much too quickly, eager to make her escape. Turners Falls streets were laid out in tidy square blocks, and following the barman's instructions was easy, even with three glasses of wine in her. The waterfront was as he'd suggested, a mix of old mill buildings and newer ones similar enough in style to retain character but unique enough to mark themselves as modern. The canal itself reflected streetlamps, and there was indeed a sense of revitalization as couples took after-dinner walks along the water, greeted by dog walkers and joggers. It had the feel of a town reinventing itself, and Lara found the Canal Bar with her own sense of purpose renewed.

A group of locals, mostly young men, sent wolf whistles and approving jeers toward her as she approached. Nerves clenched her stomach and she wished Dafydd or Kelly were with her after all. Retreating, though, wasn't an option, and she made her hands into fists, hidden by her skirts, to urge herself forward.

An older man with military-cut gray hair and a limp stepped through the group of younger men, raising his cane to smack one of the youths on the shoulder as he passed. "Your mother'd never forgive you for harassing a woman that way, Denny. Behave like a gentleman."

"Denny" swallowed a protest into a look of embarrassment as

the older man came forward to offer Lara his hand. He was in his sixties, and wore a beaten-up black leather jacket over a blue T-shirt and jeans that had seen better days. "Sorry about that, Miss Jansen. I'm Old Jake. Been waiting for you a while now." He glanced beyond her, eyebrows lifted, then looked back at her. "Where're your friends? Two men and a woman. They were expected, too."

"Expected?" Lara squeaked the word, then cleared her throat. "There are, um. Just three of us. How did you know?"

He flashed a sharp smile. "You want the hoodoo mystic answer or the practical one? You were on the news," he announced, choosing which answer she got. "But I've been waiting a lot longer than that. C'mon inside, let me get you away from these hooligans."

Bemused, Lara followed him into the bar, which was brighter and more welcoming than she expected it to be. Jake waved a waitress down, ordered himself a beer and Lara a ginger ale without asking, then gave her a sly look of curiosity.

"Ginger ale's fine, thanks. Great, in fact. How did you—"

"Know the history of Turners Falls, Miss Jansen?" Jake leaned back and folded his hands behind his head. Lara thought he might kick his feet onto the table between them, he looked so comfortable, but instead he thumped his chair forward again as the waitress hurried back with their drinks. Lara waited for the woman to leave again before giving Jake an uncertain smile.

"Not really. Only what I read on the tourist board on the main street."

"About the massacre. Does it mention the men were gone from the village that night? That it was mostly women and children who died?"

"God," Lara said involuntarily. "No. That's even more horrible, somehow."

"No, Miss Jansen, what's horrible is the men left knowing their wives and children would die, but they went anyway, or so that's what the family stories say."

The wine she'd drunk swirled up in a twist of bitter nausea. "Why would anyone do that?"

"They were given a vision, a holy duty to carry out. A woman's voice, charging the men to save an artifact before the great falls were stopped."

"The worldbreaking staff?" Lara whispered. Then even more softly, around a knot in her throat, she asked, "My voice?"

Gentleness slid across Jake's expression. "Now, I wouldn't know that, Miss Jansen. I'm Old Jake, but I'm not that old. It's just a story handed down over a dozen generations. They say the shamans asked the spirits, and the spirits said to empty the great falls before the white men came."

Despite the churning in her stomach, Lara smiled a little. "Forgive me for saying so, but you look pretty white yourself, Mr . . ."

"Jake," he said easily. "Just Old Jake, Miss Jansen. That's how everybody knows me. And bloodlines mingle over the years. My sisters, they got more of the Indian blood than me, but I'm the one patient enough to sit around waiting for a myth to come walking through the door."

"Lara. Please, just call me Lara. Jake, I'm not even sure what I'm looking for isn't a myth itself."

His gaze sharpened on her. "Now, that's not the truth, is it, Miss Lara?"

Discomfort surged over her in a toneless howl. "Anyone else would think it was a myth."

Satisfaction colored his expression, and he picked up his beer to take a long drink. "Stories say the shamans feared what would happen if the white men found the gift of the waterfalls. That it was a terrible power for the one who could use it, and that a dozen dozen men would come searching for it. That it could be kept safe, but only with the blood of the land."

Cold crept up Lara's spine, more insiduous than anything Emyr had cast on her. "Breaking your own world to protect it." Dafydd was right: the staff was a thing of dangerous power, even to mortals, if ensuring its safety destroyed communities. She wondered abruptly what price Brendan had paid, nine centuries earlier, to bring it across the ocean; wondered how his own world had been shattered in the bringing, because she was suddenly certain it had been.

Jake nodded again, his satisfaction turning grim. "And so the warriors took it away, and left their families to die, because they couldn't stay and not fight. And one of us has been waiting ever since to give the burden to the one who comes for it."

"How do you know it's me?"

He steepled his fingers over his beer, then noticed it again and lifted it to drink. Lara glanced at her own untouched ginger ale and left it alone, the wine in her stomach more than enough to make her feel unwell already. Jake set the half-empty beer glass down, wiped his upper lip, then flicked answers off on his fingertips: "Her companions are a giant, a wise woman, and a spirit man. She will know the truth of the stories when she hears them." He paused, giving her a hard stare, and Lara nodded to both, though the descriptions of her friends struck her as a little funny. Kelly would never think of herself as a wise woman, but after the levelheadedness she'd displayed throughout the day, Lara could hardly think of a better descriptor.

"And," Jake finished pragmatically, "she'll be the only one with the knowledge to look for it. I saw you on the news, and knew you'd come here today. I expected you to be earlier."

"We took the long way around. Did" —Lara swallowed—"did the news say anything about Detective Washington? Is he all right?"

"Not dead yet, anyway, and where there's life, there's hope." The platitude had the strength of conviction behind it, unusual enough to make it sound true. Jake leaned forward, pushing his beer aside like it blocked his view of Lara. "What will you do with it? With this thing we've protected all these years?"

Lara shook her head, eyes closed briefly as images of the Barrowlands, of Emyr's shining citadel and the sprawling black opal Unseelie city, and of the people, one so bright and one so dark, and both unhealthy with it, washed over her. "The legend I've been told says it's a weapon to break a world. That it's been used already to destroy. But a scalpel can help cure as well as kill." She opened her eyes again, meeting Jake's gaze, and willed truth into her voice. "If you'll grant me the burden to carry, I'll use it to try to heal a world."

Satisfaction slid over Jake's face again. He nodded once, sharply, then hefted his cane from beside his chair, and laid it on the table between them with a resounding smack.

"I thought it would be bigger." There was nothing extraordinary about the cane: it was a polished length of aged wood, knobs and lumps still giving it character. Lara stared at it until it swam in her vision, sending a spike of pain through her eyes. She rubbed them, then looked again at the cane, then Jake.

Smile lines made deep crevices around his mouth. "They say it used to be. They say the one it's meant for will reveal its true form." His eyebrows waggled with the last words, and Lara, despite herself, laughed.

"Do you believe any of this, Jake?"

He sat back with a laconic shrug. "I believed you'd be here today. Believed you'd be looking for this. Guess that means I believe it all enough. So how does the reveal work?"

Lara glanced at the cane again, squinting against another stab of unreliable vision. Dafydd's glamour had done that to her, once she'd known it was in place. "Oh! Oh. I can almost see through—um, would you like to take a walk with me, Jake?"

"Can almost see through?" Jake finished his beer in a few long swallows, eyed Lara's untouched ginger ale, then gestured to his cane as he stood up. "A walk sounds terrific."

Lara folded her hands behind her back like a child resisting temptation. "I'd like you to take it out of here. I'm not quite sure what will happen when I touch it."

"Curiouser and curiouser." Jake scooped the cane up and made a show of using it to herd people out of his way as he led Lara to the door. The youths outside scattered guiltily as they left, though one of them whistled and called out a congratulations to Jake as he headed down the canal street with a woman young enough to be his granddaughter. Lara grinned, and Jake gave an unapologetic shrug. "Small town. Everybody gets in everyone else's business."

"I grew up outside of Boston, but everyone still got in everybody's business. I think a lot of people went to church just for the weekly gossip."

"Big Irish-Catholic community?"

Lara nodded. "My family are mostly Dutch and Norwegian, but four of my friends growing up all had the last name Murphy. Different families."

"Makes the paperwork easy when people get married."

Lara laughed. "Except these were all girls. The laws might allow it now, but their mothers might never recover if any of them married each other. It was a pretty conservative community that way." She looked over her shoulder, judging the distance they'd come and the other people out walking along the canal. "Okay. I don't think anything really showy is going to happen, but I didn't want to risk it in the bar."

Jake offered her the cane again, ill-disguised interest in his eyes. "Risk what?"

"Looking at that gives me a headache." Lara took a breath to steady herself. "That might mean it has a glamour on it, a . . ." She trailed off, uncertain of how to explain a glamour without sounding absurd, but Jake gave the cane a little shake, obviously eager for her to take it.

"Something to make it look different from how it really is."

"Right. And I'm a truthseeker, so it's possible that just holding it will strip away the glamour."

"You're killing me here, Miss Lara."

Lara looked up at him with a smile. "No, I'm not." Buoyed by that simple exchange of exaggeration and truth, she took the cane in both hands.

Power sparked dissonance against her palms, a vivid shock of what she felt not matching what she saw. A headache flared and she crushed her eyes closed. The cane's gnarly polished surface faded from her mind's eye, her hands instead telling her the truth. Patterns were marked against her skin, the cane's circumference much larger and more varied than what she'd seen. Relieved song swept through her, washing away the last vestiges of untuneful falsehood. She whispered "It's all right" as if she spoke to a living thing, and squeezed the column in her hands. "Show your true form. I'm the one you've been waiting for."

Jake, reverently, said, "I will be God damned," and Lara opened her eyes to look at the ivory staff lying across her palms.

It was as it had been in Dafydd's vision: hollow, carved with intricate Celtic patterns, and considerably longer than Lara stood tall. The ends were solid, as if they'd been capped to give them strength to stand against the wear of use. Despite its age, the ivory was still a rich gleaming white, unyellowed by time, and it tingled with power, as if pleased to be reverted to its natural form.

Oisín, Lara realized very clearly, was more exceptional than she'd known. The staff in her hands *wanted* to be used, like it had a will of its own that it could work upon the bearer. If he'd carried it as long as he had without turning its power to any ends of his own, then his willingness to be no more than he was was extraordinary. She looked at Jake, who still gaped at the staff, and found herself shaking her head.

"Did you never have any impulse to try to use this for anything? Did it not . . . tell you it could be used?"

Jake's eyebrows furrowed and he shook his head. "Not for anything more than a cane, Miss Lara. Why, does it say something to you?"

Maybe it responded to inherent magics. Lara tightened her fingers around the staff, hope surging through her. If her mortal magic could make the staff sing, then Dafydd's Seelie talent might awaken it far enough to heal him. "It almost makes promises," she whispered. "Like it's alive. What it says . . ." She breathed a laugh, and gave Jake a lopsided smile. "What it says is, I'm going to have to be very careful with it. Thank you, Jake. Thank you for bringing this, and for trusting me."

"The world needs healing, Miss Lara. Good luck to you, if you're the one to do it."

Twenty-Nine

"That didn't take long." Kelly eyed Lara's staff as Dafydd, looking a little refreshed, came from the largest copse of trees available in the park. He studied the staff even more avidly than Kelly, and Lara handed it to him wordlessly.

Color flooded back into his face within seconds. He sagged, but with an air of relief rather than the exhaustion that had dogged him. "It feels like home," he whispered. "I can hardly believe an artifact of such power has been here for so long and I never sensed it."

"It was in disguise," Lara said carefully. "I'm not sure you'd have sensed it even if you'd known to look for it. Someone was waiting for me," she added to Kelly. "I think they sort of had been for four hundred years. So it didn't take long."

Kelly looked faintly disapproving. "I thought finding mystical artifacts was supposed to take great trials. Or at least, I don't know, Nazis chasing after you."

"Only, I think, if you're Indiana Jones." Dafydd smiled at Kelly, then wrapped his arms around the staff, putting as much flesh against it as he could. "With this and a wild place, I would be well restored in a matter of days."

"I don't think we should wait days, but we can at least stop for the night in one of the state forests," Lara offered. "We should be able to get five or six hours' rest, even if we want to try to get to the Catskills by morning."

"But perhaps we should just push through to the mountains," Dafydd murmured.

Lara shook her head. "I don't know. It's already after ten and we've had a long day. I could use the rest."

"A long day," Kelly echoed. "Is that what you call it? I was thinking more like a horrible, terrible, no-good awful day, and I want a nap. Dafydd, is that thing going to make riding in the car easier for you? Because Lara's right, we should get away from town sooner rather than later. We can head northeast and get a little farther away from where anybody might expect us and then sack out for the night."

"The staff will make it much more comfortable, I think. All right." Dafydd curled a hand around it protectively, then drew in a deep breath and straightened his shoulders. To Lara's astonishment, his glamour slipped back into place, changing the staff to a cane and taking the elfin edge off his looks. His visage still fluctuated and twisted to her eyes, but to other people, he would look normal again.

Kelly muttered, "That's flipping freaky, man," and more clearly said, "Can you make yourself, I don't know, short, forty, and balding? Because that would be a much better disguise for tromping back to the car in."

"I'm sorry." Rue flashed across Dafydd's face. "It would take several hours to build a new glamour, and weeks of practice to be certain it would hold under even mild scrutiny."

"Guess we'll just have to make a run for it."

"All the way to the sidewalk?" Lara wondered. "Didn't you move the car down here to the park?"

Kelly opened her mouth and shut it again. "No. That would have been smart. I left it back up on the main drag where we parked earlier."

"Oh." Lara twitched a smile, and offered Dafydd her arm as they left the park. He leaned on it more heavily than she might have hoped, the staff clearly not having helped as much as it could. "That's a relief, really. You've been so competent and levelheaded all day, but if you didn't think of that maybe you're not a criminal mastermind in the making."

"It's my first attempt," Kelly said with a sniff. "Give me time."

"Time," Dafydd murmured, "is one thing we do not seem to have in abundance."

Reminded and chastened, they hurried back to the car.

The Corolla bumped down a rutted road, all three passengers gritting their teeth so they didn't bite their tongues. Cicadas squealed loudly enough to be heard over the engine, announcing their lovelorn state to the world. Dafydd, apparently undisturbed, all but fell from the vehicle before it had come to a full stop in front of a reed-ridden pond, and took several long strides away as Kelly killed the engine. Both women got out of the car as Dafydd turned back with a joyous smile.

"This will do," he said. "This will do wonderfully. Thank you, Kelly. Thank you for everything. I owe you my life."

"You actually mean that, don't you."

"I do. It's not a phrase I would use lightly." He took a breath and closed his teeth on it, like he was actually eating the fresh air. "Resting under the risen moon will do me good. Thank you again," he said, then took a few steps and disappeared.

Lara startled and Kelly made a noise of disbelief. "Where'd he go?"

"He's . . ." Lara blinked hard. "I can kind of see him." There was no double vision of glamour, but the trees seemed to accept and camouflage the Seelie prince in a way they would never do with humans. "I guess he was right. The forest likes him."

"I guess so." Kelly watched the trees in silence a few moments, then spoke in a low voice. "I always thought it would be cool to have somebody say 'you saved my life' and mean it. I thought, you know, that it'd be happenstance, just being in the right place at the right time to be a hero. I didn't know it would really be this kind of blind panic, running to try to do the right thing while everything else got fucked up."

"Kelly, I'm sorry."

Kelly wiped a hand under her eyes before speaking snappishly in an attempt to keep further tears at bay. "It's not your fault. If those—*things*—hadn't attacked everything would be okay. Reg wouldn't be hurt and Dickon wouldn't have flipped out, but they did, so we're just going to have to deal with that."

"You shouldn't have to." Lara folded her arms around herself, then thought better of it and edged closer to Kelly, putting an arm around her shoulders. "At the most it should be Dafydd and me dealing with it."

"Yeah." Kelly sniffled. "Because you live in a vacuum, or something. We were all there when Reg got hurt. There wasn't going to be any parceling out of whose fault it was. We all looked bad and there was no way to explain it."

"Maybe I could've made them believe us."

Kelly, red-eyed and puffy-nosed, gave her an incredulous stare. Lara ducked her head. "Okay, I might've convinced them we believed we were telling the truth."

"And then they would've carted three of us off to the funny farm and the fourth to a government lab. There wasn't much choice. I just didn't know an adventure would feel like this."

Lara sighed, images of Emyr and Ioan and of black-clad warriors meeting a silver-armored tide of enemies flashing through her mind. "Yeah. Neither did I." She put her mouth against Kelly's hair. "Maybe Dickon will—"

"Get over it? Adapt? Calm down? I donno, Lar." Kelly's voice thickened up again and she twisted to wipe her nose on her shoulder. "I actually think he'd have handled David being an elf if Reg hadn't gotten hurt. I mean, he's a big guy, he likes to ride his Yamaha, he does a little of the rebel without a clue thing, but he's pretty squishy inside. Law-abiding. And I just went and . . ." She trailed off into a shudder that was more exhaustion than sobs.

"And proved yourself devious beyond any of our expectations." Lara hugged Kelly harder, a mix of guilt and gratitude tangling inside her. "You really did save his life. Thank you."

"He's an *elf*, Lara. He's got pointy ears. Did I just throw my whole life away for an elf?" She put her face in her hands, dragging a deep breath through her palms. "We should have kept going. I wouldn't have to think so much if I was still driving."

"Look." Lara nudged her toward the car door. "Crawl into the backseat and sleep for a few hours, okay? I'll stay awake, and maybe things will seem better when you wake up."

Kelly sniffled again, then nodded as she climbed into the car. "Aren't you going to tell me it'll be okay, that Dickon loves me and that if he doesn't forgive me he doesn't deserve me? The rest of my friends would."

"Yeah," Lara said softly, and closed the door as gently as she could before whispering, "But you and I both know the truth's more complicated than that."

The silence of the upstate forest was nothing like the silence in the enchanted forest surrounding the Seelie citadel. There, the silence was absolute; here, if she listened hard enough, Lara could hear mechanical things. Distant airplanes, the *thrum* of car engines or horns; even voices raised where no one had seemed to be. But Dafydd had gone into the woods like a child seeking solace, and the quiet was a gift even for Lara.

The common phrase would be "there had been no time to think." But there had been, long hours on the road in enforced silence, neither Lara nor Kelly eager to speak and disturb what rest Dafydd could get. The staff had eased the last hour of the journey, but traveling in the car was clearly bad for him when his glamour was released, and he'd made no effort to continue holding it once they reached the vehicle's relative safety. So the silence had reigned, leaving her to her own thoughts.

She crouched at the pond's edge, dragging her fingertips through it and watching ripples rebound against the incoming laps of water. Magic seemed like that to her, bouncing in unexpected ways. The staff Dafydd clung to had perhaps changed his world once already. Even with her best intentions, using it there could have unforeseen consequences.

"Changes that will break the world." She sighed, then pushed to her feet and went into the forest more deliberately than she had the last time she'd entered a wood. Then she'd been hurt and angry and trying to escape. This time, if anything, she was searching for something.

For some*one*, truth be told, and for Lara, it always was.

It took longer to find him than she expected, as if he'd been wholly embraced by wilderness and it chose to deliberately hide him from her. It was absurd, but she was given no less to the fancy when she came on him sitting in a pool of moonlight, his shirt abandoned.

He looked like what he was, half-clothed and silver-skinned under the stars: an alien being, ethereal and beautiful and so terribly inhuman. A handful of half-interested bugs darted around him, even landed on his naked skin, but left again without tasting him, as if they knew his blood was wrong.

Moonlight was his friend in a way sunshine was not. He looked carved of it, looked like he was brother to it, and looked, Lara thought, as though he was drinking it in through his skin, vitality restoring as she watched. The staff lay across his lap, his palms resting on it, and even it glowed in the moon's light, making it more ethereal and inhuman than before.

She stood where she was a long time, watching him in silence as the shadows changed and made leaf tattoos on his skin. There was peace in simply standing there, wrapped in calm, but eventually she whispered, "Does it help at all?"

He didn't startle, didn't so much as change the steady slow draw of breath, but after a little while he spoke. The words were music, incomprehensible at first, but as the moments went by, their meaning became clear. Seelie language and truthseeker magic wound together, making a story of sorrow and pain.

"A little," Dafydd breathed. "The moonlight here is cooler. At home it would burn a path to my heart, strengthening me."

"What will happen to you if you stay here?" Lara had an answer for that, one she didn't want to consider, and Dafydd's sigh said her fears were well founded.

"I don't know. With the staff, I think I would survive. Without it . . . your world can only give me a fraction of what I need." Dafydd put his hand to his chest, a spasm of pain tightening his features as he did so. "There is a wound here, Lara. An empty place where I once was connected to the Barrow-lands. I'd never noticed its presence until its absence told its tale. The pale magics of your world might flood it, but they will never fill it. I reach for things here, for the sounds of nature, the taste of the wind, the cool light from the sky, and they fall away from me." His hand rose again, this time to capture one of the insects in his palm. "Like these biting creatures, your world simply does not recognize me well enough to give me sustenance. I might become a wraith if I stayed here. Like the nightwings became, before they took that man."

"I won't let that happen."

He smiled suddenly, brilliant in the moonlight. "No. I don't think you would, at that." Finally he opened his eyes, then put out a graceful hand, inviting Lara to join him. She knelt by his side, then leaned in to kiss him.

"Good," she whispered. "You're still real. There are so many things I need to ask you, Dafydd."

He nodded, gaze solemn. "So many things to talk about." Then he smiled again and drew her closer. "What was it you said? 'Shut up and kiss me'?"

Lara laughed. "I only said shut up."

"That," Dafydd said, eyes bright, "I can do." Then, for all the honesty in his voice and promise in his words, he added, "You came for me. Thank you, Lara. You might not have."

Lara put her forehead against his, lost for a moment in simply wanting to touch him. His skin was cool, almost cold, and she took his hands to warm them as she sat back on her heels. "There was never any chance I wouldn't."

"Unless you'd been lost to the Barrow-lands forever. How did you come back? How did you open the door?"

"Me! What about you? You disappeared in the middle of a war! How did that happen?"

"I've had months to wonder about that." Dafydd shook his head. "The Barrow-lands will only permit someone of royal blood to cast that spell, and it certainly wasn't me."

"Well, it certainly doesn't seem very likely that it was Emyr, and I'm sure it wasn't Ioan."

"Hafgan, perhaps. The Barrow-lands will heed Unseelie royal blood as well as Seelie."

"No, it wasn't Hafgan. Ioan's been ruling in his name for centuries, maybe longer."

"Ioan has *what?*" Dafydd gasped and Lara dropped her gaze to their entwined fingers, gathering herself before answering.

"Hafgan abdicated and Ioan took his name. For consistency, maybe. Your brother is king of the Unseelie, Dafydd."

Astonishment kept Dafydd still, though his gaze went through Lara as if he saw something distant. "Not for consistency, but because Emyr would take abdication as a folly. He might have seized the opportunity to attack the Unseelie court, to push an old enemy out of sight when they were at their weakest. Hafgan can't be dead, can he?" He refocused on Lara, leaving her with the alarming impression that she should have many answers she lacked.

"I don't think so, but Ioan said it was so long ago that the Unseelie have all but forgotten someone else used to be king. How long would that take?"

"Too long for it to have any meaning, Lara, or even any number I might name for you. Oisín keeps some mark of the years, but our nature doesn't incline us to. I don't see how the Unseelie court could forget their king was once a different man. Our memories fade until even our own lives are nothing more than stories and legends, but Ioan's Seelie coloring would forever remind them."

"Ah." Lara puffed her cheeks. "I wouldn't have known he was Seelie if he hadn't told me. He says the Unseelie used to be pale, too, but living underground for so long has changed them, so he chose to change, too. He's dark-haired now."

"*They*? He thinks of himself as one of them?"

"Didn't Merrick think of himself as Seelie?"

"Not so much that he let our magic work subtle changes to his coloring. I didn't even know that could be done." Dafydd fixed his gaze on the black pond. "So my blood brother truly is of another people, while the brother of my heart lies dead and I am, perhaps, trapped in a world not my own. I suppose it could be worse," he said eventually. "It could be raining."

Lara shot a look toward the sky, then shouldered him. "Even I know better than to say things like that."

Dafydd flashed a brief smile at the stars. "I'm a weatherman. It permits me a certain leeway. Am I forgiven my follies, then? I should have told you about Merrick," he said more quietly. "I am sorry, Lara."

"I know. And yes, you're forgiven. A year in jail is more than enough penance. I didn't mean for that to happen."

"You didn't cause it to happen. I spent a great deal of time worrying about you, Lara. It seems impossible it was only a day."

Lara shook her head. "I know. I spent hours reading news archives on Kelly's computer. It was like reading a past history of a world that never was. But it could have been much worse. You were gone from the Barrow-lands for ten days, and a century passed here. I could've been missing for a decade."

"Some aspect of the spell I used to hold time in tandem must have clung to you. Either that or a truthseeker's will can find its way through time as well as the space between worlds."

"In that case I need to work on my timing."

"Well," Dafydd said in a wonderfully mollifying tone, "it was your first time."

Lara laughed aloud. "Practice makes perfect, is that it?"

Dafydd took the question for invitation, brushing his mouth against hers and murmuring, "That's the human expression, yes."

"I'd just as soon not have to practice that, though. I can think of better things that might need perfecting."

"Really. Like what?"

Lara sat back, trying to look serious. "Well, the cut of your shirt. It's all right when the glamour is working, but right now it looks like you borrowed your big brother's clothes. And—"

She shouted laughter as Dafydd tackled her, knocking her back into moss and soft earth. "My dress! You're going to destroy it! I made this, Dafydd!"

"My deepest apologies." The phrase was teasing, not sincere, and Lara pursed her lips uninvitingly as he tried for another kiss. "Ah, is a man not allowed to offer perhaps slightly insincere apologies to salve his lady's heart?"

"Not with me. It grates on my skin." Delight flooded Lara, though, turning her sour expression to another smile. "His lady?"

Dafydd looked discomfited. "It's absurd, I know, Lara. We've spent barely a day in each other's company—"

"And you still haven't learned when you're talking too much." Lara touched her fingers to his lips. "Shh. We can give it some time before we start putting the absurd into words. Right now—"

"Right now nothing." Kelly's voice came out of the shadows, and after a moment she appeared to lean against a tree. "If I had a bowl of popcorn I'd probably just sit down and watch, but since I don't, we should probably hit the road."

Thirty

Lara lifted her head to give Kelly a halfhearted glare. "You're supposed to be sleeping."

"I woke up," Kelly said apologetically. "One of those oh-my-God-I-slept-through-the-alarm jolting awake things. I figured we were better off with me driving with adrenaline in my system than half asleep, so I got up."

Lara looked down at Dafydd, who had gone rabbit-still. Rather like she had, she thought, when Emyr had happened on them in the Barrow-lands glade. "Do you think it's a sign?" she asked, more light-heartedly than usual. She'd been embarrassed when Emyr had caught them; now she was only amused. "Do you think someone is trying to tell us we shouldn't have sex outdoors?"

"Yes," Kelly said helpfully. "I am."

"I meant in a grander scheme." Lara sat up, hands on her hips. "This is the second time we've been interrupted like this. We were outside both times." She started buttoning her dress, saw disappointment dart through Dafydd's expression, and gave in to a laugh as she leaned down to kiss him again. Her world had been turned upside-down. She had lost months of time, had battled vicious monsters, had run instead of helping when a decent man was struck down, and still, somehow, she was happy. Dafydd ap Caerwyn offered her that: an unexpected delight in life, even when so many things were going wrong. She kissed him again, then got to her feet, shaking her skirt straight. "You're the one who told me I should be more adventuresome, Kel. I'm just trying to follow through. I've never had sex in the woods."

"Look at it this way. You'll be incredibly grateful to me in a couple hours, when you're not trying to discreetly scratch mosquito bites in seriously indiscreet places. Now come on. Get your skinny elf boy dressed and let's go find his world."

"Lara." Kelly's whisper broke through the fog of half-sleep that rendered Lara's name almost meaningless to her. She wasn't awake, but was just aware enough of the world around her that it impinged on her dreams. The road's curves made her sway in the seat, and she knew it, but in her dream she was on the ocean, tossing and weaving in a small boat at the whim of waves. The slowly brightening sky was sunrise, but in the dream it came in bursts of light that promised a path out of the storm.

Kelly said, "Lara," more insistently. Lara drew in a sharp cold breath that balled itself in her throat like a hiccup from the other direction, and her eyes popped open.

The sky shone red over nearby mountains still blue and misty with night. Lara stared at them, then shivered, part in response to their otherworldly appearance and in part her body's objection to waking from the fugue it had been in. The road behind them faded into haze in the sideview mirror, distance and fuzziness a reflection of Lara's mental state as well. She mumbled, "We've gone a long way," and dropped her face into her hands, trying to wake up.

"Yeah, and now we've got a problem. Guy coming the other way just flashed his lights at me."

Lara lifted her head again, uncomprehending as Kelly slowed the car and pulled toward the side of the narrow road. "So?"

"So my headlights weren't on high, so if he was flashing me it means there's probably some kind of trouble up ahead. Either somebody hit a deer or . . ."

"Or there's a roadblock." Exhaustion burned away, leaving Lara's spine tense. "We're a hundred and thirty miles from Boston. They can't possibly be putting up blocks this far out." Hope, not truth, ran through her words.

"What do you want to do?"

"I don't know. How far are we from the mountains?" They looked close, but they dominated the horizon, making her perspective uncertain.

"Ten, maybe fifteen miles before we're really in them. We could walk it," Kelly said dubiously.

Lara lifted her feet a few inches, displaying the heeled sandals she wore. "I didn't know when I got dressed yesterday that I'd be going on the lam or I'd have worn hiking boots."

"You don't even own hiking boots. Okay, so we ca—" Kelly broke off to stare at Lara. "You don't own hiking boots."

"I know. I was kidding."

"You don't kid like that."

Lara caught a protest behind her teeth and held it there, looking at Kelly in astonishment. She was right: it wasn't the kind of joke Lara made, its inaccuracy lying too close to falsehood for her comfort. But there'd been no twinge of dissonant music, no out-of-tune keys played as she'd spoken. They were more distressing in their absence than their presence ever could have been, and her voice went light and heady. "It didn't feel like a lie."

"Holy crap." Kelly sat up more enthusiastically than Lara liked. "Does that mean you're losing your power?"

"Impossible," Dafydd murmured from the backseat. Both women twisted to look at him. He looked worse again, the vehicle sapping his strength for all that he still held the staff. "Lara's magic is mortal. Even if the Barrow-lands are closed away forever, her talent will never fade. At most it's only changing. Maturing."

Truth rang clear and reassuring in Lara's mind, relaxing her shoulders a little. "I thought developing it would make hearing, and telling, lies worse. But it's like, what's the phrase? 'Close enough for government work.' It didn't matter that I wasn't perfectly truthful. It was like it understood nuance."

"Lara!" Kelly caught Lara's hand, expression bright as she put away their troubles for a moment. "Lara, does this mean you might develop a sense of humor?"

Lara, injured, said, "I have one. It's just not very—"

"Nuanced?" Kelly suggested happily. "Seriously, Lar, this is great. Think how much less hideous it'll be if your wacky talent doesn't make you turn green when somebody gives the polite answer instead of the truth."

Dafydd, far more gently, said, "I've never known a mortal truth-seeker, or even one of the Seelie talents. You can already do more than you could—"

"Three weeks ago?" Lara asked wryly. "A year and a half ago? I honestly don't know which way to count it. Either way, though, you're right. I can do more than I could, and for the first time I'm wondering if maybe I could learn to turn it on and off." The idea sent a shock through her, relief tangled with fear, and she unwound to gaze out the windshield at the mountains again. On one level, the idea of turning the truth sense off seemed like casually removing her arm. The idea also made her aware, as she'd never been before, how tiring it was to always be on guard against falsehood.

She heard herself say, "It doesn't matter right now," and ached with the weary truth running through it. "We're going to have to keep going, Kel. I can't walk ten miles in these shoes, and maybe all that's up there is a dead deer."

"If I were stronger," Dafydd said from the backseat, his voice low and frustrated.

Lara shook her head. "If wishes were horses." Chills ran down her spine, this time from awareness that her talent didn't object to the phrase. "I've never said that before. I've heard it, but it just made me uncomfortable. If wishes were horses, beggars would ride. I never would have said that. It's too improbable. It's not *true*."

"It's true enough," Dafydd said. "If wishes were horses, beggars probably would ride."

"But wouldn't a beggar be more likely to wish for a house and food and clothes?"

"It doesn't say if wishes came true, only if they were horses."

"Will you two shut up already? Ye gods." Kelly put the car back in drive. "If I'd known you were going to start deconstructing axioms I'd have left you to sleep."

"No." Lara smiled, unexpectedly cheerful. "You wouldn't have."

"How many times do I have to tell you you're not supposed to *do* that?" Kelly shot her a scolding glance. "You better hope it's a dead deer, or I might just turn you over to the cops."

"No," Lara said again, and smiled at the road. "You won't."

Kelly said "Oh, be quiet" without rancor, and both women laughed. It was better that way, Lara thought. Better, certainly, than the tension that slowly ebbed their laughter away as they made their way down the road.

She wasn't, she realized, afraid of being arrested herself. She could employ the newly acquired knack of making people hear the truth in her voice if she must, though it was still an unpalatable solution. One that would probably end, as Kelly had suggested, in straitjackets and padded walls. And prison was hardly preferable, though there at least she'd be less likely to face psychotropic drugs meant to ameliorate the insanity of claiming to have been attacked by fairy-tale monsters. There would be a chance of parole from prison, as well, should she be convicted of manslaughter or murder. Aggravated assault, a more hopeful part of her suggested, or attempted manslaughter; those were lighter sentences, and there was no word yet on whether Detective Washington had survived his injuries.

Anxiety relaxed its knotted hold in her belly, loosened by faint curiosity. Lara had never thought of herself as particularly brave, but she recognized the pattern of her thoughts: she was looking for ways to accept all blame herself. None of them had done anything wrong, beyond being caught up in extraordinary events, but if the worst should come to pass, there was no reason for both Kelly and Dickon to suffer.

It would be easier if she had a weapon, so she could claim she'd forced Kelly to help her at gunpoint. But the true voice might help there, if she could vocalize a command that even authorities might find impossible to ignore. Two weeks ago she never would have imagined her talents might stretch that far, but now, watching the mountains come closer, she was certain there were innumerable aspects to her truthseeking, and that in time she would learn to use them all.

Lights flashed in the distance, a curve in the road hinting at a hollow and the interference the oncoming driver had warned of. Lara squinted, trying to see more clearly. "If it goes badly, we'll need a distraction. Something to let Dafydd get into the forest."

"I could always take my shirt off," Kelly offered.

Lara blinked rapidly at her friend. "You could what?"

"To distract them while Dafydd makes his getaway. You said we'd need a distraction."

"Oh. Oh! I didn't think I'd said that out loud. I was just thinking. They won't be able to find you if you get into the trees, will they, Dafydd?"

He said "No" with utter confidence. "I'm surprised you were able to find me earlier."

"I can see through your glamour," Lara reminded him. "I should be able to see you when you're not hiding behind it."

"Okay, guys, here we go. Dafydd, lie back down, put your seat belt on, cover yourself as much as you can with your coat. I'll tell them you're sleeping if we get pulled over."

Dafydd did as he was told as the road straightened, leading down into the hollow they'd glimpsed. Four vehicles, three of them emergency vehicles, were spread across the road. The fourth, a compact car bleached of color in the oncoming sunrise, was half off the road, a black, indistinguishable shape of an animal sprawled across its hood. Kelly slowed the car, then slowed further, almost coming to a stop as Lara muttered, "I *said* they couldn't possibly have roadblocks up this far out."

"Your triumph," Kelly said sourly, "is misplaced. It doesn't really matter if it's technically not a roadblock when it's effectively blocking the road. God, what'd they hit?"

"I can't tell." Lara leaned forward, but shook her head. It was large, at least deer-sized, but early-morning shadows and the flashing lights from the emergency vehicles made it impossible to recognize. "Ambulance, forest ranger, state trooper. Two out of three ain't bad."

Kelly shot her another sharp look. "I'm not handling you using idioms very well, Lara. Can you go back to being your usual literal self until we're out of this mess?"

"Sorry," Lara whispered, and meant it. "I feel like someone's taken a rubber band from around my thoughts. I never would have even thought to say 'two out of three ain't bad' before now."

"Well, it's not usually true. *Crap,* here comes the cop. Did it have to be the cop?" Kelly put the emergency brake on and rolled down the window as Lara put her elbows on the dashboard, supporting her chin with her hands as she looked out the windshield. She could see almost nothing, gaze unfocused while her heartbeat soared, but she hoped her fingers would help obscure her features. The ranger would have been less likely to have seen their images, but she was kneeling intently by the dead animal.

Kelly pitched her voice in a loud whisper, calling, "Hey," to the trooper. She made a loose finger-over-the-lips hushing gesture, explaining, "My sister's sleeping in the backseat. Is everybody okay? Are we gonna be able to get around?"

The trooper's tense expression faded and he flipped a flashlight on to glance at the backseat without really looking. "We've got some people pretty badly banged up. I was able to let the last guy through, but the paramedics just got here. It might be a while."

"Well, getting hurt people to the hospital is probably more important than getting to Mom's house for waffles before seven. What'd they hit, a deer?" Kelly's soft voice sounded perfectly normal: concerned, polite, a little rueful. She'd been right, Lara thought; they'd needed her. Lara would never have been able to sound as casually interested, much less come up with easy lies about the sleeper in the backseat or their destination.

Tension sprang to life in the trooper's expression, barely visible from the corner of Lara's eye. "Something big, anyway. Look, you three just sit tight and I'll wave you through as soon as I can, all right? Keep your windows rolled up. I'll knock if I need to give you any more information."

"No problem. Thanks, Officer. I hope everybody's all right." Kelly rolled up the window as he walked away, then carefully put her hands on the steering wheel too low for him to see if he glanced back. Her knuckles went white in the dawning light, forearms rigid, though her face remained smooth and pleasant. "I think I'm gonna puke."

Dafydd, muffled, said, "Please don't. Being encased in steel is uncomfortable enough. Adding the scent of bile would be a cruelty beyond compare."

"That was amazing," Lara whispered. Both she and Kelly slumped in their seats, Kelly flipping her hair over one shoulder to mask her face as she looked at Lara. "Really," Lara repeated. "I couldn't have done that. You were perfect."

"Yeah, but did you see his face when I asked what they hit? 'Something big' isn't an answer. What's big out here you can hit? Deer? Bears? Maybe a cougar?"

"That's not a cougar. Cougars are tawny and that thing's black." Lara dared a glance toward the damaged car. "I don't think there are any wolves out here. Maybe it's a bear."

"He would have said if it was a bear."

"You think it's something from my world." Dafydd pulled his coat down, the rustling making both women start to turn before they flinched back, remembering the person in the back was supposed to be sleeping.

"I think we're too far away from any nuclear sites or chemical dumping grounds for animals to mutate into something that a cop won't identify beyond 'something big,'" Kelly said. "So, yeah, I think maybe something else came over with you."

"The nightwings," Lara said abruptly. Dafydd shifted like he wanted to sit up, and she reached backward without looking, searching for his hand. His fingers, still as cool as they'd been earlier, slid through hers. She squeezed, reassured and reassuring. "But how did they find us?"

Kelly's gaze fixed forward. "How did they find you at all? Lara, you've been home for weeks now. David's been here all along. How come those things didn't attack until this afternoon?"

"They wanted us both in the same place," Dafydd suggested.

Kelly shook her head. "You were in the same place when she visited you in prison."

"But we didn't touch," Lara said with sudden certainty. "When he came out of the courtroom today I hugged him. Maybe that was the trigger. What kind of spell calls the nightwings, Dafydd? Is it like the scrying spell Emyr was trying to cast? One that takes a lot of time and concentration? We were still holding hands when they attacked."

"Our enemy would have been holding it in preparation," Dafydd said thoughtfully. "Like I'd done with the worldwalking spell, Lara. It would've been much less dramatic if I'd had to spend a few hours concentrating to open that door, so I'd done my preparation earlier, and held it behind the final word of the spell. Our enemy wouldn't want to risk losing our scent in the time he prepared, so he would have had it waiting."

"Then why didn't it attack the moment we touched?"

Dafydd shifted again. "Time isn't the same in the Barrow-lands as it is here. From our enemy's point of view, it could well have been instantaneous."

Kelly's gaze dropped to their entwined fingers. She smacked them and Lara loosened hers, first insulted, then alarmed. "Ow. But we've touched a lot since this afternoon, Kelly. If the nightwings were using that as a trigger, they'd have found us again by now."

"No." Dafydd sat up as he spoke, clearly forgetting he was meant to be sleeping. "It would have been a spell set to trigger once, like the attack when I returned to the Barrow-lands. Setting a cascade of triggers would exhaust anyone, even my father, beyond an ability to pursue anything else. No one would risk it."

"Well, then what changed? If we're being tracked by something from your world, what pointed it toward—" Lara broke off, staring at the staff Dafydd still held clenched across his lap. "Oh, no. I broke the glamour on that, and you've been clinging to it for hours."

"There's so much iron in your world it would be difficult to pinpoint its location," Dafydd said. "And it's been in transit. But we've been on this road heading south a while now."

"And that thing came from the south," Kelly finished as all three fixed gazes on the creature sprawled across the nearby car.

Sudden life twitched through it, and Lara heard her own whisper echoed by the other two: "Oh, shit."

Thirty-One

Kelly braced herself, hands high on the steering wheel. "Should I rush it? A thousand pounds of metal ought to put it down for the count again, right?"

"You can't. There are too many people." Lara got out of the car without thinking and pulled Dafydd's door open for him. Kelly let go an aggrieved yell and pushed her own door open, half standing in the driver's well.

"What the hell are you doing?"

"I don't know! Stay in the car!" Lara ran forward, whispering the brief exorcism she knew under her breath. It wouldn't be enough, and she cursed herself for not having memorized a longer one in the days before Dafydd's release.

He was at her side, stronger again now that he was no longer trapped in a vehicle and with the staff once again bright in his hand. Still pale, still fragile, but the sunrise did him the favor of lighting his golden eyes to fire. In that light there was no pretense of humanity about him, his hair too fine, his bone structure too delicate. Panic caught Lara under the breastbone and she hissed, "Dafydd, get back in the car! You can't—"

"I can hardly allow you to face that thing on your own," he said just as softly. "You have no weapons, no armor—"

"No way to protect you! Get back!"

The trooper had looked up as soon as their car doors opened and came striding toward them in the dawning light. "I'm going to have to ask you to get back into the car—" He broke off, gaping, and an orchestra crashed raw song through Lara's mind. Too late; it was too late to hide Dafydd or herself, and if she had any doubt, it was belied by the trooper drawing his sidearm as he advanced on them. "Down on the ground, both of you!"

Lara put her hands in the air, slow actions that made her vividly aware how she was disobeying the trooper's command. She poured conviction into her voice, steeling it with truth and willing the man to hear that truth. "Officer, that thing they hit, it's dangerous and nobody's equipped to stop it. You need to get everyone out of here now."

He wavered, halting his approach but not retreating. "I said on the ground!"

"Get on the ground, Dafydd. *Do it*," Lara snapped, when the Seelie prince hesitated. "He's more likely to shoot you than me. You're male." And exotic, she wanted to add, though she suspected the trooper would use the word "weird" instead. The creature twitching on the car hood no doubt verged on too much strangeness already. She didn't want to add to it, not when it could mean Dafydd's life.

Dafydd, reluctantly, did as he was told, lying on his belly with his hands out, though he continued to clutch the staff defiantly. The trooper scowled at him, expression barely hiding fear, then leveled his weapon at Lara again. "Both of you!"

"I'm unarmed, Officer. I'm smaller than you, and I'm wearing high heels. I can't possibly rush you. I'm no danger to you at all. You know I'm telling the truth." Lara's throat hurt from the effort of making the words true, so the officer couldn't doubt them even when he wanted to. That was power, real power: she recognized it even as she struggled to command it. "None of us is a danger to you. That thing over there is, though."

"That thing is dead!"

"No." Lara spoke at the same time the ranger did, startling both herself and the officer, who shot a quick hard look toward the other official. The woman stood up, her mouth a thin grim line. "It's badly injured, but not dead. I'm going to have to . . ." She stepped toward her truck.

Lara, barely audible even to herself, whispered, "Don't."

The thing—the nightwing, though it was far more massive than the little demons they'd encountered before—lashed out with a limb so flexible it could have been a tentacle. But no tentacle gleamed the way this did, like it was ridged with cartilage. It seized the ranger's legs and yanked backward. She jerked to the earth, unable to catch herself, and Lara knew without seeing that the bones of her face were broken. One of the paramedics shouted and ran forward. *Stupid*, Lara thought, but she did it herself. She heard Dafydd scramble to his feet, and heard a shot fire, and then Kelly's scream.

Nothing else could have taken her eyes from the nightwing. Lara spun, fear gutting her as she saw Kelly fall to the ground. A misstep brought Lara low, skirt tearing as she hit the asphalt, and another tentacle lashed out, snapping through the air where her torso had been an instant earlier.

Lightning shot out of the clear morning sky and severed the tentacle. It dropped on top of her and she screamed, struggling to throw it off as it writhed and twitched and then, terribly, began to contort. Wings stretched and split from its crackling shape, then claws, then burning eyes and a mouth full of dagger-sharp teeth. Whatever horror the nightwings had become, they weren't confined to it: separated from the whole, they took on their old shapes again, and this one leapt at Lara.

Its claws scraped asphalt as she rolled, eyes wide and searching for weapons. There was nothing: no rocks, no branches, the modern highway system too tidy to present her with a chance for survival. The nightwing pounced a second time and she flipped onto her back, catching its throat as she'd done with one of its brothers what seemed like a lifetime ago now, back in the Barrow-lands. The useless exorcism rose to her lips and was drowned beneath a shriek as the monster caught her forearm in clawed feet and raked upward, leaving deep scores in her skin. Powered by a sudden rush of pain, she flung the thing away and scrambled to her feet, determined to kick it to death if she could do nothing else.

Instead, Kelly Richards appeared above it, and rained death with a dozen sharp blows from a crowbar.

For an instant she and Lara stood facing each other, Kelly's face alight with triumph in the gold light of sunrise. Her friend was beautiful, Lara thought suddenly, beautiful with violence, beautiful like a Valkyrie, full of passion and strength. With her hair spilling around her shoulders and a bloody crowbar in her hands, she made a convincing modern warrior woman. For an instant outside of time and thought, seeing her seize the opportunity to become someone so extraordinary was wonderful and even fun.

Then she threw Lara the crowbar and ran like hell for the car as the trooper shouted, "Put down your weapon! Put the weapon—put the weapon *down!*"

Lara, incensed, shouted, "Shoot the goddamned *monster!*" and threw herself toward the amalgamated nightwing, crowbar raised like a sword.

Some part of her recognized that she herself had become a warrior in the past few days. There was no other answer for the boldness that drove her to charge the massive creature enveloping the car that had struck it. She was armed with a crowbar and passion, nothing more, but the pairing proved formidable: a tentacle wrapped around the bar and she swung like a pro hitter, smashing the glittering black thing against the wrecked car's door. Ichor splattered and the damaged piece fell away, beginning its terrible transformation into a nightwing, into a component piece.

Lara bashed it ruthlessly, turning it to spattered goo before it became what it had been, and swung again as another tentacle lashed at her. The thing was formless, shapeless, creating of itself what was necessary to attack, and she couldn't imagine how the ranger or the officer had thought it an animal at all. Unless—and it seemed possible—it had held some near-earth shape as it hunted, simply so it wouldn't draw attention to itself. That need was gone now: Lara and Dafydd were its prey, and the law enforcement agents and paramedics were nothing more than collateral damage.

The trooper was still torn between his enemies, clearly wanting to choose Dafydd as the comprehensible one, but too afraid of the conglomerated nightwings to ignore them. A black mass slid up behind him, threatening to end his dilemma permanently. Lara screamed and Dafydd lifted his hands, the staff held high in one and his other palm forward.

Power surged from the staff. Lightning arced around the trooper and exploded into the roiling creature of darkness. The trooper fired wildly, terrified by the lightning, then realized he hadn't been hit. He whipped around as nightwings erupted from the section of monster Dafydd attacked, and chose his side: gunfire blazed repeatedly, every shot counting as bullets buried themselves in the monster.

Dafydd dropped to one knee, visibly fading, even with the staff's support. Lara's heart caught. There was no time, not to fight the creature the way they'd been doing. The Seelie prince would die before they triumphed, and bitterly, they would likely not triumph at all should he die. For an instant that held her in place, staring fearfully at Dafydd, and then the nightwing came again in a surge of darkness and rage.

She didn't think it out clearly; didn't think it out at all, in truth, and truth was her talent, so she ought to heed it. She was surrounded, like the nightwing wanted her drawn in, and so in a spate of madness she dove forward, taking the fight to it. The truth could build a way of its own. Lara had followed such paths three times now, those stark roads of white light and irresistible power.

There had to be a spark of that brilliance buried somewhere in the nightwings' makeup: they were creatures of dark, perhaps, but dark couldn't exist without the light.

That thought wobbled fearfully, bringing with it the image of a starlit sky, brilliant diamonds scattered through velvet night. She could imagine each of those diamonds winking out, leaving nothing but darkness behind. Terror squeezed her chest, leaving her hands clammy. There was no telling what lay in the dark, no way to protect herself when the world was only black. Perhaps it was light that couldn't exist without dark.

That thought twisted, too, turning her inner vision to nothing but blazing, pure light. It was as meaningless as the blackness: no contrast, no shadows, no color, only brilliant pain that matched the fear of darkness.

They wound together, pain and fear twining to make a world of shadows and color. Gold painted the edges of her vision, reminder of the sunrise. As if it were a guide, that soft shade made her grasp that pain and fear were part of the truth that might destroy the nightwings. She was reluctant to embrace them, but the music pounding in her ears soured as she shied away. Jaw tight, she nodded acceptance, and felt her limbs go thick and numb as ugly emotion rooted inside her. They weren't comfortable, she realized abruptly, but they were necessary. Without pain, without fear, humans had little way to gauge danger; personal experience could be too deadly a cost. Somehow that made them easier to endure, and they lost a degree of their paralyzing power.

Suddenly bold, Lara thrust crescendos, pieces of who she was, of the magic she commanded, out of herself, like they were a weapon themselves. Music rushed out of her, throwing a challenge to the dark Seelie creatures that had crossed into her world.

The world roared back, an entity of its own, *alive*.

Put that way, into simple and obvious terms, it rang with such truth that Lara blushed to have never noticed it before. Of course it was alive; it supported all the things that lived. But she had never imagined it to have a voice of its own, a presence and a power that threatened to overwhelm everything that she was.

It was the sound of earthquakes and waterfalls, thunder so profound she felt, more than heard, it. If it had music, it was lost to her. She staggered under its weight, then dropped to her knees and put her hands against the asphalt, trying to gather support from the same ground that threatened to drag her under.

Pain reached a crescendo, then drained away as the world searched and found her magic, the thing that had garnered its unfathomable attention. For a brief eternity Lara felt she was a mote under a microscope, turned and twisted for examination. Urgency fled as the earth's vibrations reached into her marrow, shaking it loose. It seemed to her that she belonged where she was, all but mindless, a single beacon of song and light so small as to be obliterated by the earth-storm all around her. Her sense of self was lost, a speck in the maelstrom of life, and she drifted forever.

Forever, a speck that was still Lara Jansen whispered, *forever is a very long time, to immortals.*

And the world, in so much as it could, laughed. Ease and recognition rolled through thunder, not reducing her awe, but at least making it a more comfortable thing to hold inside her. She belonged to this world; her strange magic was born of it, and it accepted her, though welcome was still far removed. Satisfied, it released its hold on her. Lara, trembling, bent all the way to the ground and rested her forehead there in thankful relief.

As it retreated from her awareness, she caught a glimpse of music so old, so vast, that she understood she had been on the edge of a chord for all the time she'd been in communion with the planet. It belonged to a song so impossibly huge she could barely grasp that it was played at all, and she knew with a sudden, aching breathlessness that the very earth itself was no more than a single instrument in an orchestra spanning the stars.

Her hands made claws, trying to snatch the endless concerto back; trying to reach beyond the earth to grasp the melody of the moon, the sun, the planets.

It was cold, the space between notes. Cold and endless, with no promise of warmth or forgiveness. The moon, dead world that it was, had a refrain of its own, but it was lost to her, lost long before she could understand it, long before she reached so far as the music of the sun. Through despair she wondered if that was perhaps for the best: surely any fraction of sound she could capture from a star would incinerate her, and yet she would have taken the risk if she could have stretched so far.

She fell back inside herself, bereft of the solar system's song; bereft of everything but the thin tune that was her own sense of truth, and which now seemed puny in the face of what she'd seen. She turned blind eyes toward the sky, aware of the heat of tears on her cheeks, and saw nothing, only felt the loss of a symphony she would never be large enough to hear. That, *that* was a truth of terrible proportion, and it cut her apart, releasing all the music inside her. Notes shattered outward, their edges like knives, and they lanced the darkness around her.

It came apart with a scream, with a hundred screams, as nightwings were torn asunder from one another. Lara caught her breath, a single tiny retraction of the power flooding from her.

The nightwings saw it as weakness, and struck.

Thirty-Two

Lara felt them like the earth hadn't let her go. Wounds opened up across her skin, great bloodless slashes that rent her to the bone, for all that her eyes saw no such scours. Cramps seized her kidneys and fluttered with agonizing intent, as if her body was trying to reject a wrongness it had no understanding of. Every instinct said to curl down around her own pain, to wait it out, but the part of her that still held a fumbling grasp on intellect remembered what the nightwings were, and how to fight them. Breathless with hurt, she forced her eyes open and staggered to her feet.

New sunlight cut through the distant mountains, illuminating their hollow until it became a cup of fire. Nightwings flooded it, marring its brilliance, but even their numbers were unable to disguise how it sliced apart the world. Lara stood bathed in brilliance, and knew that the handful of men and women who fought with her looked like warriors of legend in its light.

Beyond that slash of daylight lay the rest of the world, bathed in comparative darkness and on the verge of never waking from that night. Lara knew it with a clear thunder of truth: they would defeat the nightwings here, giving all to do so, or something would tear in the fabric of her own world, and might never be mended again.

She didn't know she spoke, only heard the words linger on the brilliant sunrise: "Changes that will break the world."

As if she'd called them, the nightwings came to her.

They burned bright, their once-black shadows gray with distance from their own world and reflecting pale gold with morning sunlight. It made them worse somehow, made them seem more solid and more real than they had been when she'd wrestled one to the ground in the Barrow-lands.

The Barrow-lands were a place of magic, she thought, the idea unexpectedly clear in the face of demons swarming toward her. They were lands of mist and magic and insubstantiality, of illusion and impermanence. A scrying spell might open a window to another place, might permit people to speak to one another, but it lacked the physical presence of her own world's telephones and video cameras. Those things remained, here, always ready for use, but another spell would need to be cast, another whole communications array built, for a second "call" to be placed in the Barrow-lands.

Reversed, that could mean the nightwings grew evermore material the longer they remained in her world. The short exorcism hadn't worked on them. Maybe that failure was as much an increase in their reality as the brief exorcism being only the beginning of her world's version of a spell.

Crystal thoughts, all of them, more standing out in her mind as sudden epiphanies than as any progression of logic. The nightwings were on her, vicious screeching bats whose claws tore her dress and, she was faintly aware, her flesh as they attacked. One hit her chest-on, driving her backward, and lightning exploded from the clear morning sky yet again, rupturing the thing that attacked her.

Sudden blazing anger ate away her fear. This was her home, and she wouldn't surrender it to nighttime monsters from another world. Nightwings were ephemeral things in the Barrow-lands, but the idea that they could survive and breed in her world rang violently true. She swung with her crowbar, feeling satisfaction as it crunched into thin bone and cartilage. Somewhere nearby Kelly was shouting, the trooper was firing his weapon; somewhere there were screams, and she thought that all the nightwings hadn't come for her, after all.

Lightning split around her again, crashing into the mass of demons. They fell, making a brief clear space around Lara: clear of demons, clear for thoughts, and only then, finally, did she realize where the attacks were coming from. She swung around in the little space of safety he'd made for her, voice breaking as she cried, "Dafydd, *no!*"

Too late: too late; much too late. Dafydd stood in a ring of crackling electricity. No, didn't stand. Floated, as if the air itself was so ionized it had to lift him a few centimeters above the earth. He drifted in a half-circle, staff held tight in both hands, as though he drew power from it. He did: Lara was certain of it, and doubted even its power could sustain the Seelie prince for long. His hair, his fingertips, his very breath seemed alive with voltage, and as Lara watched, another burst of power erupted from him. He sagged, strength waning, and Lara ran forward even knowing there was no more chance she could reach him than the nightwings could; the Tesla cage surrounding him was too dangerous. But there were fewer of the monsters than there'd been: a few dozen now, where there had been uncountable numbers before.

It was enough, Lara whispered to herself, and willed it to be true. Dafydd had depleted their numbers enough: they could end it without his help. "Dafydd, stop! We'll find a way to finish them! *Stop!*"

Song poured off her as she shouted, conviction in her voice turning the words white with power. Dafydd's crackling electricity was puny next to her own relentless outpouring of strength; next to a determination so profound it made her courtroom demonstration seem like child's play. She spoke the truth with the will to make it real, and her world, her own thick and slow home, whose own magic was so long-muted it barely existed any more . . .

. . . *responded*. Sluggishly, yes, but it responded, shifting to align itself with the command Lara laid out. *Find a way to finish them*. So

278 ᵔ C.E. MURPHY

vague, so terribly vague, but her world's magic was so long-quiet that she felt that delicacy and fine-tuned requests would go un-heeded. There was no time to cajole, not with her friends and the others losing the battle. Dafydd blazed where he hung in the air, coils of electricity still snaking toward the nightwings, but with each monster's attack the cage that held him faltered a little. The trooper had run out of bullets and raced for his car with a swarm of nightwings after him. The paramedics, like the ranger, were down, but Kelly had a tire iron to match Lara's crowbar. She stood within the safety of the Corolla's open door, bashing every nightwing that came near.

Only Lara was out in the open and still standing. The nightwings were gathering; her power, blazing though it was, only needed to miss one of them and she would fall. She could feel something still changing in the world, acquiescing to her demand, but her heart's acceleration beat a story that the world would answer too late. That was the price of old magic, of power called in a place that no longer recognized its own strength: it could only rise in its own time, and she had no time left.

She only saw it from the corner of her eye, the small gesture of Dafydd raising his head, and panic soured her stomach. She knew, she *knew* what he intended, because she would have done the same: would have gathered all her power to her with the same gesture he did, crossing his arms over his chest as he offered a brief, but not re-gretful, smile. He would burn himself out to save them, as Lara would have done in his position.

As she would have done, and in so doing, would have rendered it all meaningless.

Lara threw the crowbar at him.

Cold iron smashed into his web of lightning. Electricity crashed toward it, ionized air losing its tension. Dafydd fell, knees crumpling as he hit the earth and lost his grip on the ivory staff. The crowbar it-self dropped to the ground a few feet away, not close enough to have touched him, but close enough to disrupt his power, to ensure he couldn't use the last of what sustained him and die trying to save a scattered handful of mortals.

Relief ricocheted through Lara's heart, then turned to dust as Dafydd ap Caerwyn collapsed into insensibility.

She barely knew she moved, and though she wanted to go to Dafydd, a different need sent her elsewhere: to the worldbreaking staff, lying alone and abandoned just out of Dafydd's insentient reach.

Power cascaded through her as she scooped it up, turning her body rigid with pain and excitement. The staff *sang,* an unholy shriek of exultation: its very purpose was chaos, and it had been bound too long by an order. Released, that power could do what she needed it to: defeat the nightwings and save Dafydd. Save her world, perhaps, and the truth of that burned through her until she lifted the staff and drove it into the earth.

The world cracked, rivulets of light slicing out from Lara and bashing into the ground. She heard it more than saw it, an endless tumult of bells, as though she'd been caught in a tower as the church below tolled out a greeting to the first light of morning.

Asphalt tore beneath her, a long jagged line opening up. Music poured out, rising into the sky, and the rip followed it, splitting apart earth from heaven. It rushed toward a vanishing point, toward the ball of fire just over the horizon, like a road reaching for the roof of the world.

Oisín's voice danced through the music, whispering "Truth will seek the hardest path." Lara, staring at the ripped hole in the world, thought she'd never seen a path that looked harder. She jolted forward, forcing her knees to unlock. Her ankle bent to the side, a reminder that she wore strappy sandals. She scrambled forward regardless, afraid that if she paused, the shredded earth would close again, and whatever answers lay on the road before her would be gone forever.

A nightwing screeched, the sound harsh against truth's music. She swung with the staff, and the nightwing exploded on impact.

Lara ducked as another flew in, and felts its claws snag at the back of her dress. She would have to start wearing sturdier clothes than her favored linens and silks if she was going to live under constant attack. Leather, at least, or perhaps Seelie armor, simply as a matter of course.

She recognized the calm, wry idea as panic's close sister, something irrelevant to focus on so her fear seemed less important. She threw herself forward, feet clumsy as she tried to clamber up the path of light and music soaring into the sky.

Shock jolted her heart as hard as the ground jolted her foot as she slammed downward through the path. Lara tumbled forward through insubstantial light, catching herself on her hands and rolling to gape in offense at the shining road that wouldn't support her weight. A nightwing backwinged above her, falling like a bird of prey, and brilliant gold from the sunrise glittered just at the top of her range of vision. At least she would die with the light in her eyes, if she had to die at all.

She was looking for a phrase, a way to shape truth, to save herself, when a black-clad warrior spilled down the path of light and eviscerated the nightwing as he passed.

Watching him, Lara knew she'd never really seen someone fight before. The battle with the Unseelie had been too busy, too crowded, for her to watch any one person, and her other encounters with violence—mercifully few, excepting the past week—had been either brief or laden with magic, neither of which allowed for a man with a sword to do what he did best.

He was Unseelie; he had to be, if the armor of hammered midnight meant anything. He wore a helm, obscuring his face even if his back hadn't been to her, and the blade he used was liquid gold in the sunrise. The nightwings came to him like moth to flame, drawn by a likeness or by the path of light he'd entered on. They came to him, and they died.

There was no pattern, but there was grace and surety of movement to their dance. He seemed to know where they would strike
from, always twisting or stepping away. Flame, weak in the morning
light, washed off his armor when they spat it. At that, a handful of
them scattered, screaming defiance, then rushed at each other, col-
liding in a spatter of dark above the ruined highway.

A single creature rose up where there had been many, and others
retreated to dive into its blackness. It contorted as they crashed together, gaining strength and size until it became a sinuous black ser-
pent, winged and fork-tongued and spitting fire. Clawed feet burst
out of its chest, and it coiled its tail beneath itself and used it to
spring forward. Lara screamed and skittered backward, but the Unseelie warrior met the creature with a leap of his own.

They came together in a clash, armor and cartilage rattling. Fire
gouted over the knight's head, the monster's flesh absorbing his
sword's blow. Absorbing in part, at least: a howling nightwing fell
away and the whole of the thing became fractionally smaller. Lara,
wide-eyed, sought her crowbar and found it lying almost directly beneath the conflict, alongside Dafydd's too-still body.

Sickness grabbed her belly, but she pushed onto her hands and
knees, crawling forward as the battle fell to the side, both combat-
ants requiring the earth for leverage. They struck again, metal
shrieking as the giant nightwing's claws dug into armor, but a second wounded nightwing fell away. Lara closed her fingers around
her crowbar and edged closer to the fight, swinging with both it and
the staff when one of the smaller monsters came close. Her hands
were icy, so thick she could barely feel either weapon, but she would
not leave their rescuer to fight the amalgamated nightwing by himself.

He was the answer to her determination. How, she didn't know,
but she had no doubt that she'd called him. That the staff had torn
her world asunder and ripped open a road between the Barrow-
lands and here because she had spoken truth. She'd promised their
little army would find a way to defeat the nightwings without pay-

ing a cost in Dafydd's life, and a chaos magic had responded. The earth still rattled and shook around them, and she no longer knew if it was the staff's work, or the battle with the nightwings.

One came too close to her and she rose up on her knees, smashing it against the asphalt. Kelly, sounding miles away, let out a triumphant shout and tore toward the fight, joining Lara in crushing slices of midnight the warrior hacked off the larger beast.

They were mindless, Lara thought, driven only to destroy. They weren't by nature cooperative, not from what she'd seen in the earlier battles, and yet they had twice now joined together to make a single creature more dangerous than they were individually. Something had to be guiding them, using creativity and cleverness to turn many small demons into a single vast one.

She whispered "Amazing grace" and turned her gaze from the falling bits of monster to the larger one still battling the Unseelie warrior. Song settled in her blood, focusing her power to know truth, to hear it, to *see* it, and their master came clear.

He rode the giant nightwing, ghostly expression full of the mixed concentration and glee of a bronco rider. His features were smooth, beautiful as all the Seelie were, but looking on him made her eyes hurt, as if she was looking at something that both was and wasn't there. She dropped the crowbar and clawed her hands around the staff, trying to draw more of its strength into herself so she might see more clearly, but that, it seemed, was not one of its gifts. Only destruction, and perhaps healing. No amount of pouring herself into the song, seeking truth, would alter that.

The nightwing changed shape as she struggled to see its master more clearly. New heads sprang up as the knight cut pieces away, until it was a hydra, all heads and almost no body. Kelly still smashed the injured nightwings with her tire iron, and finally the warrior struck one head off and a new one didn't arise. A second head fell, and the rider's face contorted with rage. He glanced up, seeking escape. Lara bellowed, "No!" with all the energy she had left, and for an instant he met her eyes and froze.

Then the hydra leaped forward, striking directly at her. Lara fell back, swinging with the staff, but the black knight was there, skewering the hydra's breast. Ichor sprayed out and another head fell before the thing dissolved into a handful of weak and broken nightwings. Kelly jumped on the closest ones, pounding them into the asphalt, and the Unseelie warrior dispatched the last two or three with less vigor, if no less thoroughly. Lara collapsed onto her elbows, wheezing with relief as their rescuer stood still a long moment, clearly searching for any further danger.

Then, breathing hard, he pulled his helm off and Ioan ap Annwn turned to offer Lara a hand up.

Thirty-Three

"What are you—" Lara fumbled the words, tongue too big for her mouth as she stared up at Ioan. He was gore-spattered, black smears across his golden skin, and he bared his teeth at her half-asked question, though his extended hand remained steady.

"I have been trying to follow you for hours. The worldwalking spell is difficult even for an adept, and I have very little practice with it. It was only when I heard your call for help that I was able to open a door at all. Will you stand?" He spoke with impatience so polite Lara hardly recognized it. She put her hand in his and he drew her up, then brought his sword to the ready as Kelly approached with the tire iron gripped in both hands.

"Lara, who is this? What's going on?"

The trooper drew their attention by amending her question to, "What the *fuck* is going on?" He was crouched behind his open car door, a shotgun balanced in the rolled-down window, so all that was visible were wide eyes and a double barrel.

Lara sensed, more than saw, both Kelly and Ioan cede the right to answer by taking half-steps backward. The right to answer and the position of responsibility, she thought a little wryly, and stepped forward. "We're the good guys."

"You're wanted for assault!"

Incongruous hope slammed through Lara's chest. "Just assault? Detective Washington's alive?"

The shotgun wavered as the trooper raised his head a few more inches, staring at her incredulously. "'Just' assault? That carries a fifteen-year prison term, lady! Whatever you did to him was bad enough that the whole damned East Coast is on alert, looking for you three."

"We didn't do anything to him. It was creatures like these ones." Lara nodded toward the shriveling nightwings, then took a second look and swore. "They're disintegrating."

"Not entirely." Ioan nodded at the largest of the nightwings, which twitched like a lizard's tail, life gone but nerve impulses remaining. Its body changed shape more than withered as Ioan spoke again. "Whatever sustained them will be left."

"Something *sustained* them?" Lara said horrified. Then, more urgently, she added, "Nobody's going to believe any of this without a body. Do you have a camera, Officer? Ioan, can you, I don't know, can you put a stasis spell on one of them or something, so it doesn't disappear?"

Both men exchanged glances, but the trooper, looking like he wasn't sure why, exchanged his shotgun for a cell phone and approached the largest dead nightwing to take pictures. He muttered, "The camera in the car will have caught the fight, too," somewhat dubiously.

Lara shared his uncertainty: it seemed somehow unlikely that magical creatures could be caught on videotape. On the other hand, Dafydd had spent years as a TV weatherman, so maybe there was hope. "Ioan?"

He shook his head. "Any spell I cast would only last as long as I remained here, and I have no intention of staying to explain any of this. We're weaker here, Truthseeker. Legend said we have always been. No one from Annwn stays in your world long, not if they can help it."

"Fairy tales," Kelly whispered. She'd knelt at Dafydd's other side and looked up now, eyes shining with worry. "In fairy tales if the fair folk stay in our world it's usually because they're trapped somehow and aren't strong enough to get away. Like Tam Lin except in reverse."

"And it was mortal love that saved Tam when he rode back into this world with the queen's host," Ioan said. Lara looked between them, bewildered, though Kelly's expression said she knew the story. "Had Janet come to Annwn to rescue him, she never would have been able to free him. We're weakened by this world," Ioan said again, "and Dafydd is weaker yet than he might have been, because his link to the Barrow-lands has been stolen from him."

"How did you—?"

"Know? Because no denizen of the Barrow-lands would be so wasted unless he's been cut away from the source of our power. Was it you?"

Lara nodded miserably. "I was trying to stop the nightwings from coming through a breach between the worlds. I closed it. I was afraid they'd take on a life of their own."

"As they would have. Or stolen many, more likely." Ioan frowned at the largest nightwing, which the trooper stood over, still filming. It had nearly reverted to shape, and bile rose in Lara's stomach as she recognized the shape.

"It's Officer Cooper. Oh my God." Her hands went to her mouth, half shock and half holding back illness. "Oh my God. This is the man the nightwings . . . took refuge in. Hid in. Oh my God, Ioan, what happened to him?"

"They required a host. Sustenance, so they could survive. Their maker would have been able to control a man infested by them, Truthseeker. Not easily, perhaps, but in time, with such an infection, the purveyor of disease would inevitably dominate the host. And the host's perception of himself as an individual being would have permitted the nightwings to act in concert the way we saw." Ioan sounded admiring. "It would take a magic user of great skill to accomplish all this."

"And a lot of innocent lives," Lara snapped. Ioan had the grace to look slightly abashed, as Kelly slowly came to Lara's side, looking down at the contorted dead man.

"No wonder it took awhile for him to catch up with us," she whispered hollowly. "Cooper would have been fighting for control over his own body."

"And losing," Ioan said without pity. "You're fortunate he had the strength of will he did, else you might have been destroyed hours since. And you are equally unfortunate that there was such corruption in his soul that he was susceptible at all." He fell silent a moment, looking at Cooper's body. The police officer looked tortured, Lara thought, and as though he'd aged years in the hours since she'd seen him last. Black threads stained his skin, like the blood vessels were filled with poison, which wasn't, she imagined, far from the truth.

Ioan finally turned his attention back to her. "You probably saved your world from an infestation, Truthseeker. And no wonder, then, that I had such trouble crossing over, with the path so thoroughly closed. Following you took everything I had, and even now I'm uncertain how it was accomplished."

Lara curled her fingers around the staff she still carried, reluctant to suggest it as the source of power Ioan had sent her searching for, or as the conduit that had allowed the worldwalking spell to work again. He only knew that he'd wanted a weapon, not what it looked like, and she had no intention of giving it up. Instead, after a moment's silence, she shook her head. "It doesn't matter, does it? You came, and you saved us."

"As I would now save my brother. I would return him to the Barrow-lands, Truthseeker." Ioan's voice cooled, as though he expected a challenge, and Lara for once found herself glad to meet that expectation.

"Why would I let you take him anywhere? As far as I know you're the one who killed Merrick and started this whole mess."

For a sudden moment she saw what Emyr might have looked like if he'd ever displayed a sense of humor. It cut through Ioan's face, biting but true: "I have done no such thing. I have, indeed, done my best to protect him. He faced some manner of trouble on the battle-field, Truthseeker. That was why I usurped his power and thrust him back to this world in the first place."

"You *what*? You laid the compulsion?" She hadn't expected her suspicions to be confirmed so easily, but Ioan's voice rang out over hers, strong and angry.

"No. I stole his power, Truthseeker, but not his will. I was watch-ing you during that battle, through my silver pool."

Lara, under her breath, said, "I thought scrying was an ice spell."

Ioan, unexpectedly, interrupted himself to answer that. "Ice is only frozen water, and water is my gift. I was watching," he re-peated. "To find you, but Dafydd rode close to you, and so I watched him as well. I saw him struggling with the compulsion, and I saw his lover bind him so he could drive himself away into the heart of the Unseelie army. I took the only path I could see to keep him safe. I wrenched his own magic away and forced the worldwalking spell he held at the ready to be cast, sending him back to your world. But he is dying now, Truthseeker. He will die if he stays here."

Lara's ears turned scarlet and she bit back a heated denial of the term Ioan had used for Aerin. He'd spoken only truth, and she knew it. Knew, too, that Aerin had been Dafydd's lover, but she hadn't allowed herself to put it into words, and was surprised how much they stung when voiced.

It wasn't a sting she could allow herself to pursue right now. Not with the truth of Ioan's words rushing over her. "Then, take me with you."

Ioan made a sound outside of words, a breath of regret and help-less humor. "I can't. The Barrow-lands will tolerate one passenger when the worldwalking spell is used, but I cannot force it to more. Much as I need a truthseeker, Dafydd is my brother, and dying."

"I can't just let you take him!" Fingernails on chalkboards, screeching untruth in her protest. She could; she would have to. Lara knelt and curled Dafydd's hand in her own, squeezing like she could waken him by force of will. "How can I trust you?"

"You're a truthseeker," Ioan whispered. "Ask your questions, but do it quickly. He has very little time."

Dafydd's hands were warm in hers. That seemed wrong, when he was the one lying so close to death. Lara stared at him dry-eyed and, dry-voiced, said, "Did you, Ioan ap Caerwyn, called ap Annwn, by any action or inaction of your own, force Dafydd ap Caerwyn's hand to murder Merrick ap Annwn?"

Soft, ferocious: "I did not."

Lara nodded once, a stiff ungainly motion. "Do you mean Dafydd ap Caerwyn any harm?"

That same sound again, the unhappy breath of laughter. "He's my brother, Truthseeker. I mean him no harm."

Lara nodded again, still jerky, then forced her gaze from Dafydd to his brother. He was beautiful, more beautiful than Dafydd, a per-fect creature cut from amber and garbed in night. She wanted to hate him, and could find nothing other than fear to knot her heart: fear for Dafydd, and fear that her gift might somehow fail her and she might be sending him to his doom. "Do you know a way for me to get back to the Barrow-lands?"

A spasm crossed Ioan's sharp-etched features. "Find the one who's done all of this to us. He must be in your world, Truthseeker. With the world walls closed, there's no other way he could have controlled the nightwings. He's here somewhere, and must himself be able to work the worldwalking spell. Find him, and maybe you can return."

Lara pressed her lips together, nodded a third time, and climbed to her feet. Her stomach was a solid mass, tight and heavy inside her, and her own expression felt like a stranger's, a mask of ill-concealed rage and frustration. She stepped back, giving Ioan the space he needed to kneel and lift Dafydd's body. When he'd straightened again she said, "Ioan."

"Truthseeker?"

Stranger's face, stranger's words; Lara had never said anything like what she said now. "If anything happens to him, Ioan, I will kill you."

Ioan ap Annwn afforded her the scantest bow, all he could manage with Dafydd's weight in his arms, and said, very softly, "I believe you."

Sunlight wrapped them, and they were gone.

Power erupted from the staff again as the walls between the worlds closed. Lara staggered, planting the weapon against the ground for support, and felt a shudder beneath her feet. Kelly bellowed in dismay as the earth lurched. "Pick it up, pick it *up!*"

"Pick what—?" Lara heard her own voice distantly as she took a few hopeless steps forward, dragging the staff with her. Overwhelming weariness drained all other emotion away. There was no lingering doorway, no break in space that might permit her to follow the two elfin princes. Visions shattered behind her eyes with each beat of her heart, pictures of the fanciful world she imagined every time she thought of Dafydd ap Caerwyn. A life with a man who grasped, instantly, what she was; a world beyond her own to explore. Now the color drained from those dreams, leaving them remote and cold.

"The staff, the goddamned *staff,* Lara!" Kelly slammed against Lara's side, bringing her back to herself enough to stare uncomprehendingly first at her friend, then at the ivory rod she herself held. It took long seconds to understand Kelly's alarm.

Worldbreaker. And it didn't seem to care what world it broke: Lara's own was as good as any other. She yanked it up, breaking its connection with the earth, but the ground continued to rumble threateningly. "This is New England!" Kelly wailed. "We don't have earthquakes here!"

"It's not an earthquake." Lara glanced upward, half expecting the sky to boil with clouds and lightning. It didn't, but a foreboding sense of *not yet* came over her, and she knotted her hands around the staff, holding it parallel to the earth. "You're done for now," she whispered to it, and exerted effort to put truth into the words. "This is my world. I don't care how much power I might wield through you. I won't let you destroy my home."

A length of ivory couldn't, in any logical way, be sentient or opinionated, but a sense of resentment built up from the staff regardless. Lara tightened her hands around it, aware that such fragile-looking bone should shatter beneath her grip, but never dreaming it might actually do so. "You waited for me for centuries. I've found you now, and I'm your master. A mortal master, at that. Oisín carried you a long time. You should know by now mortal masters can't be tempted the way Seelie can." The truth came from within her, absolute with conviction, though where it stemmed from, Lara had no idea. Oisín might know, if she ever had the chance to ask him.

Sullenness flared, but the building power retreated. With it, so did the tremors, and Lara stood breathing heavily and wondering at her own strength of will.

"I oughta arrest you both." The trooper sounded uncertain, but his voice took Lara's attention from the staff. She'd forgotten about him and everything he represented, caught up in Dafydd's weakness and the staff's living hunger to wreak havoc. There were innumerable other things to think about, and she latched on to the first one that came to mind.

"Detective Washington. Is he okay?" Speaking propelled her into action. There were injured people, perhaps dying people, who needed attention, and the trooper's indecision suggested he wasn't likely to follow through on his threat.

"Last thing anybody mentioned he was stable," he said after a moment. "Serious condition but stable."

"Thank God for that." Lara crouched by the ranger, whose eyes were wide open. She breathed through her teeth, fingers pinched against the asphalt, but she was alive. That was two, Lara thought. Washington and this woman, both survivors. It was more than she'd hoped for.

For a moment the staff felt warm in her hand again, as if offering potential power. Healing power, perhaps: that was what Lara had wanted it for, after all. The potential caught her off guard, and a sensation of triumph spilled from the staff. Lara jerked to her feet, narrowly avoiding casting the staff away in revulsion. No inanimate object should offer impulses like it did. Even if she knew how to control its power properly, the idea of doing its bidding seemed dangerous. There were humans who could affect healing much less esoterically than the staff's unknown magics might, and with only predictable side effects. "Officer, can you call for more paramedics?"

"A lot more," Kelly said unhappily from near the ambulances. "Two of these guys are dead."

"We saw it." A new voice spoke as the back of one of the ambulances opened. A paramedic climbed out, followed by a white-faced woman clutching her arm. She nodded to the station wagon the ranger had fallen by. "That's our car. We saw . . . those things . . . that you fought. We were afraid to get out."

Shocked relief shot through Lara. She'd forgotten there had been injuries in the car, that their delay had been due to the paramedics arriving and transferring people to the ambulances, and hadn't considered that anyone might have been hiding there. "That was the smartest thing you could've done. And probably getting back in and waiting for more paramedics is the smartest thing you can do now."

"Are they gone? Those things? What were they? What was it?"

Lara exchanged a look with Kelly, who said "Bats" without any conviction. It shivered tunelessly down Lara's spine, neither true nor false; bats were the closest equivalent to the nightwings that she could think of, too.

"Bats," the woman repeated, almost angry. "Bats don't do what those things did. That thing. It changed. It—they—turned into a . . . a . . ."

"Dragon," one of the paramedics supplied, then flushed as everyone looked at him. "Looked like a dragon to me."

"Little-known fact," Kelly breathed. "Bats and dragons are closely related."

That *did* run sour over Lara's skin, but she laughed anyway, a short sharp sound. "They were called nightwings. They're not bats and they're not dragons. They're more like demons, and they come from fairyland." She put truth into the words, knowing everyone would hear it. Knowing, too, that they wouldn't believe it for long, but she couldn't do anything about that. "The man who rescued us was an elfin prince," she added. "Thank him in your prayers, if you pray."

The woman stared at her a long moment. "I think I will tonight." She climbed back into the ambulance and closed the door with a resounding crash that ended all conversation for a while. Lara trailed back to their car as the trooper called for more help. Kelly joined her, earning an uncomfortable glance from the cop, though he made no effort to stop them.

"So now what?" Kelly asked eventually. "Do we let him arrest us or what?"

"No," Lara said as she got into the car. "I'm going to do what Ioan suggested. I'm going after whoever did this."

"I kind of thought so. Okay. How?" Kelly asked as she, too, got into the car.

"I'm not sure, but he's somewhere nearby. He has to be. Us killing the nightwings hurt him, I saw it. So if he needs the same things Dafydd did, he'll be in the woods, somewhere quiet and green where he can regain strength. I just need to concentrate and open a true path." Lara relaxed into the hum of truth in her own words.

Kelly cleared her throat. "Lara?"

"What?"

"I get that this whole truthseeking magic path thing is just how you roll now, and I hate to be all pragmatic . . ."

Lara frowned. "But?"

Kelly gestured at Lara's clothes. "But you're the one who pointed out you weren't exactly wearing hiking gear. If we're going chasing through the woods after bad guys, maybe we should do some shopping first."

Lara glared at her pretty, impractical sandals. "No."

"Lara, you're the one who said—"

"That was before. Besides, we're on the far edge of nowhere. There's probably not a J.Crew for forty miles."

"You've never worn J.Crew in your life."

"That's not the point!" Lara banged her palms against the dashboard. "The point is that before, we were just trying to get Dafydd somewhere quiet and safe so he could recover. Now he's almost dead and my last chance of getting back to him and making sure he's all right is out there somewhere. I'm not going to let whoever's been controlling the nightwings have an extra few hours to rest up while I find sensible shoes!"

A drawn-out silence, long enough to make her feel guilty, met Lara's tirade. She looked away, trying to summon the energy to mumble an apology, but Kelly said "Okay then" in an unoffended tone. "Let's pretend I suggested that first so my second idea would seem more palatable."

"What's that?"

"Do your truth-path-seeking thing somewhere else." Kelly pointed toward the trooper. "And right now, let's bug the hell out of here before he gets up the nerve to arrest us after all."

Thirty-Four

They crept by the trooper's vehicle like fugitives, neither of them bold enough to catch his eye. Lara wasn't strong enough to avoid it, either, and caught a glimpse of his grim expression as Kelly eased their car past his. She glanced sideways, too, then breathed, "We're going to have to try explaining this at some point, you know."

"One mess at a time," Lara whispered back. "At least half a dozen people saw it this time. Maybe that'll help with Washington."

"I hope so. God, I'm glad he's okay. He's a really good guy, Lara."

"I believe you." A little smile curled Lara's mouth. "Why are we whispering?"

Kelly gave a quick, startled laugh and an equally quick, guilty look over her shoulder to where the trooper and the battle scene were fading in the distance. "I don't know. Because the boogeyman back there might get us if he hears us?"

"I think the boogeyman is up there somewhere." Lara nodded toward the soft-lit mountains, her smile fading. "I'm sorry for getting you into this, Kelly. Maybe I should go on alone."

"There is no way I'm missing the grand finale after all this shit,"

Kelly said firmly. "I think even if it gets us killed I'd rather at least know how it turns out."

Alarm danced up Lara's spine to the tune of soprano flutes, pure sweet sounds. "Did you know you actually mean that?"

"I kind of thought I did. I'm pretty good about not stretching the truth around you, Truthseeker." She chortled. "Wish I'd thought of that. Um, so, hey. That guy was David's brother? He's cute. Sturdier than Dafydd."

Lara arched an eyebrow, both pleased and dismayed to see Kelly's flirtatious nature resurfacing. It was a way to keep her mind off Dickon, Lara knew; any other time she might have reminded her friend that she was engaged.

Not today, though. Whether Dickon could forgive Kelly remained to be seen, and Lara wouldn't entirely blame him if he couldn't. Neither, she suspected, would Kelly, and the game of looking to an elfin prince might take some of the edge away from that hard truth. "I think he chose to become stronger. The Seelie are all tall and slim. The Unseelie seemed broader, and he told me they'd changed to suit their surroundings. Maybe in another million years they'll be dwarfs," she said flippantly, and curious tones chimed around the idea, exploring it.

"I think I'll get my digs in while they're still tall, dark, and handsome, then. Beards never did much for me. I thought we thought he was the bad guy," Kelly said more quietly.

Lara dropped her chin to her chest. "We did, but you heard him. He was telling the truth."

"So basically you have no idea who's out there waiting for us. Okay," Kelly said to Lara's nod. "I'm pulling over when we get to the top of that hill, so we'll be right in the sunlight. And then you can do that voodoo that you do so well."

"I can't believe you just said that."

Kelly straightened, eyes wide. "I can't believe *you* just said *that*! Wow, you're like a real girl! Somebody call Geppetto!"

"You are not helping." Lara harrumphed at Kelly's smile, then looked ahead to the peak of the hill they climbed. Sunlight blinded her as they crested it, a lash of brilliance that reminded her of the true paths she'd created.

None of them were like the one she needed to build now. Two had simply led her home, figuratively and literally, and the third had been *seeking* indeed, searching out the staff's location. She thought the fourth had been something else entirely, less a path than a thread that pulled the world into alignment so it answered her need. That need had, perhaps, helped open a door between worlds, had perhaps helped mark the road Ioan ap Annwn wanted to take, but even that was unlike searching out a single man. An enemy, Lara thought, and made that idea clear in her mind. She was preparing to hunt an enemy, an individual with malicious intent. He'd struck at her and her friends repeatedly, and people had paid for that with their lives.

Dafydd might well have paid for it with his life.

Lara's hands clenched into fists. "No one else." Truth vibrated through the warning, its strength making Kelly catch her breath as she pulled the car over. Lara got out without thinking about it, feeling a little elfin as she did so: it seemed like being outdoors would help, even if her magic shouldn't be constrained by steel. She took the staff from the backseat as Kelly got out, and murmured, "I wish I meditated, or something. I feel like if I only had the right kind of mental discipline this would be easy."

"Think about what it's like when you're sewing," Kelly suggested. "I've seen you do it a few times. You get into the zone and nothing bothers you."

"Just stitch it all together, huh?" Lara smiled, but the idea caught, creating a tapestry in her mind. The door Dafydd had opened to the Barrow-lands began it, golden rectangle against a Seelie night, and black-winged monsters picked out in shining silk against a matte sky. There was something else there, a nebulous being whose presence was only known by his absence, but someone had set the spell to sic the nightwings on them.

The tapestry wound through the hours she'd spent in the Seelie court, reshaping itself into battle. There came the dark thread again, seizing Dafydd's will before another slash of gold cut it off when

Dafydd was thrown back to Lara's world. And then the attack in the garage, threads finally winding together to make a visible form. A hum struck up at the base of Lara's skull, the excitement of recognizing a true thing, and the staff, as if sensing her use of magic, warmed in her hands.

Encouraged, the tapestry wove itself faster, dark streak broadening until it became a violent smear of black: the scene they'd just left. Still it leapt forward, details lost as darkness raced away through white threads that turned to bells. Silver, white, pale gold, all ringing with sweet chimes. Goose bumps lifted on Lara's arms and she opened her eyes, barely daring to breathe.

For an instant she glimpsed a layer of radiation and heat; of all the wavelengths of light that human eyes and minds interpreted into sensible, comprehensible objects and colors. She could see past those constructions, could see a truth that lay outside of her ability to translate into anything meaningful. If she only knew the right direction to look she thought she might see through the heart of the universe, see all the way to its creator and perhaps through that, too. The music was that of the world again, made tenfold, far too much to bear.

Her mind folded under the strain, crumpling with the weight of too much vision and a terrible inability to understand. She dropped to her knees, staff falling away as she hid her face in her hands, and overwhelming song and sight collapsed under her cry.

The tapestry threads remained, though, black against white scoring a mark through her mind. Lara whimpered and felt Kelly's hands on her shoulders, and through incessant bells heard her friend ask, "Are you all right?"

"I can't open my eyes." Power drowned her voice, making it sound like she spoke through water. She ached with trying to contain it, her skin stretching too tight over blood and muscle. "The world hurts my mind. I can see his mark if my eyes are closed, but I can't open them."

"Okay. Okay." Falsehood, all of it: Kelly thought nothing was okay, and was verging on panic. Her fear made spikes in the music, driving into the sides of Lara's head. "Okay," Kelly said a third time, and panic faded into determination. "If I get you into the car, can you tell me where to drive without looking?"

"I think so. If I can keep my eyes closed. It's hard not to look." Mankind had never been good at not looking, from Lot's wife to now. Looking upon an angel was said to burn out the viewer's eyes, and yet the impulse to do so was enormous. An angel couldn't be so bright as the burning, bewildering world she'd glimpsed. Wanting to look hurt as badly as looking did, magic and human nature clashing with each other.

Maybe that was why humans had so little magic. Maybe their need to explore and investigate had trumped their inner gifts, forcing them to try and absorb more than their minds could handle. Her hands were pressed over her eyes, holding her lids shut, and still she *wanted* to see. Anyone weak enough to give in to all the glory magic could show them might well have ruptured with it.

Lot's wife, she thought again, and had an agonizing spike of sympathy for the woman that manifested in a lingering headache.

"Okay," Kelly said breathlessly. "Okay. Stay there a second. I think David's coat is still in the backseat. I'll make you a blindfold? Will that help?"

"Yes." Relief cracked the single word. "Yes, please." Barely a minute passed before Kelly tied Dafydd's coat over Lara's eyes, arms wound around her head and the back dangling over her face. Almost none of his scent remained in the fabric. "I can't really breathe."

"It's a modern Middle Eastern look," Kelly said. "I think it suits you." She flipped the coat back over Lara's head without loosening the blindfold. "Better?"

Lara drew a shaky breath, grateful for the physical inability to open her eyes and take in a world stripped to its essence by truth. "Much. Thank you."

"No problem." Kelly slipped her hand into Lara's and tugged her gently upward. "Can you navigate?"

Rough-woven white cloth spread out behind her eyelids, the black mark across it jagged and unfriendly. It made a schism in the otherwise pure tones of music, off notes drawing her as strongly as true ones ever had. It was exhausting, and she'd only held on to that much power for a minute or two. "As long as I don't have to get myself into the car, yes."

"That much I can help you with." Kelly guided Lara into the Corolla, buckling her seat belt with motherly efficiency, then hurried around to the driver's side. "The staff's in the backseat. Lead on, Quixote."

Lara turned her head, stymied in giving Kelly a dirty look. Just as well, she thought; with the truth burning in her gaze it might do Kelly physical harm. "That's two literary references inside of ten minutes. What did you do while I was gone, study the classics?"

"No, I studied them in college, but come on, how often do you get a chance to reference Pinocchio or Don Quixote in real life? I'm just seizing the opportunities you're presenting."

The car eased forward, startling without vision to accompany motion. Lara squeaked and fumbled for the handle above the door, curling her fingers around it. "I guess I'm glad to be of service. Not seeing where I'm going is really freaky, Kel."

"Maybe, but it makes perfect sense."

"It does?"

"Sure. You've heard the phrase 'blind truth,' haven't you? Now," Kelly said over Lara's groan, "which way do we go?"

"Lara lara bo barra don't fall asleep in the car-arra, me my mo marra, Laaaaa-ra. Wake up, Lara."

"I'm awake!" A half truth: despite the textured white brilliance behind her eyelids, only Kelly's singing kept Lara on the edge of consciousness. She was confident they'd reached mountain roads, at least. For a while the car had rattled over gravel, barely enough to keep her awake. But gravel had turned to near-silent, if bumpy, grass as they'd traveled onward, and the quietness had let her drift again. "I'm sorry. The blindfold is making me sleepy. And my head itches."

"Well, you're in luck. We have reached the end of the road, and I mean that literally. There's a mountain in front of us. If we need to go up it, we're doing it on foot. Mountain climbing blind and in high heels. That should wake you up."

"Or kill me." Lara tugged the blindfold carefully, then tightened it again. "I don't think I can take it off without going crazy. I'm still seeing white and hearing whole orchestras. I feel like an overstuffed sausage."

Worry came into Kelly's voice, distorting its usual music. "Maybe you should let go of the power."

Lara shook her head. "I'll lose him if I do."

"Blind, high-heel mountain climbing it is, then. When this is over we'll start a school for athletic businesswomen. At least you can use the staff as a, er. Well. Staff. You know what I mean. A walking stick." Kelly helped Lara out of the car and got her the staff before adding, "This is a terrible idea, you know?"

"I know." The ivory staff was cool in Lara's hands, like it had been after she shut off its power from shaking the earth. That was good: she was certain its power was part of what had stripped the world down to its barest essentials, and she still had the headache from that.

"Okay. I just wanted to make sure it was clear. The first bit's not so bad. We'll go slow."

"We're going to have to!" Even using the staff as a walking stick, the earth under Lara's feet seemed eager to reach up and grab her. She set a reluctant pace made somewhat smoother by Kelly's quick warnings of "Root, hole, branch!"—though the last proved to mean "duck" rather than "step up," and Lara clobbered her forehead against sturdy lengths of wood twice before Kelly started saying "Duck!" instead.

"Log," though, meant something to climb over. Kelly went first, grunting. "There's a kind of pit on this side, so you'll have to slide farther down than you think you will. Give me your hands." She guided them down to its softening surface, and Lara leaned there for a moment, testing it with her weight and trying to listen beyond the music in her mind. The discordant tones veered to their left, pulling the threads she'd envisioned that way as well.

"I can't see and it makes me feel like I shouldn't talk," she said after a moment. "Or maybe I'm just paying too much attention to my feet to try. We're going to have to stop more often so I can see which way to go. We have to go left a little."

Kelly drew in an unhappy breath. "Are you sure?"

Lara lifted her blind gaze, an eyebrow arched under the weight of Dafydd's coat. Kelly muttered, "Yeah, yeah, okay, of course you're sure. It's just that it gets rougher pretty fast over there, Lar. The angle goes up and it gets rockier instead of woodsy. Maybe we should look for a way around. Go up a ways from where we are and see if it smoothes out."

"You go." Lara climbed over the log and sat on it. "It'll take three times as long if I go up, and if it turns out there's no way around we'll have to come back down. At least if you go up we'll know, and if it's clear you can come get me."

"You want me to leave you sitting blindfolded in the middle of a mountain forest?"

Lara managed a wan smile. "We're probably far enough off the beaten path that the only person who's likely to find me is the guy we're after. That's sort of a good thing." Rueful truth ran through everything she said, thinning out some of the weighty song still dominating her thoughts. "We're closer than we were. Maybe we're close enough that I can let some of this power go and still track him. I'll try while you're looking for a path through, okay? It gives us both something to do."

"All right," Kelly said unhappily. "But yell if you need anything at all, will you? Even if you just don't like being alone down here."

"I will," Lara promised. "Go on. I'll be fine." She forced her shoulders to relax as she listened to Kelly scramble up the hill, then turned her attention to the raw music pounding through her mind.

She had barely loosened her hold on it when Kelly's scream ripped the air.

Thirty-Five

Magic ripped loose of Lara's grasp, music drowned beneath the sound of Kelly's terror. She yanked her blindfold off, tears flooding her eyes at the day's sudden brilliance, but her feet were already carrying her forward with no care for safety or sight. The ground seemed even more treacherous as her vision returned; Kelly had made light of its difficulty without quite lying about it. Lara scrambled upward, putting weight on the staff despite its look of fragility. She stepped on her dress skirt repeatedly, its fullness proving more impediment than her heeled sandals. In frustration, she seized the fabric and pulled it up gracelessly. No one was there to see, and all that mattered was she reach Kelly.

A vast boulder, deposited on the mountainside by glaciers many millennia past, blocked the way. Lara shot a glance off to the left, wondering how difficult that path had been, if conquering a fifteen-foot rock was the preferable choice. Packed earth made a ridge along it, leading slowly upward and reminding Lara of the pitched stone road that stretched down to the Unseelie city. That was good, she thought: any parallels to the Barrow-lands meant they were closing in on their quarry.

Dissonance thundered through the thought. Lara shouted, a raw sound of frustration as she tried to push the music away. Lies had never been comforting to her, but for once she craved their solace. Parallels with the Barrow-lands were coincidence, nothing more, but she wanted them to have meaning. She drove herself up the ridge, stepping on her skirt again as it escaped her grip. Stitches tore at the waist, making it sag further, and she wished she had the strength to simply rip the whole thing free. Deliberately destroying clothing— that was a thought she'd never imagined having.

The narrow ridge switched back as it reached the boulder's edge. Softer ground had been cut away, making a skinny V between the mountain and the half-unearthed stone. Kelly couldn't be too much farther ahead. It had been mere moments between her departure and her screams. Lara ran, staff in one hand and her damnable skirt hitched up in the other, and burst through the end of the switchback.

It opened onto a raw expanse of earth that had once been the site of a river or a landslide, with rocks strewn about it in awkward chunks. Dozens of tall thin stones stood at skewed attention, like bowling pins knocked partially aside, and innumerable round stones the size of beach balls lay among them. Kelly hid behind one of the taller rocks, arms curled over her head. Relief soured the panic in Lara's stomach and she ran forward, waving. "Kelly! Come on!"

Kelly dropped her hands, face stricken with dismay. "Lara, no! Watch out!"

A round rock as large as those settled among the tall ones came flying down the riverbed. It bounced, shattering smaller stones into shrapnel, and spun on its axis to veer toward Lara. She shrieked and ducked, the rock flying overhead. It bounced once more, then crashed into a ravine a little farther down the mountain. Heart hammering, Lara straightened to gape after it, and Kelly's warning shout came a second time. "Get *down!*"

Another rock came smashing down toward her. Lara shrieked again and ran for one of the standing stones. A third rock bashed its top off, sending dust and shards over her, and she stuffed her hand in her mouth to keep from crying out again.

"It's—" The thunder of another stone rushing toward them drowned Kelly's words and ended in a shuddering crash that shook the earth. *"Fuck,"* Kelly bellowed, "that one hit my pin. It's ninepins, Lara. We're the pins."

Bewildering truth shot drumbeat rhythms up Lara's spine. She stuck her head out from behind her rock regardless, trying to meet Kelly's eyes. "Who the hell's throwing the balls?"

"I don't know! Giants!"

"There's no such thing as giants!" Half a dozen stones came smashing down toward them, giving the lie to Lara's assertion, for all that it rang true in her mind. She flinched back, staring as another one flew overhead and bounced into the ravine. "It's got to be him."

"He's a *giant*?!"

"No! I mean, I don't think so!" Lara pressed her spine against her standing stone, then dared another glimpse toward Kelly. They were separated by no more than twenty feet, with one of the pin-stones offering shelter between them. "Stay there!"

"Like I was going to go anywhere!"

A giggle rose up and gave Lara the nerve to launch herself into a run, aiming for the nearby standing stone. A hailstorm of smaller rocks exploded down at her, pebbles pelting her arms and ribs as she ran. One, a fist-sized rock, connected solidly with her thigh and she stumbled as bone-deep pain bloomed. The rest of the stones rattled off the ninepin rock as she rolled into its lee. Kelly's voice broke over the last clattering of stone: "Are you okay?"

The ache in her leg was dull but comprehensive, setting her whole body off-kilter so she wanted to both curl over the injury and to throw up. Lara put her hand against it, gasping, and managed a weak "Yeah" in response.

Kelly's silence was filled with another rattling of stone, at the end of which she said, "You're still a terrible liar, Lar."

"No, I'm okay. I'm just . . ." Lara exhaled like the ache would rush out on her breath, then inhaled again deeply. "That hurt."

"I'll come the rest of the way to you." Before Lara had a chance to protest, Kelly burst out from behind her rock, running pell-mell across scattered stones. She slid behind the ninepin rock seconds before another round stone came rolling down the hill to batter their protective wall. "You shouldn't've come after me, you idiot. But thank you."

"You sounded like you were dying! Why didn't you just turn around and come back?"

"Look." Kelly nodded toward the switchback and Lara pushed herself up to peer at it.

The mountainside had closed, no hint of the passageway visible. Lara, incredulous, said, "That's not even possible, is it?" and Kelly laughed.

"Lara, hon, we're well on our way to six impossible things before breakfast. We—eep!" Rock shattered over their heads, the top of their standing stone exploding under the impact of another thrown stone. "We can't stay here."

"No, I mean, it's really not *possible*." Lara scowled at the blank mountainside, searching for a way to see through what she was certain must be illusion. *Truthseeker* was better suited to words, she thought, to hearing and speaking the truth. Seeing it was too complicated, the human mind poorly constructed for truth's visual tricks. She clutched the staff, frantic to call its power to help herself see through the impossible, but it remained cold and quiet in her hands. Like it resented the limitations she'd put on it and was punishing her for it. The thought was absurd, but there was no hint of mistruth to it, and Lara found herself staring at the staff in bewildered distrust.

Kelly caught her arm, shaking her from half-formed thoughts. "I *know* it's not possible, but that's not stopping it from happening! That rock that hit you . . . can you run?"

Lara rubbed her thigh again, residually aware of the ache there. "Yeah, I'm fine. It's a bone bruise. A week from now after I've forgotten what happened it'll turn purple."

"If you can manage to forget what's happening I want your therapist's phone number. Come on, maybe we can get over the edge of the ravine and it'll protect us."

"No, we need to go up." Lara peeked around the edge of their rock, then yelped and flinched back as another barrage came rolling down the mountain. "It feels right, and besides, that's where the stones are coming from. I'm going to get this guy even if I have to fight giants."

"With *what*?"

Lara pushed herself up. "With the truth."

"Oh, good. You've got a truth shield, then? One that's going to keep enormous rocks from flattening us?"

"Sort of." Lara closed her eyes, listening not for the next rumble of stone, but for the music that was a part of her. The nightwings had strained at that tune, making it ugly, though she hadn't recognized that until the third encounter. But it meant something; it had to.

It meant that, like the breach between worlds that had let them through, they weren't a *true* thing. They undoubtedly existed, but like a flaw in cloth, a woven bit gone wrong. It pulled at everything else, warping it the same way an out-of-tune piano warped a song.

There were no giants. Not in this world, not now, if there ever had been. Lara clung to that as a truth she could be certain of, and it hummed comforting agreement. "There aren't any giants, but giants are throwing the stones."

"What?" Kelly half-swallowed the question, letting Lara ignore her. Music trembled, unable to fuse *there aren't any giants* and *giants are throwing the stones* into a cohesive whole. One couldn't be true without the other, and the first part carried more weight.

"There aren't any giants to throw the stones. I want the stones to *stop*."

Shocking silence surrounded them, as alarming, in its way, as the rockfall had been. Lara crowed triumph and swung around the edge of their standing stone to glare defiance up the mountain. "They're an illusion. That must be his talent."

"An illusion?" Kelly surged to her feet, gesturing at herself. Scrapes lined her hands, her shoes were dusty, and a bruise was forming on one cheekbone. "That's a hell of an illusion, Lara. Packs a lot of punch. And the nightwings sure as hell weren't illusions! How'd he make them if he does illusions?"

"The nightwings were something else. I mean, Dafydd knew what they were, so it's got to be a spell the Seelie can work as a general rule, cutting away pieces of the night sky to make an attack beast. And anything can hit hard, Kelly. *Air* can hit hard." Lara began picking her way up the riverbed, gaining speed as her certainty grew. "That's got to be it. You can't see the air, but it's got presence. His talent must be giving it form, making it real."

"Air's one thing, but those were rocks!"

"No." Lara turned around, catching Kelly's hand and nodding toward the passage they'd just climbed. "Look."

The ninepins stones still stood, rickety and tall in the ancient sluiceway. But they grew up out of flattened stones, grass working its way between the cracks. There were no lumps of round stones to be seen, though dust still settled where they'd crashed into the earth. "Look," Lara said again, softly. "He stopped holding his concentration, so they disappeared."

"That's not possible. They almost killed us."

Lara let go a quick laugh. "Maybe it's not possible, but it's true. It's just like the military trying to use compressed air for nonlethal weapons." She started back up the mountain, hearing Kelly follow close behind. "The only difference is this guy can add a visible component to the attack. I'm sure of it." She felt like she was floating on the music, confidence shoring her up.

"The military can't turn compressed air into visible rocks," Kelly muttered, but the argument had run out of her. "Lara, what do we do against somebody who can turn illusion against us? I mean, he could be hiding in plain sight."

"I don't think it'll work on me now that I'm looking for it. Dafydd's glamour wouldn't, anyway. I knew he was using it, but I still saw him as he really is."

"Good," Kelly whispered. "In that case, can you please tell me that I'm not seeing the Headless Horseman riding down on me?"

Lara twisted around in time to watch blood splatter from Kelly's face.

She saw nothing: no horse, no cloaked figure, no sword; nothing but Kelly spinning with the hit she'd taken. There was no sound, not even of Kelly hitting the earth, much less hoofbeats against the stone. Two, she thought clearly: two upstate New York legends so far, and though she didn't like fairy tales, Lara knew these things usually happened in threes. She said "Two is enough" under her breath, and slipped down yards of grass-riddled rock to Kelly's side.

Her friend's eyes were wide but glazed, and the cut along her cheek scored hideously deep. It had caught the bone, narrowly missing her eye; narrowly missing the fleshy cheek, where it might well have severed her face. The strength Lara had wished for earlier roared through her and she savaged the skirt of her dress, tearing off a strip to ball it against Kelly's face.

Kelly gave a thin gaspy shriek that turned to a real scream as she saw something over Lara's shoulder. Lara risked a glance as she folded herself over Kelly. There was nothing there, a promise she shouted into Kelly's screams. The truth was a shield and Lara its manifestation; no new scores opened in Kelly's flesh, though she whimpered again with fear.

"It isn't there, Kel. It isn't there." Truth pounded through the words, but not enough: even if Kelly wanted to believe her, the monsters were too real. Lara, shaking with determination, bent her head over Kelly's until their foreheads touched. "I'm going to show you. I have to show you, so you're not afraid. So it won't be able to hurt you. This will work," she promised. "It has to work."

The music had always been internal, even when it had opened a path from one place to another. Even when she'd sung aloud to focus it, the power had come from within, bound by her flesh.

It wasn't enough. Not this time, not now. She reached for the staff where it lay to the side, abandoned when she'd collapsed at Kelly's side, but it remained sullenly quiet, unwilling to offer her any of the strength it had shown when she'd struck it against the earth and broken open a path to another world. Frustrated, she wished for an instrument, for some talent to share music directly with others through something other than her voice. A lifetime of hearing truth's song, and she'd never thought to learn to play anything. She would, she promised herself. She would do that, when she was free of the complicated world Dafydd had introduced her to.

The words woke a snatch of music in her mind, a phrase of gospel song. Eyes closed, she whispered the lyrics, then struggled to strengthen her voice. "Great God Almighty, I am free, I am free at last."

She whispered the will to be free toward Kelly; freedom from the illusions of the world, from the comforting lies, from the terrible things hidden by falsehood. Freedom, most especially, from the magic that convinced her of the Horseman's presence. Such a conviction could hurt her, even kill her, if she believed hard enough.

Song and strength poured out of her in a rush, leaving her temporarily bereft and in sudden silence. Kelly, though, screamed again and surged upright, fingers clawing at something Lara couldn't see. "Oh my God, oh my God, no, make it stop!"

"Kelly! Kel, it's me! You're okay, I've got you!" Lara caught her, holding on hard, and for long seconds Kelly struggled, her gaze still panicked and distant. Then she collapsed, hands over her ears as she twisted away from Lara.

A mad orchestra, every instrument playing its own tune, crashed back over Lara as Kelly broke away. She put her own hands to her head, agog at the noise. It drowned out the sound of her heartbeat, of her breathing; of every normal thing that told her she was alive. The world was abruptly too much to take in, filled with cluttered, unorganized truth that no one person could possibly bear.

But she'd borne it all her life. Lara shook her head hard, trying to sort out the cacophony, and pieces of it fell away so quickly she had the impression the very world was abashed at its behavior. Notes came clearer, different instruments coming in to tune with one another, so that when a sour flute sounded she sensed it as wrong, and tried to tug it into alignment. It resisted and she pulled harder, then let herself forget it as Kelly half sat up, staring at her in horror.

"Is that what it's always like? So loud, all that music everywhere, all that pain, all that awful truth?" She crumpled and Lara pulled her close again, breath coming hard and short.

"I'm sorry. I didn't know what else to do."

"I don't ever, ever want to see things the way you do again."

"I promise," Lara whispered. "I promise, Kel. I'm sorry. I know you weren't meant to see things like that. Only I am." The world was calmer now, cymbals of discontent settling into more regular chimes. Distortions still rippled through it, tunelessness striking again, and this time she recognized it as the same dissonant warning the nightwings carried with them. It was closer, reluctantly closer, and she remembered how she'd pulled at that off-tone, trying to make it match the rest.

"Well done," said a bitter male voice. "Well done indeed, Truthseeker. I had never meant to come this far."

Bewildered, bloody, angry, Lara lifted her gaze to see a young man—as all the people of the Barrow-lands were—standing before her, his dark hair shadowing equally dark eyes. He had his people's beauty, but it was marred with a glimmer of madness. "Ah," he said, mocking. "But you don't know who I am, do you."

"You're wrong. I do." Lara, full of calm certainty, got to her feet. "You're Merrick ap Annwn, and this is all your doing."

Thirty-Six

"When did you know?" Strained curiosity filled the Unseelie prince's voice, as though he strove to make light of being discovered, and fell just short.

Lara gave a deprecating laugh. "Not until just now. Not until I started thinking what could be done with illusion. I just don't understand why. What do you get out of starting a war between the courts?"

"Power." Merrick shrugged. "You should have seen that much, Truthseeker. What else does any ill-favored son covet?"

Kelly, unexpectedly, muttered, "A father's love, usually. It's all very Oedipal, or something. Lara—"

Lara hissed a warning, trying to silence her friend. Merrick's gaze flickered to her, then back to Lara, a dismissal that caused Kelly to draw offended breath. "*Tscht!*" Lara said, and splayed her fingers backward, trying again to cut Kelly off without ever taking her own eyes from Merrick.

His attention, though, was drawn to Kelly a second time. "You mortals have a saying, I think. One that suits my situation. 'Better to reign in Hell,' is that not what you say?"

"Not most of us." Kelly subsided as Lara shot a despairing glance over her shoulder. The wadded-up skirt Kelly held against her face was black and wet with blood, and something in the way her mouth pinched told Lara that sharp commentary was meant to distract Kelly from her injury. But the truth wasn't a shield that could protect her, and so Lara was desperate for her silence, not wanting Merrick's regard to linger on her.

"For most of you," Merrick said softly, "there are hundreds, perhaps thousands, of others between yourselves and absolute sovereignty. For me there are four. It's a surmountable number, and most easily achieved through war." His voice sharpened. "A war that should have been met within hours of my 'death,' were it not for mortal interference."

"Mor— I didn't get to the Barrow-lands for almost two weeks." Lara turned back to Merrick, her hands clenched with worry.

"But Oisín made his prophecy and stayed Emyr's hand for those critical few days until my dear brother could bring you from the mortal world to ours. How is Dafydd?" he added, voice gone oily and smooth. "Shall we see, Truthseeker?"

He made a familiar gesture, fingers clawing the air to rip a shining door between one world and the next. Lara's breath caught and she started forward, but Merrick lifted an imperious hand. "Do you know what a scrying spell is, Truthseeker?"

"It lets you see across—" "The Barrow-lands" was how the sentence was meant to finish, but Lara swallowed it along with bitter recognition. "Across space," she said instead, and Merrick's smile turned pointed with approval.

"Very good. It's no small feat to turn the worldwalking spell to a scrying window, but let us see what's to be seen. Think of Dafydd, Truthseeker. Think of your love."

Anger and fear stung Lara in equal parts. Merrick knew more than she did, as if he'd been watching them all along. The frequency of the nightwing attacks struck her, and she thought perhaps he had been, right from the moment she'd crossed into his world. She didn't want to give him an even greater advantage by playing his game, and yet . . .

She'd escaped the Barrow-lands through a twist of magic she had no idea how to command, much less replicate. Merrick's torturesome offering could far too easily be the last chance she would have to see Dafydd ap Caerwyn. She crept forward, gaze locked on the glittering window between worlds.

The image on its other side swam, blurring with the thickness of melting glass, then slowly came clearer, focused on a single man. Dafydd lay in a bed of ermine, impossibly pale against the soft black fur. He didn't move, not even to breathe, so far as Lara could tell. She muffled a cry, inching closer, and became aware that she was almost within Merrick ap Annwn's reach. She froze in place, unwilling to risk his presence even when distance from the window lost details that might have eased her heart.

His surroundings were semi-familiar to her, the Unseelie palace's black opalescent walls reflecting light from the scrying window. A white-haired woman moved into the image, tall and confident in her moon-silver armor: Aerin, who in no way belonged at the heart of the Unseelie palace. She knelt beside Dafydd, then slipped an arm behind his shoulders, helping him to sit, and offered him a drink from a goblet like the one Ioan had shared with Lara.

Childish envy made Lara's eyes hot. She dashed the heel of her hand against them, trying to turn misery into anger. "She shouldn't even be there. What's she doing there?"

Answers flooded her without Merrick speaking aloud. Aerin was one of Dafydd's oldest friends; Ioan might well have sent for her, or even stolen her the way he'd done Lara herself, so that someone Dafydd knew would be there to care for him. Someone of his own people, rather than an unknown Unseelie. Ioan might even be wary of showing himself to Dafydd; he had no way of knowing that Lara had already betrayed the secret of his change to the younger Seelie prince.

And the more hateful answer was even more obvious than those. They were lovers, Dafydd and Aerin, perhaps even meant to wed someday. Lara was an ephemeral thing to them, barely lasting a moment. She could never offer what Aerin might: a lifetime of inti-macy for a man whose years spanned aeons.

Dafydd took a wracking breath, doubling against Aerin's side. Hope leaped in Lara's heart: he was alive, at least, and she hadn't been at all certain he would be. He'd been so weak, so close to burned out entirely, all for the sake of protecting her and her world. A life like his lost for a planet full of mortals who would neither know nor care would be criminal, and that ache rang true in Lara's breast. Aerin helped him to lie down again, smoothed his hair, and stood, leaving the scrying window's frame.

Lara whispered, "No. Follow her." Dafydd was sleeping; he would remain that way without her worried supervision. The window, at Merrick's command but at Lara's wish, trailed after Aerin until she entered another room, more grandiose and brighter than the one she'd left.

Ioan ap Annwn stood alone in that room, looking through a win-dow of his own. Lara imagined he looked over his city, and won-dered how many of his people had returned. Not enough. If even one was lost, not enough had returned.

Merrick made a startled sound as Aerin said, "Ioan," and for an in-stant Lara's gaze strayed to him. She'd told Dafydd of Ioan's trans-formation, but Merrick, true son of the Unseelie king, hadn't known about it. He must have expected a man as pale as Dafydd to appear in his scrying window, and a strange twinge of sympathy jolted Lara. He had been traded away and now it was revealed to him that he had been replaced more thoroughly than he ever would have dreamed. No one would take such a change of fortunes easily.

His crimes, though, had been developed well before he had made this discovery. Lara tightened her stomach muscles, trying to liter-ally harden her heart, and turned her attention back to the window between worlds.

"He's dying," Aerin said in response to something Ioan had said. Then she shook her head and sat gracefully, as though she wore a court gown rather than armor. "Worse than dying. His fire is gone,

Ioan. Everything that makes him Seelie is burned away. He's . . . *mortal*."

Something akin to disgust filled the last word, but Lara's hands went icy with hope. Mortal meant a life span like hers, a lifetime that could be shared. Her heart hammered with a painful, misplaced joy. If she could return to him even briefly, then she might convince him to come home with her, where they could be together without magic or monsters to confuse their future.

Selfish, she whispered to herself, but repugnancy crossed Ioan's face as well. Wouldn't it be better, she reasoned, to make a home and a life in a world where everything was mortal, than to always be an object of pity and disgust in the land that had once been his?

"I can open the door," Merrick said. Truth shivered through it, proof of his royal blood. "You could bring him back here. It would be the end of everything you tried to do in the Barrow-lands, but it would be a future for both of you."

Without thinking, Lara breathed, "Open it," and the window winked back to Dafydd's chambers. Light exploded everywhere, gold and blinding, but she ran forward, staying just out of Merrick's reach as she dove across worlds.

She hit the black mother-of-pearl floor with as much dignity as she'd landed in a sandbox weeks earlier, but this time she was able to roll to her feet and run to Dafydd's bedside. The furs were soft, so soft she wanted to bury herself in them and hold Dafydd forever. She could, she promised herself. She could hold him, but not here. His skin was cool beneath hers as she caught his hand and brought it to her lips.

Like a fairy tale, his eyes opened at her touch. They were brown now, such an ordinary mortal color, and confusion rose in them as he frowned. "Lara?"

"Come with me. Merrick's holding the door open—" She glanced over her shoulder, making certain it was true. Merrick stood in her world, grim with concentration against a backdrop of stones and mountain grass. He made a gesture: *hurry,* and she twisted back to the exhausted man on the bed. "Dafydd, you used too much power.

You burned out your magic, but you're alive, and you're . . . you're mortal, Dafydd. Come with me," she whispered. "We can be together in my world for the rest of our lives. But we have to hurry. It's a terrible thing to ask without any warning, I know that, but there isn't much time."

"I'm not . . . I'm not sure I can." Dafydd laughed thinly as Lara scooted her arm under his shoulders like Aerin had. "I barely remember what happened, Lara. I'm very weak."

"I know. The nightwings, the hydra—" Lara shook her head. "I'll tell you everything later, but if Aerin comes back—"

"She won't stop you." Aerin's voice, cool as glass, came from the doorway. Lara flinched toward it, awed all over again at the woman's tall beauty. She'd set aside her armor in the little time that had passed, and looked the part of a queen in her castle, garbed in white that spoke of a bride's gown. "He would only be a reminder of what we've lost," she said. "It's better for all our people to make a new start together."

Ioan entered behind her, putting his hand under hers. He was resplendent in black, groom to her bride, and his handsome features were pinched with sorrow. "This war has offered us that much, at least. We're no longer enemies, and reparations are being made to the Unseelie people. Emyr is reluctant, but dares not stand against the rising sentiment of all our peoples. Take Dafydd," he murmured. "Make a good life. Do not come here again."

Lara, heart breaking, whispered, "We won't," and helped Dafydd to his feet. He hesitated, looking toward the brother he didn't know and the woman he did, and then drew strength from somewhere, straightening himself to walk, unbowed, through the door that Merrick held open.

It blinked out behind them and Dafydd dropped to his knees, exhaustion greater than pride. Lara fell with him, trying to support him. Relief mingled with joy and terror and sent her heart hammering. A life with her; he had chosen a life with her, and no amount of worry could undo that. But now he turned his gaze slowly upward to examine Merrick ap Annwn. "You were dead."

"It was a trick." Merrick's lip curled. "A trick that has not played out how I meant it to. I meant to be the crowned head that it seems Ioan ap Caerwyn now is."

"But we were brothers."

"No. I was a hostage to my father's good behavior, and no amount of time could have made me more than that within your father's court. What else was I to do, Dafydd? Spend all of history waiting to sip from a cup that would never come?"

"You—" Dafydd stumbled on the word, turning a weary gaze to Lara. "Is he right? Does he speak the truth?"

Lara bit her lip unhappily. "Dafydd, he—"

"Lara." Kelly, at her side, pressed the staff into Lara's hands, and said, very steadily, "David isn't there."

Illusion shattered.

It came apart like crystal hit by stone, fragments rupturing around her. Dafydd's image schismed and became glittering bits of light before it fell apart. Lara cried out, reaching for the bits of an imagined life, and choking on sobs when they cut her fingers and faded away.

So close, it was *so close* to what she wanted that she had invested her own truth in it, made it almost real. Her talent had always told her when someone else was lying, as long as they *knew* they were lying. Never, never in her life had she wrapped truth so carefully that even *she* couldn't tell she was lying.

Truthseeker's gift, she thought, double-edged. Strong enough, now, to make it possible to lie to herself. A little stronger, and maybe Merrick's illusion would have become reality. Maybe Dafydd would have crossed worlds with her, mortal for the brief time he had left.

And then she, not her world, would have been responsible for his death. Lara shuddered violently, wanting to curl up, curl in, to hide from truth and life itself. But anger flared, a small bright ember that forced her to her feet. Illusion, such a strong illusion, so carefully based in something so close to truth, had almost turned her into a monster, the same way it took star-filled night skies and made them deadly.

Merrick ap Annwn blanched to see her face.

His window between worlds was still open, its closure nothing more than part of the story he'd shaped for her. The story she'd shaped for herself, with all the parts and parcels laid out for Merrick to use. Her envy of Aerin; her awe of the Unseelie palace; her impression of Ioan, who had taken the place Merrick sought as his own. He stepped back, hands lifted, and Lara advanced on him, blazing with rage.

"You shouldn't have let me go. You should've made certain there was nothing that would break the illusion, because now I'm going to do whatever it takes to follow you. I'll find a way, Merrick. I'll expose you to your people, to all of them, and you'll *never* rule in Annwn." The world's true name rang like gunfire, louder even than the crystalline shattering of illusion.

"But only royal blood can open the pathway," Merrick whispered. "Where I go, you cannot follow. I'll have my victory, and you'll be here, lost with your power, alone without a lover, while Annwn becomes my own. Good-bye, Truthseeker. Good riddance."

He twisted and leaped for the door, its golden outlines rupturing as he passed through. Lara bellowed, *"No!"* and ran forward, willing her truth to be the only one. Power flared in the staff, responding, finally, to her passion. *No,* he would not escape her; *no,* the door would not close; *no,* this would not be the end of the life she'd dreamed of having.

Music thundered, endless crescendos, and the collapsing door shivered, then froze.

Kelly, behind her, shouted, "Lara!" and in her voice was all the things to be left behind. Family. Friends. The job she loved, the world she knew. Lara went as still as the door, then turned back, breath coming short.

"Don't look like that." Kelly came forward, bright-eyed but smiling past the cloth she still held wadded against her cheek. "Don't look like that. You're going, I know that. I just wanted to say good-bye."

"I might not be able to come back." Falsehood rang in the words and Lara fought the truth before admitting it in a whisper, regrets swelling: "I probably won't come back. The time difference . . . even if I came right back it could be years. Your wedding, Kel. I'm going to miss your wedding. I can't—"

"If I'm getting married." Kelly's voice broke, then cleared. "I will someday. And I'll put a fairy princess doll in your place. Okay? I'll think of you." The tears she'd held back spilled down her cheeks. "I'll think of you all the time. Now go on." She gave the trembling doorway a sharp nod. "Go."

Lara laughed, quick crack of a sound edged with loss, and stepped forward to crush her friend in a brief hug. "Thank you. Tell my mom what happened. I love you, Kel. Live happily ever after, okay?"

Kelly's smile flashed through tears. "You, too. I love you, too, Lar. Now go on. Go rescue your prince. I'll see you later."

Unexpected, gratifying truth flared in the promise. The fist around Lara's heart loosened a little, and she stepped backward, closer to the door. "Count on it."

One more step, and she walked between worlds.

TO BE CONCLUDED IN

Wayfinder

COMING SOON FROM DEL REY

ABOUT THE AUTHOR

C. E. (Catie) MURPHY is the author of two urban fantasy series (The Walker Papers and The Negotiator Trilogy) as well as The Inheritors' Cycle, which includes *The Queen's Bastard* and *The Pretender's Crown*. Her hobbies include photography and travel, though she rarely pursues enough of either. She was born and raised in Alaska, and now lives in her ancestral home of Ireland with her family and cats.